TOP HAT

HAT TRICK

TOP HAT

LUKE CHMILENKO
AND
G. D. PENMAN

Podium

Cover design by Mansik Yang and STK Kreations

ISBN: 978-1-0394-5420-0

Published in 2024 by Podium Publishing
www.podiumaudio.com

Podium

TOP HAT

CONCERNING OUR JOURNEY SO FAR

In a hole in the ground, there lived a kobold. The hole was vile, he was wretched, death would have been a sweet release from his mindless bug-grubbing existence. Then along came me, the greatest thing to have ever happened to anyone, let alone a kobold. A wizard's hat that was capable of speaking into his mind, teaching him the High Art of magic and instructing him in how to survive the dangers of the Badlands in which we found ourselves. Under my wise tutelage, Ig grew into as powerful a mage as an overgrown rodent with a skin condition might become and mastered a few of the absolute basics of magic while doing his damnedest to piss off literally everyone that we met. This list included a horde of werewolves, an entire city of ogres, a horny necromancer, and miscellaneous woodland creatures. This was hardly ideal, but so long as he listened to my advice, we survived.

So needless to say, the moment that he stopped listening to my advice he promptly blew us both up, trapping him and me deep in the bowels of the earth. We were separated by several tons of fallen rubble, just because he was too much of an idiot to listen when I told him that launching a fireball was not actually a good solution to every problem. This is a recurring issue with young wizards, not just kobolds.

In the company of one of the adventurers we had encountered, Ig made his way back to the surface and joined a circus. Our companion Ildrit got bitten by the werewolf ringmaster. Remember that. It will become important later.

Meanwhile, down in the depths of the world, I was rescued by a hirsute young dwarf by the name of Cygni. Technically, all dwarves are female except a few special drones that are used by the "King" for procreation, but as a rule they all behave as though they are male. Remember that. It will become important later.

Forsaking tradition and duty, Cygni took pity on me for my plight and carried me off from the dwarven city of Knute's Crack, through mines, dungeons, and the dark places of the world. She studied magic, just as Ig the kobold had, but unlike Ig, she had no natural capacity to retain Quintessence, and as such could cast only the tiniest of spells before passing out from exhaustion. One apprentice with all the power he could ever need and no brain, another with all the brains and no power. I had to hope that my third and final apprentice, if I should ever elect to take on another, would have an even balance of both. A Goldilocks apprentice.

In our travels we encountered several unpleasant places and creatures, including a dragon so elderly it could no longer see and a bound monster that insisted that it was a god. It was the escape of the latter that resulted in our rather hasty ejection from the underworld. Thankfully by this point we had found some condensed Quintessence for Cygni to use to fuel spells so melting our way up through half a mile of rock and topsoil was relatively simple business really.

Up on the surface we encountered a traveling circus that was headed in the right direction, reunited with Ig, and then killed the ringleader—who had been using his ability to convey the curse through biting as a means of social control and blackmail. This happened to coincide with the arrival of all the other werewolves who had been relentlessly hunting Ig since the Badlands, so that worked out nicely. All the nice doggies were freed from their curse, Ig inherited the circus on the basis that he was somehow the best qualified and least annoying person there, and we all set off for Arpanpholigon once more. The city of magic from whence I had come.

On arrival we performed some moderately impressive magic to try and attract some attention, succeeded in attracting the wrong kind of attention, got in a scrap, and eventually, after what felt like over two hundred thousand words of traveling, we arrived back at the Invisible College, where we were to be presented to the archmage, who would decide what to do with us.

This was relevant to me in particular, because I was working off the assumption that whoever had murdered me would have also supplanted me as the leader of the college, ergo I was about to finally meet whoever had managed to outwit me, kill me, and consign me to eternal hat-damnation.

So imagine our collective surprise and confusion when the person in charge of the Invisible College of Arpanpholigon turned out to be me.

CHAPTER 1

CONCERNING THE UNTIMELY AND TRAGIC DEATH OF ABSALOM SCRYNE

I wasn't dead.

This came as something of a surprise to me, as I had, until this moment, been operating off the assumption that the transubstantiation of my soul into a hat was the sole logical explanation for my current state of being.

The fact that I was sitting there behind my desk with a condescending sneer on my face, looking out at the gathered associates who had assisted me in returning to Arpanpholigon so that I might avenge my death, was a subtle hint that I had not actually died. This puzzle would of course occupy the greater part of my mind for quite some time to come, but in the exact moment that my other self turned to look upon us, I was instead seized with an awful realization. To my companions, I was a friend, mentor, confidante, genius, leader, but to the gentleman seated over there filled with pomp and power, I was none of those things. I was merely a hat. As such, I could predict some significant problems arising.

"Is me hat," Ig declared before I'd gotten over my initial shock.

"I can assure you that it isn't," Absalom Scryne replied. "I've been looking for that hat for months."

No. He was not Absalom Scryne. I was Absalom Scryne. This imposter must have been shrouded in some sort of illusion to make him appear as though he were me. There was no other explanation. It wasn't as though there could be two of me. I was alive, I had a soul—admittedly it was bound inside of a hat rather than a human body, but that did nothing to diminish the fact that I was a real person.

"You is fake!" Ig proclaimed, complete with a shaking finger pointed at the archmage. "Hat is real Scryne."

The wizard cast a glance to Ildrit and Cygni, who both helped out immensely by shrugging in confusion at what Ig was trying to say.

Be silent, you fool. If he is an imposter, an imposter with power enough to slay me in my prime, I might add, then he will kill you before letting that secret get out. He'll kill everyone in the room!

"Weh?!" Ig squealed in sudden terror. "You is real! Hat is fake. Me sorry."

"What in the nine hecks is that kobold gibbering about?"

Ildrit stepped forward. "Perhaps we can explain . . ."

The step was arrested scarcely an inch after his foot had parted with the rather expensive-looking rug in my office. The complex floral pattern from that rug had coiled up and bound his ankle the moment he tried to move. I'd forgotten just how many magical protections I'd piled into this room. Protections that were now serving to keep my usurper safe from me.

"No explanation is necessary." Scryne pressed on unfazed. "You and your pet have discovered my property and traveled some distance to return it to me. Something for which I will gladly reward you. Just as soon as you hand over my hat."

Do not give me to him. I am the only evidence that he is not the real Scryne, and if he's powerful enough to have defeated me, then he's certainly powerful enough to strip my essence from the hat.

"Me no give!" Ig snapped, flinching just a moment after the words were out as though expecting to be immediately struck down.

"I'm afraid that the situation is more complex than . . ." Ildrit attempted again before I cut him off. Well, not me. The other me. The faux-Scryne.

He said, "There is nothing complex about it. Return my property to me. Now."

"Prove it," Cygni barked. Silencing all of us.

"I beg your pardon." His eyes flickered over her. There was a very brief moment of indecision on his otherwise stern expression. "Sir or madam?"

"Prove it's your hat."

That was actually a rather clever play on her part.

"Clevers?"

Indeed. Proving ownership of me will delay matters for long enough for us to devise a solution to the situation.

"Certainly," UnScryne declared, snapping his fingers. We had been escorted in by several of the inner circle of wizards from the school, who now stepped forward promptly. "Is that or is that not my hat?"

The wizards didn't even look at Ig and the hat before declaring, "That is your hat, sir."

He smiled then, and I wondered if I ever had such wickedness in my grin when I won so petty a victory. This fake was truly an evil cretin. "While you will doubt the word of the Archmage of Arpanpholigon, Master of the High Art and

Dean of the Invisible College, I am sure that you will not consider both Sabrinia the Blue and Danyeel the Dramatic to be liars too?"

Drat. He is as clever as he is good-looking. There is no way to pretend that he is being unreasonable now.

"Hat is not wanting to go to you," Ig announced as though it would settle matters.

The fake Absalom Scryne opened and closed his mouth before turning back to Ildrit. "I am choosing not to acknowledge anything that your pet says from this point forward. I admit that it is rather impressive that you've taught a kobold to speak, but as it is talking nonsense exclusively, I do not believe that pursuing conversation with it shall be fruitful."

"It does more than speak," announced Sabrinia, drawing Absalom Scrynot's attention to herself despite anyone of good sense doing everything they could to avoid said attention. "We have seen it doing magic."

"A kobold casting spells?" The wizard masquerading as me scoffed at the very idea. "What is next? The dwarf doing magic?"

"Actually," Danyeel droned, "The dwarf was also doing magic."

"You are mistaken," the fake Scryne informed us all forcefully. "It is more likely that a kobold might be able to muster up a spark of Quintessence than a dwarf. Clearly you have been deceived. One must assume by this gentleman here."

All eyes turned to Ildrit, who was as perplexed as I'd ever seen him. "I'm literally the only person in the room who can't do magic."

"Dubious," the imposter said, stretching the word out and narrowing his eyes.

"Use your wizard eyes or whatever you do. I'm no magician," Ildrit snapped.

If I had not been looking for it, I would not have seen the little sideways smirk that Scryne gave to Sabrinia before raising a finger and hissing, *"Fragor."*

A bolt of golden flame zipped out from my finger. His finger. I really needed to work out the pronouns situation.

Ig had impeccable reflexes as always, flailing a hand towards the incoming Potassium-infused death bolt and catching it in its arc, freezing it in midair. The imposter's gaze jerked around towards Ig. Pinning him in place.

Sabrinia smirked. "Told you so."

"Well that is rather interesting, however, I will still require the return of my property."

Ildrit finally managed to shake off the surprise of the situation long enough to growl, "Did you just try to murder me to make a point?!"

Which was about the moment that everything went entirely off the rails. It had happened quite a bit faster than I had anticipated, but I had anticipated it.

Sabrinia had been spoiling for a fight ever since we'd dunked her in the mud. She already had a spell ready to go, a sphere of shimmering azure light that would contain all of the magic being flung around in the next few moments. She may have been quite desperate to beat our faces into the ground, but she did have the good sense to protect her precious invisible college from the inevitable fallout. She'd always been rather good at shielding as I recall. Not as good as me, obviously. But competent enough that we wouldn't be making a run for it.

So we were trapped in this sphere, in the imposter's place of power, facing down three of the most powerful wizards in the world.

"I am Absalom Scryne, the greatest wizard of my generation. I have no clue who you might be, imposter, but rest assured you will be unmasked before this day is through." There could be no mistaking my voice, and even as I spoke, I could see the color draining from the imposter's face. Oh, he knew who I was when he heard me. He knew that the jig, as they say, was up.

It certainly surprised Sabrinia and Danyeel to hear their master's voice coming out of a kobold. They both stuttered in their own casting and instead cast their gaze to the imposter, thinking that he was throwing his voice with some parlor trick.

Just the opening that we needed.

Like a well-oiled machine, all of my allies leapt into action. Which is to say, they all stood around looking gormless.

"Give me my hat!" the fake me yelled, thumping his fist down on the desk. It was not a blow idly struck. Quintessence flooded out from the point where he had struck into the spells bound into the wood. The brass workings around the outside of the desk's rim disconnected themselves, transforming before our eyes into living mechanical insects akin to dragonflies, assuming every one of a dragonfly's legs ended in a knife, and its wings were made of knives and . . . let's just say they were some extremely sharp bugs.

Ildrit might not have had the slightest inkling of what was actually going on, but his body had been honed into a finely tuned weapon of war, the instincts refined and sharpened to the point that even without a brain driving the motion, his body still moved. Kicking out, he knocked poor Cygni off her feet, leaping aside in the same motion as the torrent of brass bugs swarmed through the space where they had once stood in a hurricane of blades.

He rolled to his feet, drawing the black blade Widowtaker from where it had hung across his back. The wizards would never have bothered to disarm him. After all, they were wizards. What could a man with a sword ever hope to do to a wizard before their magic overwhelmed him?

It was not that he was faster than a normal man, or even all that much stronger, though you could of course see and admire all the sinews in his arms straining as he brought the blade around. It was just that he seemed to know precisely where his sword needed to be without thinking about it.

As the buzzing swarm of knife-wings came back around in a tight spin, his blade rose through the torrent of brass, severing wing from body and blade from joint. A solid half of them were destroyed in that one blow, and the other six flitted off in every different direction to avoid another assault wiping them out.

Had we only the one magical assault to defend against, I would have said that we were doing well, but unfortunately for everyone involved there were actually three wizards trying to kill us, and they had not been caught off guard the way that we had, or at least not for very long.

With a flex of his shoulders and a whisper of Archaic, Danyeel vanished from sight, leaving only his fluttering robes standing where once he had been. I could only hope that this was an illusion intended to distract us and that he had not actually shucked them to run around naked and invisible.

As one wizard committed acts of invisible indecency, the others were casting too. My doppelganger involved in something vast and complex, as would befit me, and Sabrinia doing something rather clever to contract the barrier that she'd laid around us, limiting our mobility. She had the grave misfortune of casting her spell entirely too close to where Cygni had fallen, however. Others, more honed in the art of magic, would have reached immediately to counter Sabrinia's spell. Even more advanced wizards likely would have taken the opportunity of this distraction to land a spell of their own. Cygni was not yet so far along in her training that such things came naturally to her. In no small part because she had squandered valuable training time shacking up with Ildrit.

But she did still have some sense in that blocky head of hers, and it was that sense that made her realize that regardless of what specific spell Sabrinia was casting it would not be to our advantage. She took a hold of the other woman's foot, and as Cygni surged back to her feet, Sabrinia the blue was toppled. All her gathered Quintessence blurted out of her with a heavy huff of breath as her back made contact with the floor. The rather nice rug took some of the force of the fall away, but the grasping tendrils of the embroidery made no distinction between friend and foe. Mostly because to a wizard in a position of power like my imposter, everyone was a potential foe.

It wouldn't take her out of the fight, but it stopped her from bubbling us, and for that I was extremely grateful. All of which meant that Ig had only one wizard that he needed to deal with himself. The most powerful wizard. The false Absalom Scryne who had slain and supplanted me. Without hesitation, Ig screamed out *"Fragor!"* at the top of his lungs.

What should have followed, since he had been concentrating upon Potassium, was a bolt of golden flame that would soar through the air and ignite the pretender. What actually followed, since Ig was Ig, was a banana.

It shot from his outstretched hand and soared across the room.

Sensing Potassium being invoked and recognizing the extended paw of the kobold as indicative of a directed assault, the fake version of me did precisely what the real version of me would have done, abandoning the spell he had been casting, taking the same Quintessence and reforming it into a mixed-element barrier screen that would stop the *Golden Flames of Galgalagrin the Great* in its journey to burn out his bones.

Alas, what would have held back golden flames did naught to halt the flight of the banana. It soared in a gentle curve across the room to poke him directly in the eye, drawing a prolonged warbling yelp from betwixt his whiskered lips.

Served him right for stealing my identity, really.

With a moment's breathing space I called out to Cygni and Ildrit. *"Pull together, we need to escape."*

They both responded, as I knew they would, by entirely ignoring me. Ildrit had spun on his heel to intercept one of the brass blade birds with his sword's pommel. Cygni had clambered over Sabrinia to start pounding a fist into her face.

At least I can rely on you, Ig.

He was making a sound in the back of his throat somewhat akin to a piglet that had stepped on a rusty nail. Adrenaline flooded through his system, putting him over the edge of panic and into downright terror. He shook and quivered with terror. His mouth became dry. His vision blurred. I could barely make out the fake me behind my desk mouthing out some spell in Archaic, and only my own highly attuned arcane senses gave me the opportunity to warn Ig of the impending doom flying his way.

A simple bolt of flaming death, we might have been able to cope with by dodging, but my counterpart was not leaving anything to chance this time around. Rather, he had readied a plethora of destructive spells that flitted around him like hummingbirds, just awaiting the call to arms.

"Fragor!" Ig belched again, consumed by his own mortal dread. His concentration was all over the place. Flicking back and forth between the various elements he had been taught to invoke. To everyone's dismay, he seemed to have settled on Carbon.

Instead of a precise bolt of golden flame or heckfire darting across to interrupt my replacement's casting, what was summoned in more or less every direction was a sudden puff of soot.

The pristine office that I had maintained throughout my tenure at the Invisible College was smeared black. Every person within it, also covered in schmutz. This did not include the occluded form of Danyeel, though his position was somewhat given away by the human-shaped outline left on the wall where he'd been hiding.

Ildrit dashed to where the wizard had once stood, deflecting another brass bat with a flick of his blade. Its flight had already been knocked off course by the blast of carbon, and its mechanisms had seized as every moving part was clogged with now-oily dust.

His blade lashed through the air where the wizard had stood, and I fully expected to see an eruption of blood paint the walls that were, frankly, already pretty messed up after the soot-ball explosion. Instead the black blade swept through the empty air harmlessly and I let out a little sigh of relief.

Danyeel might currently have been something of a pain in the old kobold tail, but that didn't mean that I particularly wanted the boy bisected. There was still potential there untapped in all his frippery with illusions, and I did not mean to see it wasted on the edge of some blade.

Throughout the soot-splosion, there had been no pause from Cygni. A cloud of dust had never stopped a dwarf before and it wasn't about to start now. Just as a mining pick rose and fell rhythmically, so too went her fists. Up and down. Up and down. I doubted that Sabrinia would still be capable of casting at this point, what with so many of her teeth lying scattered around her and her lips being so swollen, but it seemed that Cygni was not willing to take that risk. Either that or she still held a grudge about the whole "being frozen alive" thing from earlier in the evening.

As to the imposter and his flock of vicious invocations, he had thrown up a screen to protect himself from Ig's latest outburst to the net effect that the chamber was now neatly divided in two by that same barrier spell. One side of it facing us, completely coated in soot and impossible to see through. The other . . . we couldn't see. Because the barrier was impossible to see through.

I was not so naïve as to hope that the massed spells of destruction on the other side of that soot curtain weren't going to come flying our way at any moment. Even with only the computing power of Ig's feeble little brain at my disposal, I was able to come up with a dozen potential solutions to being blinded like this, though judging from the snippets of Archaic I was able to pick out, it seemed that he was constructing a seeking spell to lead all the rest home to Ig's little fluttering heart. Removing ourselves from this situation promptly would have been my preferred solution, but with a seeking spell and bad enough luck on our part, the imposter's attacks might still reach us.

We had to do something to dispel our enemy's unseen attacks. Something drastic unless Ig had developed a handy immunity to torrents of lightning fire and miscellaneous other causes of gruesome death.

I glanced to Cygni, hoping that perhaps with her mastery of all the elements and her markedly more advanced education in the Archaic tongue she might be able to compose something worthwhile that might avert disaster, but alas, she was still intently pummeling poor Sabrinia into the rug. It is said that dwarves are stronger than humans and in a sense that is so. Anyone who spent all day and night mining would inevitably have a little more muscle mass than those of us who flounced on the surface doing as little physical activity as possible. But it wasn't her greater strength coming into play here; it was the relentlessness of her nature. She would hit and hit and hit again for so long as she drew breath. It did not matter that Sabrinia was no longer capable of casting, or indeed eating anything other than soup, because Cygni had set herself on a course to violence, and like the great trains that the dwarfs ran beneath the surface of the earth, she would carry on along those tracks until anything under her wheels was ground to mush.

One might consider it quite lucky that I was looking to Cygni in that moment given that it was the precise moment that Danyeel's invisibility faltered while he attempted to bring a knife down on her back. He was a wizard so of course this was no ordinary knife, nothing so plebeian as an actual stabbing for him, oh no. This was a spell-wrought blade fashioned from frozen methane. Chilling, poisonous, and a guarantee that regardless of how she was prepared, she would leave behind a very stinky corpse.

In a terror, Ig flung up his paws, unleashing a tide of low magic that cleanly slapped the fart blade from Danyeel's hand and sent it spinning end over end into the shrouded half of the office. From beyond the oppressive dark barrier, the imposter who had slain me and masqueraded around wearing my image yelped, "Shit."

If there was ever any further need of evidence that he was not truly me, surely this lack of vocabulary was it. I could cuss far more creatively, even in a pinch; in fact I was quite in the mood to do some very serious cussing right about now.

Perhaps the fleeting passage of the fart knife served to distract the wizard from his casting, or perhaps we were simply lucky—contrary to all evidence up until this point that luck was fixed firmly against us—but when the barrage of spells was unleashed from beyond the darkness, they went awry.

Some of them flew straight for Ig, but with the air thick with Quintessence and his will already fully extended in every direction at once, it was a surprisingly simple matter for him to simply catch them. A more educated wizard would of course have realized that such a thing was impossible, but I had absolutely no intention of informing Ig that he couldn't do the things that he'd been doing up until now that kept saving our lives. I also had to admit to taking some small delight in the flabbergasted noises that more thoroughly educated wizards made when confronted with Ig's impossible acts. Both Danyeel and Sabrinia had seen this very same trick down in the fairgrounds yet still the two of them were taken aback.

Well, Danyeel certainly was. Sabrinia had more pressing concerns to deal with. Many more causes to be taken aback, such as the fairly existential realization that even if one has mastered all of the elements and can command the universe to bend to one's whims, it doesn't actually help all that much when there is four feet of furious dwarf attempting to pound her way through your face.

The only real blessing of all this was that the passage of the various lightning bolts, firebolts, and other miscellaneous bolts of lethal energy cleared a good portion of the soot off the supposedly invisible barrier across the center of the room. Allowing us a wonderful view of the false Absalom Scryne and all of his wicked workings.

Un-Scryne was casting again, of course, because when confronted with any problem, that is where a wizard will go. He will seek the solution in magic regardless of how much easier it would be to circumvent it with literally any other method.

Cygni and Sabrinia had been relatively safe thanks to their prone position. Ildrit, meanwhile, had been saved by the fact that he was constantly in motion. Still fighting the good fight against those little brass bat bladed bird things that had been relentlessly pursuing him around the room. With a sweep of Widowtaker, he smashed one, sending it careening into another, which in turn intercepted the lightning bolt that had until that moment been crackling its way to his heart. If you had asked him how he did this, I imagine that he would struggle to tell you because there was no rational part of his mind plotting these motions out. It went beyond instinct into something else entirely, almost as though he were simply following the flows of fate where they led him. As though his course through the chaos of battle was predetermined. I had never seen anything like it, but then again prior to becoming a hat I didn't really get out much.

Danyeel had been kind enough to just stand there after being disarmed of his whiffy dagger, directly in the path of one of his alleged allies' firebolts. If I had not changed in the time since I had departed this ivory tower then I would have allowed the flames to consume him. After all, he was my enemy at that moment. He was doing his level best to kill me and my friends, so wouldn't it be only reasonable to return the favor? I cannot pinpoint the exact moment where Ig's sentimentality poisoned me. It must have been somewhere between crossing the first river in the Badlands and the second, because I had definitely gone a bit soft by the time that I met Cygni, and recall that I'd said some nice things to Ig before he'd attempted to blow us all up with heckfire. Which had the rather unfortunate result of giving him enough confidence to mess around with the heckfire to begin with. Regardless of exactly which moment had brought me to this shameful state of affairs, it was still a nudge from my will that set Ig into motion, catching the flaming orb with his low magic before it could render my former academic associate down into tallow.

He had just enough time to look confused at his ongoing survival before the pommel of Ildrit's sword caught him in the temple and knocked him out.

That actually opened up a whole line of questioning that I had not yet considered about that enchanted sword of his. If Danyeel had been married—which I sincerely doubted he was, thanks to his avowed status as a bachelor about town—then would his husband have been rendered unconscious by that blow? Or was it only the lethal strokes of the blade that were shared?

"Cygni, stop punching!" I was forced to shout out the order just to cut through her bloodlust, and it was only thanks to a lifetime of being a diligent dwarf drone that even that worked.

Her head jerked up, and I must admit even I was a little taken aback by the glazed expression in her eyes. "What?"

Ildrit was the one to answer her, flicking out Widowtaker with a flick of his wrist to smash the final mechanical menace from the sky. "She's done."

Cygni glanced down at Sabrinia and the purple hue that her once blue robes had now taken on in the neck and chest area. "Oh."

Perhaps she might have had some moral crisis after beating an unarmed woman into bloody submission in other circumstances, but in all honesty, I considered it quite justified given that Sabrinia would have gladly spherified us all if given the opportunity. That said, there was no time for moralizing now. Not with the imposter readying his next volley.

With a barked command, the barrier that had been so sullied with Ig's soot-bomb didn't dissolve so much as it shattered. Fragments of carbon-smeared nothingness burst out towards us like someone had just kicked in a particularly large window, and once more it was only Ig's remarkable ability to split his attention that saved us all from being impaled with extreme prejudice. The innumerable razor shards of wind that had been heading our way hung in place in the air and dispersed; the rest gave my office an extreme makeover. It is lucky that I was not overly attached to the tapestries, paintings, or even the books stored on shelves in this room, because they all suffered a moderate to severe shredding. Not to mention the gouges put in the hardwood floors.

Very deliberately, I chose to ignore the horrific damage being done to my study, and attempted to focus on what mattered. *"We must depart with all haste, my friends."*

"Why's that?" Ildrit drawled, treating my fake counterpart to a sneer. "Seems like we've got this guy right where we want him."

We did not.

Thus far, the pathetic excuse for an Absalom Scryne had been flinging his own magic around rather than relying upon the various defenses built into the room, with the exception of the desk and rug. As a result, he had been faring rather poorly. To my mind, this lent further credence to the idea that the imbecile was an imposter who did not even know what protections I had assembled for myself, but I will admit that it was possible he was simply so arrogant that he did not believe their use had been necessary before now.

My opinion definitely tilted more in the direction of the latter option when I realized that rather than casting yet another flurry of easily intercepted zaps our way, he had flung out his hands and sent Quintessence flowing into some of the prebuilt spells stowed away in the walls of the chamber.

For all of his flaws, Ig had a keen sense for danger, and while he may not have rationally grasped that the imposter was pouring Quintessence into inactive, but fully functional, constructed spells, there was some keening animal part of him that was afraid. Not just the usual base-level anxiety that typified his existence, but the sharp spike that typically preceded something truly terrible happening to him. "We need go! Now!"

When I said it, they didn't listen. When the kobold said it, suddenly it became vital. I don't know what is wrong with these people that they prefer an imbecile's commands to mine, but I was firmly unimpressed.

The trouble was that even though they wanted to listen to Ig, there was no actual physical way for us to leave the room. Despite having been knocked out—and then some—Sabrinia's sphere still enclosed us. We either had to break out of a spell intended to reflect all magic back inwards, or we needed to render it temporarily permeable. If I were in my own body, then it would have been a relatively complex procedure to allow myself to slip through the sphere. Probably something that involved rendering myself gaseous and the sphere permeable enough for my gassy self to pass through it. But with all of Ig's mastery at my disposal, we were stuck.

The dynamic duo of Ildrit and Cygni had flung open the chamber doors and rebounded off the barrier by the time that I got my head around what we needed to do to escape the situation. A situation that was worsening by the minute, as the various mechanisms of magic behind us began to activate.

Pass me to Cygni.

"Me no want do that." Ig was swift to reply. Obviously a little nervous about his chances without a far-wiser wizard guiding his actions.

Pass me to her now, Ig, that we might escape this situation.

"We is running?" After all of our time together, and all that we had experienced in that time, I could swear that this marked the first occasion on which one of my plans made Ig sound excited rather than riddling him with dread.

I consider myself to be quite even-tempered, all things considered, but his reluctance to do the only thing I was asking of him was irking me somewhat. Still I retained my cool demeanor, even as my doppelganger readied his next assault.

Not if you don't pass me to Cygni.

The stubborn kobold made a mad dash across the room to the chamber doors, ducking and weaving all the way as though there were impending fireballs already in flight. Fireballs would be the least of our worries once the study's defenses all swung into action. Already the tapestries and paintings had begun to shift and the characters within were readying themselves for war. Having faced down a full-size dragon not so long ago, I had to say the prospect of being assaulted by several six-inch-long ones was a little less imposing, but I suppose it is not how big the dragon is but how one uses it.

Making a leap, Ig separated me from his flaky scalp and attempted to dunk me directly onto Cygni. A dunk that most likely would have been successful were she not so wired. Instead, I was plucked from Ig's head, plunged into darkness, and only returned to reality a full twenty seconds later, atop the dwarf's head, with an aching in her elbow that was surely a match for the dent in Ig's chin.

What a delight to be reunited with you before you could beat anyone else unconscious.

Cygni scowled. "She had it coming."

That I cannot deny, but perhaps stopping sometime before you could see fragments of skull on the rug might have been preferable.

"Why are you on me?"

What a charming creature she was. Small wonder that I preferred being atop Ig, an actual imbecile, to her.

We must break free of the sphere in which we are contained as swiftly as possible so that we can make a tactical withdrawal.

"And how do you suppose we're going to do that?" She grimaced as the hypnotic patterns of the rug began to swirl.

The correct answer, as would have been taught in this very college, was to find a way outside of the bubble and then collapse it from the outside. But I found myself reluctant to abandon my companions to their fate within the bubble for even a moment, given just how much of the lethal defenses of the chamber were now buzzing, roaring, crackling, and yawning into action.

If I was unwilling to leave any of my party inside, then my options became to transport all of them outside via whatever mechanism I concocted to escape the inescapable, or to burst the bubble.

The latter option may have sounded easier but came with its own unique set of risks, given that the destructive energies that would be required to over-power something designed to contain destructive energies would likely have to greatly exceed the amount of destructive energies that we were liable to survive in here with.

Cygni's mind was racing at a similar pace to my own, though obviously her grounding in magical theory was considerably less solid than mine. Luckily her education was being supplemented by the presence of the mind of a genius currently co-occupying her brain meat. Unlike mine, however, her solution did not have to be purely theoretical. With a growled word, she unleashed a bolt of flame at the barrier beyond the door.

Working as intended, the sphere reflected the blast back inwards, though thankfully Cygni had angled her attack in such a way that it did not immediately incinerate her, instead rebounding towards the ceiling, where it encountered a swooping eagle recently unleashed from the frieze painted there, flooding the room with smoke and the scent of scorched paint.

How this particular data point assisted her in her decision-making process eluded me at this time, but at least provided a practical example to Ig, who I feared might have done something similarly foolish if he had not directly wit-nessed how it would have played out for him.

Across the room, I got a brief glimpse of my fake counterpart grinning as all the myriad magics I had prepared for my own protection were turned against me. Had I been in his seat, I must admit that beneath my far-better-trimmed beard, I might very well have been smirking like a loon too. Weeks, months, and years had gone into the preparation of all of these spells, and I cannot deny that even from on the receiving end of them, it was exciting to see how they would all play out.

The dragons from the tapestries had formed flocks, which now took sweep-ing and diving paths through the air to assault us from all angles. The flightless creatures of fantasy that had been included in the paintings around the walls were making their way in our direction, but it was markedly more difficult, and several of them had sprained limbs dropping down from their respective picture frames, slowing their progress even more.

As fun as it was conceptually, having the contents of pictures come to life and jump out just wasn't very practical. Either you had the arcane constructs scale up to their actual size on escape from the pictures, which would likely have caused a great deal of congestion at the portal point, not to mention the issues with crowding when they got out here, or you kept them small and the majority of them were laughably useless.

An elf fired an arrow that sailed across the vast gulf of space between his little army and us, and it lodged harmlessly in Ildrit's boot.

So that one may have been a bit of a bust, but all of the other defenses I'd concocted were most assuredly more lethal, and it was mere moments until they activated. I needed a solution now to the impenetrable sphere containing us.

Wait.

I had it.

Tightening her grip on the shard of Scrynium in her pouch, Cygni bellowed out the word of Archaic that I had just squeezed into her frontal lobe along with the complex balance of elements that would be required to pull such a spell off. *"Motus!"*

For an instant, it echoed around the room, around the sphere, and it seemed that all of our efforts had come to naught, but I was not so foolish as to believe that without a showy splash of colored light, magic had failed. The greatest acts of magic have ever been the most subtle.

I seized brief control of Cygni's voice box and cried out: *"Now run!"*

Ildrit pointed helplessly to the milky barrier beyond the door; Cygni tried to frown up at me about my stupid statement, even though that simply wasn't possible given the angles involved. The only one who was as good and obedient as expected was dear sweet Ig, who took off sprinting at the barrier, clearly expecting that he would pass right through it unharmed. He splatted against the barrier with a simultaneously wet and crunchy noise. Then let out a very tiny whimper. "Why?"

"All of us, together."

With somewhat more trepidation than the now rather bruised Ig had shown, the other two approached the milky barrier and pushed their hands against it. Ildrit sighed. "Still solid."

Solid it may be, but no longer is it locked in its place, so push with all your might, my friends.

The penny finally dropped for Cygni: she dropped into a half squat, set her shoulder against the sphere's interior surface, and bore down on it with all the strength in her stout body. It shifted as she pushed, not only outwards, but spinning downwards too. Rotating around its central point, as though we were lab rats in a wheel. Exactly as I planned.

My evil twin had not moved from where he stood behind my desk, nor had he taken any real action since his activation of the preprepared spells. Likely considering anything more to be overkill, or a waste of his energy. Little did he suspect the nonsense that was about to engulf him.

It was all to do with the parameters of Sabrinia's spell. The containing sphere did not interact with the material of the walls, the ceiling, or any of the inanimate fixtures. They could pass through it entirely unharmed so long as they were not in motion. But the spells, the people, anything alive and capable of magic inside of the sphere would be trapped by its encroachment.

The sphere turned, rolling out of the office doors, and descending with us down the staircase that had led us to my counterpart, but even as the front of the ball went where we wanted it to, the rear end went precisely where my nemesis did not want it to. First slapping him in the back with such an upward spin that it launched him onto his desk, and then descending towards him. The top of the ball dropped into the room as we went downstairs with it, crushing all of his magical constructs flat against its surface, and soon the floor as we descended.

As we lost sight of the imposter, I strained my ears for but a moment to try and hear whether there might have been the satisfying crunch of victory, but alas it was not to be. He was gibbering out something in Archaic that would doubtless save his hide, prompting me to find a whole new way to slap him around.

As for us, we were the ones exerting force on the sphere, so we were at its turning point, safe for now.

By memory I guided my companions back down through the college, making only one or two wrong turns when I encountered renovations that had taken place after my departure, or murder. It was something of an inevitability that any place of learning where people learned to harness the arcane arts would have a degree of turnover when it came to architecture. A fireball here, a lightning bolt there, and what had once been a solid wall rapidly became a charming new bay window, and what used to be a ballroom floor became a brand-new, minor version of the eternal acid pit of Arpanpholigon.

Needless to say, after that incident, any jokes involving whether or not wizards had any balls were punishable by transmogrification into a pigeon.

CHAPTER 2

QUINT
OR PERISH

Still, we made it a remarkable distance in the time that we had, truly impressive, even if I do say so myself, before we reached the Quint and the sphere shattered around us with a thunderclap.

Sabrinia and Danyeel's unconscious forms were no longer being repeatedly rolled up the rear surface of the sphere to bounce around with the arcane constructs that had fallen dead and useless in a heap the very moment that we departed from my office. Instead they were dumped out into a heap upon the grass. Rather unfortunate that they'd been brought along for the ride, but at least we hadn't accidentally mashed them. I probably would have felt quite bad about that, eventually.

The popper of our bubble was none other than my wicked counterpart, who now stood with my own bloody staff in his hands, held horizontally like a barrier. "You shall not pass."

It was more or less the nightmare image of every student present on the Quint, given that it was exam season.

But of course, we no longer needed to pass; the bubble containing our magical workings was gone and we were free to cast and escape with all haste as we saw fit. Except Ig hadn't quite mastered teleportation yet, so he'd probably end up fused with a wall, Cygni couldn't handle mass teleportation with so many separate elements to keep track of mentally, and Ildrit was pretty much just a paperweight now that we were in a magical battle.

Right. A plan.

The other Absalom Scryne was not content to wait while I concocted a solution to our situation, instead launching a complex barrage of spells in our direction. I recognized them all, of course, as I was a master of the arcane, but they came at such speed that keeping track of them all separately was beyond even my impressive faculties. Particularly since my faculties were somewhat limited by the bullet-head that I was perched atop.

Some elements, Cygni recognized for herself, launching out the appropriate opposing elements as counterspells with huffs of *"Scutum, Scutum, Scutum."*

But the sheer volume of the fake me's assault could not be stemmed. It was only through the intervention of a kobold—which I suspect is diametrically opposed to divine intervention—that we happened to survive.

Throwing up his little paws, Ig snatched curses and fireballs out of the air with his low magic, tossing them aside like they were hot potatoes before they could explode and, somewhat accidentally, destroying the Quint with his deflections of the sustained artillery fire.

It was enough to make the students scatter in terror, but also sufficiently impressive to make my counterpart's jaw drop, giving my face a truly gormless expression. "You can't do that! That's impossible."

"That's what I said!" I inadvertently replied before realizing that hearing the voice of the person that he was impersonating coming out of the mouth of one of the people he was fighting might have given the game away somewhat.

"What?" He cocked his head to one side.

Cygni shrugged. "What?"

Not wanting to be left out, Ig attempted to say the same thing, though it came out as, "Weh?"

Ildrit held up his hands, Widowtaker having been returned to its sheath now that he realized just how surplus to requirements he was. Bringing a sword to a magic fight was somewhat similar to bringing a knife to a ballista battle, except for the fact that the person with the knife wasn't attempting to split ballistae with the knife as they were flung at their face. Key point: he was extremely underequipped for the current conflict.

"Gentlemen, we don't need to fight." He attempted a charming smile. "This is all just a misunderstanding."

The other Absalom's eyes narrowed. If he were really me, which obviously he wasn't, since I was really me, then his response to some big bully boy trying to smirk his way out of trouble would have been an abrupt fireball. After all, if he were really me, then he would have had a long and arduous adolescence marked by smirking, handsome, buff boys like Ildrit would have been a few decades back shoving his head down the toilet.

Which just goes to prove that I am the real me, and this imposter was a fake, because he did not respond with a fireball. He threw a lightning bolt instead. Totally different.

Ildrit flung himself aside, but the lightning curved to follow him. It was the curse of the warrior to always be wearing some amount of metal, either in the form of weapons or armor, that would draw electricity towards them. Making the lightning bolt a more solid tactical choice than a fireball. Not that I was impressed with the decisions my imposter was making, obviously. He was a fake, and I was real, and it was probably entirely coincidental that he was making all the decisions I would make if I hadn't been on my little journey and had all of my usual brainpower at my disposal.

Cygni's quick invocation of Holmium grounded all of the crackling bolts of lightning into the courtyard paving, but from Ildrit's rather strained expression, it was apparent that he was beginning to feel a little concerned about our prospects of survival.

Were this the real Absalom Scryne, I would have been concerned too. Absalom Scryne, which is to say, I, was one of the most fearsome arcane combatants in all of history, and poor Ildrit was standing up to him with nothing but a sharp bit of metal at his disposal. Not him. Me. I . . . never mind.

"Leave my boyfriend alone," Cygni snarled.

That seemed to replace all of Ildrit's fear over his impending electric death with a far more palpable terror. "Boyfriend?"

Now really isn't the best time to . . .

Cygni's glare snapped around from un-Scryne to her companion. "You've shared my bedroll every night since we've met. What else should I call you?"

"I mean, I just didn't realize we were at that stage yet, putting labels on things." If it were possible for a hat to cringe, rest assured, I would be cringing as I had to listen to this. "Making that kind of commitment. I just . . . our lives are in flux at the moment and I don't know if . . ."

"Really?! 'Boyfriend' is too much commitment? Where I'm from we'd have been wed before . . ."

At that moment the fake Absalom Scryne burst into flames, sparing all of us the horrors of having to endure another moment of this conversation.

He said, "Yeargh!" and flailed his arms around a little before adding, "Aaaagh," and "Aaaah!"

Ig had not been caught up in the drama of Ildrit and Cygni's relationship the way that the rest of us had. Kobolds had no real concept of relationships, and therefore no concept of the dramatics involved. Their breeding was accidental, and each mistaken copulation resulted in such a volume of kubs—the technical term for a baby kobold of course being spelled with a k—that the species continued to survive and propagate. The closest that any kobold had ever come to this sort of awkwardness was when two of them started chewing their way along a worm, not realizing another kobold had already begun chewing the other end. It did not end in smooching, so much as flailing and attempts to pry partially chewed worm out of an opponent's mouth. Regardless, his lack of interest in their impending bickering had surpassed even that of my counterpart, who as a wizard of the highest order was meant to be above such tawdry gossip. And as such, he had been able to creep around behind the other Absalom and unleash a great gout of heckfire.

"Aagh!" the faux-Absalom announced, before pausing a moment to contemplate his circumstances and adding, "Yeaaaaaaagh!"

I'd like to think, after everything I'd learned about myself and the world during my journey, that after a moment of watching my greatest foe slowly burn to death, I'd have felt compassion for them and put the fire that was consuming him out, but if I am to be entirely honest, the reason that I had Cygni combine Hydrogen and Oxygen into a casting of *"Uligo"* to put him out was not compassion. I wanted to see who was under the disguise. I wanted to know the face of my murderer before I scorched him to death.

Unfortunately for the fake Absalom Scryne, while he had constructed no defenses against heckfire, thinking that nobody would ever be so utterly stupid as to unleash it in a built-up area, he had prepared for aquatic assaults. As the splash of water leapt from Cygni's hands towards him, it was caught in some prepared dweomer that sent it flowing around him like a river before unleashing it back in the dwarf's surprised face—somewhat lesser in volume after its transit, thanks to the amount that had become steam while orbiting the blazing pillar of fire that was the imposter.

With a noise somewhat akin to a large sack of glass being trampled on by a horse, the imposter defended himself at last. From the heart of the inferno shone a purple light, spreading out and turning blue as it broke through. It spread throughout the fire, carried out by the licking flames themselves until the whole thing was encompassed, then, in a snap, the fire turned to ice, and encased at the center remained the shadow of my shadow-self.

That frozen silence persisted for but a moment before the great shattering was upon us. With a thunderous smash, the frozen flames exploded out in every direction, peppering us with jagged shards of ice that Ig was able to halt but the rest of us simply had to endure. A thousand tiny cuts appeared across Cygni, every one a tiny stinging distraction, spreading chill out from each point of impact until she was almost entirely numb.

From the epicenter of the explosion stepped the man who looked like Absalom Scryne, looking somewhat the worse for wear. His robes were scorched and blackened, the silk melted into his skin in places. His beard was almost entirely absent after the heckflames had licked his face, and what remained was streaked with black soot. But burning brightest of all was the fury in his eyes. "You dare to conjure the fires of heck here, in this most sacred place?!"

In terms of religion, the Invisible College was not a sacred place. Not by any stretch of the imagination. Our experiments were often described as playing god, our actions called abominations; even our magic itself was viewed with suspicion by those people who put more stock in asking their imaginary friends for help than in advancing the sum of human knowledge and creating solutions for themselves. If anything, the college would have been considered an unholy place by most major religions. The only ones that might have considered it holy were those religions with a very limited number of members, and deities with considerably more tentacles that tenets. Yet despite not being a cultist of any sort, I could feel the truth in this fake Scryne's words.

Before I had been cast out, before I had been made a hat, I had always held a reverence for this place, and considered it a blessing that I got to remain here throughout the years of my life. To me, these halls and chambers were hallowed ground. Learning was as close to a religious experience as I'd ever had. All of which is to say that the fake version of me must have really done a lot of research before taking my place so that he could provide such an incredibly detailed and deep performance. Bravo, murderer, you impersonate the corpse so well.

Ig tried to launch another burst of fire at the other Scryne, given how well the first one had worked, but this time the human wizard was the quicker on the draw, barking out, *"Retro,"* and invoking Oxygen.

The heckfire, filled with the snarling faces of the damned, poured from Ig's hands towards his foe, screaming its heckion scream until it had traversed half the distance between them, then a sudden gust of wind escaped from un-Absalom, blasting all of that lethal fire right back into Ig's stupid little face.

My beloved kobold companion was entirely engulfed and had neither the training nor the wherewithal to escape from his predicament.

There had been a great many times that I had heard Ig scream during our time together. I may have actually heard more screams from him than coherent thoughts. But this time was different. He'd been hurt before, but never so badly as to unleash a sound so animal and sharp. Throughout all our travels, I'd made light of him, of his pain and discomfort, but now, hearing him in genuine suffering, my heart ached. Or at least it would have, if I had one.

Poor Ig was in no way prepared to become kobold flambé, and given that I'd never intentionally taught him to channel heckfire, I certainly hadn't taught him any of the various countermeasures to ensure that it doesn't scorch and consume you if the wind blows in the wrong direction.

"Holy water. Quickly! Someone douse him in holy water!" I cried out in horror, before Cygni seized back control of her voice. "Where the heck are we going to get . . ."

The fake Absalom Scryne scoffed at us and vanished in a puff of nitrogen, repositioning himself somewhere not between a rock and a heckfire place.

My memory has suffered somewhat as a result of my mind being printed onto fabric instead of the juicy folds of my prodigious brain. In addition, the dark god we found down in the depths of the earth slurped a fair bit of my recollections down like a rather chunky milkshake, but there was holy water here, somewhere. I just had to remember where.

Cygni had darted forward valiantly, shielding her eyes from the flames with a sleeve, but her own half-hearted attempts to conjure water to quench the flames did nothing.

As previously mentioned, the academic and ecclesiastical worlds rarely had much crossover and the "chapel" attached to the college was unfortunately devoid of any sort of religious leader who might be able to furnish us with a blessing. All that you were liable to get if you went to the chapel was bullied. Or possibly some sort of sexually transmitted disease from the pews, as my understanding was that the small building's perpetual state of abandonment had made it a regular meeting place for lovebirds. Why, when I was . . .

Ig's screech cut through my reverie once more. Ah yes. Dying kobold.

Holy water. The laboratories! They'll have a holy water shower in case of demonic ichor spills and splashes. Quickly, take him to the laboratories.

Ig was still engulfed in flame. And this presented something of a problem when it came time to pick him up and carry him anywhere. If the situations were reversed, Ig could have quite easily reached through the fires and lifted Cygni with his low magic, but for Cygni such a raw application of power remained too difficult. She would not believe that she could hold him through the blazing Quintessence of the flames, and what the mind did not believe the magic could not achieve. It was the inverse of the principle that allowed an idiot like Ig to perform impossible acts of magic simply because they were too stupid to know that they were impossible.

Which was when Ildrit burst back onto the scene, smothering the kobold and fire with the cloak torn from his own back and scooping the whole flaming bundle up.

Would that it were normal fire that could be smothered so easily. Heckfire did not need to draw air to go on burning. You could drop it to the bottom of the ocean, and it would continue to scorch. Small wonder that we didn't teach apprentices to summon it really. All things considered.

On the plus side, while the fire could not be put out so easily, and was already scorching through the cloak, at least Ig's noises were now muffled as Ildrit took off running. He did not know where the labs were, but the great thing about being a hulking man with a sword was that people were very excited to answer any questions that you might have had.

Cygni set off to follow the rest of our party, only to discover that her feet were stuck. Glancing down, she could see that the grass had grown up and woven itself around her ankles. "Huh?"

I knew it! This proves that he is an imposter. I would never use druidic magic! I think druids are smelly hippies!

Cygni's brow furrowed. "Was that in question?"

I . . . no. I'm me, so he can't be. But it is still nice to have some evidence so that we can prove . . .

The lightning bolt caught Cygni right between the shoulder blades, lancing down through her spine and legs and scorching away the grass that had held her in place long enough for my counterpart to blast her.

If you've never been electrocuted before, you don't know what you are missing. It is a unique kind of pain, one that almost verges on pleasure, as every muscle the lightning passes through tightens up and releases involuntarily. Like a really good sneeze, but with more ruptured blood vessels and burning.

Cygni dropped to her knees on the seared black grass beneath her and let out a tooth-chattering groan. If she'd had her beard, it would have all been standing on end.

The Absalom Scryne fake stepped out from the cloak of shadows he had cast about himself and sneered down at the defeated dwarf. "I don't know who you are, and I don't much care. You will return my hat to me now, or you will face the lethal consequence of disobedience."

This guy sounded like a real dick. I hoped that I'd never spoken like that.

"You . . . don't know . . ."

Another lance of lightning crackled from betwixt my doppelganger's fingers to rake across Cygni once more as he strolled across the grass towards her, looking insufferably smug. "I know more than you could even comprehend the possibility of knowing, not to mention all that I know. You are a nothing, a nobody, and I am the Archmage of Arpanpholigon. Absalom Scryne, the greatest living wizard of our time. Master of the High Art. Commander of the . . ."

Alright, he is going to be distracted for a while listing off all his titles. Here is the plan . . .

She interrupted my nemesis's barking. "Never knew you were a druid, Mr. Scryne."

It was such an off-the-cuff comment that it didn't even stop un-Scryne's rambling until a moment later. "What?"

"Grass round my ankles." Cygni grunted as the last of the electrocution tremors ran through her. "Druid magic, right?"

"Why . . . yes, I suppose technically one of those dirty hippies could have achieved the same effect, but of course I made use of the elemental properties of . . ."

It was a minor tragedy that I never got to hear how my counterpart was going to explain himself, given that I, in truth, have made sufficient study of the druidic arts to very simply achieve the same effect by borrowing certain turns of phrase from them, and I could have used an excuse in my back pocket in case I ever had to rely upon them. I had to find some solace in the fact that his explanation was cut short by the sudden impact of Cygni's balled-up fist in his crotch.

This is the thing that nobody ever talks about when it comes to dwarves. They talk of how fearsome they are in battle, how stalwart and strong and highly trained, but I suspect that the greater part of the fear that elves and humans alike experience when facing off against the diminutive and hirsute people is that every blow is a low blow when you're fighting someone whose head comes up to your belly button.

Fake-Scryne made a high-pitched warbling noise as he folded in around his brutalized crotch and dropped to his knees. Cygni's second punch caught him under the chin, lifting him right off the grass to land in a moaning, groaning heap. "That's for Ig."

She stepped in and gave him a kick. "And that's for the real Absalom Scryne."

He did reply to that second one, but unfortunately Cygni could not hear his answer, given that it was spoken in a voice so high-pitched only dogs were liable to pick it up, and dwarves' ears were built with low-frequency sounds like distant rockfall in mind. Perhaps Ig might have been able to hear him, if the kobold were not currently being hauled off to be purged of heckfire.

I must confess that when the time came to put my imposter to question, I had assumed it would be after he had been overcome by magic rather than a couple of swift punches, but that assumption had been foolish. If this other wizard had not assumed that magic was the solution to everything, then he wouldn't currently be trying to ease his testicles back down out of his body.

"Here's how it's going to go . . ." Cygni began as he whimpered helplessly. "Going to ask you a question. You're going to answer me. Anything else, I start cutting bits off. Got it?"

This false Scryne was a coward at heart. He had endured no hardships in his life to climb to the top of academia beyond enduring some annoying dissertation challenges and occasionally having to study late. Meanwhile I had been off on an adventure, I had grown as a person, and if I were punched a few times and threatened with dismemberment, I would like to think that the version of me that I had now become would be able to resist such threats instead of whimpering and nodding.

Cygni crouched right down over him in a squat, met his eyes, and growled. "Who are you?"

All of this time, ever since the very moment I became aware of my existence as a hat, I had been waiting to find out who had murdered me. That may sound morbid to some of you, but for me it wasn't just a matter of vengeance—though you can be assured that the vengeance was going to be bloody, or burny, possibly acidic, I hadn't decided that yet—it was because whoever had managed to kill me had bested me. They had beaten me. The man who could not be beaten by anyone. When I had spoken the words, "I am Absalom Scryne," that is what I had been saying. *Invictus.* Undefeatable. And so whosoever had managed to end my life had robbed me of that.

Without a blink of hesitation, the imposter answered Cygni, "I am Absalom Scryne."

Cygni sighed and reached for the knife on her belt.

Do remember not to remove anything too vital until we have our answers, please.

"What are you doing? I'm telling you the truth." Panic spread across my face, so close that I could see every wrinkle, freckle, and wild growing hair. "I am Absalom Scryne!"

She caught hold of his wrist and waited for me to consent before she folded down all his fingers but the smallest and readied her blade.

Before our eyes, I could see some sort of epiphany passing over the imposter's face. Then he said it one last time with fierce certainty. "I am Absalom Scryne."

She lifted the blade to chop down into his finger-meat and was launched bodily across the Quint by the raw Quintessence released from the faux Absalom in a concussive wave. With the same mastery of the flows of magic that I had always shown, this fake levitated back upright and unleashed heck.

A bolt of black fire leapt from his fingertips to explode across a hasty carbon shield that Cygni only just barely got up in time.

"I am Absalom Scryne, and you dare to lay a hand on me."

Another blast rocked Cygni back, not fire this time but a blast of what I assumed was air. The invisible gas washed over her, making her ears pop, and when she tried to draw breath to cast for herself, whatever she breathed was most assuredly absent any oxygen. She gasped, drawing in more, but that achieved nothing but to bring darkness rushing in at the periphery of her vision.

"I am Absalom Scryne, Archmage of Arpanpholigon. Master of the Secret Art. Tamer of the Primal Elements. Here in my place of power, surrounded by my servants and students. And you dare to threaten me?!"

The world seemed to shake with the impact of his words upon us. All dimmed into darkness for but a moment, then we came back to reality with a crash, air forcibly driven down Cygni's throat to bring her back from the brink by the wizard now looming over us. His foot rested on Cygni's wrist, and with a little grinding, the pressure of his soft leather shoe uncurled her fingers from around the shard of Scrynium.

He plucked it from her grasp with a flex of low magic, bringing it up to hover atop his palm. "And here we have the secret of your magic, revealed at last. Not some lost scholar in the dwarven hives or some clever teacher, come from without, to convey wisdom to you, but a trick. A gimmick. Quintessence cultivated into solid form. An impressive piece of industry, no doubt. But it takes more than raw power to make a wizard, young lady."

He stepped away again, leaving a perfect simulacrum of himself in place, standing on her wrist. The other was bound to the dirt of the Quint, not by grass this time, but by a solid bar of carbon, pinning her down. Not that it mattered much at this point. Without the Scrynium, she couldn't cast a thing, even if she were free.

"I know you aren't the real Scryne," she tried to call out, loudly and dramatically so that anyone still lingering around the site of the battle could hear. Most unfortunate that the gas she had inhaled in copious amounts was helium, and her voice had gone from throaty and gruff to somewhere in the range that one imagines mice in children's books might sound like.

Still, the imposter managed to maintain his composure, apart from a small twitch of the mustache hiding his smirk. "Then who exactly am I?"

"A fake. A murderer. You killed the real Scryne and took his place." She was still shouting in her squeaky little voice, hoping to spread dissent among the enemy ranks, but honestly, she was probably barking up the wrong tree there.

Even if I was very good at magic, I'd never exactly been the most popular boss, and if this gentleman had killed me then most people in the college probably would have considered it: a) a relief; and b) a very rational career choice on his part, given the hundreds of years that wizards can easily live if they aren't assisted in departing early to free up their seat at the big-boy table. The only thing they might have questioned was why he'd felt the need to hide it or disguise himself as me.

"I am very sorry to tell you this, madam, but you have been led astray by some false information. I am Absalom Scryne, and I remain resolutely undefeated and un-murdered. Nor am I making use of any sort of illusionary spell, given that there are many enchantments around the college deliberately built to strip such disguises." He sighed, mostly to himself. "You would not believe the pranks that supposedly full-grown wizards inflict upon one another if left to their own devices."

That last part is true actually, why didn't I think of that?

"You tricked the enchantments." Cygni pressed on, even as internally, I tried to work out if what she was saying was even possible. "Ordered them not to strip you. You're the top boss, in charge."

"I am but the latest in a long line of custodians of this place of learning. No more its master than you are the master of the stone you carve in the depths below. The only difference is that I sculpt young minds, while you carve statuary, or whatever it is that you dwarves do with all that rock." He treated her to a surprisingly benevolent smile. As if this were all just a game that they were playing with one another and not going to end in anyone being thrown off the top of a floating college.

If you'd thought the bird strikes were bad, just imagine what a mess suicides would make of the old town below. The mental health support that students of the college received may not have been the most robust, but it did place a heavy focus on alternate ways for even the least competent wizard to expunge themselves from this reality without jumping the outer wall. Severe reinforcement of the umbrellas below would have been required otherwise.

Cygni ignored my tangent. "I know you're a fake, because I know the real Absalom Scryne."

"Madam, I'm afraid that you may have been taken in by an impersonator. Did this 'real' Absalom Scryne of yours want something from you? Something that you were unwilling to part with?"

"He wanted me to bring him here. To find you . . ." I could feel doubt beginning to prick at Cygni's mind. "To take his place back."

"And for some reason you believe that this imposter is the true version of me, even though I am standing before you, while your little friend is nowhere to be found. Interesting." There was a sharp precision to the word *interesting* that slipped between Cygni's ribs before she even felt it.

I think I liked him better when you had him on the floor sobbing.

She wet her lips. "How do I know mine is the real Absalom Scryne . . ."

Because I am, obviously.

Whoever the imposter was, I must admit to being at least a little impressed with him. Copying the mannerisms of a man is one thing, but copying those moments when his base instincts take him over and make him behave in a manner in which he never intended to . . . that takes an entirely different degree of acting talent. If young Danyeel had not already eliminated himself from suspicion then I would likely have assumed that it was him, as a master thespian.

Before our eyes, the concentrated, calculating fury of Absalom Scryne engaged in battle melted away into an almost childish glee to be presented with a logic puzzle that he had to pick apart. "You must admit that it would be considerably easier to trick you, than to trick the dozens, nay, hundreds of highly trained wizards that I encounter every single day."

There are certain spells with hypnotic elements to them. But the fake was not casting any of them. Instead he was simply trusting in the weight of his words to carry him to victory. Not the most reliable tactic, but for some reason he had lost all fear of the bloody reprisal now that he and Cygni were in reversed positions, and she'd been deprived of magic. "But my one has all the memories of the real Absalom Scryne."

"Does he though? Are you so intimately familiar with my life that you can ascertain that with certainty?" A wry smile settled on the imposter's face. "Or was the only thing that really proved your imposter was me, the fact that he had my hat on?"

The fact that our minds have converged and you have shared in all of my most intimate memories is probably a subtle hint that I'm the real one. Just a thought!

"He doesn't look like a real wizard." Cygni conceded the point. "Not like you do."

Conjuring up a tuffet from the green to sit upon, the Un-Scryne settled down to continue the debate with the supine dwarf. "So beyond the hat, which this fake decided to give you to wear for some reason, there is no real evidence that your Absalom Scryne is the real one."

"He can do magic," Cygni pointed out.

The other Absalom just scoffed. "Magic. Anyone can do magic, present company excluded. All you need is two brain cells to rub together."

"He knew a lot about it," she countered.

"I would suggest that this may be another matter similar to the memories, where your own ignorance of the subject matter rendered you susceptible to deception. How could you know that the lessons in magic that he taught you were of any value?"

And that was when I had him, because while there could be a great many besmirchments of my character, the one thing that nobody could say about me was that I did not know magic, or that I had not taught it to my two apprentices to the best of their abilities. Cygni herself had performed some frankly miraculous acts under my guidance, ascending from the depths of the underworld with a single cast, defeating a dark god . . . well, inconveniencing something that claimed to be a god at least.

She knew that I knew magic inside and out, because she had experienced it. So I need not worry in the slightest about her loyalty to me.

Her brow furrowed. "I think you might be right . . ."

"Aha! You see, with enough time and the application of reason, any deception can be undone." He clapped his hands together happily. "Now with this little misunderstanding settled, would it be too much trouble for you to return my hat to me?"

Don't listen to him, Cygni. Don't you do it! He'll destroy me. A wizard of the caliber required to keep up with both you and Ig will be more than capable of tearing through the feeble defenses I've stitched for myself and pillaging all my memories. His deception will be completely impervious should he place me atop his head and absorb all the real me's memories! Not to mention all of the power he'll get once he has my knowledge. And he will destroy the final fragment of my soul teetering on the verge of oblivion and complete the murder that he committed, setting off this entire chain of events. Don't give him the hat!

She waited patiently until my ranting was complete, then said, "You can't lizardman him?"

It was only then that I realized what she had been playing at all along. *Alas no, it would be akin to wresting all the Quintessence from the dragon. Draining so great an amount would burn me to threads as surely as it would kill him.*

"I beg your pardon?" the fake Scryne said.

"The guy that said he was you. You don't want to go after him? Get revenge? Turn him into a newt?" For a people entirely incapable of lying most of the time, Cygni was certainly getting good at a certain degree of quick-thinking obfuscation, I must say.

The fake me tittered, like a tit. "Oh, I can hardly hold it against someone for wishing that they were I. Who would not long for the glamorous life of the archmage? Though I suppose I should question them as to how they got their hands on my hat to begin with. Last time I recall having it, I was surveying the new protection spells cast on the Badlands Great Wall and a gust of wind swept it off. Whoever found it must have both known me and been traveling beyond the bounds of civilization. What an odd person they must be."

What?

Cygni's heart seemed to thump a little harder, for reasons I couldn't discern at present. "It wasn't stolen?"

"Merely lost." The false Scryne's brow drew down in mild irritation. "And then you refused to return it, for reasons I can't discern at present."

He's lying, he must have . . . he must have disposed of me, my body, beyond the wall, and lost the hat as a result.

"Right," Cygni announced. "I've heard enough. He wasn't going to admit to being a fake when we had him on his knees, but he should have admitted it when he had me on mine. To gloat. You wizards all love a gloat."

I will confess to enjoying a degree of gloating once in a while, yes, but that doesn't mean . . .

"We aren't getting it out of him." Cygni began shifting herself around, bending her knees, and tucking her feet below her body. "That's all there is to it."

Surely there is something that we can do to . . .

The other Scryne's frown deepened. "Madam, who exactly are you addressing?"

She jumped. Both rings of jumping had been placed firmly upon her fingers earlier in the conflict. It was an awkward jump, from an awkward position with her arms pinned down at the wrists, but there was strength enough in her leap that no matter the odd angle, it was going to drag her free. She was torn loose of the simulacrum and carbon bar with an awful jolt to her shoulders, launched in a great flip head over heels, and then landed a good distance back from the wizard that had been so certain she was his captive until only a moment before.

Yet more evidence mounted that I was the real Scryne and this fellow a fake when I saw the gormless gaping expression on the imposter's face. I had never looked that stupid and surprised in my entire life. Not once. Composure in the face of the unknown is a necessity for any wizard. Just proving that this buffoon was my inferior in every way. Even if we couldn't currently beat him in a magical duel.

Which was, unfortunately, the situation that we now found ourselves in once more. Going toe to toe with a wizard who I will concede was nearly as good as I was. Which was still light years ahead of both Ig and Cygni. Particularly when Cygni had been deprived of the Scrynium she needed to cast.

The imposter readied a spell, invoking what felt like Flerovium. There would be a flash of light as the spell washed over us, and then any living tissue would be gone, leaving only a heap of clothes, a bag of holding, and me, intact.

Lead! I cried out helplessly, already knowing that it was pointless. Even if Cygni did have the wherewithal to cast a shield before the spell struck, the drain on her bodily Quintessence would kill her all the same.

With only one final moment together, she reached up to touch my brim. "It's been an honor."

The spell was unleashed. The blazing sphere of death soared across towards us, leaving a trail of blighted grass beneath us. Death had arrived to claim Cygni, even though I was the one with the long overdue appointment.

Then the floor beneath us collapsed.

Cygni landed in Ildrit's big strong arms, which I couldn't help but note were now horribly scarred by the licks of heckfire. Contorted, sneering, demonic faces in every red whorl of wounded tissue. The sort of thing a certain class of warlock would spend a small fortune on in tattoos.

Ig looked . . . less good.

I would not like to give any false impressions that heckfire merely leaves one looking like an incredible badass wherever it touches and warps the flesh as it did for Ildrit. The fact that he had survived transporting Ig so far as the laboratory showers was frankly remarkable, and I suspect his current barely wounded status to be a direct result of the curse affecting him providing immediate and ample payback for the good deed of snatching the poor little creature up without a second thought for his own well-being.

Ig looked like a kobold still, vaguely. In shape at least there could be no denying his koboldness. The basic structure was all there, but it had all been layered over with horrific scarring the color of a well-boiled lobster that entirely covered his body. His eyes peered out from amidst that swollen mass of raw and tender flesh, and you could already see them watering from the pain of mere air touching him. When he opened his mouth to speak, I could see tattered tendrils of flesh trailing from the upper to lower jaw that stretched and snapped apart. "Me help."

Around us were the laboratories, perhaps the most important and dangerous parts of the Invisible College.

While your average institution for higher education typically judged the quality of the service that they provided based on the rate of students who successfully passed examination, matters were assessed on a different metric for schools of magic, where the most successful had the lowest mortality rates. Though rarely did even the best of the best ever manage to get that number down below the 50 percent mark.

Magic was inherently dangerous. The study of it possibly even more so than the practice of it, as in practice we merely repeated those spells known to work and not turn one inside out, while in studying and devising new spells and elements, we ran the far greater risk of encountering a fully unknown conundrum that could only be unraveled through practical experimentation.

The laboratories were where such experimentation took place, and they also represented the precise geographical area where the vast majority of the almost 50 percent mortality rate of this college was generated.

Once upon a time, an entire wing of the college had been dedicated to vast, carefully constructed and shielded chambers where our students and graduates might experiment, but when the whole thing blew up, it left the college lopsided and drifting to the left. After the center of gravity was reestablished, it had been decided that a smaller, more compact and central facility would be more practical, and fit better into the yearly budget. The question had then become, where should the laboratories be placed?

For some strange reason none of the various departments of the college wanted to live next door to a ticking timebomb of wizardly curiosity. Indeed, not even the administrative block, typically devoid of much power in inter-departmental debates, had refused to be shackled with it. But to everyone's delight, I had ascended to the role of archmage of the college amidst the debate—the position having been left vacant due to the prior archmage having been performing a small experiment of his own in the old laboratories at their time of detonation that may, possibly, have been the cause of the cataclysm.

There was one very obvious place, in my mind, for the new laboratory to be constructed, and that was directly underneath the Quint. I had lived through my student years with a certain disdain for the Quint, the enchanted frisbees being tossed about, and the happy couples dry-humping on its benches. If anyone was going to be annihilated in a pillar of arcane disaster, then I felt that the school would miss the kind of students that hung around on the Quint, the least. After all, if they were truly devoted to their studies, they wouldn't have been out there cavorting instead of being in the library, like good and sensible students. Like me.

What luck then that my prescient decision had placed Ig directly below us at this most vital of moments.

"Gods below!" Cygni bellowed. "He looks like a sausage that fell off the grill."

Nice. Tactful.

Ig's already watery eyes now brimmed with tears. "Snausage?"

Ildrit stepped in before the kobold could cry. "We need to get out of here right now. I don't know who your fake wizard is, but we're not prepared to face him."

"You are right, of course. Though it pains me to flee the battlefield without this matter resolved." Cygni was getting better about conceding control of her vocal chords but she still didn't like it.

Once she was back in control of her voice, she used it to bitch at me. "So we're all just going to pretend the hat didn't lead us in here like lambs to the slaughter?" She pointed at Ig. "Look at him! Look what you did to him!"

I did nothing . . . he . . . he made his own decisions . . . and these are the consequences . . . he'll just have to . . . I couldn't do it. I couldn't even think it. This wasn't Ig's fault. Nothing was Ig's fault, except perhaps for the rather unpleasant eggy smell in the room. He had been out of his depth from the moment I dragged him out of his hole in the ground, and the suffering he now endured was the inevitable consequence of that. I had been so proud of him, my little creation. My finest student, a creature that should have been incapable of even speech, taught the highest art. But just because he was the wisest and most powerful kobold to ever live, it did not mean that he could compare to a real wizard in his prime. I had filled his head with promises and nonsense and this was how my treachery had been repaid. *The poor . . . poor thing.*

Cygni's pity for Ig mingled with her contempt for me into a soup of self-loathing. The first course of a misery banquet that I was almost glad that my evil twin leapt down into the labs to interrupt.

"You cannot escape my wrath so easily, you treacherous . . ." He paused to take in the scene. "Oh . . . you're all here. Well . . . that is certainly more convenient than having to track you all down individually. Let's not have any more dramatic escapes, shall we?"

He raised a hand above his head, and Quintessence swirled into it to form a ball of pure magic. Not nearly so condensed as Scrynium, but a feat of control that was beyond impressive. Beyond what anyone in the whole Invisible College could achieve, other than me. Showboating. "Any last words of penance before I wipe all three of you away?"

"Snausage?" was Ig's rather dazed contribution.

"Get bent, longshanks," was Cygni's. Not particularly helpful either.

At least Ildrit could be relied upon to be sensible. "This has all just been a misunderstanding. Surely we can talk about this . . ."

The fake Absalom Scryne cast before the end of Ildrit's sentence. The same flesh-cleansing wave of destruction that should have consumed Cygni up on the Quint blasted towards us, and nobody had the magic to stop it or anywhere to run.

Cygni invoked lead and threw up her arms.

The shield wasn't very good. It only lasted barely a fraction of a second, with so little Quintessence fueling it, but it was sufficient to do two things. The first of which was stopping the Flerovium blast, and the second of which was vacating her whole body of every single particle of Quintessence.

She dropped dead, even as the spell dissipated harmlessly.

No. No. No. Unacceptable. No! Get up! Wake up!

"No!" Ildrit screamed, dropping Ig's lobster body to the ground and charging forward with his hand already reaching for Widowtaker.

There wasn't much Quintessence left in me after all of our adventures together. I'd been able to keep myself topped off, and sentient, by sipping at Ig's supplies along the way, but without the proper channels to store it, what I wasn't using for bare minimum survival tended to dissipate away. I dumped it all down into Cygni. Infusing her flesh with what little power I had left, hoping against hope that my tiny spark would be enough to reignite the apparatus of life inside her.

Ildrit was almost to the fake Scryne when she drew in a ragged breath, suddenly loud in the silent laboratory. The lust for vengeance that had contorted his face into something monstrous and fearsome melted away into sheer joy as she met his eye. He looked like a child receiving his first winter's day gift. "Cyg?"

From the juicy patch of tiles where he now lay, Ig groaned.

And it was about at that moment that the last vestiges of magic were drained out of me and sentience with it. I became, for the very first time, a hat in mind as well as body.

"Hat saved me," I could hear Cygni say. Though the words meant nothing to me.

The Scryne-imposter scoffed with contempt, "There was no enchantment on my hat that would protect you from that. What are you people playing at?"

What do we do? Cygni thought to me, as if a hat could think back.

Hat? What do we do now?

"Oh no." She whispered.

CHAPTER 3

THE ONLY ONE TO EVER DEFEAT ABSALOM SCRYNE

There was some mourning happening above me now that I'd been scooped off Cygni's head to be cradled in her lap. Ig had crawled his painstaking way over too, reaching out his grabby little claws in my direction.

As for me, my consciousness was withering away to the great black nothing more and more with every passing moment. It was consuming me as surely as Nun-Mhorgoth had done. The crushing weight of inevitability.

Distantly there came the sound of gloating. "I do not know what it was that you hoped to achieve here today, but let me assure you that it was doomed to failure regardless. Do not feel too badly about yourselves just because you were incapable of defeating the undefeatable Absalom Scryne. Nobody can."

I was so close to gone entirely by then that I scarcely heard him. But the truth of what he said resonated within me. Nobody can beat Absalom Scryne.

As Quintessence flowed into me from the brush of Ig's fingertips, life roared back in. Just a tiny spark of power, barely enough to keep me in existence, but enough. I tried to give some subtle sign that I lived. *I'm alive!*

Could someone put me on their head so my thoughts can be heard? It came out rather plaintive and pleading, but luckily it also wasn't heard. Wouldn't do to ruin my reputation after all.

With his red raw hot-dog fingers, Ig plucked me from Cygni's loose grasp and put me on his head, probably in an act of mourning. Softly he whimpered, "Me sorry. Me let you down."

Ig. You have never done a thing wrong from the moment I met you. You are perfection itself.

"Feel like I can still hear his voice . . ." Ig sobbed.

You can hear my voice, you tit. I'm alive.

His head jerked up, sending a whole ripple of agonies through his ruined flesh. "Weh?"

I'm alive, but you won't be in a moment if you don't get off your backside and fight!

"Hat alive!" Ig cried out in delight.

The false Absalom paused in his casting of some new and terrible curse to ask, "I'm terribly sorry, did you just say that my hat is alive?"

I did not draw deep on Ig's Quintessence, for I had no need. There would be more than enough Quintessence where I was going.

Enough running. Enough hiding.

I pulled Ig up to his full height, which currently was approximately bugger all, given that he couldn't even stand. But I gave myself whatever dignity I could muster before I announced to my enemy, *I am Absalom Scryne. You asked how we knew that you were an imposter; this is how.*

The false Absalom Scryne, the nemesis who had damned me to this hat-based heck, who had run rings around my apprentices, blasting all and sundry who crossed him to kingdom come, blinked. "Once again, terribly sorry, just to clarify, you, the kobold, are claiming to be Absalom Scryne? The wizard. Who is directly in front of you."

Ig made a little strangled noise as I seized control once more with exasperation. *No, not the bloody kobold. The hat! Your hat. I mean, my hat. I'm Absalom Scryne.*

The fake cocked his head to the side. "You seem to be rather confused."

Kobolds aren't really built for shouting, so much as squeaking and screaming, but I got some good boom out of Ig's voice when I made my declaration. *There is no confusion. I, Absalom Scryne, was murdered, and my consciousness transposed into my hat by the immense amounts of magic that it had been exposed to. Ergo, you cannot be the real Absalom Scryne. Ergo, you are an imposter, likely the one who murdered me to take my place.*

"Might have Er-gone off track near the end there," Cygni piped up.

Then the imposter made the last mistake of his life. He smirked. "I am not sure why you think that I have been murdered, or indeed that anyone would be capable of murdering me, but I am pleased to inform you that rumors of my demise have been greatly exaggerated."

If I was not dead, then how do you suppose that my consciousness transferred into my hat? I shot back.

Cygni had been looking back and forth between us this whole time, as though attending a game of verbal tennis, but once more she felt compelled to weigh in. "Could just be a copy."

"What?" the fake copy of me barked at the same time that I very reasonably asked, *What?*

Cygni was suddenly on the receiving end of two angry stares. One being projected through a kobold's beady eyes, from somewhere down amidst the mangled mess of Ig's fried features. But despite glares that should have pinned her in silence as they had a million students before them, she shrugged her shoulders and pressed on. "Been talking to the two of you through this whole day and . . . you're the same."

"*How dare you . . .*"

"How dare you . . ."

We had both spoken in harmony, with the very same timing and cadence. I will admit that the imposter was very well practiced in my impersonation, but this was getting annoying.

"I cannot be compared to a piece of headwear," he cried, as I decried him, "*I cannot be compared to this pathetic excuse for an imposter.*"

"Stop doing that!" We both shouted in perfect time. "*Stop doing that!*"

The other Scryne got ahead of me at last, bellowing, "Enough!" and putting an end to that annoying interlude.

He paused for a moment to be sure that he had silence, then proceeded. "There is a very simple solution to this problem, that I suspect will not be to your tastes, but you cannot deny will be efficient." Once more a pause for any interruption, but none came. "I am going to destroy you, all of you, and the hat, utterly. Thus eliminating this entire tiresome side quest. I shall then proceed to drink copiously in the hopes that I can also eliminate it from my memory. Any objections?"

Ildrit, Cygni, and Ig all raised their hands. I then raised Ig's other hand.

"Good, nobody that matters has an opinion." He nodded firmly. "Goodbye!"

Now that he was no longer trying to preserve my existence, or the existence of the college around him, thanks to the well-shielded walls of the laboratories, there was no longer any need for complex or clever spells to assassinate us. Cygni had no Quintessence with which to cast, Ig was an absolute horror show of molten flesh and agony, and Ildrit had no magic to begin with, so could not be reliably useful as anything other than a blunt object.

He readied a lethal and catastrophic spell that Ig wasn't sharp enough to catch the components of through the previously mentioned agony, and was about to unleash it, killing us all, when I took matters into my own hands.

Or rather, Ig's paws.

I reached up, snatched myself off his head, and flung myself across the room like a discus.

The more skeptical among you may have thought that I was attempting to preserve my own life by escaping the blast cone of the spell that was about to be cast, but my aim was true despite the ruined mess of Ig's musculature. My hat form flew gracefully through the sky to land atop the fake Scryne's head.

Now let's see who you really are.

I pulled with all my might, all my will, all my everything. The emptiness where the Quintessence that kept me alive usually floated was filled in a moment, and my memories were flooded with the past months where this imposter had taken my place, continuing my delicate research projects diligently, managing the complex administration and finances of a college that exists simultaneously in multiple different realities and time zones, even attending the awful interdepartmental meetings that had ever been the bane of my existence, all without complaint or any thought of the great victory that he had won over me.

"What in the seven hecks?!" The imposter beneath me cried out as his spell collapsed back in on itself and the Quintessence he had used to form it was sucked back up his channels, through his body, and up into me.

I began to glow and smoke as the massive buildup of Quintessence started tearing me apart from the inside out, but I was not done. This was going to kill me in a very real and permanent way, but only by completely draining every drop of Quintessence from my murderer could I be sure that I'd take him down with me.

Magic began to discharge all around us as I overloaded, tiny lightning bolts shattering beakers and rebounding off the warded walls, resolving into veritable tides of tiny bunnies that scampered about underfoot, covering tile with an extremely fuzzy carpet.

Cygni cried out in despair as she realized what I was doing. That I was heroically sacrificing myself to save them all. She'd been sad before when I'd heroically sacrificed myself just to save her. With the added heroism of saving her boyfriend and Ig, I was probably going to draw actual tears from the dour dwarf.

"You cannot do this to me, I am Absalom Scryne!" he bellowed, and then he began pulling back, ripping power and memories from my grasp even as I yanked more out of him. Glimpses of what he was taking passed before my figurative eyes as he tore me apart.

The ogre laid low by a banana. The necromancer's questionable décor. The werewolves. Scrynium. The dragon. My loathed roommate who always practiced the lute when I was trying to study. The faint and distant remembrance of my mother's face, now long faded to almost nothing.

"How could you know . . ."

On one side of his brain he was being flooded with my memories, and on the other I was dragging his out as fast as possible. The fateful day that he dropped his hat while flying over the Badlands. His irritated searching, that had turned up nothing. The annoyance at having to order a new one so intense that he'd simply never bothered. The latest argument between the thespian illusionists and the statistical analysis department about who had claimed use of lecture hall C on Thursdays. The first time that I had drawn Quintessence, the sweet burn of power in my veins after a lifetime of being powerless. Knowing that I would always have this. The certainty that I would become great in the art of magic purely based on that first brief sensation of Quintessence all around me, binding all reality together.

"You . . ." he choked out.

You . . .

The draw of memories and magic had become a churn now, the speed of it accelerating, the memories flooding into both of us, mingling together, blending into one coherent story of my life, even if for a time it featured two simultaneous timelines, coming together into one, right about . . . now.

All of the magic in the room stilled. The balance of it between my body and my hat finding equilibrium and all of my senses returning to me for the first time. I could feel it all. All of the universe was within my grasp now that I was back as myself again. I took a deep breath, filling my own lungs with air, feeling the creak in my lower back like an old friend and the itch where one bit of golden thread protruded through from the embroidery on my robes to tickle at my knee, just as it always did when I wore this set.

I remembered everything. Everything from my whole life. I was complete again, but more so, I was changed. I could remember what it was like to be the Absalom Scryne who had never been a hat and never gone on an adventure. To be so dreadfully lonely but never admit it, to be closed-minded and angry and think of others as lesser players in my own story. If you had asked me but a moment before, I would have said I was still the same man as I'd been on the day my hat parted from my body, but the truth was that in the few brief months of our separation, the hat had lived more than I had in the past decade or more. It had done more, learned more, become . . . better.

With a sigh, I opened my eyes. "It is over, my dear friends. I have . . ."

Ildrit was swinging Widowtaker for my neck.

For any other wizard I have no doubt that this would have spelled instant death, but I was not any other wizard. I was Absalom Scryne, improved and upgraded and combined into my most perfect form. My incredible mind was back in my incredible brain, and connected to all of my incredible reserves of Quintessence, accumulated over decades of hard work and growth. Magic enough to drown continents, raise mountains, and make even the gods themselves, if there even were such things, pee themselves a little.

I was also, conveniently, dumped back amidst all of the familiar and typical layers of protection that I had assembled over years of paranoia, expecting one of my myriad lesser enemies in academia to assassinate me by means both fair and foul. In short, for the very first time since my grand adventure began, I was actually equipped to deal with the problem in front of me. A talisman of a bent-bowed tree on a silver chain, laced around my left wrist underneath my voluminous sleeves, began to glow, unseen, and a barrier of thickened air sprang to life betwixt Ildrit and me. Dragging at his swing until it was comically slow.

I took a step backwards, out of reach, and then tried again. "My friends, it is me. The Absalom Scryne that you know and love."

It was a testament to the impression that I had made on both of my apprentices that at that moment each of their entirely differently constructed faces made the same shifty-eyed expression of "not really."

Ildrit's furious expression had not changed, however. He was trying to avenge the hat he had befriended with the same brutality that he had attempted to unleash for the death of his girlfriend. It may have somewhat reduced the romance of the prior situation that he seemed to be perpetually waiting for an excuse to unleash the most gruesome violence imaginable as soon as he could justify it with some upset.

"Ildrit, it is me," I told him, knowing full well that he could hear me just fine inside the thick air. "My consciousnesses have fused into a single person once more. I never died."

"Told you so," Cygni felt obliged to say, despite many more pressing matters.

"Yes, truly you were the only one who could possibly have picked up on all the nuances, such as the two of us thinking and speaking almost identically, our magic being perfectly matched, and our behavior perfectly reflecting how the other would have behaved in the same situation." I rolled my eyes. It felt so good to have eyes again. "I definitely wasn't aware of all those things but in denial because I wanted to eke out some vengeance on the one who had put me in so terrible a situation."

"Yeah, yeah." She smirked. "I told you so."

"Me liked you better as hat," Ig opined from where he lay on the floor.

"That is just charming, thank you so much, Ig," I grumbled before turning back to Ildrit, who was still in mid-swing and showing no signs of stopping. Though judging from the way the muscles in his legs were bunching up, he was intent on launching himself that little bit farther forward so that the blow would again make contact. "I know you can hear me in there. Please do stop trying to murder me so that we might have a conversation?"

The furious rictus remained unchanged, so I sidled around the frozen warrior to go and see to my beloved, non-murderous companions. "First thing is first."

With my own brain back, synapses were firing at the speed they were supposed to be. Leaps of logic that I'd been quite incapable of as a kobold or dwarf with their differently structured brains now flooded through me. Sodium, hydrogen, and oxygen to purge. Then oxygen, carbon, hydrogen, nitrogen, calcium, phosphorus, potassium—of the non-banana variety—and sulfur to put a little evil in him, as was true and correct of all sentients; sodium, chlorine, magnesium, then traces of fluorine, bromine, boron, silicon, vanadium, nickel, and a handful of other tiny elements that would scarcely require mentioning. They'd have to be adjusted on the fly to suit the kobold body, but with a brain as quick as mine, it went from an impossible task to a mere chore. One that I'd more than willingly undertake for my dear sweet kobold.

"Sanabitur."

Copper, iodine, and chromium were added to the mix too as I realized that the kobold body needed them. And despite the obvious temptation to make improvements on the clearly faulty design of the kobold body, I managed to resist and remake Ig as he had been before his encounter with heckfire.

The outer layer of scar tissue that had entirely covered his body burst like a colossal blister, with several pints of saline spattering across the floor. And there within that soggy cocoon lay Ig, remade once more in his own image, rather than the image of a deep-fried spicy sausage.

"Ow," he said, habitually. Though I felt quite certain he would have experienced naught but a little pressure.

Next I turned to Cygni, who, having seen the breadth of the gifts I was bestowing, began backing away in a scramble. "Oh no you don't!" I called with glee. "It is time to repay you for all the kindness you showed me."

She turned and tried to run, but fast as her little stubby legs might have been, they could not outpace my magic. This was a more complex working than simply reconstructing Ig's body back to its original parameters. Initially, I had meant to grant her some sort of external arcane device that she could use to store Quintessence and wield it as she had with the Scrynium, but feeling inspired after seeing the mess of all Ig's internal organs to make something better, I now felt equipped to give her precisely what she had desired all along.

"Vias Aperire."

I shall not bore you with the complexity of all the elements that I invoked to spread the channels within her body back to the way that nature had intended, given that it ultimately ended up as a combination of around one hundred of them in varying amounts and orders. She was lifted bodily from the ground by the force of the spell's work, and landed with a groan. She did not say, "Ow," as Ig had, though I imagine that her experience was considerably more painful.

Oh well, she'd soon forget that pain when she felt . . .

"Cor Aperire."

That one probably felt like someone reaching down inside her, planting an explosive and setting it off. But the extra spike of Quintessence that I sent surging in afterwards to fill her newly expanded reserves should have more than made up for her brief segue into an agony bordering upon the hinterlands of death. I filled her soul up to bursting with magic, and let it flood out through her. Restoring that which nature had failed to furnish her with properly, making her the first dwarf in millennia to be naturally capable of casting magic.

She flopped down directly onto her face with that spell completed, and I turned at last to Ildrit. Looking at him now with all my arcane senses attuned, I could see the curse, hanging over him like a vast praying mantis, just waiting for its opportunity to strike.

Changing bodies, even changing the channels that magic might flow through a body were relatively minor in comparison to the working that would be required here. Whoever had laid this curse upon him had tapped into some primal and fundamental force of the universe, hooking his personal fate to the complex balancing act of all reality. Unpicking it had been beyond the Bonetaker, and any other wizard that Ildrit had taken it to, not because breaking such a curse would be so complex and difficult, though it obviously would be, but because any minor mistake might knock the balance of the entire cosmos out of whack. Such a thing could be catastrophic. Apocalyptic, even.

What luck then that he had found his way to Absalom Scryne, the greatest wizard of his generation, and the most willing and capable of dissolving such a curse. Why, I messed around with the cosmic balance just to boil my breakfast pot of tea most days, shifting the boiling point of water at this altitude wildly around until it achieved the temperature that I desired. Even the loss of my hat, or myself, depending upon which version of me you were following, had been amidst a period of time in which I was temporarily convincing the force of gravity that I did not need to be noticed for the time being. For a friend as true as Ildrit, I'd have been willing to topple the universe into chaos six times over, and even then, we'd only have to face consequences if I were to make a mistake—and that, dear friends, is the only thing that I, Absalom Scryne, am incapable of doing.

Oh no, there is also losing. Making mistakes and losing, the two things that I cannot do. And while I realize that you may be thinking that my omission of losing initially might constitute a mistake, you would be incorrect, as I corrected my very minor error instantly, before any consequences of that error, such as you misunderstanding my ability to lose, or make mistakes, could come to pass.

"Ildrit, I can see the curse set upon you, and I believe I know how best to remove it, but beforehand I really do need you to stop swinging that sword around, would you?"

Gasping from a wet heap on the floor, Ig cried out, "No, let him help. Is worse than when he try kill you."

The groaning from Cygni seemed to be in agreement.

"Oh come now, you two, in but a moment you'll both be fully recovered and able to enjoy the benefits of the gifts I bestowed upon you. Surely you would not begrudge Ildrit that same freedom." I will admit that I may have been a little manic in my delight at having gotten my body back. Usually I would have been at least a few degrees more conservative and considerate before throwing so many spells around in quick succession, but who cared? I was me again. And I finally had the power to make all that was wrong with my friends right. Why wouldn't I?

"I'm releasing you from the spell now; resist your urge to hit me with your sword." I paused for a moment before actually casting the counterspell and added, "Please."

Ildrit completed his leaping cut towards the place where I had been standing and then spun on his heel, readying his sword once more. His eyes remained dark, locked on mine as though he could stare right down into my soul and steal the answers he sought. "How do we know you are who you say you are?"

"Well, I just had you all entirely at my mercy and delivered onto two thirds of you your greatest desires instead of blowing you up?"

He took a careful step towards me, waiting for any sign that I was casting against him. "That doesn't prove you're still the hat."

"Well, I suppose that if one were to get philosophical about it, I am not the hat." I stroked my beard as I thought. It was a bit of a mess after my brush with heckfire, but it felt so incredibly good to be back in a bearded body again. Stroking Cygni's had never felt the same. "Both versions of myself have formed a gestalt mind. Though judging by my actions thus far, I'd argue that the hat version of myself seems to have been the more dominant of the personalities in the mix, given that I've lost a good deal of the . . . dislike that I maintained for all of you prior to our recombination. One might even say that I consider you to be my friends."

Ildrit's eyes narrowed. "Tell me something that only the hat would know."

I thought back through everything I knew about Ildrit, and those few private moments that we had shared together, searching for anything that only the two of us would know, out of everyone in this company. "You almost definitely had sex with the Bone—"

Once more he leapt, but this time it was to clamp his hand over my mouth midway through the sentence. He laughed loudly to drown out anything I might have been saying. "Haha! It is you after all." He leaned in close and whispered in my ear. "Don't ever mention that again or else . . ."

I never got to hear the *or else* because we were intercepted by a flying kobold. Had he been a little more substantial, we may both have been knocked over by Ig's hug, but since he still appeared to be made out of blotchy skin draped over bird bones we were simply rocked by it. Cygni trudged across after him and flung her arms around the huddle too, though I suspect that was at least in part because she was struggling to stand upright on her own without assistance.

"We won," Cygni murmured.

"We is winning," Ig concurred.

"Finally," Ildrit said with a smile. "It is over."

For a man so intimately connected to the tides of fate, one would have thought that he might have had a little more sense than to tempt it with a statement like that.

CHAPTER 4

TABULAR ROTATION

After all of the hugging was done and we'd parted in awkwardness, coughing and failing to make eye contact, I realized that I had rather a lot of tidying up to do. Not to mention a not-insubstantial amount of explaining myself to everyone in the college, and most specifically to those members of the college's faculty who had been beaten bloody and knocked unconscious by the people who were now going to be invited to stay here for the foreseeable future as I worked on their training, and in the case of Ildrit, cured his curse.

Needless to say, the majority of that explanation had to be done considerably more publicly than I would have liked since the fighting had spilled out into the more public areas of the college, resulting in a great deal of the story of my journey, as a hat, also becoming public knowledge. This was not ideal. It is difficult to maintain one's image as the undefeatable, all-powerful master of all magic, while simultaneously acknowledging that your survival beyond the safety of the college walls had been predicated almost entirely upon luck and the quick thinking of a kobold. But if I were to become a laughingstock as a result of my sojourn in hat-dom, then so be it, so long as each of my friends received the reverence that they were due for their part in my rescue.

Overnight they became celebrities about town, and the circus that Ig was technically still the ringleader of became the town's latest hot spot. Resulting in him making masses of money that he didn't need, which was promptly shared among the various employees who then swore their eternal and undying loyalty to him. Meanwhile, Ildrit and Cygni finally had some peace and quiet to explore their burgeoning relationship without the prying eyes of a wizard atop either of their heads. Their celebrity could be parlayed into a decent table at any restaurant in town, and since I hadn't touched a penny of the pretty substantial salary that I drew as archmage of the college in the last century or so, I was more than happy to clear any tab that they managed to run up, regardless of how ridiculous it may have been—though it is helpful to note that if you have a reputation for being impossibly savvy and can turn people into snails for trying to cheat you, you will very rarely be overcharged for anything.

I was returned to my rightful place in a hastily reconstructed office, where I made private apologies and offered reparations to both Sabrinia and Danyeel. The former of which seemed to surprise them so much that they didn't even try to make any obscene demands as part of the latter.

With my full memory now at my disposal, it became clear that I had never actually apologized to anyone ever in my earlier life, pre-hat, and as such, the sudden switch in my personality was considered to be so much of an oddity and blessing that they were willing to put up with a few bruises in exchange for having facilitated that change.

Which left only three matters to attend to.

Item the first: discovering how my hat had become a copy of my consciousness.

Item the second: the breaking of Ildrit's curse.

Item the third: Ig.

The first matter was one that would require significant amounts of study, and for which I was forced to pry poor Cygni away from her lover boy for some substantial amount of time to undertake a little carving work.

Some experimentation with Cygni showed that the hat maintained an up-to-date copy of my current self, operating in parallel to me until we were recombined again, allowing the possibility that we could have a pair of Absalom Scrynes operating simultaneously, which provided a massive boon to my research projects, which I could now undertake twice as many of. It also meant that I would, once I had a suitable host body, be able to bounce ideas off the only person in the world who was as smart as me. Which was just wonderful in every way.

This led to poor Cygni being commissioned with a secondary task that she seemed to relish, while everyone else in the college had shied away from it, due in no small part to the danger of bodily harm that it involved.

Item the second proved to be somewhat more difficult, as Ildrit was oddly reluctant to spend the time with me that I required to decipher the fine details of the magic laid upon him. Much of the time he claimed that he was expected to meet with Cygni somewhere, and—unwilling to interfere with, or hear too much about, their relationship—I was always keen to let him go. But soon a pattern emerged when it seemed he was trying to avoid my assistance regardless. After so long trying to find someone who could rid him of his curse, I couldn't really understand that reluctance, but it soon faded into the background of my concerns when it came to Item the third.

I found Ig on the Quint, several days after I had healed him, and somewhere in the midst of my various apologies, explanations, and requisitions for new construction materials to repair the parts of the college that we'd destroyed.

He was sitting on the ground in the dirt, digging for grubs.

Given that I had turned over my personal chef and directed all of the kitchen staff in the depths of the college to provide the kobold with any delicacy that he requested, without any thought to cost, this was somewhat odd.

"Ig, my dear boy. Whatever are you up to?"

"Weh?" came his vacant reply.

Looking up at me, there was clearly nothing going on behind that heavy-lidded stare. Even more so than usual. Where before, as a resident of his mindscape, I could hear the gentle plinking sound as his one brain cell bounced off one side of his skull and then the other, now even that gentle motion had been stilled.

I crouched down beside him despite the varying protestations from my ankles, knees, hips, and back. I will say, I had not missed being old when I was a hat. "Ig, can you understand me?"

He nodded his head slowly, snout drifting up and down at an almost geologically slow pace.

Okay, there was still some sentience there. "Why are you digging, Ig?"

He pointed to his mouth. Food. Hungry. Dental hygiene. There were many possible interpretations of the gesture, but I leaned towards the first one as being the most likely.

Perhaps sentience was too much of a stretch; even a parrot was capable of speech, and I'd hardly call those bright feathered bastards sentient. I'd call them a lot of other things. But not that.

"Ig, you know that you just need to go to the kitchens, and they'd be happy to provide you with whatever you need."

Ig blinked at me, very slowly, then once more made the same sound as before. "Weh?"

This was concerning to say the least. I had not been giving Ig a great deal of attention since arriving back at the college, simply because my duties had taken precedence. Although I'll be the first to admit that my counterpart or prior self or whatever we were calling him had done a bang-up job keeping things ticking over in my absence. In my absence from Ig's day-to-day life, I had not been present to observe the warning signs that he was slipping back into his natural kobold state. Which is to say, approximately as intelligent as if one had left some milk out in direct sunlight for about a week.

The Council of the Wise is not called often. In part because everyone has a very busy schedule, in part because each time the Council of the Wise is assembled, everyone who is not a member begins having a strop over not being considered sufficiently wise. A course of action that they would not undertake if they were wise, as it marks them as distinctly unwise, and unlikely to be invited to future iterations of the Council of the Wise.

The other reason that the Council of the Wise is not often called together is a fundamental problem with all wizard-kind, and academics in general, in that if you are to place two of them into a room with one another, they will immediately zero in on the one thing in magical theory that they disagree about and have a century-spanning argument about it, with citations aplenty, and humbling volumes of research produced to back up their own particular case. In fact, I remain convinced that if one were to take a single wizard and lock him in a small room without anyone else around, he would have an argument with himself until working out a way to schism himself into two sentient beings, each holding the opposing viewpoint.

As such, when one called a Council of the Wise, it was rare that any actual conclusion would be reached, and their value typically lay in getting a look at the current interdepartmental political posturing and inciting any underperforming members of said council into stepping their game up so that they might be a more effective antagonist to everyone around them the next time.

This particular Council of the Wise had new members who previously would not have even been considered as viable options. Two were faculty members who had found their way onto the Council of the Wise as some sort of favor for assisting the archmage of the college. One of the few concessions demanded from Danyeel and Sabrinia. But the other two were not even wizards, so far as the rest of the council was concerned. They would concede that yes, the dwarf lady did seem to be able to use magic to some degree and had memorized a starkly terrifying amount of magical theory since her arrival at the college and before, but that did not make her a wizard. Where were her robes and pointy hat, for instance? Where was her publication history in peer-reviewed scrolls? Just because one is capable of performing some magic utilizing every single known element on demand, does that make them a wizard? I personally would have argued against such a thing in my previous life, but since I was the one who wanted Cygni present for the council, I had to reverse my position and argue for the radical fringe who believed that being able to do wizardry actually mattered more to being a wizard than having the appropriate attire, education, and credentials.

These additions to the council rounded it out to twelve members, with the other eight broadly representing the most important fields of magic within the Invisible College and beyond.

Archimendo, the Lore Master of Ancient Tongues, Balthazagar, Evocation Master of the Elements, Iomedania, Mistress of Research and Divination, Poindextrous, Calculating Master of Statistical Analysis, Maximus Arturo, Portly Portal Master of Dimensions, Copernicrust, Indifferent Master of Balance, Philodephina, Quadratic Mistress of Quintessent Studies, and myself of course, Master of All Magics.

Before they had even shuffled into the conference room, the fighting had already begun. "I'm not saying that the drag of interdimensional drift isn't the generating force behind Quintessence, I'm merely stating that all evidence to that effect has thus far been anecdotal."

"Anecdotal?" Philodephina cried in horror. "A three-year study conducted by some of the finest researchers in the world has concluded that . . ."

From the sidelines, Balthazagar sniped, "I'm not sure I'd consider weed-gnomes to be the finest researchers . . ."

"Ladies and gentlemen." I raised my hands for silence.

"How dare you talk about my researchers like that. You cannot seriously believe that the Quintessence generated by dimensional drag is insignificant to the concentrations we have available to us?! How do you explain portal balancing?"

"There is no balance in the creation of interdimensional travel, only equal opposing forces," Copernicrust opined without looking up from his book.

"They're talking about the release of Quintessence from the rupture points in m-space," Iomedania explained, apparently to herself as nobody else was listening. "You cannot discount the m-space rpq!"

"I doubt that your output ever even equalizes to your input." Archimendo scoffed. "It's all overspill from badly constructed spells."

Arturo flung himself up from his chair, face already turning puce with rage. "My spellwork is tighter than a badger's back end!"

"Ladies and gentlemen!" I tried again, a little louder this time.

"You'd know all about badger's back ends, wouldn't you." Philodephina delivered each word like they were envenomed darts being shot into a king's back.

"I beg your pardon," Arturo bellowed, as though volume won arguments.

Poindextrous sneered out from behind glasses so thick you could have used them to start not-insignificant forest fires if the sun was right. "Ev-everyone knows about your little puh-puh-polymorphed adventures, you lecherous old . . ."

"SHUT UP!" Ildrit bellowed with such force that a few of the wizards physically wilted down into their seats. Where had he been all my life? How many meetings that could have just been notes could have been cut from multi-hour fiascos to a quick conversation adjudicated by the scowling warrior?

I cleared my throat again. "Thank you."

Pausing a moment to see if the rabble would resume, I was pleased to discover that it would not.

"I have gathered you here today for two reasons. The first of which is to offer you some explanation as to the events of last week when there was some minor damage dealt to the college, and the second of which is to pose you a hypothetical question with some very real consequences for all of us."

Danyeel and Sabrinia shot each other smug looks. This was the Council of the Wise, and they already knew something that everyone else didn't. Did that make them the most wise of the whole council? The ones held highest in my estimations? Could this mean that their futures were assured so long as I held power? Or that one of them might be named my successor when the time came?

It was more a matter of proximity, unfortunately for them. They knew about what had happened because they were the ones who happened to be closest by when it happened, not because they were particularly special and dear to my heart. And if truth be told, I would rather have kept the full details of my own transformation a secret. This would have been a crime against academia of course, concealing such an interesting effect of long-term Quintessence saturation on an inanimate object, but at the same time, I really didn't fancy dealing with all the problems and accusations and whatnot that would come with it.

Alas, the state of Ig had forced my hand and now I stood before these lesser minds with my hat held in my hands, begging them for help, because while in my previous state I would have slogged away at the problem alone in perpetuity, I was now mature enough to abandon my own ego and ask for help when I needed it.

That is called growth.

Admittedly none of these people were as smart as me, nobody ever was, but they were specialized in areas of study that I might have overlooked with my more generalist, all-encompassing knowledge. Which meant that even if they couldn't provide me with an answer, they might have at least sparked the right question in my mind.

"At some point in the duration of my ownership of this hat, the saturation of raw Quintessence combined with proximity to one of the most magically infused brains in the world to produce something hitherto unseen and unheard-of. Sentient life, born of magic alone."

Copernicrust weighed in. "Um, actually, I'm pretty sure that we conjure sentient life all the time out of pure magic. If you refer to the *Treatise on Golem Creation and Enhancement* by Progten Antilles, then you'll find . . ."

I cut him off before he could get going with the citations. The man was like a living library, in the sense that practically all the information inside of him was completely irrelevant to the situation. "Intelligent life does not occur in an emergent fashion as a result of proximity to heavy magic usage or the world would contain a great many talking wands, staffs, staves, mirrors, and suchlike."

Balthazagar raised a hand. "The world does contain . . ."

I spoke over him quickly to try and get them back on task. "Once again, I must remind you that we are discussing intelligence that formed on its own without direction by an external magic user."

"Um, actually . . ." Copernicrust started again before I spoke just ever so slightly louder.

"The form that this intelligence took was that of my own. A perfect copy of my mind at the last moment that I was wearing it, give or take a little fraying of memories at the edges."

"So we're discussing an emergent doppelganger?" Maximus sat forward in his seat and began stroking his beard. "That's a relatively common effect in inter-dimensional travel."

"That is a completely duh-different effect." Poindextrous rolled his whole head when he was rolling his eyes. Like he'd never quite worked out how the different parts of his body were connected. "When you have emergent dop-pelgangers in interdimensional travel, you're encountering alternate reh-reality reh-refractions spawned off from the fracture point in m-space, not . . ."

"Not a doppelganger," I added for clarity. "Only a copy of my mind in a hat."

"If one were to approach this matter from the angle of philosophy, what is one if not one's mind?" Archimendo began. "And what is a copy of one's mind if not a doppelganger? And more importantly, once we have divorced ourselves from the physical, which, from that moment of divergence, is the true you? Or have you merely created a branching point in your person which can later coalesce back into a single being?"

The man's droning voice and ambling thought process may have brought me to the verge of tears, but to my surprise, he'd actually hit on something real in the midst of his ramble. "Oh, we did that, actually. When I put the hat on, we merged. And when I take it off, we diverge again."

Iomedania pushed her glasses up her nose. "This is a fascinating hypothetical that challenges everything that we know about the nature of self."

"Yes, it is," I was quick to agree, "but also no, it is not, because this is an actual thing that has happened."

"Imagine what it would be like to be confronted by a divergent version of yourself, an offshoot that had an entirely different experience." Archimendo now leaned back in his chair to expose the full length of his belt-tickling white beard to the room so that he could begin to stroke it in full view of the group. "Imagine learning how much walking the path not taken might have changed you . . ."

I had to cut him off again as he meandered off into philosophy instead of useful answers. "I don't actually need to imagine that, because it happened, and we tried to kill each other when we first met up, because we didn't understand what had happened, and then we merged and now I'd like to think that I'm a better person for my experiences as a hat, but it seems so ridiculous to say that I'm inclined to plagiarize your line about the path not taken."

Usually so slow, he was surprisingly sharp in his reply. "You're welcome to it, though I will expect shared credit if you publish using it."

I was so frustrated by this point that I was tempted to just abandon the whole Council of the Wise and start over with just Ig for advice. At least he didn't go off on tangents like this. "Publishing my findings and receiving credit is not my primary concern at present."

That was enough to silence the whole table in shock. With the exception of Ildrit and Cygni, who knew as much about academia as I knew about . . . well, alright, I know about almost everything, but they didn't know much about academia.

"You certainly have changed," Philodephina said with an odd cheer to her voice. "I call for a vote of no confidence in Archmage Absalom Scryne."

That was enough to prompt an uproar, and I was very much among those up and roaring. "I beg your pardon?!"

"Were my body taken over by a mind-demon, should I expect that it will remain as Quadratic Mistress in my place? Shall it teach my lectures and guide my students?"

Maximus rolled his eyes. "You can hardly compare a mind demon to . . ."

Copernicrust felt obliged to be pedantic. "Um, actually, they are both external intelligence that integrate themselves into . . ."

"Buh-but the external intelligence is huh-him." Poindextrous shut that argument down fast. I was finding unexpected allies at the table this day.

Until now, both Danyeel and Sabrinia had remained silent, probably trying to get a feel for things before putting their foot in it, but now that things had degenerated so rapidly into chaos, Sabrinia piped up. "He is considerably nicer and more pleasant to be around now."

"Nicer?!" Iomedania spat. "If we had wanted a nice archmage then we would have elected a halfling! The real Absalom Scryne was a vicious old bastard who hated all of us, and was hated by us in return, and we liked it that way, because we could rely on him. We could understand him. This thing standing before us asking us politely for help with a major magical accident that he has admitted responsibility for? That is not him."

Philosophically, they were technically correct. I had changed from the man that I was when first selected for my high station in the college.

"Are you the same woman that you were when you first became Mistress of R&D? Are you the same woman as you were this morning?" Danyeel came out swinging. Bringing all of his impressive thespian speech-making talents out of his bag of tricks to sway everyone to my side. "All of us change. All of us grow. To do otherwise would be to welcome stagnation."

I wasn't sure which play or story he had pilfered that particular speech from, but I'd have to borrow it from him at some point; it sounded very good.

"There is a very simple solution to this difference of opinion," Philodephina said, still smiling. "We put it to the vote. That's what a vote is for, isn't it?"

This didn't look good. They were going to depose me. Every single one of the existing council members had good reason to be rid of me, and the votes of two people I'd just inducted and two people who'd been disqualified for reason of not being part of the college were not going to turn the tide. I'd only just gotten back to all the glorious resources available to an archmage of the Invisible College and I wasn't ready to give them all up again so soon. I had to do something. Something to impress upon them that I was still the old Absalom Scryne. "I believe that you are forgetting the problem with a vote, Philodephina."

"And what might that be, oh Archmage?" she asked wryly.

"The problem with a vote is that it must occur among equals." I said it all lightly, as though I were conducting a lecture to my students. "Lest the votes carry different weights."

Poindextrous's brow furrowed. "And you duh-do not feel that thu-those assembled at this table are equal?"

I stood at the head of the table and slammed my hands down on its ancient surface. "None of you are my equal."

Silence fell over the gathered wizards. Eyes darting from side to side, to see who would first respond. A wizard is, ultimately, a creature of ego. How else could we look at the very nature of creation and proclaim that we know better than the universe how things should be? A wizard without an ego is like a knife without a blade.

As such, I knew that not a one of them could abide my quite factual statement that I was better than all of them.

"Are you suggesting that you would not abide by the decision of this council?" Arturo asked, as delicately as he could.

I let just a trickle of the Quintessence that I had stored inside this wonderful old body of mine out. Letting it flow into my words in the common tongue as I would have words of Archaic. They resonated with power. "I'd burn the whole world down before I let you rule over me."

The assembled wizards once more cast glances to one another. Trying to work out who would be an ally, and who would stab them in the back, who would use this as an opportunity to oust me or to get into my good books.

To my surprise, Copernicrust was the one to speak up. "You might be able to best one of us, Scryne. But not all of us."

And that, dear reader, is where he was incorrect. "Iomedania is the quickest; she'd activate the personal shield on her anklet that she thinks nobody knows about. Second quickest is, surprisingly, Archimendo, who would lead with a rubidium fire enforced by that magic girdle that he doesn't think we know he wears. A spell that Iomedania's shield will easily deflect after I launch her into its course using nothing more complex than low magic. Angling off her shield, the rubidium will neutralize Poindextrous's niobium constructs before they fully form before scorching him and putting him out of the fight. The anklet shield has a recharge cycle of around one third of a second, meaning it will be up again when Philodephina unleashes neodinium rays at us through the wand she carries up her left sleeve, deflecting them back into Copernicrust and killing him instantly. Sadly, the shield will still be in recharge just as Maximus Arturo's classic dimensional shear passes through Iomedania on the way to me. Archimendo and Balthazagar should both launch their respective evocations at about that moment; Archimendo will fall back on habit, rubidium fire once more, but Balthazagar . . . oh, he's a wild card, it could be a few different complex spells that might interact in different ways with rubidium, although all of them will result in an explosive effect knocking both of them out of the fight, at least in the short term. That explosion would also take me out of the fight, had I not spent all of this time preparing a counterspell to reverse dimensional shear, carrying me in one piece back to the shear's point of origin. I will manifest directly in front of Maximus, duck as Philodephina makes a second stubborn attempt with the neodinium rays, annihilating him from the waist up—sorry, Max—and then turn to deliver a killing blow to Philodephina, probably with something laughably simple like the Golden Flames of Galgalagrin the Great. After that, it is just a matter of mopping up whatever remains on the floor and going about my day."

It is a rare thing indeed to see any wizard speechless, let alone an entire room of them, so you can imagine that I savored my moment before, blustering, Balthazagar sputtered out, "You . . . couldn't do all that."

"Two spells is all it would take. And I wouldn't even need to tap my reserves for either." I forced confidence into my words and smugness onto my face.

"That isn't how we wuh-would . . ." Poindextrous began, but I held up a hand to forestall further sputtering.

"Not anymore, not now that I've informed you of how it would have played out. But even now you're scrabbling for other ideas of how to beat me that don't rely on your ill-kept secrets and your strengths, and I must sadly inform you that they shall not work either. I know your minds better than you know your own, because I am just that much smarter than you all." I leaned forward with a cruel smile. "So do please call your vote, see how it ends for you."

There were yet more looks being exchanged around the table, but Philodephina did not meet anyone's eye. She rose to her feet defiantly and cried out, "I call a vote of no confidence. All in favor of stripping Absalom Scryne of his position and title, raise a hand now."

The silence was palpable.

From the periphery of my vision, I saw Cygni raise her hand, only for Ildrit to grab it and force it down again. There was some hastily whispered conversation, with all I could decipher from it being Cygni's plaintive, " . . .but I want to see him do it."

With her vote defeated, Philodephina sighed and held out her arms to her sides. "Do it, then."

I raised my eyebrows. "Do what?"

"I defied you." She actually seemed offended at my feigned ignorance. "You're a tyrant. Do what tyrants do."

Taking care not to scrape the polished floor, I pulled out my chair at the head of the table and sat down, turning my attention to Archimendo. "Have you ever come across any historical accounts relating to the accidental creation of magical artifacts?"

Relieved that nobody was blowing him up at present, he practically gushed, "There have been a great many reports to that effect throughout the centuries, but typically they are imbued with a lesser enchantment rather than something so complex. Perhaps it was due to the proximity to the thing being copied? It is my understanding that in several of the historical cases, regularly used tools took on enchanted effects related to their use and the expertise of their owner. As your most commonly used tool is your brain, perhaps that is why . . ."

Philodephina interrupted the rambling. "Is that it?"

"Hmm?" I glanced her way.

"No punishment for defying you?" She looked quite put out. "No torturous curses?"

"Madam, this is an institution of learning, not a dungeon." I scoffed before turning back to the lore master.

"I'd say she's learned her lesson," Cygni piped up before Ildrit could stop her, ratcheting the tension that I was trying to abate right back up to ten again. I manfully resisted the urge to chuckle.

Archimendo had been bumbling on, almost entirely unaware that we'd all had our attention elsewhere. " . . . If I'm entirely honest, I doubt the veracity of the accounts of emergent enchantments. My suspicion is that they merely learned to activate already enchanted items, or undertook to have said items enchanted but lived in areas where the use of such magic was frowned upon. Very rarely do we see any artifact to speak of being manufactured without someone taking credit for the spells involved."

That piqued my interest. "So you are suggesting that perhaps someone placed the rather complex enchantment upon my hat with the intention of having it clone my mind?"

"I suggest nothing, sir," Archimendo mumbled. "I only cite the accounts . . ."

"Philodephina." I said her name and savored the way that she suddenly sat bolt upright in her chair. "This seems like it is most relevant to your area of study. Saturation with Quintessence in vast quantities has been known to change the behavior of some materials, has it not?"

"I . . . yes?" She was quite flustered.

Shifting the spotlight of my undivided attention across the table, I asked, "Iomedania, research into new magic is most assuredly in your wheelhouse; perhaps you have some insight?"

She was not flustered at all, in fact she seemed entirely delighted with how the whole vote-of-no-confidence matter had played out, judging by her smile. "I should need to examine the hat in more detail. Take it apart, perhaps, to see how it works."

"Alas, the deconstruction of the artifact is not going to be possible, as it contains a copy of my consciousness, which would experience that deconstruction rather torturously." That idea needed to go and die in a ditch promptly.

"But surely we are not acknowledging the alleged sentience of this duplicate. It is a hat. An object. It can hardly hold the same rights that we would afford a living creature."

"Um, actually, philosophically speaking . . ." Copernicrust began.

Poindextrous snapped his fingers. "Yuh-you are the hat, sir. You still think of it as you."

"Well, yes." I was not clear on where he meant to go with this. "It's me."

"Thuh-that is why you fear it being deconstructed, buh-because you don't know which of you is the real you."

"Both of them are," Cygni called out from the side of the room. She may not have been afforded a seat at the table, but nobody was going to argue about her standing on the sidelines.

I held up my hands for silence, and this time, wouldn't you know it. Everyone actually fell silent. "I did not call you here to discuss my time as a hat, nor to expound on philosophy of the self. Or even theoreticals about the creation of my pointy-topped self. This was all simply background information that I needed to convey before we could move on to the actual crisis that we are facing."

"What crisis is that?" Arturo asked guardedly.

I prepared myself to regale them with the tale, carefully editing it in my mind so as to remove any references to Ig wetting himself, or me wishing that I could wet myself despite lacking any of the necessary plumbing. "In my travels as a hat, I became acquainted with a certain kobold . . ."

"We've met." Iomedania sounded profoundly disgusted, as though occupying the same room as a kobold had somehow sullied her good name. It wasn't like I'd asked them to kiss, just exist on the same plane of existence as one another without resorting to brutal murder.

"Yes, well, this kobold . . ." I began.

"Keeps digging up the green in the Quint." Copernicrust huffed.

"Lowering the standards for entry to allow dwarves is one thing, but . . ." Sabrinia trailed off after making accidental eye contact with Cygni.

"Smells disgusting," Balthazagar opined.

"We have a menagerie for a reason," Iomedania whispered, with her whisper somehow being louder than everyone else's usual talking.

Poindextrous nodded in agreement. "His puh-presence in a school is a huh-health code violation."

"This kobold," I declared, loud enough to drown them all out, "is sapient."

CHAPTER 5

PURELY ACADEMIC

As a group supposedly dedicated to understanding the universe in all of its infinite diversity, this did not provoke the degree of interest—or indeed wonder—that I had anticipated.

Philodephina raised an imperiously well-groomed eyebrow. "And?"

"Are they not normally?" Danyeel seemed to be genuinely perplexed.

Sabrinia took a different route, trying to steer the conversation to something less contentious. "How does one define sapience . . . really?"

Sadly this set off the living library recounter Copernicrust once more. "Um, actually, sapience was defined first in the writings of Sir Arugula Lomagon in the year of . . ."

I was practically shouting at this point. "He acquired sapience as a result of exposure to my hat."

"Well, bravo for him then." Danyeel probably wasn't being sarcastic when he said that, given that his presence on this council was only by my good graces, but it sounded more sarcastic than anything else I'd heard all day all the same.

"Yes, three cheers for the sapient kobold. Can we get it off the Quint though? It is playing bloody murder with the lawn," Copernicrust complained.

It was genuinely flabbergasting to me that newly emergent sentient life had been created by magic, and not one of them seemed to give half a damn. "I feel like you may be overlooking the significance of this. We have now the capability to make creatures that were hitherto non-sapient into sapient creatures."

"Wouldn't it be quicker to just conjure a magical construct in the shape of whatever animal you wanted?" Balthazagar had a practical streak wide enough to blot out the sun. Usually an advantage in a place where everyone else had their heads in the clouds, but at present, shockingly useless. "You could make it say whatever you wanted to."

"In terms of planar navigation, there are very few applications, given the incorporeality of the forces at work. Nowhere to hang a hat, so to speak." Arturo tittered. I suspected that he had only spoken because he liked the sound of his own voice, and nobody had said anything that he could filibuster about in quite some time.

"Sapience is overrated, I'd say." Philodephina said it quite flippantly. But you could tell that she was quite serious from her smile. She never smiled when she was joking.

Copernicrust started up again at that prompt. "Um, actually, from a philosophical standpoint there is certainly an argument to be made that . . ."

"Really? None of you think that this is significant?"

There was a great deal of shrugging and gazes turned aside.

Cygni raised a hand, so I turned to her.

"I do." Everyone was staring at her. "I think it's significant . . . probably really important."

There was a long silence broken only by a cough.

"And are we to understand that you made the dwarf sapient also? Because the process may not have stuck."

For such a crusty old man, Archimendo could be a real bitch sometimes.

"Dwarves are all sapient creatures," Iomedania said kindly, as though she was showing extra politeness by acknowledging that a person in the room was capable of thinking. "They simply sublimate all individual thought to their matriarch's will because of societal pressure."

"No I bloody don't." Cygni began to reach for a weapon that was no longer there, having been lost somewhere on our long journey through the nether regions of the world. It would be quite some time before she reached so naturally for her magic when enraged, something that I suppose we should all have been thankful for.

As for myself, I must admit that, now I was reattached to all the glands and things in my body that produced all the chemicals that make one behave in irrational manners, my temper was fraying somewhat. How I'd made it through so many meetings with these people prior to my going off and becoming a better person by suffering as an item of clothing, I shall never know.

"I am going to explain to you in very simple terms why this is so significant for those of us who claim to study magic in all its myriad forms, and then we shall move on to the actual problem I have gathered you here to address." I glanced around the table for any signs of disagreement and was met with the typical bored stares. Honestly, the fact I had never fireballed every single one of them into ash was nothing short of miraculous.

I reached out my arms to my sides and let the part of my mind that had been so embroiled with Ig's that they were indistinguishable take over. I slipped it a sharp memory of stubbing my toe on the very chairs that my guests were currently seated upon, fed it fear of that pain, and then, like magic.

All of the seated council members began to levitate. Lifted from the ground by low magic alone.

In itself, this obviously was not particularly impressive as far as acts of magic go, but the fact that it had been achieved without casting on my part seemed to catch their attention.

Maximus Arturo was the first to lose his composure. Presumably because, as he was the most portly among us, he had the most to lose if dropped. "How in the blazes are you doing that?"

Keeping my concentration on all of the various places that it needed to be was simple once I had realized that I didn't actually have to give it any attention, not when the screeching animal of my brain stem was on the lookout for anything frightening.

"A spell cast on the chairs in advance and then veiled?" proposed Iomedania.

"Nuh-no chance." Poindextrous shook his head cautiously, still peering down at the floor. It was a six-foot drop to the rug; even for a man as unathletic and top-heavy as him, it was hardly dangerous. "How could he manage the tuh-timing."

"Some sort of trigger?" Archimendo asked the room at large.

Both of my younger allies looked quite smug in the knowledge of how the trick was done, so I lowered them graciously to the floor, and let them speak without the risk of wobbles.

I'd expected it to be Danyeel, ever the showman, but Sabrinia rose before him. "Low magic."

It was hardly fair to give her any credit, given that she'd seen it done before, up close and personal, but I gave her a nod all the same. "Low magic. No more, no less."

"You have some cohorts in the wings lifting chairs to impress us?" Contempt dripped from every word out of Philodephina's mouth. "We aren't schoolchildren, Scryne."

"Incorrect once more. My magic and my will alone hold you aloft."

"Nonsense," Balthazagar grumbled. "There were nine of us up there. Nobody can split their focus in nine."

It was time to deliver the death blow to any argument about Ig's importance going forward. "A kobold can."

"A kobold?!" Copernicrust scoffed. "Um, actually, kobolds cannot use magic because they lack the prerequisite sapience . . ." He trailed off before citing anything at all.

I granted him an encouraging smile, though I suspect it was masked by my whiskers. "I see that you have finally arrived at the same destination as I."

"You are telling me that you learned to split your focus from . . ." Iomedania looked queasy and stopped before she said the word. Gathering her resolve, she tried again. "You learned from a kobold? You? Master of All Magics?!"

I lowered everyone carefully as I could back to the table before I genuinely lost all concentration and dropped them. "As it turns out, we have a great deal to learn about magic from the other people of our world, and I think that we can agree that any wizard should be, first and foremost, a student. Intent upon learning instead of asserting what is already known as the sum of all knowledge."

They weren't quite as flabbergasted as I might have hoped, but I could practically hear the wheels spinning behind their eyeballs. The possibilities of being able to direct not one or two spells simultaneously but a dozen or more. The interplay of different elements that could never be achieved before. Low magic was just the beginning. Once this technique had been codified and explored, we were looking at a whole new world of modular magic, with various elements and components of spells being separately cast and then combined on the fly.

Iomedania arrived at the conclusion faster than the rest of them and held up her hands. "I will concede that this development does cast new light upon your fixation with the kobold. And on your journey as a whole."

Iomedania might have arrived first, but now that the rest were catching up, the excitement in the room was palpable.

Copernicrust was on the edge of his seat. "What else did you learn from the kobold?!"

Philodephina was practically shouting at this point. "Forget the kobold, what did you learn from the dwarf?!"

"I suppose it bears mentioning that as a hat, I also briefly experienced life as an adult dragon."

What had been an uproar now became a riot. Everyone in the room was up and yelling, even if it had taken Archimendo several attempts and a quick assist from Danyeel to actually haul himself out of his chair on such short notice, and he was still kind of folded forwards as if he were still in it. In the midst of all this there came a knocking at the chamber door. Probably just one of the staff making sure we hadn't accidentally opened a portal to heck.

"We're going to have to found whole new schools of magic just to explore these discoveries. New departments for each of the methodologies extracted . . ." Sabrinia's usual icy exterior had entirely melted in her excitement. She actually looked rather flushed.

"From the dwarves, I initially learned a more perfect way of categorizing and memorizing elements and their interplays. But in our joint exploration, we have also discovered the means of condensing Quintessence into a solid object, binding unstoppable elemental forces, chaining together multiple casters into a single spell, runic magic as yet unknown to the surface world . . ."

Danyeel was hastily conjuring illusionary sheets of paper and had enchanted pens scribbling down every word that I said. Balthazagar was holding on to his head as though it may explode at the revelation of the dwarvish system of memorization. Maximus Arturo was bouncing up and down on the spot with a visual effect not dissimilar to that of a lava lamp as he heard about the different things that I had learned in my travels.

At the mention of Scrynium, Philodephina looked as though she might actually faint, and then she was peppering me with questions about it that I couldn't hear over the general roar of excited babbling. At some point in the chaos she crossed the room and scooped poor Cygni up in her arms. An impressive feat, given that dwarves typically make up for their lack of height in bulk and Philodephina had the upper body strength typically associated with wet noodles, but passion apparently carried her through with the act all the same. Cygni looked frankly terrified. I don't think anyone had ever picked her up before.

Iomedania kept clapping her hands to try and get my attention back to her as she slowly mouthed the word "dragon" repeatedly. Unfortunately, there were a half dozen other questions being flung my way at every moment so I didn't really get a chance to discuss what I'd learned from my few seconds as a dragon. Though I suspect that what I did learn was probably a deciding factor in my ability to re-carve Cygni's Quintessence reservoir into its current burgeoning state given the vast quantities of magic that a dragon has stored and is required to channel constantly simply to maintain its existence as a truly unlikely creature.

Eventually the chatter and babble died back to a less deafening level. Quiet enough that I could hear Ildrit laughing his ass off at Cygni's affronted expression, at least.

Once more I held up my hands and waited for quiet. Though I did have to wait a fair while.

"All of this bounty and more, I have learned from just two creatures in this world that previously had no access to magic. And all of it I have learned in the briefest span, just from spending time in their company. What will happen when there are more? When we have a lifetime of study and exchange of ideas? When we unite every creature of the world in the High Art? Can you even imagine the possibilities?"

Everyone at the table looked as though they were overwhelmed before I said that. Maximus Arturo had actually extracted a pipe from somewhere about his person and was now sitting back in his chair with a post-coital glow about him, wreathed in blue smoke, occasionally passing it across to Poindextrous, who seemed to be puffing it just to try and calm himself down a little. With the revelation that the revelations were going to just keep on coming, their eyes had all glazed over a little.

"What do we know of goblin magic? Of ogre magic? The magic of gryphons or lamassu or any of the million myriad creatures we share our world with? Elves and humans have held a monopoly over magic for so long as it has been taught, and we have plumbed the depths of questions that nobody in the beginning would have even thought to ask and come out the other side with an incredible bounty. But now we have the means to throw the gates of learning open and encompass all the world's people. They will have questions we never thought to ask, answers to questions we could not even have conceived of. The possibilities are truly endless."

There was another knock at the door. *Bugger off, housekeeping, I'm in the middle of a speech here.*

It was a pretty solid speech, if I do say so myself. Leading them to the conclusions I wanted them to reach without getting too preachy. If it hadn't convinced them all already as to why what I'd achieved was so incredibly important, then the constant nagging thoughts about those endless possibilities would inevitably win them over. With just the discovery of Scrynium, we'd shattered preconceptions and breathed new life into a half dozen fields. With Ig's multi-casting, we'd begun a full overhaul of how magic was learned and taught. When they learned of his ability to use Low Magic to intercept and influence spells that had already been cast, they were liable to lose their minds all over again, but thankfully neither Sabrinia nor Danyeel had brought that up just yet. What with the decent odds of it entirely destroying people's perception of reality and all.

In all likelihood, we could quite easily have spent the rest of the day, nay, the rest of the week, just talking about the possibilities of the fraction of things that I'd learned, with each new possibility blossoming out into a million more, but Balthazagar seemed to have a slightly better memory than all the rest of them. Or at least a more practical mindset about matters. "So what's the problem?"

"I beg your pardon?" I blinked at him.

As haggard and hairy as he was, it was easy to forget that he was one of the cleverest people in the world, at least until he spoke. "You told us that you'd brought us here to solve a problem, not to hand us the next millennium's syllabuses and research projects on a platter."

"I did indeed. As I said before, I raised Ig to sapience through him wearing me. And now that he is no longer wearing me, I am confronted with the decline of his faculties back to their previous standard. He has managed to maintain his ability to cast for the most part, but as of late his behavior is becoming less and less wizard and more and more kobold. This is cause for concern."

"So having devised a unique manner in which to render a non-sapient creature sapient, you now wish for us to devise another to maintain that sapience in your absence?" Iomedania had been having such a nice time up until now that I was surprised at just how cutting her remark was.

"Just so," I was forced to reply.

The various members of the Council of the Wise looked around at each other, as though pondering, then Danyeel piped up before any of them said a word. "Can't you just put the hat back on him?"

I opened and closed my mouth a couple of times. "I'm not entirely sure that would be wise."

Cygni frowned. "Why not?"

"My dear girl, I don't want to have a schism of the self again." I sighed. "I am back in one piece, body and soul, and asking me to fragment myself once more to serve as a sort of long-term disability aid for a chronically stupid creature seems a little unfair."

"Doesn't have to be long-term, does it?" she asked before any of the wise and learned gathered here could say the very same thing.

"I believe it does."

Because I wasn't willing to let him slip off into oblivion. Because he was my friend.

"Couldn't he wear your hat for a bit to keep his intelligence topped off, then you could go back to being your combined self afterwards?" she asked, rather pointedly.

"I was hoping for a more elegant solution than perpetual spiritual bisection."

Balthazagar was smiling, all of the yellowed peg teeth that had somehow survived his centuries of life on display. "Elegance is the antithesis of practicality." His broad grin turned into a smirk towards the end as he added, "A very wise wizard once told me that."

Quoting my own words back to me. What a bastard.

At least I could rely on the other wizards to see a complex problem and do everything that they could to make it more complex.

"Um, actually. Intelligence isn't really a single factor," Copernicrust piped up. "To increase a creature's intelligence would be to manipulate a whole variety of different factors. It doesn't really exist as an abstraction in itself."

"There is a biological component that you'd need to overcome; the physical structure of the brain is most likely reasserting itself after being twisted out of shape by your presence, and the natural structure may just be . . . dumb." Sabrinia had gotten her hands on one of the conjured scraps of paper and was scribbling down her own calculations and notes without looking up.

"Education, brain structure, emotional development . . ." Iomedania began listing off component parts.

There was another knock at the door, but I was far too embroiled in all this to pay much mind.

"Wuh-what about the chaos factor?" Our dear statistical analyst weighed in, "Two people might have identical biology and education but produce wholly duh-different intellects."

This was helping, technically, but not as much as I'd have hoped. "So what I'm hearing is that we need to create an external abstraction of intelligence to work on, as one does not exist at present."

"Of course, why wouldn't we just jump over all the middle steps and arrive first at the gates of the impossible?" Iomedania rolled her eyes.

"We are wizards, my dear." I gave her a nice contemptuous smile in return, just so she remembered who she was dealing with. "The possible isn't really our purview."

"Might I suggest education?" Archimendo spluttered for a moment, then started up again. "I've found that even the most piteous mind can be improved with education."

Arturo let out a belly laugh. "Do you mean to teach the kobold classes?"

Iomedania wiped a smudge off one of her nails. "I'd suggest that you do so, since your research has been at a dead end for years now."

Maximus Arturo was on his feet like a shot, even though it took some of his chins a little while to catch up to him. "How very dare you besmirch the good name of Interdimensional . . ."

"Ladies and gentlemen," I cut them off. "I have spent the past month being pursued by werewolves, ogres, and all other manner of monsters, yet I find your bickering to be considerably less civilized. Do you think we might conduct ourselves like adults?"

"But she . . ." Arturo began.

"Everyone knows that dimensional research is a slow and arduous process, and nobody begrudges the time that your truly vital work takes. You are being deliberately needled." I stopped him before we could get into name calling and hair-pulling. The ogres really had been easier to deal with.

"Let us approach the problem from a practical standpoint. Directly interfering with the brain structure is likely to produce lethal results, so it will have to be something external. I intend to construct an artifact that will allow Ig to retain intelligence independently of my influence, so that he might have the opportunity to grow and become his own person." I smiled softly. "It is the greatest gift that I can offer to a creature who saved my life, time and time again."

"Um, actually, you were perfectly safe here the entire time." Copernicrust wilted under my stare but still went on speaking all the same.

I acted as though he had not spoken, in the hopes that he'd take a hint. "How might that artifact be constructed?"

Sabrinia looked up from her notes. "A crown or helmet would be best. With all due respect to your former self, a hat is a pretty poor choice to be made into an artifact. Too fragile to contain the forces involved."

"Right, good." Once again, it wasn't much, but it was better than nothing.

"I could forge you a wee crown for him," Cygni offered.

I waved her off. "I need you to maintain pace on your current project."

"And we all need Ig to be smart again so he doesn't try to fireball himself up some dinner and kill us all," she snapped back, clearly annoyed at my affected contempt. I would have to explain the precariously balanced social situation to her in private at a later time.

"The fact of the matter is . . ."

The knocking at the door had gone from sporadic to insistent. Which suggested that whoever happened to be on the other side of that door either had a burning desire to live out the rest of their life as a newt, or they had no idea what meeting they were disturbing. I might actually go so far as to say the knocks had become brusque. The whole slab of wood was shaking with each mighty thump. "Be a dear and get that, would you, Ildrit?"

That would put whatever bloody stupid student was bothering us off. One look at Ildrit would have been enough to convince most people that time spent in his company should be minimized if you wished to maximize the number of limbs that you would leave the conversation with. Wizards might be more capable of rendering you down to your component atoms or inflicting some terribly inventive curse upon you, but you process that information intellectually, which takes some time. A big scary man with muscles hits you right in the brain stem.

I turned back to the assembled council. "With the concept of a crown in mind, what is our next step of development?"

"The Quintessence input and storage would be dependent on the exact functionality you were looking for," Philodephina conceded. "If you're attempting a flat increase in intellect or something multiplicative so that growth is quadratic rather than linear."

Balthazagar's bushy eyebrows appeared to be attempting to mate with each other in the middle of his face. "The forces involved will be complex. We shall have to consult all known texts to identify various cultural associations with intelligence and specific elements."

Copernicrust looked terribly pleased with himself. "Um, actually, I believe I can be of assistance in that matter. You see, a new cataloging system was introduced by Archimendo's predecessor alongside our existing one which . . ."

"We do not speak of the alternate system," Archimendo barked furiously.

"Guys." Ildrit tried to catch our attention, but it was not terribly successful.

I talked right over him. "If this alternate system happens to be the one I'm thinking of, its intention was to create nigh infinite duplicates of our existent books so that they could be catalogued in all relevant sections of the library. Old Gertrude had begun the construction of a master index, with every book addressing a specific topic included."

"Wouldn't an index like that be as large as the library itself?" Cygni asked, quicker at the math involved than anyone else in the room.

"Why else do you suppose she was consulting me?" Arturo groaned.

I affixed both Arturo and Archimendo with a pointed finger each. "Between the two of you, do you believe you will be able to unlock the secrets of the index?"

They looked at each other and shrugged. With Archimendo eventually wilting a little bit. "We can give it a go."

"Guys, I think you need to listen to . . ."

Iomedania had her chin cupped in her hand as she puzzled through the question. "Conceptual abstraction isn't entirely unheard of, but it is usually emergent from elemental studies rather than conducted in reverse. Not to mention the difficulty of identifying the specific effects from said element that you wish to make use of while eliminating all of the others."

Sabrinia had now entirely snatched all of poor Danyeel's papers from him and was simultaneously correcting his notes and scribbling out designs for a hypothetical crown. As seen in the fifth dimension. "With the multi-target techniques that the archmage has offered to bestow upon us from his, uh, consultant kobold, I believe that we could actually install a converter into the mix during the phases of casting, turning the excess energy being misdirected into different output forms back into the loop as Quintessence to refuel the enchantment."

"Elemental purification is a pipe dream!" Balthazagar bellowed. "Better wizards than you and I have spent lifetimes in pursuit of that particular golden goose."

"Better than you maybe," Sabrinia sniped back without looking up from her papers.

There was a gasp around the table as the older members of the Council of the Wise were intensely offended on the behalf of Balthazagar. How dare this upstart speak to him in exactly the same manner that all of them spoke to him? They moved past it quickly though, when they cottoned on to the idea that the impossible dream of Elemental Purification—procuring the result that one desired from invoking an element without all of the associated side effects—might actually be possible.

It would be essential, in truth, to the project of improving upon Ig's mind, though I'd been too lost in the big picture of my plans to see so fine a detail. If mercury were associated with intelligence—as I suspected it would be—there would have been no way to divide it from the poisonous aspects of the element, demanding that we include some counter-element to neutralize it, thus also negating the greater part of its effectiveness. Only through the application of Purification would we be able to extract the specific results we desired, and only through the simultaneous creation of a feedback loop, dissolving some conceptual parts of the conjured element back into Quintessence, could we maintain the incredible Quintessence costs of such a thing without draining poor Ig dry. The kobold drew Quintessence like a thirsty man a week in the desert supping up water, but he'd have no chance to use it if all of it was being directed into the crown.

"Perhaps . . ."

Ildrit slammed his fists on the table, shutting everyone up and, in a few cases, causing grown wizards to cringe in fear of being stuffed in a locker. "The king of Arpanpholigon wants to see you. Now."

"King?" Cygni instantly perked up. Probably thinking that the king was going to be a birthing female at the center of the human hive rather than the rather more depressing reality.

"I'm terribly sorry, Council, it seems that my duties as the representative of the college demand that I depart." I pointed to Cygni. "Keep them talking. Keep them thinking."

"But I want to see the king."

I tried to work out how to phrase my response so that it wasn't technically treason. "You aren't going to be missing much. I can't imagine that this is a social call with . . . His Majesty."

Restraining myself from calling the king any of the various things that I thought of him as was something of a testament to the strength of my willpower.

It wasn't that he was a particularly bad ruler—he was actually one of the select few capital-G Good rulers in all the world, a kind and just king who did everything in his power to care for his citizens, make sure that nobody died that didn't need to, and generally oppose all evil things. But despite his many positive qualities, he did have the terrible misfortune of the city-state that he called home happening to also be the home of the Invisible College. As such, when dignitaries from foreign lands came to visit, it was more often than not me that they came to see on arrival to the city, assuming that I was the de facto ruler. This had of course also occurred with my predecessor and indeed every other predecessor since the college had put down roots here. As such, there was some degree of resentment and professional jealousy. It also didn't help with that jealousy that while I was technically one of the subjects under his rule, I could at any moment turn him into a chicken with barely more effort than it took him to rise from bed in the morning. I had always tried to be convivial with him, given that we were forced by circumstances to work together frequently, but I will admit that there were times throughout our shared history when I became a little competitive too.

As I've mentioned before, I went through some considerable emotional growth while living as a hat and not an awful lot beforehand. So yes, I sometimes got into pointless pissing contests with the king and made fun of him for having no magic and possibly was involved in his daughter running away with a stable boy while they were both transfigured into swans.

I understand that they're both very happy together, and I was invited to be godfather of their cygnets but could not attend the naming ceremony on account of my busy schedule.

What luck that while I was unwilling to engage in treason, the rest of the council were more than ready to pick up the slack. Balthazagar rolled his eyes in disdain. "He's still king?"

Poindextrous tittered, "Wuh-we haven't been bored enough to duh-depose him yet."

The king's herald was standing right outside the open door listening to all this, but the sad fact of the matter was that even if he did decide we were plotting against him, treasonous, and evil, there was approximately bugger all he could do about it, what with every single wizard in this room having power enough in one little finger to wipe the floor with his entire army.

"Please forgive my academic associates, good knight." I tried to come up with some sort of excuse for them but honesty seemed the best policy. "They're . . . uh . . . dicks."

Ildrit cleared his throat. "Herald Knight Uhp is here to accompany us to the castle."

"Let me go fetch my cloak, staff, and kobold." I hoisted myself out of the chair, where I must admit I had been doing some lounging. "Meet me at the entrance.

Uhp glanced after me with a confused expression. "He's got a kobold?"

CHAPTER 6

HERALDS OF DOOM

Knight Herald Uhp was from one of the border provinces of Arpanpholigon, and given that this was a city state, that basically meant suburbia. He scraped and groveled and bowed extensively to me in thanks for so politely acquiescing to accompany him after only a half hour or so of ignoring him. Given how some of my predecessors had treated some of his predecessors, I could understand why he was so obeisant. I actually think that one of the quail scampering around the Quint was once a knight herald, though I could be wrong. I haven't a clue about the lifespan of quail. Just as likely it was a knight herald's grandson nowadays.

He might have been terribly respectful to me, but that did not seem to extend to my entourage. He looked at Ig with confusion, Cygni with contempt, and Ildrit with slightly narrowed eyes, as if he recognized him from somewhere. I do not know how good the likeness was on Ildrit's bounty posters, but it was just good enough to prompt suspicious thoughts in our guide to the castle.

Ah, my entourage. When the king invited me ever so politely to appear before him, he was strictly only inviting me, but at some point in my travels, this ragtag group of weirdos had become a part of me. A part that I not only wanted around, but that was an essential piece of the apparatus that I used to think. It had not even occurred to me to approach the intrigues of court without the grotesque triad of my closest friends in tow.

I was never clear on why anyone needed a guide to the castle. It was the biggest building in the whole city, visible from miles around. Although it had lost a little height from some of its towers at one point when some of the janitorial staff in the college knocked the controls for the levitation spell that keeps it in the sky. Nobody important died, so it was all brushed under the rug, but I must admit that the reconstruction efforts carefully avoiding brushing up against the cloud-line had rendered the place a little bit squat looking in comparison to other keeps of its size.

At no point would I ever have attempted to imply that the king was trying to compensate for anything with his massive sprawling palace. But I had to admit that it made a very good metaphor for the relationship between the ruling class of Arpanpholigon and its wizards. They could grow and grow as much as they wanted, but they could never reach the heights that we started at for fear of self-destruction. It was rather poetic really.

"Big." Ig nodded solemnly. It was the most intelligent thing that we had gotten out of him in days, and the sound of his little ratty voice scared the heck out of Uhp, who jumped a foot in the air.

"Did that thing just talk?"

Cygni rolled her eyes. "Aye, I talk too. We all talk."

Uhp, recognizing a verbal minefield, quickly switched targets. "So, Master . . . Ildrit? Do I know you from somewhere?"

There was a very tense fraction of a second as Ildrit tried to work out how to lie without karma smacking him on the backside for it, but thankfully Cygni intervened. "The circus? He performed in the circus until just this week."

"Oh!" Uhp said, as though that explained anything.

We trudged on for a moment, and then, as though dreading even a moment's silence, Uhp flashed a smile to me. "Master Scryne, I've heard tell that you had some sort of adventure in the Badlands. Is that true?"

"In a sense," I replied as vaguely as possible.

He went on prying all the same. "And that is perhaps where you met your new . . . uh . . . companions?"

"Perhaps," I conceded.

Ig interrupted whatever Uhp's next thought might have been. "Me wears him."

Unable to parse that particular sentence, the knight herald just blinked.

Cygni let out a filthy chuckle in Ildrit's direction and opened her mouth to say something I would never, ever be able to scrub from my mind, and which would cast my relationship with Ig into truly horrific territory. I cut her off with a slightly raised but thoroughly withering voice. "You all wear on me."

Ildrit was sweating. I'd seen him face down small armies with less obvious stress than just walking through the streets of a civilized city in broad daylight. The guards wouldn't need a "wanted" poster to identify him at this rate; all they needed to do was listen to the radiating waves of guilt pouring off the man.

"Perhaps bringing all of you along wasn't entirely necessary," I said to him pointedly, but he shook his head ever so slightly.

"Always wanted to go to the castle," he said with a little chuckle. Given his prior career, I imagine that he'd intended to put the whole city to the flame and plant his backside on the throne after cleaving the king into multiple bite-sized pieces. Oh how the tables turned.

"Oh, you'll love it," Uhp said. "Some of the finest architectural work and illustrative carvings in all the world."

That actually served to perk up Cygni's interest. "Stone?"

"Marble, I believe." He looked a little uncomfortable at the sudden scrutiny. "For the most part. Though I imagine there's something else underneath to give it stability."

"Marble's plenty dense," Cygni replied, picking up the pace and forcing Ig to jog to keep up with us.

He had been sounding increasingly bewildered with everything as his faculties declined, but at least now he had a good reason to look bewildered. "Why run, nothing chase us?"

"Architectural interest," I called back over my shoulder as I struggled to keep up myself. I had entirely forgotten just how rickety this old body of mine had gotten before I lost it. A month of riding around on comparatively athletic young kobolds and dwarves had served as an excellent reminder of exactly how much I'd neglected this bag of bones in favor of expanding my mind. I had no regrets, of course, one must specialize to succeed, but at moments like this, when confronted with the vile and wretched beast *cardio*, I felt the full weight of my hundreds of years of life upon my aching bones.

Ildrit, Uhp, and Cygni arrived at the keep a good few minutes ahead of Ig and me, and Ig was wheezing from the weight of carrying me draped across his narrow shoulders. "Hat . . ." He made a sound like someone stepping on a geriatric accordion. "Was lighter."

We both collapsed into a heap at the base of the stairs, equally pathetic in our levels of physical fitness. Cygni squatted down beside us with an as yet unreadable expression upon her face. "The kobold, I understand. But wizard . . . why didn't you use magic?"

Dear god. I'd forgotten I could use magic.

It had been so long since Quintessence came at my call, so long trapped in one useless body after another, that it had entirely slipped my mind that I could use magic as easily as these buffoons could use their legs. Why, there had been days, nay, weeks at a time during the heights of my time as the archmage of the university when I had not moved a single muscle in my body, floating from room to room, enchanting food to leap into my waiting maw, and conjuring spirits to turn the pages of my books for me and take notes.

Honestly, the fact that my decrepit body was as functional as it was after a lifetime of neglect like that, was frankly amazing. The fact that I could function at all was a testament to the human body's tenacity in the face of willful neglect.

So yes, a little exercise had probably been good for me, but by heck did it feel like it wasn't. I'd been through a living heck as both Ig and Cygni, not to mention other brief heads I'd occupied, yet none of those things had hurt like trying to make my own creaking bones swing into motion the way that they were meant to do naturally without any sort of effort. Being old is terrible, and I made a mental note to myself to undo it just as soon as I'd cured Ig of his declining intellect and Ildrit of his universe-warping curse. The trick would be reversing the physical aging without also reverting my mind to an earlier state, though I supposed that I could simply copy my mind into the hat and then reload over the earlier version of my own awareness. The possibilities of off-board sapience could not be overstated.

When I finally managed to drag in a breath, I replied, "Exercise . . . is good . . . for you."

Given that it appeared that I was approximately a twelfth of a second from death, it was not very convincing.

Cygni hauled me back up to my feet, and Ildrit crowded in on my other side, less like he was trying to support me, and more like he was a duckling trying to tuck under his mother's wing. He thought that my influence could protect him from the consequences of his criminal activities, and he was probably right, but given that he'd spent the past two months of my story looking cool and suave while I was stuck as a hat, I felt quite justified in letting him sweat a little. Regardless, we strolled the remaining distance up to the palace with our heads held high, or at least as high as a dwarf and a kobold can hold their heads, only to be brought to a halt by two knights standing guard.

"No monsters in the palace," snapped one through his closed helmet, clad in a red and green tabard with a goose on the front.

"And don't go philosophizing about who's the real monster, because it's the kobold," added the other, bearing a brown surcoat with black crosshatches.

"This is my apprentice, Ig." I managed to wheeze out almost a full sentence that time.

"No Igs allowed." The gentleman in brown said it directly to Ig, in a manner not dissimilar to a schoolyard bully.

Uhp stepped forwards to champion our cause. "Knight Protector Racha, Knight Protector Lhoin, surely you would not deprive an old man of his pet."

"Knight Herald Uhp, if you do not wish to obey the rules handed down by His Majesty . . ." began Knight Lhoin before Knight Racha interrupted.

"We'll cut you down like dogs."

Funnily enough, this whole interaction had actually made Ildrit begin to relax a little. Laws and justice being done were abstract, frightening things to the man, but two idiots in armor threatening him with violence, that was a normal day for him. He took his arm off my back, where he'd been subtly supporting me, freeing up his hand to draw his blade. I hoped that neither Lhoin nor Racha had a blushing bride at home, because in a moment they'd become widows, then immediately die after Widowtaker's stupid enchantment slew them.

"Knight Racha," the other knight began, "such language is unnecessary and unseemly of a courtly gentleman."

"Knight Lhoin," Racha snapped back, "You've been pushing my buttons all day, and I'm not letting some wretched rat-dog into the palace just because you are too soft."

Knight Uhp opened his mouth, presumably to say something sweet and defuse the situation, but both guards' helmeted heads snapped around and they snarled, "Stay out of this, Uhp," in harmony.

"You need to remember that we are knight protectors, not savages." Lhoin was back on target.

"And you need to remember that fighting is our jobs." Racha leaned in closer across the gap between the two guards. "Not making pretty noises for the nobles."

"I don't think anyone could mistake us for nobles . . ." I began before a visor-slit glare from the guards silenced me too.

"If violence is the only thing that you understand, then perhaps we would best settle our dispute on the dueling field?" Lhoin drew up to his full, and not inconsiderable, height.

I truly thought that our problem was about to solve itself then and there with the shorter knight shortening the taller knight by a head, but instead he leaned in ever closer and sneered. Something quite difficult to do when your entire face is covered by a helmet and visor. "And cede ground, saying I can't settle things with words, proving I'm the savage you think me? I think not."

It seemed to me that regardless of whether the two knights intended to come to blows, Ildrit's patience was drawing thin. On reflection, I really should have expected something like this. We had taken him from his natural habitat of adventuring in the wilderness, dumped him into a densely populated city, and expected him to adapt seamlessly just because he happened to be a human. It was most unfair of us. All of his life before being an adventurer, he was an outlaw, and I couldn't even imagine how long it had been since he'd had to deal with something like this.

Ig had the same idea as I regarding the survival of the guardsmen's spouses if Ildrit drew his sword, although he had of course arrived at it quite a while later, as he blurted out in the midst of all this, "You is married?"

The knights both froze and looked down at the kobold, with the hotheaded Racha shaking his halberd and snarling, "How did you . . ." and the cooler-headed Lhoin stopping him before he got any further. "It was always going to come out eventually."

Cygni's finely attuned sense for gossip had her eyes darting back and forth betwixt the three knights, as Knight Protector Lhoin let go of his shield, letting it crash to the ground and revealing his left hand and the gold band upon his finger. Knight Protector Racha made a sound like a sob, echoing metallically out of his helmet, and let his halberd fall too, reaching out and taking the other guard's hand.

"I'm tired of keeping it a secret. It shouldn't be a secret. I want the world to know I love you," Knight Protector Lhoin said with a tremor in his voice.

Racha was blushing so hard that a little steam was rising out of the slotted grill on the front of his helm. "You complete me."

The two of them abandoned their duties entirely, seizing one another in their arms and clanging their visors together with a fairly catastrophic noise, akin to two frying pans meeting. There was a continued sound of scraping metal as they turned their heads from side to side, clearly trying to better angle their kiss, but utterly failing still to recognize the visors in their way. I leaned closer to Knight Herald Uhp and whispered, "Can we just go while they're busy?"

The man seemed a little shell-shocked but he nodded and led us inside all the same.

Within the palace was precisely the degree of opulence that one would have anticipated. Lush, thick red carpets along pristinely aligned flagstones that you just knew were making Cygni's dwarf senses tingle. Tapestries that must have taken bored wives of nobles literally decades to complete while they festered in loveless marriages. Gold leaf also featured heavily in the decor. I only recognized that it was leaf, rather than solid gold fixtures, thanks to the persistent influence of Cygni's viewpoint upon my own, but I supposed that having solid gold everything was probably a bad investment, given the softness of the metal. You'd need to scoop the drooping candelabras up and recast them every few years.

Uhp was blind to the luxury around him due to overfamiliarity; Ildrit took it in with a hunger; Cygni examined fine details of things that nobody else would have even thought to look at, nodding in satisfaction at a good joint in the vaulted ceiling; and Ig . . . it is difficult to say how much Ig understood what he was looking at by this point in his degeneration. To his mind, it may very well have just been a very brightly colored hole that he'd crawled into. Or he could entirely grasp the centuries it had taken to construct such an edifice to glorify a bloodline of people who just happened to have been left sitting in the big chair when the music of early violent history stopped. Who could say what was happening behind his beady little eyes? Not I.

What followed was a procession of large grand rooms where we had to stand around for several minutes as Uhp explained in detail who we were, why we were to be allowed farther in, and that we should be allowed through more swiftly, followed by buttock-numbing periods of sitting around waiting for the bureaucrats of the court to ascertain that we were in fact who we were, we were in fact to be allowed farther in, and we should have been allowed through more swiftly. Then we would rinse and repeat in the next room, and the next. With increasingly lofty titles attached to the people stopping us and decreasing patience across the board.

No longer needed the guards and pedants of the king's keep fear Ildrit's mighty blade, for I was on the verge of turning them all into salt. Even Ig was getting irritated, and he was the kind of person who would happily sit and stare into space for days at a time. Though what the wrath of a semi-sapient kobold might look like, none could say. I assumed he'd piss on the tapestries, personally, but that might have just been wishful thinking.

Every so often, when you were hanging around with Ig, as we were at present, you got some strange sensations. Perhaps it was only because of my own sensitivity to the flows of Quintessence, but after long enough in his company you did get the sense of movement. Just a slow and steady drift towards him, like we had felt at the periphery of the dark god's tomb down in the deep places of the earth. Even though he no longer seemed capable of using magic, he was still drawing more Quintessence into his reserves instinctually. The pattern of behavior established before he had forgotten it being established. The buildup of power within him, relentless.

The crown I meant to set upon his brow had been a priority before, but with this revelation it became a vital necessity. All of that power with nowhere to go would begin to leak out in wild magic. Worse yet would be if it didn't leak out, and the Quintessence within him continued to build and build and build until finally his containment catastrophically failed, and then we'd be cleaning Ig off the walls and ceiling, or at least the rubble where those things used to be. Assuming any of us survived the explosion.

The key point was, we had to get Ig back to normal—new normal, not old normal—or risk catastrophic kobold failure.

"His Majesty will see you now."

I was startled out of my reverie by the sudden appearance of an elderly gentleman dressed in extremely somber clothes, contrasting sharply with the audaciously overblown fashion of the day. Everything about him screamed "butler" except for the fact that he worked in a castle, so he'd be a castellan, or a steward? The chamberlain? Lord of the Privy? I have no idea. He was ushering us through to the throne room all the same.

The king of Arpanpholigon was a gloriously rotund gentleman with a beard like burnished gold. Or at least, it had started out that way before age grayed it and tobacco stained it a rather different yellow. Opulent robes covered his nigh-spherical form and a crown was perched at a jaunty angle upon his increasingly balding head. He didn't rise from his throne to greet us—that probably would have been too much respect—but he did wave us over the moment he caught sight of us with a big smile.

Down in the depths of that voluminous face of his, two eyes peered out, black as beetle shells. Each blink seemed to chitter, as he took in me, Ildrit, Cygni, and Ig, before returning to me once more. At a glance one might have thought him a buffoon. A lounging lummox with no more care for his kingdom than a cat for its keeper. But in this you would actually be quite incorrect. Behind those beady eyes was a calculating and cunning mind. One that in the correct circumstances likely would have been cruel and depraved, but luck had placed him on the throne of a peaceful kingdom, so all of the energy that he would have had to put into plotting and planning and backstabbing and manipulating others was left to linger. He channeled it into his hungers, I suspect, hence the stains and bulk, and the long chain of bastard offspring he'd sired across the countryside with all and sundry each time he went on one of his "hunting trips" that never seemed to produce any game.

There had been assorted queens through the years, every one of them convinced that they could change him, but none had yet succeeded, though it should be said that succession in other areas definitely would not be an issue, as the number of heirs lingering around the city was probably more than sufficient to start up some sort of royal-only sporting league.

"Archmage!" he called out joyously. "It has been too long since we've shared company."

It was an act, of course. He loathed me with the kind of passion you can only find in bullies confronted by someone unbullyable. But it was a useful act. Pretending to be friendly was a sensible course of action if we intended for both the city and Invisible College to go on coexisting peacefully.

"King!" I cried back with similarly falsified excitement. "What a pleasure to see you!"

I did know his name, it was right on the tip of my tongue. It would come to me in a moment.

He never took his gaze from me, even as my own eyes glazed over trying to remember his name. "My dear man, you must introduce me to your new friends . . ."

I started with the easiest and worked up from there. "This is Ig. He is a kobold. The first of his kind to undertake the study of magic."

Ig, bless his little heart, waved.

The king nodded, clearly nonplussed by the kobold's existence, let alone presence in court. "Mmhmm, very good. Shows initiative."

I moved along swiftly. "This is Cygni Khnutesdottir, a dwarven princess who traveled with us to the city."

"Mmhmm, seems like the kind of person someone should have brought to the palace for introductions, but go on . . ."

"And this . . ." I looked at Ildrit, pale and sweaty.

There were a few different directions that this could go. I could be honest, believing that the king's spies in the city had already identified Ildrit, possibly throwing him to the wolves, and possibly allowing me to position myself as a sort of warden promising his good behavior. I could lie blatantly, and trust that nobody in court could recognize Ildrit from any of the wanted posters that had been circulating a decade or so back.

He wasn't actually all that recognizable in his current guise. His hair was a lot tidier, and tied back. His stubble was mostly under control. He wasn't slicked from head to toe in the blood of the innocent. You could probably mistake him for just another adventurer.

So really the gamble was on how good the king's spies were.

"This is Ildrit Elfbane, infamous across the lands for his acts of great violence and evil. Wanted for his terrible crimes, in particular against elf-kind, ergo the name."

There was not even the slightest flicker of surprise upon the king's face as I said that. He had known all along; lying would have just lost us any moral authority we might have claimed in the argument that was sure to follow. I had made the correct choice. "And might I ask why you thought it wise to bring this bandit lord with you into the very bosom of Arpanpholigon?"

"Why, isn't it obvious, Your Grace?" I managed to force a smile back onto my face. "Because he is rehabilitated."

Both Cygni and Ildrit had been tensing up for a fight throughout all of this, but now they turned to gawk at me.

"Rehabilitated?" the king repeated back to me with barely concealed contempt.

"Allow me to elaborate," I began, taking Ildrit by the hand and bringing him closer still to the throne, so the king could look directly upon him. Ildrit did not care for the scrutiny, but if he didn't want people staring at him then he probably shouldn't have become infamous. "Rehabilitation is the process or act of restoring a person to a state of health or normalcy following illness, imprisonment, or immorality. In this case, we are discussing the transformation of a previously criminal individual into one who is ethically . . ."

"I am familiar with the meaning of the word," the king interrupted. King Cuspid? No. That wasn't it.

"Me not," Ig opined from somewhere in the skirts of my robes where he was cowering.

"So you were wondering at the confidence that I hold in my good friend Ildrit's rehabilitation?" There is a certain showmanship to politics that I had never much cared for, but I believe that the flair for it had finally made its way into my repertoire of tricks after our stint with the circus and the planning of our grand stunt to draw the college's attention.

King Clavicle—no, that wasn't it—made the universally recognized hand-rolling gesture to get on with it. "That is more to the point I was making, yes."

"Ildrit, my good man. I hereby give you my leave to do whatever evil thing you want. As does the king. Slaughter anyone it pleases you to slaughter. Pillage whatever you desire. Have at it."

King Cadence—definitely not—asked, "I give permission, do I?"

"You do indeed," I replied without hesitation.

"Alright then, let's see this villain in action." The king looked . . . bemused. "Guards, let him do as he pleases."

The knight protectors scattered around the room did not actually look less tense after being told that they could slack off. Quite the opposite, really.

Ildrit shifted uncomfortably from foot to foot. Everyone was staring at him.

Like I was trying to encourage a flighty animal from its cage, I spoke softly to him. "Go on now, Ildrit. Anything you want to do, you can do. There will be no consequences at all."

He glanced around the room, eyes passing blindly over the omnipresent wealth, until they set upon Cygni, then he shuffled awkwardly back over to her and took her hand. She looked absurdly pleased at this outcome. Meanwhile Ig had settled down on his rump and begun gnawing on his own tail with apparent fascination.

"Sufficient demonstration?" I asked King Caecum. No, that wasn't it either. It was definitely a C name. I was sure of that much. Something to do with the body, and the letter C.

There were clearly cogs turning behind the eyes of the king, the machinery of a mind that had been designed through generations of selective breeding to pick out hidden meanings in words and actions, to ferret out traitors and tricksters in court and turn them into very pointed demonstrations on why the royal family was not to be crossed. He was turning all of that hyper-specialized mind on the problem of me bringing Ildrit here, trying to discern my purpose in doing it, and I knew for a fact that he did not have enough information to inform a decent answer to that question, because the sad truth of the matter was that I had not approached this particular situation with any intelligence or planning; I had simply wanted my friends with me.

The very prospect of friendship had always seemed so very alien to me. Like some abstract concept regarding the binding of atoms to one another through resonance of purpose. People connected to other people, people who enjoyed spending time with one another. The whole thing would have seemed farcical to me in my youth, as I did everything in my power to avoid the company of my peers and focus on my all-important studies, but now, since my time as a hat, I truly saw the value in friendships. In interpersonal relationships in general. Eventually there would always be a problem that brute magical force could not solve, and turning to others was the only solution.

"I will accept your word, if you claim that he is reformed, but should he commit any wrongdoing while within the territory of Arpanpholigon, then rest assured that . . ."

You could tell that he wanted to make some grandiose threat in the manner of his forebearers. To have Ildrit drowned in blood or skinned alive and made into a cape. One of the absolutely ridiculous things that kings sometimes do just to show off how tough they are. I stepped in before his imagination could catch up to his mouth. "You'd have to race the lightning bolt I was sending his way to catch him before me, Your Grace."

This seemed to sate him for now, and he settled back into his throne once more.

King Cartilage? King Cranium? King Cruciate? What the heck was his name?

Ildrit took a bold step forward, still clinging to Cygni's hand like she was a cuddly toy that he'd become overly attached to. "Good King Salivar, I thank you for your wisdom and your trust in my better nature. I shall do my best to bring no trouble to you."

Salivar! That was it. Idiot.

"It is funny that you should mention bringing trouble to me, Elfbane . . ." King Salivar said, ever so casually, before trailing off. The whole court was on tenterhooks, leaning forward to listen in as he spoke ever more softly. "Would I be correct in saying that you accompanied our mutual friend, the archmage, on a journey through the Badlands recently?"

Damnation, his spies really were good. Even when I'd physically been here the whole time, he still somehow knew about the little sojourn that my mind and spirit had been on. That was some impressive spycraft. Either that or there was a little birdie nested in the college that was twittering in the wrong ears and would soon be flung from its nest up in the clouds. After I'd clipped its wings. Figuratively; I'd never do that to an actual bird. Unless it was sapient and spying on me for the king. Oh, let's be honest, I'd probably just fireball the thing, the same as I'd do to whoever had been telling tales out of my school.

"That's correct, Your . . . Radiance," Cygni piped up when it seemed I was momentarily too flabbergasted. "Your wizard here, he was checking on your big wall when . . ."

"I don't think we need to trouble His Majesty with every paltry detail of my Badlands tour, thank you." I cut her off before we could get into any hat-related discussions. "All that matters is that I did indeed travel beyond the wall and take in some measure of the forces arrayed against us out there."

"Initiative, again. I appreciate it." The king nodded encouragingly. "And did this have anything to do with the veritable tide of werewolves that came scrambling over the Great Wall just a short while prior to your return to Arpanpholigon and your rightful station?"

Ah.

"I believe that the two events may have been related, yes." I stalled for time as my brain tried to catch up to my mouth. "It is most likely that they were related, in fact. Given that I encountered werewolves on multiple occasions in the Badlands, before returning here, after they had my scent. It was also related to a great many of your citizens having been cursed and banished beyond your borders as the result of a single vicious individual who my party disposed of with all haste, returning that alleged tide of werewolves back into a village-worth of rather charming farmers." I paused for a moment to catch a breath and mentally applaud myself before adding, "You're welcome."

The king let out a little snort. Somewhere between confusion and amusement. Not quite the bemusement of before, as this time it had definitely tilted more to the side of confusion, but not sufficient confusion to prompt a violent or negative response, I supposed. Or at least, not yet. "While I'm appropriately grateful for you bringing a swarm of werewolves down into the undefended farmland that is the sole food source for the entire city, I must now ask about the ogres."

"Ogres, Your Majesty? A single drop of sweat had formed beneath the rim of my hat, and was now threatening to descend.

"There appears to be a deputation of ogres at our walls, quite irate over the destruction of their city, and demanding the head of a kobold wizard."

"Oopsie," Ig mumbled.

Ah. Right. That.

The king pressed on. "I'm inclined to give them the kobold so as to avoid any further unpleasantness."

Ildrit tutted loudly enough for the whole court to hear him.

"Does something meet with your disapproval, Elfbane?"

It was interesting seeing the change that had come over him, now that he was no longer acting like the man we had come to know and love, or at least tolerate, and was instead putting on the mask of the bandit king that he had once been. "You've never dealt with ogres before, have you?"

"I cannot say that I have had that dubious pleasure, no." The actual king still looked upon him with a degree of suspicion that felt frankly justified, yet in spite of that suspicion, you could see that he was weighing Ildrit's words all the same. As if he meant to find the grain of truth in the plume of sand he was being doused with.

"An ogre only respects strength. If it thinks it can demand something and get it from you, it won't just be once, it will be back every day, asking for more. And it will bring all of its friends too, once they've realized that you're a soft touch." He said the last words as though they were venomous. It was a potent argument that probably would have been effective even if everything he was saying weren't true.

"Big oopsie." Ig added his own gravitas to the statement.

With a little chuckle, King Salivar looked around at his courtly vassals. "So you'd advise against removing one monster from my city so as to prevent the intrusion of a dozen more?"

There was some tittering from the gathered bobbleheads.

"Not going to be intruding, are they?" Cygni said gruffly. "Not with the wall."

Salivar managed to look intensely bored with the whole proceeding. As if trying to convey to us that it was impressive just how little he cared. "It would be preferable not to have one of our borders under siege by a tide of monsters, I must say."

There were more murmurs in the court. Complaints about the college and all the trouble we literally and figuratively rained down upon the city. Complaints about my leadership, and the selfishness of not letting the king dispose of my little pet. All of the usual bitching and moaning that those more accustomed to court probably learned to drown out, but which I, usually uncontested master of my domain, struggled not to take to heart, and take offense at.

Rationally, I did know that we were being baited, but that did little to stop me from coming to the inevitable conclusion that I knew the king wanted us to reach. We could have prevaricated about it all day, but I had neither the time nor the patience, given the ticking time bomb of Ig. I jumped to the end. "Allow me to address the problem for you, Your Grace. Since we were the cause of this inconvenience."

His Royal Highness King Salivar the Third looked surprised and delighted that I'd jumped on the bait so readily, but then you could practically hear the cogs between his ears spinning up to speed once more as he tried to grasp what advantage he had just given me without realizing it. Too much conspiracy is bad for the brain. After just a moment of wincing internally, the king said, "Much obliged, my dear Archmage. You must come visit again with us soon."

Ig repeated, "Sorry," many times as we departed court on cue, first to the king as we backed out, then to the nobles that we passed by, to the other people awaiting their audience with the king, even to a tapestry that he brushed up against. If I'd been atop his head, I could have silenced him without anyone noticing, but as it was, we were being observed and listened to, both by the myriad ears and eyes of court but also by our knight herald guide, so interrupting his rambles would have drawn unwanted attention.

On arrival at the main entrance, this time from the inside, there was no sign of the charming married couple tasked with guarding it. There was, however, a steady rhythmic clanging going on in the nearby shrubbery that we all very pointedly did not go to investigate. Uhp looked extremely red in the face until we were off the grounds entirely, and even then, you still could have probably fried an egg on his cheeks. He pulled down his visor to obscure his face and, with a metallic echo to his voice, said, "Right, see you later."

Only then did I finally seize Ig by the scruff and tell him to shut the hell up. "You have nothing to apologize for."

"Me brought the ogreses." Ig began to wail before Cygni's hand clamped his muzzle shut.

I had to crouch to be nose to nose with him, which my hips quite firmly did not appreciate. The hiss to my voice was both from whispering and pain. "The ogres are a minor issue. Your constant conceding of responsibility for their presence is not."

"But they is so strongs . . ." Ig began, the moment that Cygni let his face go.

"They were an issue when you were alone, dear Ig, because at that time the closest thing that we had to a competent wizard was you. I shall be quite capable of wiping out their whole civilization with a gesture then heading off to drink some tea." I offered him a smile. "Do try to keep up."

I clapped my hands together, bringing our little conglomeration to a halt. "Right, does anyone need to visit the privy before we go?"

"Go where?" Cygni's eyes narrowed.

She was typically the most intelligent of my companions, so I was somewhat surprised that she hadn't already worked it out. "The Great Wall, of course. To see what is going on and commit some minor slaughtering if it proves necessary."

"Me not need go," Ig piped up. For a moment I thought he meant that he did not intend to accompany us, then realized he was answering my question about going to the bathroom.

Tapping into nitrogen, oxygen, and a couple of other trace elements, I spoke the spell. *"Lanuae omnes ad murum magnum quaeso."*

Our mortal shells shattered, our flesh turning first to ribbons then to vapor as every part of our being unwound. If it had been slower, it would have been the worst agony imaginable, but my magic worked faster than the speed of pain.

For a moment all that we could conceive of was the blur of passing motion, the tug of the currents of air upon our gaseous forms, then to flesh we were returned.

Ig and Cygni stood to either side of me for maximum dramatic effect as we appeared atop the Great Wall in a burst of whipping wind. A sound like a thunderclap echoed out as what was there before was forcibly pushed out of the space we now occupied. The guards arrayed along the wall, previously occupied with peering down at the gathered congregation of ogres, all startled to attention with my sudden arrival. And the shock of the archmage popping up was apparently sufficient to distract them from the fact that my companions were somewhat unusual.

Ig let out a little whimper. "Me did need go."

CHAPTER 7

OGRE AND ABOVE

It was probably for the best that he had abandoned the practice of wearing robes sometime during his mental degradation, as cleanup would now only involve a mop, not a launderette.

"Alright, gentlemen," I cried in my most booming wizardly voice, "what seems to be the trouble here?"

"Wizard." Cygni tugged at my sleeve, but I ignored her for now—first impressions were important when you were meeting commoners for the first time; they had to have it impressed upon them that you were not to be ignored.

"Bunch of ogres, ain't it," said a young gentleman who was either a transmogrified peach, or too young to grow a proper beard. To my immense distress, he was the most senior amongst the guards who were meant to be watching over Arpanpholigon.

"Quite so," I pressed on regardless of his rather glib tone. "And how long have this bunch of ogres been lingering outside the walls?"

Another tug at my sleeve. "Wizard!"

"'Bout a week?" He turned to his coworkers for assurance and received some nods. "Yeah, about a week."

"Did you try driving them off at all, or . . .?"

He looked at me like I was mad when I asked him if he had actually done his job. "Don't get paid enough to fight no ogres, sir."

"Wizard!" Cygni was shouting now.

"Excuse me one moment," I said to the guards, before turning my attention to Cygni. "What?"

"You forgot Ildrit!" She was doing her best not to yell directly in my face, but there was still definitely some degree of hostility in the way she had seized me by the front of my robes.

"What?!" I cast a glance around, and to my immense surprise, the hulking swordsman was not here. I took a quick stroll over to the edge of the wall and glanced down, just to make sure he hadn't made some sort of accidental catastrophic splat, then returned to Cygni and Ig. "Well, I cast the blasted spell right."

Her eyes narrowed. "You meant to leave him behind?"

"No, of course not." I held up my hands to ward off her glare. "I'm merely saying that his absence is not due to anything that I have done."

One would think that it would be difficult to be intimidated by a dwarf, what with the height disparity, but in truth, when a creature is made almost entirely of hard, chiseled muscle, you tend to give it the due respect regardless of whether it towers and looms or not. "Well, he isn't bloody here, is he?!"

"It would appear not." She drew back a four-fingered fist before I could add, "I shouldn't worry about him; if the spell failed to take hold of him, it won't have rendered him down to his component atoms and scattered him to the wind, he'll simply have been left in Arpanpholigon. I'm sure that he can manage without us for a half hour or so in an entirely peaceful city."

"Won't stay peaceful with him left alone half an hour." She growled, releasing the front of my robes, but leaving behind some serious creasing. "He's a wild man."

I shuddered.

"Every time you imply anything about your romantic relationship with Ildrit, I cringe so hard it takes several years off my life, I hope that you realize that? You realize that you are killing me?"

"Grow up." She tutted, with a little bit of a smirk she was trying to hide. "What if he gets in a fight?"

I tried to smooth out my poor crinkled robes, but it was to no avail, I would be walking around with a stubby grab mark on my chest all day. "Then we'll retrieve him from under the pile of people he has massacred when we get back. Could we please focus on the task at hand instead of your boyfriend?"

She tutted, pointedly. "Can't believe you forgot him."

That touched a little too close to a nerve, if I'm being entirely honest. As I too was unclear on how exactly I'd managed to fail to include Ildrit in the spell. "I forgot nothing! My mind is a steel trap."

"Rusty?" she snapped back.

I drew myself up to the full height of my pomposity and declared, "Madam!"

"Sir?" the guard called from behind me.

Ah yes. Guards, ogres, walls.

"Ah yes, my apologies." I put a hand on Ig and Cygni's shoulders and steered them towards the stairs down to the gatehouse. "We shall nip down to the gates and have a word with the ogres, see if there isn't a diplomatic solution to the situation."

"Haven't been much bother really. They just want some kobold called Ig, figured it'd be easy enough to find one." He blinked and seemed to focus on Ig for the first time since our arrival. "Look, there's one."

"Me is Ig," said Ig, helpfully.

The guard cheered up a little. "And it's already got the right name!"

"Me is Ig!" Ig was positively delighted that someone was happy to see him for a change, not entirely aware that they were happy in the same way that a high priest is happy when he spots a particularly plump calf among the potential altar toppers.

"Come on, Ig." I sighed heavily. "Let's get this over with."

Cygni caught me by the sleeve once more as I was heading down the stairs, barely out of earshot of the guards. "Send me back to town to make sure Ildrit . . ."

I cut this nonsense off. "Ildrit is a grown man who is quite capable of taking care of himself. A few minutes without you clinging to him isn't going to do him an iota of harm."

She met my glare with one of her own, one that was considerably less watery in the cold wind atop the wall, if truth be told. "I'll do it myself then."

"Go ahead," I called back over my shoulder when she stubbornly refused to follow us down the stairs. "Just remember not to leave your molecules spread across all the distance between here and there and to invoke the correct balance of elements so you don't rapidly dissipate. It would be a shame for you to cloud yourself."

"If I get clouded, it'll be because you didn't help," she shouted down, all pretense of civility slipping.

"If you get clouded it shall be because you are a rank, arrogant amateur dabbling in arts you are still barely a student of, touching powers far beyond your reach."

Ig and I rounded the corner, and I fully expected to see her capering down after us to continue the argument, but to my surprise, I instead heard the soft popping sound of someone teleporting away. She had actually done it. I was both surprised and impressed at her gumption. The previous supervised teleportation that she'd experienced had either been under my hatty guidance or controlled entirely by me in some manner. I know that I may have waxed lyrical about how impressive my dear apprentice's capabilities were, but each day I was impressed anew.

Meanwhile, Ig had stopped halfway down the stairs because he got distracted excavating something from his ear with a claw.

"Ig."

He seemed to notice where he was again. "Weh?"

"Try to keep up, dear boy." I tried not to let my despair show too plainly on my face, even though I realized that at this point he was probably too stupid to even parse what my expressions meant.

The sooner I could get him back to normal, the happier I would be.

Beyond the portcullis, the ogres awaited us. There was very little snarling or thrusting of arms between bars as one might have expected from a monstrous incursion into civilized lands. Rather, there was a somewhat awkward ogre in a suit that had been poorly tailored to him, standing at the front of the group with a little leather briefcase. The leather, admittedly, was green, and had likely started off as the skin of an orc, but there could be no denying that the pince-nez glasses on the ogre's face helped to offset this peculiarity in the otherwise entirely official-looking getup. "We is 'ere for the kobold wizard known as 'Ig'," he announced without preamble. "He burnt down our city and we is wanting reven—justice."

Ig, showing a surprising degree of common sense for a creature usually deprived of it, had fallen into step behind me as we approached the gate, remaining hidden from sight behind the skirts of my robes.

"Good day to you, sir," I said to the ogre with as much politeness as I could muster. "I am the Archmage Absalom Scryne, and it is my duty to represent all wizards in matters of diplomacy and politics."

"We is wanting the Ig please." He remained focused, I'll give him that.

"With all due respect to you"—I've always been fond of that phrase, "with all due respect," it had a wonderful flexibility to it—"might I ask on what authority you are demanding that I turn over a creature in my care to your . . . justice?"

He started pulling papers out of his green briefcase. "We is the represemble of the sovereign city-state of New Orc . . ."

I cut him off. "I'm terribly sorry, but I don't believe any such place exists. Ergo, you have no authority to demand I turn over anyone."

"New Orc be biggest city in the Badlands!" the ogre snarled.

"Are you certain?" I resisted the urge to smirk. "I was rather under the impression that all you had out there was a heap of ash? Isn't that your entire complaint?"

The ogre flushed with rage, but instead of smashing his meaty hands against the bars, he reached up and carefully adjusted his necktie. "Allow me to consulate with me clients."

"By all means." I maintained a professional smile.

I glanced back to Ig where he was cowering. "I can talk them out of this, don't worry."

He stared at me blankly. Asking a kobold not to worry was rather like asking a fish not to swim.

The ogre returned with his temper at a high simmer. "My clients pustulate that there was New Orc City before your rat got there, ergo you give him, or we smash this place up. And your face."

"If the city-entity heretofore referred to as New Orc City is no longer in existence, then I do not believe that it can exercise any legal authority. Perhaps you should wait until you have a client to represent before supplying demands." I took a breath. "And regarding threats of property and facial damage, I feel obligated to remind you that you have not, thus far, been in any way capable of penetrating the Great Wall of Arpanpholigon, nor are you liable to do so at any point in the future."

The ogre opened and closed his mouth a few times. It was difficult for them, to be presented with a problem that couldn't be solved with overwhelming violence. It would be like taking my magic away, or Ig's cowardice. A fundamental part of who and what they were was being restrained. It was for this reason that I considered the work of Sour Ron, the now-deceased mayor of New Orc City, to house-train his ogres to be particularly cruel. They were not meant for legal debates; they were meant for smashing faces. Forcing them into suits and obligations like this wasn't improving them, it was detracting from the perfection of what they are.

This is not to say that no monster is deserving of civilization, of course—just look at Ig to see how well they can take to it, and how much it can do to improve their lot in life. But there is a vast difference between choosing the life of a civilized creature and being forced into it. Ig had been forced into it too, if I were being honest, but once he had developed a sense of sapience and self, he took to it well. These ogres had not been pulled through any magical transformation to open up their minds to the wonders of paved roads, administration, and politeness; they had been bullied into behaving contrary to their nature. Which led, inevitably, to situations like this.

The ogre flung himself at the bars, cramming his big meaty arm through and trying to grab me despite the sensible distance that I had kept from the portcullis. I tried not to look too contemptuous, as that makes negotiations trickier, as a rule, but it was difficult to keep a straight face when he got one of his comically oversized biceps stuck and the other ogres had to awkwardly shuffle over and tug him free with no small amount of grunting and groaning.

The worst part of the whole spectacle was that this was the one ogre out of the lot that they had democratically elected to be the most sensible, level-headed, and capable of lawyering.

After some ahem-ing and straightening out of suits, the negotiations for Ig's life began anew.

"What you is doing is bearing," the ogre said, once his temper had settled somewhat.

"I beg your pardon?"

He nodded knowledgeably. "Is like badgering, but bigger and worse."

"I am terribly sorry, sir," I conceded. "I may have been trying to push through these proceedings without taking your feelings into account."

His broad shoulders slumped and he let out a held breath. "Thanks."

"Let us work from the assumption that you have some standing from which to advance your position, and move on to why you will fail regardless."

"Unthanks," he grumbled.

I pressed straight into the meat of the matter, ignoring him entirely, as I suspected would become the trend of this conversation. "Are you familiar at all with the Genieva Conventions?"

The ogre pinched the bridge of his flattened nose. "The what-va whats?"

"During the great Genie War, all of the various powers and dominions gathered to lay down specific rules of warfare, which, if broken, could be punished by the summoning of genies to annihilate whoever broke them from history via wishing them away." I could see that he was starting to lose focus from the way that his eyes were slowly uncrossing to stare off to either side of me, so I snapped my fingers to get him back on task. "It was decided during said gathering that it was wrong to torture prisoners of war, and in particular, it was not allowable to punish any prisoner of war for attempting to escape, as it was entirely within their entitlement as a sapient being to seek freedom."

The ogre was staring at me blankly.

"The genies were quite particular about that part of the conventions actually . . . not entirely clear as to why . . ." I stroked my beard for a moment, relishing having a beard to stroke once again.

Apparently enough time had passed from my explanation of the conventions that the ogre's brain had begun turning over again. "What's genies got to do with . . ."

I cut that path of thought off before the ogre could get lost down it. "It establishes the legal precedent that it was entirely acceptable for my client, the aforementioned kobold Ig, to do whatever was necessary to escape confinement."

"He burned our whole city down!" the ogre roared, spritzing me with spittle despite the protection of the portcullis.

Raising my voice would have led to a shouting match, which there was no way anyone with lungs so much comparatively smaller was liable to win, so I pressed on to my next point with the same genteel tone as I'd employed before. "As to that, I must now ask about the construction of your alleged city. Was it built to the standards mandated by the International Guild of Architects and Stonecutters?"

He blinked. "The what by who?"

"Was the mandated space left between those buildings deemed to be constructed of materials that were a fire risk, as prescribed by the International Guild of Woodworkers, Oilers, and Miracle-Workers?" I knew it wasn't, because I'd seen the whole tinderbox of a town before it went up in flames.

Until now the lawyer had been predominantly angry; now he mixed in confusion. "What's that?"

Gripping my robes by the lapels and feeling mildly smug about my successful attempt to shift blame, I smirked back. "It sounds to me, my dear man, like you need to take your case to whosoever was in charge of planning rather than to the unfortunate kobold who merely served as the catalyst for the inevitable disaster that consumed your city."

"Sour Ron is gone." And anger was back in full force now. Low and sinister instead of high and flaring. The kind of anger bred of deep-set hatred, not momentary annoyances.

Getting them to see things from my perspective shouldn't have been impossible, it would just take a little work. And once I'd contorted their worldview into something more useful, we'd be all set. "Something that I would think would be pleasing to you, as he has now paid the maximum penalty available under law to slumlords and the like who construct homes in such a manner as those in New Orc City."

The ogre looked affronted. Not a common look for an ogre, who are typically quite happy-go-lucky until they're murdering you. Actually, they're usually even more happy-go-lucky when they're murdering you. It is their favorite thing to do, after all. "Ron was the boss!"

"I'd go so far as to say that whoever killed your Mayor Ron was doing your city a great service, perhaps one that was worthy of reward. Perhaps a reward of a full pardon for any crimes?"

"Ron is the . . ." the ogre began to shout, and then what his ears had taken in filtered through to his brain and left him mouthing at the air like a fish out of water, albeit only briefly before he managed to whisper, "Ron is dead?"

Ah, perhaps I'd overplayed my hand a little there.

I replied coyly, "One would assume."

The ogre's eyes narrowed to slits, almost invisible in the vast, meaty slab of his face. "How you know Ron's dead?"

What luck that thinking quickly on my feet is one of the many kinds of thinking that I excel at. "Well, I assume that were he still alive, he would be the one here presenting your case."

Like a dire terrier with a bone betwixt its teeth, the ogre did not let go. "Did you kill Ron?!"

I rolled my eyes, making sure that even this dimwit could see my contempt for the question. "Of course not! I have been here in the city the entire time. Ask anyone."

"Did the rat-runt kill Ron?!" It seemed that I had mildly underestimated the intelligence of this particular ogre.

I supposed that he must have been moderately intelligent to serve as the group's lawyer, and certainly smarter than the average ogre, what with his ability to tie his own tie. That said, it wasn't that ogres were inherently stupid in the way that creatures like kobolds were.

"I'm not familiar with anyone by that name . . ."

He cut off that deflection with another bellowing roar. "The kobold!"

I wet my lips. "That would depend entirely upon whether you intend to extend him a full pardon for any misdemeanors that may have taken place while he was passing through your city. Misdemeanors which would already be considered perfectly legal under international law due to the Genieva Conventions. And a city we no longer acknowledge as an entity because it is burnt down."

"He did!" he called back over his shoulder to the gathered ogres. "The rat killed Ron!"

"There is absolutely no evidence to that effect," I shouted over the sudden uproar from over on the ogre side of the wall. "No proof that Ig slaughtered your mayor and the whole hunting party that you sent after him."

"Give us kobold or we kill you all!" bellowed the lawyer-ogre. Restating his demands in a very succinct manner.

"With all due respect . . ." I began before being shouted over rudely once more.

"Give rat-runt or we smash!"

That certainly seemed to be the consensus among the ogres, as they were all screaming and roaring things to similar effect. The ogre at the portcullis had now seized hold of the bars and started trying to bend them. He wasn't liable to have much luck, as despite how strong any given ogre may be, they aren't quite a match for enchanted carbon-steel rods. I suspect he had also failed to consider that given his prodigious girth, he would have to proceed to bend a third bar after the first two so that he might make ingress.

Being the reasonable person that I was, I waited politely for him to work all the frothing-at-the-mouth frenzy out of his system. At one point he did make the bars squeak ever so slightly, which was better than anyone had managed before, but it was still insufficient to affect their curvature, which remained uncurved.

"As I was saying . . ." I began when I thought he was done, only for his eyes to bug out of his head, all the veins in his muscular arms to bulge out, and a second attempt at bar bending to begin. The other ogres had now come charging in to make their own attempts at the bars, but without my direct antagonism, they seemed to lack quite the same degree of berserk rage. They couldn't even get a squeak.

I checked my nails were clean as they grunted and roared and a few of the dimmer ones threw themselves bodily at the bars ineffectually. Eventually they began to settle down again.

"Have we all got that out of our system now?"

The lawyer was panting for air after all of his exertions, but he still had strength aplenty to lift up a finger and point it at me. "We is coming back and we is going to demol . . . We is going to demo . . . We is going to smash down your wall. And then we is going to smash you up!"

"Might I advise you to seek some assistance in that regard?" Alright, I will admit that I was actively antagonizing them by this point, but they had irked me. I was irked. "You seem to be sorely lacking in the necessary firepower."

They all stormed off, roaring and baying for blood, as is their wont.

I turned back to Ig at last, who was now fully fetal on the ground. "There, that was easy enough, I don't expect we shall be seeing them again anytime soon."

He made a little hiccup or belch and curled up a little tighter.

I sighed. "Ig. You can get up now."

When he failed to move once more, I prodded him with my toe. "Up you get."

So softly I had to strain to hear him, Ig whimpered, "They is wanting murder me."

"Well, that is hardly news, is it?" I rolled up my sleeves and tried to pick the kobold up, but he had gone entirely limp, and dangled back to earth no matter how much of him I lifted. "Everything has been trying to murder you since I first met you, and a fair more things have been trying to murder you since before you were even born. One might say that the entire world has sought your death at one point or another. There is hardly any point in taking it personally."

He shuddered in my arthritic grip. "They comes all this way to murder me."

"Well, they are somewhat peeved that you annihilated their entire civilization. Which is a pretty good reason to be annoyed, as far as these things go."

Ig shivered all the more violently as I spoke until he slipped through my fingers entirely to rest in a coiled heap once more.

"Me should just die," Ig announced with another hiccup that may have been a sob. "Me so stupid."

"Ig, my dear boy." Crouching despite the unhappy noises from my knees, I laid a hand atop his greasy scalp and petted the kobold as best I could without bile rising in my throat. "If the price of stupidity was death then I would walk this world alone."

"Me sorry." Ig sobbed onto the flagstones. "Me so sorry."

I took one look at him down there, looking every bit the most piteous lump I had ever laid eyes on, and within my heart I felt a crack.

"No."

It was incongruous enough to his self-pity that he looked up at me. "No?"

"You are not sorry. You are a wizard. A wizard is never sorry, because to be sorry implies that they made a mistake, and a wizard makes no mistakes." I towered over him, by virtue of not being a kobold, but in this moment I stood not as a man but as a pillar of truth and faith.

Philosophy was not my strong point. My interest had always been in the practical applications of power rather than the metaphysical implications of it, but there was one stricture to which I had been raised.

"To be a wizard, one must have unshakeable belief in oneself. In the rightness of one's actions. There can be no regrets, no looking back and wishing that another spell had been spoken or another fate woven. We are the arbiters of reality, and there can be no sorrow in us, for what we decide reflects what was always meant to be."

"But me burnsed down the . . ."

I cut him off with a raised finger. "You used the tools at your disposal to depart from a situation that you did not wish to be in, with the minimum necessary force."

"Me did?" He cocked his head to one side.

"You recognized that you were being held captive."

He cocked it to the other side. "Me did?"

"You cast a spell, utilizing the exact element that would cause the maximum amount of distraction."

"Me did." He nodded timidly.

"And then you made your escape from hostile territory, only deploying magic again when it became vitally important to halt pursuit."

"Me did!" Ig was finally nodding like he believed it. "Me did!"

"Then, dear Ig, what in the world could you possibly be sorry for?" I gave him the best approximation of a fatherly smile that I could muster. I'd never experienced one myself, and the depictions in text never seemed very specific about what such a smile was meant to look like.

"Me am wizard." He took my extended hand and hauled himself back to his feet.

"Yes you are, my friend." We smiled at one another, inasmuch as a kobold can smile without lips, until I exploded us both into a mixture of gases and flung us across the countryside.

CHAPTER 8

THE CROWN OF COGNITION

I would like it to be stated for the record that as a rule, wizards are the most incorrigible and obnoxious individuals that you will ever have the misfortune of working with. In all likelihood, if you were to ask one to light a torch for you, they would end up researching the optimal methods of doing so, decide that they are all inferior, invent multiple new methods of lighting a torch that are in fact inferior, and eventually get annoyed because the paper that they are currently attempting to author and have published in a peer-reviewed journal about the effects of star positions on torch lighting is impossible to write in the dark; why won't someone light a bloody torch?

Alternately, if you asked two wizards to light a torch, you could expect a three-month-long debate over which of them was responsible for torch lighting, a demand that they receive the torch-lighting request in writing so that they can take credit for it, open warfare breaking out over who of the two had been asked to light the torch, or, worst of all, a co-authored paper on the effects of star positions on torch lighting full of constant academic backstabbing as they try to one-up one another with their superior knowledge of torch lighting.

In short, when we arrived back at the Invisible College, my expectations were extremely low that anything would have been done regarding my request to the Council of the Wise, and I had a more than sneaking suspicion that the various departments would have broken out into open warfare about the hierarchy that they would all occupy in the wake of the revelations of our earlier meeting.

So you can imagine my surprise when our arrival on the Quint was intercepted by a cleverly constructed elemental anchor, whipping our molecules out of the place I'd meant to set them and down into one of the deeper layers of laboratories where various members of the council were awaiting us.

For a moment after our arrival in this unexpected and somewhat dingy place, I was battle ready, Quintessence flowing through me, mind buzzing with the respective positions of my targets and the ideal spells to break through their defenses. Then I realized that they were all holding clipboards. Nobody goes into battle with a clipboard. They were doing the only thing that could possibly have been more dangerous than an all-out wizard war. They were conducting research.

Sabrinia and Danyeel, as the youngest and lowest in the pecking order, had been assigned the thankless task of shepherding Ig away from me and into the various testing stations that had been set up around the room. Surrounding each of these was a variety of complex pseudo-medical magical apparatuses, and surrounding those, a preponderance of graduate students.

"By heck you moved fast!" I exclaimed to Iomedania as she approached, garbed now not in the robes of her station but rather more sporty gear topped with a lab coat. When it came to magical research, looking good ranked lower in the priority list than being able to run like hell when the bunny you've pulled out of a hat starts ticking.

"Before any solution can be constructed, research is always necessary."

"Quite so."

"Ah good, I had concerns that you would not consent."

"Ig is his own man . . . kobold . . . whatever. It is his consent that you need if you want to poke around his brain."

"Leave that to the grad students and the dabblers." She smiled as sweetly as I'd ever seen her smile. Which is to say, frostily. "I'll be working with you."

"A problem you need me to look at?"

She spoke to her enchanted quill, and I watched as it copied out her words on the clipboard floating in orbit around her. "Test Subject A is being willfully ignorant."

"Test subject . . ." Her meaning finally clicked. "Now see here, I'm not some critter in a cage for you to poke and prod at, I am . . ."

She knew who I was. "Subject A is Absalom Scryne, Archmage of Arpanpholigon, male human, mid to late two hundreds."

I gasped in dismay. "I'm only one hundred and six, you cheeky little . . ."

"Subject A is belligerent when ignored. Hypothetical: lack of social interaction caused mental degradation in cloned mind?" She cocked her head to the side as she left that last note and sounded quizzical. It made her seem all the more like some sort of automaton.

"Quite the opposite, I'd say," I answered her, even though I was well aware the question hadn't actually been posed to me. "I'm accustomed to having my thoughts to myself for most passing hours. With Ig, my mind was forever filled with his thoughts, his feelings . . . mostly fear, and hunger. Not to mention all the rest of them that we were constantly having to talk to."

She had started fiddling with some machinery as one of her grad student minions carefully placed a wooden cone of approximately hat size on the bench. "I refer to the period after removal of the mind-cloning device."

I dragged my eyes back to her. "Wait, you think Ig went stupid because he's lonely?"

Even though I'd already seen Copernicrust on arrival, I still jumped when he warbled from behind me. "Um, actually, in individuals with a pathological need for attention, the loss of that constant validation can make life uncomfortable, sufficiently so that self-destruction may be preferable."

I rolled my eyes. "But Ig doesn't need constant attention."

"Who said we were talking about the kobold?" I could hear her smirk before I turned to look at Philodephina. "We are referring to the alter ego of yourself that was granting the kobold sapience."

This had been what I was worried about. Giving them too little information had sent them scurrying off down branching paths of thought experiments instead of investigating the actual issue.

"There was no . . . I didn't leave a copy of myself in his brain. I simply . . . expanded out his brain so there was enough space for me to occupy. Everything that is in there is him."

"Are you quite certain of that? From what I've ascertained from Danyeel and your dwarf friend, it seems that you weren't even aware that the hat contained a fracture personality until it reintegrated." Copernicrust hadn't looked up from the papers he was scrabbling through on his own clipboard throughout the entire conversation. In fact, I struggled to recall a time when he hadn't been reading something in the entire time I had known him.

Bloody Danyeel. I should have known that he couldn't keep his flapping face shut. Though I was somewhat surprised that old Crusty had been the one to schmooze him for intelligence.

As for Cygni, she may have told them all of that out of spite, she may have told them because she thought that she was being genuinely helpful, or she may have just been trying to avoid them prying her skull open too.

Figuratively.

Hopefully.

"I would like to think that if there were a fragment of myself buried in the mind of everyone who has worn this hat, they would have made themselves known by now. It certainly would have been helpful to have some duplicates around; I might have been able to have some intelligent penversation."

"The hat, if you please?" Iomedania held out a hand for it, quite casually. As though it were not an artifact of supreme importance to the future of magic.

I was understandably reluctant to remove it, given that for quite some time it had been my entire physical form. If you were asked to strip, then asked to continue stripping until you had discarded all of your skin, muscle, and bone, then perhaps you might have some notion of how it felt to me, to consider removing my hat. "Ah . . . There won't be any risk to this particular piece of headwear, will there?"

"The testing is non-invasive," a grad student replied without looking up from their devices.

"That wasn't a no."

Iomedania sighed, her hand still held out for the hat. "It is extremely unlikely that any examination that we make will disrupt the magic that duplicates your consciousness."

I took a little half step away from her. "Again, unlikely isn't quite a no."

"Um, actually, given the abuse that hat has suffered so far, it seems unlikely that some light observation is about to unravel it." Copernicrust was reaching for my hat too, but luckily, what nature had granted him in age, it had denied him in height, so my scalp passenger remained out of reach.

"Hmmm." I'll admit that I was stalling. No shame in that. This was essentially my mortal vessel that they were talking about probing. One should always consider the pros and cons before consenting to be probed.

"For the love of . . ." Balthazagar elbowed his way through the students and grabbed the hat off my head. "If the enchantment's so fragile that some light poking breaks it, then it was never going to last a week anyway. Stop being so bloody precious about it."

He handed it graciously to Iomedania, who swept off with it before I had the opportunity to say a word. I must say, it was rather strange to no longer experience absolute oblivion each time that I was removed from someone's head. I mean, every time that my hat was removed. I mean . . . my sense of self was still entirely tied to my hat, and I really needed to move on from that mindset. I needed to stop feeling as though the stay in my flesh was only a temporary visit. I needed to let go of this sense that my body was a stopping-off point on my way to the next one. I was home now. This was not just another goblin or gremlin that I was currently occupying. This was me. I was me. And the fact that I hadn't removed the hat from my head since retrieving it because I feared that my consciousness would be drawn entirely out of my head like a snail from its shell could now be laughed off as silliness, as the dread-hypothesis was provably false.

Giving the hat back to Ig no longer felt so impossible. I had all of my knowledge, safe and secure betwixt my ears, and there was no real reason for me to deny him the comfort of having me in there with him too. Whatever existential discomfort I may have been feeling at the idea of two congruent versions of me scampering around in the world was just that. Just a feeling. There was no reason that I could not simply . . . willingly divide myself in two.

I shuddered at the thought, earning another disdainful glance from Balthazagar, who probably thought I was still fussing over my hat and not the dilution of self that came with the branching of my sapience.

What followed that day and evening was one of the most harrowing and overwhelmingly boring experiences of my life. Both Ig and I were isolated, though I was assured that he was being kept safe, and then asked a series of questions designed to test our respective intelligences, interspersed with psychological probing intended to prove whether or not we were one and the same person. Meanwhile, my hat had been placed on a hastily designed mannequin head in a third room, where it was holding court with Copernicrust and Iomedania interrogating it in the same manner.

Perhaps it only took an hour, perhaps it took seventeen years, as it felt like it had, but either way, we proceeded through these rounds of questioning and puzzles while various devices of dubiously enchanted equipment were waved around us and readings were recorded. As much interest as was initially shown in Ig and myself, as the day went on, we were each left with only a single observer and a single interviewer to our names, while the tidal waves of grad students had all flowed into the third room, with the hat. Every one of them hoping to be the one to work out how the enchantment upon it worked, and how such an enchantment could have come into being spontaneously.

To wit, I was being upstaged by my own hat.

I hoped that Ildrit and Cygni were having a better time, wherever they had found themselves in the city. Not that I could conceive of any worse ways for them to spend their time. Not unless they had made a wrong turn and fallen into the acid pit. That would probably be worse. Marginally.

Finally, when all was said and done, Ig came scampering into the room and leapt onto my lap like an ill-trained dog. Quivering and shaking as was his wont. "Me answer all the questions."

"I too have completed the surveys set before us. Let us hope that they are sufficient to . . ."

Iomedania burst into the room and pointed her finger directly at me. "The hat is you."

"Yes, I did explain that . . ."

She was clearly too excited to stop mid-rant. "It has perfect recall of everything that you know. It tests to exactly the same degree of intelligence. It . . ."

I raised my voice ever so slightly. "Yes, we already established all this. What new information do we have?"

There was the faintest hint of a flush in her cheeks. A tremor in her voice. I do not believe that I had ever seen her so passionate about anything. Though admittedly, I had not spent much time in her company in the laboratories, typically avoiding the whole area thanks to my well-developed sense of self-preservation. With shining eyes, she said, "I . . . that is . . . we have a great deal of information to collate and sort through."

"Wonderful, shall we just leave you to get on with that, or . . ." I clapped my hands and stood up. Ig did not drop off as I had anticipated, but instead wrapped his arms around me. I was now wearing a kobold-skin belt.

She nodded her assent. "Return for further tests in the morning."

Ig and I both groaned.

"And we're keeping the hat overnight to run a full-spectrum enchantment analysis."

That sent a fresh spike of anxiety through my innards. "I would really prefer to have it back, actually . . ."

"Not possible at this time." She flashed me her falsest smile. "Sorry."

Ig looked up at me from my belly button, sagely informing me, "Wizard never sorry."

He was entirely correct. Iomedania felt no sorrow or sympathy. She was proceeding with her plan unfettered by doubt.

"Alas, you shall have to complete your work on the morrow." I reached out to the room with the hat and pulled it to me. The hat, not the room. There had been enough structural damage to the college already. It came at my call, the connection between our minds a clear bridge for my magic to flow along. There was a door and several grad-students between me and the hat, but what luck that my belt was possessed of magic and a close connection to both the hat and me to boot. The door slammed open so hard it almost came off its hinges, the grad student swarm was brushed aside like ants, and the hat returned to us.

In a moment of magnanimity, I moved to place it atop Ig's head, but Iomedania stopped me. "We need untainted results of him as he is now for us to make a clear judgment."

I sighed, then put my hat on. "Fine."

Since my return to human form, I had enjoyed spending my evenings in my large and comfortable bed. Often catching up on my reading, but sometimes simply luxuriating in the comfort of it all after a long month without any at all. The Absalom Scryne who had remained here had not appreciated the creature comforts at his disposal whatsoever, but now that our minds were combined once more, it was a different matter. My body, my comfort, they had always been secondary concerns to me when I was accustomed to what I had considered normalcy, but now I truly appreciated life in a way that surprised me.

Typically, such evenings had been spent alone, but tonight I had Ig still firmly limpet-ed onto me. My assumption had been that he too had been enjoying all the small joys that the college had to offer, such as the bountiful cafeteria, but since discovering him digging for grubs, I had been stripped of such illusions.

A few discreetly rung bells resulted in a lavish array of foods being laid out in my drawing room while I forced Ig into a bath to remove at least some amount of the filth he'd managed to accumulate since last I'd managed to cleanse him. There was a great deal of screaming and accusations of drowning and he emerged from the water vibrating so hard from his terror that the towel was essentially unnecessary.

On reflection, it would have been wiser to feed him then bathe him, but I didn't particularly want everything that I wanted to eat tainted with whatever the hell he had on his paws.

The result of setting a kobold loose on even the smallish smorgasbord I'd had assembled for our evening was . . . I want to say catastrophic, but that would imply something more dramatic and explosive. There were no explosions; if anything, there was an implosion, as all things were drawn in towards the central point of Ig's face.

He ate and he ate until I assumed that he could eat no more, and then he just went on eating. Whatever part of the human brain informs you it is time to stop was clearly absent from the structure of the kobold brain. I'd often wondered as to why the kobold was possessed of such wrinkly elastic skin, and as he devoured a week's worth of fruit, bread, and cold cuts, I was presented with the explanation: so that his stomach could swell and expand into a perfectly rounded little pot belly on those rare occasions that a kobold had the opportunity to eat their fill. It had become the only vaguely smooth part on his entire body, and even that was somewhat marred by the irregular shapes pressing against it from the inside. Kobolds also weren't very big on chewing, it seemed.

When there was no more food in his direct line of sight, he flopped back into a chair with what started as a satisfied moan, but soon became a groan. Though I suppose that it was possible that the chair itself was groaning. The groan eventually became his voice once more. "Me eats . . . lots."

I had managed a scant few mouthfuls before realizing the spectacle that was unfolding before me, but strangely enough, after watching what Ig had done to the food I found myself devoid of appetite.

After-dinner conversation was out of the question, both because of my queasiness after the devouring display, and because of the degeneration of Ig's faculties, leaving me feeling as though his contributions would be minimal at best, and he wasn't liable to recall much of anything at all.

If I were honest, I had expected Ig to stroll off and find some little cubby to hole up in overnight rather than hopping up onto the foot of my bed, curling up into a little ball, and falling asleep right where my feet would usually go. He was not particularly large, and one would imagine that the disruption he would cause would be fairly minimal as a result, but I am unaccustomed to sharing my sleeping space. As such, I too ended up contorted into a little ball that night, attempting not to kick Ig, while also feeling dreadfully tempted to give him a little bit of a boot for his presumption. I suppose that once you have shared your head with someone, sharing a blanket doesn't seem like such an ask.

However irritating I may have found his presence, and however my legs might have ached come morning, one thing did remain constant. Each time that I stirred in the night because of his twitching and flailing nightmares, I reached down and tucked the quilt around him anew. It was simply practical, I told myself. To prevent him from becoming ill and said illness interfering in our plans. Definitely not any sort of lingering affection that I might have felt for the little cretin.

We were returned to the omnipresent boredom of the laboratory come morning, where somehow even more graduate students had managed to accumulate. I had been under the impression before all of this that we were an extremely elite school who only took the best of the best, yet given the sheer population present in the college, I was forced to accept that this was not the case. In fact, our standards had been lowered to such a degree that just about anyone capable of reading and sparking up a little Quintessence seemed to have been added to our numbers. Why else would the room be packed from wall to wall?

In the midst of a particularly tight tangle of bespectacled and lab-coat-clad wizards sat Cygni, who had finally deigned to return to the college, and was now being put to the question regarding our time together, and more specifically, her time wearing me on her head.

My hat on her head. Not me. I am me.

"Morning," she grunted in my direction.

"A good morning to you also," I replied as warmly as I could muster, taking my seat beside her and pretending Ig wasn't climbing up to sit on my lap. He had definitely gotten clingier since yesterday's probing terrors. "Am I to assume that you found your wild man before he could cause anyone any problems?"

"He was drinking tea . . ." I raised an eyebrow quite involuntarily as she concluded, "he'd paid for."

A little later than one would have expected, Ig finally squeaked out, "Morning."

I must admit that I had not pictured Ildrit pillaging a teacup from anywhere, particularly when the teahouses of the city sold it for little more than the cost of the leaves, hoping instead that you'd be tempted by their various snacks. I tried not to sound amused. "Could it be that he is in fact not quite the agent of chaos that you assumed him to be?"

"Could be." She sighed heavily.

"Wait, did you want to come back and discover a charnel house?"

She wouldn't meet my gaze, but obviously she did want that, given that the only excuse she offered was, "Thought he was a bad boy."

I let out a little snort of dismay as various devices were attached to me and Ig's body, screwed and strapped into place as we went on chatting. "Madam, I know little of the ways of love, as you well know. My experience in this particular department has always been secondhand at best, but if I might impart one small portion of my great wisdom to you, it is this. When time comes to take your strength, when troubles are set at your table and when your passions wane, a good man will serve you far better than a bad boy."

She would have rolled her eyes even more vigorously if she too wasn't strapped into her seat. "Don't want advice."

"Then I shall refrain from giving you counsel in this matter," I replied tartly.

"Good," she replied, somehow even more tartly.

"Me needs advice," Ig piped up, as though trying to offer me comfort.

I gave him a little pat on the head. "I know, Ig."

"Me needs lots advice. Me real stupid."

"I know, Ig." I gave him another little pat on the head, turning to speak with Cygni, who could at least grasp my words. Probably.

"It shall indeed be good to turn my mind to more important matters than your happiness." I couldn't seem to keep myself from fussing over my apprentices as though they were my children. Entirely ridiculous, of course. I wasn't the paternal sort. Never had been.

Still, I did feel a loosening of the tightness in my chest when she said, "I'm happy."

I reached over with my only un-wired arm and patted the back of her hand. "And wise enough to manage your own affairs to maintain that state, I have no doubt."

"Sort your ogres?" She attempted to divert the conversation.

"Shouty," Ig opined.

We both continued as if he had said nothing at all. "They departed without any harm done."

She tried to nod firmly, but her head was locked to the headrest now. "Good."

"Indeed," I replied.

There was a long delay, not as the various experimenters got between us fiddling with things, but because Cygni seemed to be trying to swallow down something that tasted bitter. "Would it have helped if I stayed?"

Ah, guilt. That was the unpleasant flavor. Something quite unfamiliar to her given that she'd spent her whole life diligently doing exactly as she was told. Either that, or an uncomfortably familiar one, given that she'd spent her whole life diligently doing exactly as she was told under threat of excommunication from dwarven society.

I wanted to alleviate that guilt, of course I did, but I could hardly lie and say that Ig was particularly helpful in the situation, could I. "Who can say?"

"You could." Her brows beetled.

It was my turn to sigh and admit to my true feelings, much as I may have loathed doing so. "I did not intend to leave anyone behind. Better that you were with your lover, enjoying life, than off doing diplomacy with ogres."

"Right." She sounded unconvinced.

"Your company would have been appreciated, of course. As would your insight." I tried to smile at her, and couldn't tell if she could see, with the way that we had been fixed to our respective apparatuses. "I value them, and you."

She let out a contemptuous snort. "Shut up."

"I speak only the truth."

"Not in front of the . . ." The precise word of dwarvish that she used has no direct translation, but you could have possibly interpreted it as "nerd" or more literally "the kind of person who studies the same rock their entire life and is proud of that." Neither of which quite capture the venom attached to the word. It wasn't one of her usual eyebrow-curling swears, but it still took the wind out my sails for a moment.

"Madam!"

"Cygni." She chuckled. "Been in my head. Think you can call me by my name."

"Cygni . . ." It felt odd in my mouth. "I wish that yesterday had been . . . different."

"Because you spent all afternoon with the . . ." That grotesque word again. "Squad down here?"

"Because I do not wish for us to quarrel." My longer explanation was cut somewhat short by the sudden whining of telluric currents flowing all around us. Then the racking crackles of it touching down all across our mortal forms. It tickled, mostly. I'd expected at least some degree of pain along with the ozone smell, but apparently they'd done something to the lightning to render it harmless. I wasn't clear what precisely they were attempting to measure with this test, but I did know that it was annoying as heck to be tickled all over.

All of the world went white, as my beard was caught up in the static and drifted in front of my gaze.

Ig was vibrating on my lap in a manner not unlike a creature being electrocuted, but I suspected that it was simply a matter of nervousness.

Eventually the crackling passed and we were returned to the background babble of inquiring minds. I brought a hand down to pat Ig and sooth him, only for a spark to jump from my palm to strike him atop the head like the world's most pathetic lightning bolt. He let out a little yelp. But given how many times a day Ig could have been said to give little yelps, it was hardly notable, and probably wasn't even related to being shocked.

I turned to Cygni and almost guffawed directly in her face. All the hair on her head was standing aloft as my beard had done. Why the static had not left her as it had us, it took me a moment to realize. Rubber soles on her boots were preventing it from grounding.

Extending a finger, I let the lightning pass through me and out of her.

"Let's not do that one again, shall we?" I suggested, strongly, to the nearest white-coat wearer. He nodded nervously before retreating behind the safety of Iomedania's skirts.

"Please don't scare my laboratory technicians, Archmage," she said with some small amount of venom.

"Please don't bathe me and my apprentices in galvanic force, Researcher," I replied with a smile.

She mirrored the smile, though it did not quite reach her eyes. "It was necessary to map your respective Quintessence channels, Archmage."

"Wouldn't a Quintessence pulse have been equally effective, Researcher?" I asked so very politely that it couldn't possibly be taken in the wrong way.

"If we weren't trying to maintain the usual internal pressures of Quintessence in the system, then perhaps it would have been equally effective, Archmage."

My eyes didn't narrow. "Perhaps if you had consulted me on this portion of the testing we could have avoided wasted time, given that Cygni's Quintessence channels were derived entirely from a singular act of magic on my part rather than gradual development as a result of interaction with the artifact."

"Well, Archmage, perhaps if you would make yourself available for consultation rather than absconding to the palace, Great Wall, or your chambers when we are in the midst of a career-defining project, then the entire process might have been streamlined." She was almost manic in her smile now, forced so forcibly onto her features that I feared teeth might start pinging out.

I did not roll my eyes, nor raise my voice, though I feel that I would have been well within my rights to do so. "Well, Researcher, far be it from me to question your methodology when you are clearly . . ."

Cygni rolled her eyes. "Will you two just kiss already?"

"I beg your pardon?!" I barked at the same moment Iomedania snarled, "Excuse me?!"

"Get a room or get on with the tests." Cygni glowered at us both. "I've got stuff to do."

I paused for a moment, allowing my anger to pass through me and away, before affirming, "She does actually have rather a lot to do."

"If it help, me will kiss magic lady." Ig's contributions were impeccable as always.

Even Iomedania's stalwart professional expression could not hold up in the face of that threat. She gagged.

"Nobody is kissing anyone." I raised my voice to make it clear to any lookie-loos or other potential witnesses. "Human resources does not need to be called. This is not a frog-prince situation."

Cygni shook her head in disdain. "Even amphibians need royalty up here . . ."

Pressing on. "Have you come to any conclusions that I could not have already told you?"

Iomedania had recovered stoically from her brief brush with kobold romance and was back in fighting form. "Well, that would depend entirely on how much information you have withheld, Archmage."

Only one of my wrists had been unstrapped from the apparatus by a nervous-looking student thus far, but I used it to pinch the bridge of my nose in the hopes that the mounting headache of this entire experience would not develop further. "Let us assume that I have not withheld any information deliberately and start fresh, shall we?"

"You expect me to believe that . . ."

I cut her off before this could turn into another pissing contest. "I may have made my own assumptions, and I'd rather that they did not taint your conclusions. We are not in competition here; I have no desire for credit in any discoveries you make. Indeed, as the subject of study I shall already have considerably more page space than I would have desired in such a matter."

"Of all the blatant lies . . ." All composure was beginning to leave Iomedania as her credulity was pushed to and beyond its limit. But to my immense surprise, Cygni piped up in my defense.

"It's true, you know. He doesn't care about credit anymore." She looked over at me and gave me a grin that would best be described with one of her dwarven swears. The one that translates as "the smile of one who eats mushrooms from the refuse heap." "He even let me name the crystalized Quintessence after me. Cygnite."

I stared murder into her soul, but the grin did not falter.

"Ah." Philodephina was there, just out of my line of sight, holding a notebook and scribbling down the word. Cygnite. Not set in stone, but set in peer-reviewed magical journals. Sealed for all eternity. "We did wonder if it had been named by its discoverer."

"Yes, me," she affirmed, never breaking eye contact even as I willed her to catch fire. "Isn't that right, wizard?"

Through a clenched jaw I struggled to force out words, but betwixt my grinding teeth they came all the same. "That's right."

"Remarkable." Iomedania seemed to be truly shocked. "The find of the century, and you're willing to just . . ."

"Willing is not the right word." I managed to force the growl out of my voice before going on. "Cygni was the first one to discover Cygnite. So the rule is, of course, that she should name it. Cygnite. A very . . . fine name. Much better than if I'd named it. I mean, what would I have even called it? Scrynium? It doesn't exactly roll off the tongue, does it?"

"I suppose not." Iomedania had backed away ever so slightly, reminding me to draw my aura of power in to better hide my emotional state. It had not been a problem when I was a hat, as I'd had no power to project my wrath.

Of course, Philodephina was relishing seeing me outwitted far too much to leave it at that. "Oh, I don't know. Scrynium has a wonderful ring to it. And it would make much more sense to name the material after the first wizard to find it rather than just whosoever tripped over it first, wouldn't you say?"

Whether she meant to sow seeds of discord between us, or simply to twist the knife, I could not say. But whatever aggravation I'd been feeling before washed away as I recognized her dismissal of my dwarven companion for what it was. "Cygni is a wizard."

That statement, to my surprise and delight, was sufficient to put an end to any more pointless chatter, and to our separate assessment rooms we were sent. It took three researchers and a pry bar to get Ig off me, and even then, only my constant assurances that they were not going to do him any harm were sufficient to attain his somewhat shaky consent.

The pry bar was required for a second time to remove my hat from my head, although at least this time I was not filled with an overwhelming terror of oblivion as it parted ways with my thinning hair. Just a minor twinge of terror. Barely a smidgeon really. Were terror to be ranked on a scale between *Ig confronted with an ogre* and *myself confronted with a warm and comfortable chair and an interesting new treatise on potential translation errors in Archaic manuscripts from the 11th century* then I believe it would have been somewhere about a 4.

The questioning that day remained consistent with the day before, at least. More of the sort of intelligence testing. The endless repetition intended to put the mind into a nigh trance-like state. I could understand Ig's reluctance to return to this relentless grind, though I suspect that if he had ever experienced standardized testing in his life, then the whole process would have been more familiar and infinitely more distressing for him.

Cygni, meanwhile, took it all like a champ so far as I could overhear. Proving to all and sundry that her intellect was easily their equal, surpassing the majority of the gathered students and only eclipsed on occasion when one of the higher-ranking faculty members weighed in with a follow-up question designed to push her limits.

All the Council of the Wise passed through that day, with the exception of Danyeel, who I suspected was still lying low after spilling my secrets out of fear of reprisal. That, or the others simply didn't consider aesthetics, illusions, and theatrics to be core components of intelligence.

For all of the sneering contempt that had been shown to my companions thus far, I would, in truth, have quite liked to see the look on their faces if Ildrit had been set down in one of these chairs and presented with the same battery of tests. He may not have been a wizard, but behind those angry eyes of his lurked a first-class mind. Turned to tactics, combat, and cunning rather than academic study, but impressive all the same. He probably could have proved himself the equal of many of the gathered wizards with his intellect, and if the situations were reversed and any one of them was set upon him with a sword in hand and a fight to win, the outcome would have been comically obvious.

Do not take me wrong, I was and am still firmly of the belief that swinging a sharp bit of metal is inferior in every way to weaving the fundamental forces of the cosmos to your will, but I had at least learned some degree of respect for the other paths through life that people could take after my sojourn.

Dare I say it? The use and study of magic might not have actually been the defining factor in whether a life was wasted or spent well.

I was shaken from my reverie by the appearance of Iomedania at the opposite side of the testing table. Not armed with sheaves of new questions, but instead frowning intently upon a single sheet affixed to her clipboard. After the endless rabble of conversation that had been plaguing me all day, I was in no hurry to break the silence that she brought with her, regardless of how tense it may have been. And do rest assured that were I of a more musical bent, there was sufficient tension in the air that I might have been able to strum out a tune upon it.

Eventually she caved and spoke first. "The difference is not notable."

Of all the bad news that I had expected her to bring to me this day, a lack of results was not one of them. I'd thought she might have told me Ig was about to explode with accumulated Quintessence that he had nowhere to store because of his reflexive cycling of it. I'd thought that she was going to tell me that his mind was soon going to degenerate past the point of even the barely understandable gibberish he currently spoke. No notable difference was so far from the realm of possibility that I had not even considered it.

I blinked. "What?"

"The kobold and the dwarf were both exposed to the intellect-improving powers of the artifact, yet there has been no degradation of the benefits they reaped from it since its removal." She laid her results down on the desk betwixt us and sighed. "They are testing the same now as they were the day they arrived."

"You didn't test them the day that they arrived, you tested them . . ."

She stopped me with a raised hand. "All cards on the table, the faculty and I have been magically probing you and your companions since your re-assimilation in addition to having students ambush you with pop quizzes to ascertain any change in your abilities."

"I did wonder why so many terrified apprentices kept jumping out to ask me questions . . ." It had seemed so inconsequential that I'd overlooked it entirely. What was the point of students in an institution such as this if they were not asking banal questions of far superior minds all day? "I'd hoped that I was simply projecting a more friendly and approachable persona after the changes brought on by my sojourn as a hat."

She stared at me blankly from behind the thick lenses covering her eyes. "You haven't."

"No change at all?" I was dismayed. "Not one . . ."

She poked at the paper on the desk angrily. "If anything, the kobold is testing as smarter today than it was yesterday, now that he is more familiar with the tests."

"So . . . why is he regressing? If his intelligence is unchanged then . . ." The grim expression on her face brought me to a halt.

"You know, as I do, that there are . . . softer arts than that of magic. Ones that are more . . . fuzzy in their results. Areas of academia that we typically over-look in our pursuit of the more perfect truths of universal constants and arcane knowledge . . . It is my belief that the kobold's slip back into old behaviors may result from one of these. From . . ." She shuddered as she said it. "Psychology."

"Oh, disgusting."

"I know . . . I know . . . but when we are confronted with a problem that hard facts cannot put to rest, we must turn to soft areas of academia." She looked more uncomfortable now than when I'd seen her submerged up to the elbows in demonic ichor during vivisections.

I threw up my hands. "So why in heck is he behaving as though he is getting stupider if he isn't?"

"Well . . . I have consulted with a . . . psychologist." A word she spoke with the same venom as most would reserve for describing a horse dropping squishing under the sole of their shoe. "And they are of the belief that he is becoming less intelligent because he believes himself to be becoming less intelligent. Because he believes that without your presence in his mind, he is just a stupid kobold."

That particular phrase hung in the air for a moment before I conceded, "I mean, there can be no denying that he is a stupid kobold."

"Of course not. But his belief in his own intelligence has been undercut by his longer standing belief in his own insignificance and stupidity. Resulting in a regression to pre-sapient habits." She rolled her eyes. "Or so the . . . psychologist says."

It took me quite a moment to put this new information together, then immediately I let out a sigh of relief. It was as though the tension that I'd been carrying around with me all of this time had suddenly left my body. "Excellent news."

Iomedania blinked. "I beg your pardon, Archmage?"

I graced her at last with a genuine smile after so long inflicting my professional one upon her. There was no reason that we could not get along, and if that meant showing some degree of vulnerability by admitting I was happy about good news, then I'd gladly be the first to let loose the battened-down hatches of interpersonal communication. "If it's all about belief, then I simply have to force my beliefs on him. As an educator, that is one of my core skills."

"So all of this wasted time to prove a negative is just . . . an acceptable loss to you?" She was utterly mystified by my response. Previously, this sort of dead-end research probably would have resulted in demands for her head on a platter and threats to her grants and budgets, but I was far too happy to think about all that.

"Madame Researcher, we have our entire lives to pursue our studies. You, a good century or so more than I, by my estimation." Who said that flattery wouldn't get you anywhere. She blushed behind her goggles. "I would consider a couple of days wasted lab time to be a small price to pay in exchange for the ongoing existence of the world's only kobold wizard."

She mustered a little smile of her own. "So you have a solution in mind?"

"Observe!" I declared, finally rising from the hard-backed chair and waddling with half-asleep buttocks into the laboratory at large. Upon some various tables, set back from the room, there were a variety of other experiments and projects that had been shoved aside for all of my very important business, and amidst them there lay a cardboard box of scrap parts.

From within, I dug around and drew some wire and metal, and with a little infusion of carbon and flames . . . "*Facti coronam.*"

They lifted from my hands, contorted and wove together in a blinding blaze of heat and industry, and then plopped back into my grip. Warm, but not uncomfortably so.

"Ig!" I called out, only to see him come scampering from his own sequestered chamber with great haste. "We have a cure for you!"

Were a kobold capable of having big puppy dog eyes, I'm sure Ig would have been looking up at me with them then, instead of the weird squint he was instead treating us all to.

"This . . ." I held up my junk heap creation. "Is an artifact derived from ancient and powerful magics, designed to enhance the mind of whoever wears it to the utmost."

Ig stared up at the hunk of junk with awe. "What called?"

I hadn't thought of that yet. "I, uh . . ."

"The Crown of Cognition," announced Iomedania, playing along without a second thought. "So secret and powerful a creation that you could look in every book in our library and find no reference to it."

She was a far better liar than any of us gave her credit for.

"Just so!" I perched it atop Ig's head with a grin. "And now you shall be more intelligent than ever before. Smarter even than me, in time, once the magic has taken hold."

"Wow!" Ig said.

Everyone else in the room was looking at us as if we were insane, but it didn't matter.

"Me can feels it!" Ig declared, straightening up from his hunched position. "Me is getting smarter! Me can . . . me can do anything!"

I nodded my thanks to Iomedania, and she didn't even attempt to insinuate that I owed her one. A happy kobold was thanks enough. Either that, or she meant to backstab me with the truth at the most inopportune moment imaginable, but we could cross that bridge when we came to it.

All around Ig, tiny sparkles of light began to form as he muttered an incantation under his breath. A simple spell, invoking neon, but one that by all rights he should not have known, because I never taught it to him. He remembered it, he remembered me teaching it to Cygni. All of the memories that he had access to while I was in his mind had been left in place, and he was smart enough to put the pieces together! The whole room fell silent at this display. Not because he was casting a light spell, like any toddler worth their tiny wizard robes could do, but because he was casting a dozen of them simultaneously.

Something that none of them would have even considered attempting. Jaws dropped. Eyes widened. Amazement abounded at the mastery of the arcane that was personified in this kobold.

Then all of the sparkles turned into bananas and fell as one to splatter on the ground.

"Oops."

CHAPTER 9

CONCERNING CURSES

Arpanpholigon was a vast city. A gorgeous city. With layers upon layers of houses and shops and taverns and churches and anything else that you might have wanted out of a city. Beautiful canals lined with tree-shaded walkways. Indoor plumbing as far as the eye could see. Filled to the brim with denizens from all corners of the world, drawn to this beacon of civilization and progress. Even those other city-states nearby would never have considered waging war upon her, not with the college hanging overhead like a bird of doom, ready to swoop down at the first sign of trouble. It was a prosperous place, at the nexus of a hundred different trade routes by land and river. An architectural marvel, blending styles from cultures and civilizations that had been separated not just by continents of distance but millennia of time.

There is nowhere like it in the world, it is unique, a treasure that in all honesty, I have never treasured so much as I should have. Always I had been up in the college looking down on it both literally and figuratively, when I should have been down in it, amongst the many people living their many lives, every one of them as fascinating to me now as my books and study had been to me before. As I walked the byways of the city, I saw children chasing a conjured illusion of a goat, mimicking its brays. I saw cooks on carts lining the streets, producing culinary wonders for which I did not even know the name, let alone comprehend how to describe the colors and scents and . . . I actually was quite sure that one of them was selling grilled troll fingers in gigantic buns, but without venturing over to examine the surprisingly pleasant smell further, I would never know with certainty.

And even beyond the people and the buildings, the place had a personality of its own. The umbrella quarters where everyone jogged from one awning to the next out of fear that a bird should splatter upon the college above and come tumbling down to land on them. The regions of the city where the roofs were all flat, as no rain ever fell there thanks to the source of the looming shadow that covered them instead. The giant acid pit. No other city on the planet had a giant acid pit.

It bubbled over with industry. It was a shining beacon of invention and wonders that had naught to do with the magic we wizards wielded and everything to do with the relentless desire to make the world better that had found its place in the hearts of the common men.

Yet for all of that, it was too a city of magic. Enchantments were bound all across the buildings, crackling at the periphery of my arcane senses, and laid long before even I had begun my tenure at the college. Little gifts from the academics to the world below. I marveled to see a street sweeper with a small army of enchanted brooms clearing a whole street in a matter of moments. A city guard who simply touched his hawk-shaped helm and could gaze out across a whole marketplace to keep watch for pickpockets. Even the most destitute itinerants who had found their way to the city were well fed on conjured bread, manna from the heavens being perpetually dumped out by practicing students and very rarely turning those who consumed it into any sort of bizarre creature.

And the creatures! Unicorns in livery leading pumpkin-shaped carriages. Winged cats, swooping to snatch rats from the canals. Winged rats, swooping to ambush winged cats and make off with their lunch money. Sentient tortoises that would exchange their ancient wisdom for any greenery that was going to waste. Whole ecosystems of creatures that did not even exist anywhere else in the world.

Every inch of this city was a miracle made flesh, and all of this time I had overlooked it.

Finding a single man in a city of thousands should not be a simple affair. There should be clandestine meetings, and shadowy alleyways. There should be murky taverns and cloaked figures who may not even be human. It should be, if not an adventure in itself, at least an effort.

Instead, I simply allowed my magical senses to guide me towards Widowtaker, on the assumption that Ildrit couldn't have gone far from it.

Given his history and disposition, I suppose that one would have expected to find Ildrit in those shadowy alleyways and murky taverns that I'd managed to sidestep in my search for him, but the reality was all the grimmer. He was sitting upon a bench, beside a pond, throwing breadcrumbs to a gathered cadre of ducks with the fixed and glazed stare of the man awaiting his turn at the gallows. I had not known what he did with himself when Cygni was working on the project I had assigned her, but of all the sordid things that I thought he might have gotten himself up to with the stipend I was paying him, slowly crumbling up a loaf of bread into crumbs and dispensing it to local waterfowl was not high on the list of possibilities I'd imagined.

"I have been informed that's meant to be bad for them." I sat myself down beside him, despite him giving no indication that he'd seen me at all. "Bread fills up their stomach and prevents them eating food that actually nourishes them."

Ildrit groaned and shoved the remaining bread back into the paper bag from whence it came. "How's anyone supposed to know what's wrong, when even the stuff we're told is good is bad?"

"Morality in the modern world is complex," I opined, suspecting that we were not in fact discussing ducks anymore.

"You go through your whole life thinking ducks like bread, that you're giving them a treat and making their life easier, and then it turns out you've been starving them or something." He was so lost in thought that he didn't notice that some of the ducks had proceeded up the muddy incline towards the bench and were now dipping their head into the paper bag.

I treaded very carefully as the ducks rustled with their feast unseen. "It is a conundrum, finding the path of righteousness when every step could be a misstep, but I do believe that making the right or wrong steps matters less than the intention with which you make them. The individual steps matter in the moment, of course, but so long as you keep your gaze affixed upon the distant horizon where good dwells and work towards that destination, I suspect that you will do right all the same. Even in ignorance."

Without even looking up from where he was staring down at the grass in this frankly charming little park that I'd had no idea Arpanpholigon contained, he waved a hand restlessly towards the water. "Tell that to the starving ducks."

"You mean the ducks that were entirely delighted to receive some bread-crumbs, and may wake a little peckish tomorrow?" I sighed, as one of the ducks in question hauled the whole half loaf out of the sack and made off with it, pursued by all of his kin. "The world is . . . fuzzy, the moral absolutes that we wish to assign to every action simply do not exist."

"But they do! There's right and there's wrong. You and I both know it. You and I have both done it." Ildrit spat on the ground, just in case anyone was mistaking him for having been domesticated. "Maybe I've done more wrong than you . . . but . . ."

I cut him off from this downward spiral. "I have done wrong in my life, this is so. But I have endeavored always to do better. Just as you do now. Before, you lived in ignorance of the righteous path, and now . . ."

"You think I didn't know I was doing bad before?" He let out a mirthless laugh. "You think I didn't enjoy it?"

I sat up straight and looked out over the pond and the battle that was slowly breaking out betwixt the varying duck clans over the flotilla of bread that had been hauled out amongst them. "I believe that you do good now, and you feel sorrow over the wrongs that you have done. Am I incorrect in that assumption?"

He threw up his hand. "Yeah, I feel bad. Feel bad I get punished for it."

"Given ample opportunity to do evil, I have seen you err towards good each and every day."

There was a low rumble in his voice, sorrow choking him, or wrath boiling up, both sounded the same in Ildrit, and in honesty I had come to suspect that was because he was sorrowful each time that he was driven to wrath. "Because I'm cursed. Because if I do evil, I get it paid back on me. Not because I want to be good. I want to be bad. You have no idea how bad I want to be. I want to . . . give the ducks all the bread. Even though I know that it's bad for them."

Out on the pond, two green-headed titans of duck-kind flew at each other, smashing their fluffed-up chest feathers together as they tried to drive the other off from the rapidly sinking half loaf.

I endeavored not to draw attention to it. "As I have already said, I feel the harm that the breadcrumbs do is likely quite minimal. And I also find it rather amusing that the darkest deed that you can concoct is feeding bread to ducks."

"It isn't." He growled, low in his chest.

I gave the particular topic of Ildrit's darker urges some wide berth, because though I had known little of his pre-adventuring days before departing from this city and living as a hat, I had acquainted myself a little better with how he had acquired his nom-de-guerre since our return. Of all the little bandit kings that had united the evil creatures and people of the world, he was far from the worst, historically, but there could be no denying that in recent years there hadn't really been anyone who could compete with him in terms of villainy.

"The trouble, as I see it, is this," I began, carefully. "So long as the curse is upon you, you will never know your own mind. You will never know if you have chosen to do the right thing because you want to do good or because you want to avoid karmic punishment."

He sank forward and put his face in his hands. "But what if you get rid of the curse and I go back to being bad again?"

I laid my hand upon his shoulder, and marveled that we were actually not so vastly different in stature. When I was a kobold, he had seemed a giant, but he was but a man. A man of no greater height than me. "My dear friend, if in your heart of hearts you were a truly evil man, I do not think that you would fear the removal of your muzzle. Would you?"

"I . . ." He choked off in something like a sob.

"If you are free to act as you choose instead of constrained by this curse, I fully believe that you will do good in this world. I believe that Ildrit unchained shall be a paragon of virtue, not because he fears the punishment of the cosmos, but because he regrets the evil that he has done." I gave his shoulder an ill-practiced squeeze that I hoped was comforting and not flirtatious. "You need a collar no more than Ig needs a crown. I believe in the goodness within you, Ildrit. Please have faith in my judgment."

He twisted to look at me, eyes red, but no tears streaming, and then he laughed. "This is weird. I'm used to your wise advice coming out of a kobold. Not some old dude."

He must have seen something in my expression because he followed that up with a choked-off laugh. "Uh. No offense."

"Some offense has been taken." I forced myself to chuckle. I knew that he really had meant no harm. "In truth I am finding my return to this body to be a little disconcerting myself."

Out there on the battlefield of the pond, the battle had already been lost without either side realizing it. The ducks still battered aimlessly against one another, but the bread, the all-important prize, had already sunk, sodden, beneath the surface and out of sight. Perhaps some parts of it might be plucked free by those industrious birds who had not involved themselves in the scrap, but to those bold warriors atop the surface, it might as well have been on the moon. Ildrit finally noticed that his bread had been pilfered, patting the paper flat beside him with a chuckle. "So how do we break the curse?"

This felt like considerably safer ground for me to discuss. A comfort zone I was returning to after my sojourn into emotional grounds as churning and fluid as the duck's battlefield. "Typically there is a specific, complex, and persistent working of magic attached to a person who is cursed, constantly refueling itself from the Quintessence in the area. Such curses are most easily undone by starving them out, sealing them off from the flows of magic and letting them untangle."

He nodded. "Okay, so how do we do that?"

"Well, dear Ildrit, I'm afraid that we don't. It was the first thing that I attempted on returning to my body, and it had no effect upon your curse. Similarly, I have taken the typical second and third steps, attempting to discern the specific structures of your curse and pluck apart the threads. Neither was successful to any degree. The nature of the curse isn't complex, but incredibly simple. And the magic is . . . Imagine you are trying to see the pattern of a tapestry with your eye but an inch from its surface. It is too vast for you to perceive the fullness of the thing, only the part closest to you. It is a kind of magic that I cannot say I've ever seen worked in any formal or academic setting. More like someone has inserted an addendum into a natural law to specifically include you and only you."

He stared at me for a time, parsing through all that I had said. It didn't take him time because he was stupid, as I would once have assumed, but because he was giving every word due consideration. Would that more of my faculty were so careful. Finally he asked, "So you can't break it?"

"Please." I snorted inadvertently while trying to laugh contemptuously. "I break sixteen natural laws before breakfast each day. I *am* an archmage, though I can understand how you may forget that given you first encountered me as an item of haberdashery."

He settled back on the bench, turning his attention from the ducks entirely as they began quacking their dismay over the lost meal. "So what do we do?"

"The curse is hinged on the same black-and-white viewpoint that we were discussing earlier. The idea that each action is either entirely good or entirely bad. The vast majority of actions that you take are neither; they are neutral, preventing the curse from having any effect whatsoever—they pass beneath its activation threshold." I spoke slowly, watching as he nodded along to be sure he was grasping the concepts involved. "What we need to do to break the curse is create a situation in which a single action that you undertake is both extremely good and extremely bad at the same time, over the activation threshold, but ambivalently so. The forces involved will pull in opposite directions and the structure of the curse will tear apart, releasing you from its grip permanently."

His brow furrowed as he contemplated my solution. "Well, what can I do that's really good and really bad at the same time?"

"That is my current conundrum." I sighed. "I had hoped to create the situation artificially, through illusion, but at present I am having trouble concocting a scenario that fits the bill."

His furrowed brow furrowed just a little more. Farmers out on their fields would have considered his forehead to be over-tilled by this point. "So if you don't actually have a solution yet, why did you track me down?"

It was my turn to glance away awkwardly. It would be so easy to concoct a deception now. To make some excuse and hide behind it. But just as I asked him to be a better person and damn the consequences, so too did I need to pursue my own path with some courage. "To inform you that you need not hide from me to prevent me from attempting to cure you. That you need not evade me at every moment. Whatever else you may be, you are still my friend, Ildrit. And I would enjoy your company. If you are willing to give it."

His face smoothed out into a bemused expression that I'd seen directed towards Ig a great many times. "You hunted me down to tell me . . . you want to hang out?"

"No. I mean . . . I have reasons beyond . . . I am a . . . yes." I gave up. "Throughout my life, I have had few friends. One might even say I have had none. And now that I have returned to my old body, I find that I do not wish to return to my old life, I do not wish to lose those fire-forged companions that I have found beyond the ivory tower of academia."

He seemed to weigh this for a moment.

"Dinner tonight? I found this place that does great dwarvish food, and I want to surprise Cygni with it." He paused in recognition that he'd just made me the third wheel on his date, ran through his mental list of people that he considered would make a suitable dinner companion for me, and came up with . . . "You could bring Ig too, if you like?"

If ever there was a damning statement on the state of my social life, that was it.

"I shall ask if he wishes to accompany us, and hope that the restaurant is tolerant of his table manners."

With a laugh and what may have been a leer, he asked, "You ever seen dwarves eat?"

"I cannot recall ever having the pleasure." Cygni had consumed her dry rations with mechanical precision as we had explored the underworld, but at the time my attention had always been elsewhere.

"Ig will be fine." He chuckled. "You might want to bring an umbrella though. Dwarves in the city, they're, uh . . . passionate about food."

"Let us endeavor to keep conversation away from the subject of dwarven passions during dinner. Shall we?"

"Hey, man." He held up his hands as if he didn't enjoy scandalizing all and sundry with his public displays of affection. "I don't have any control over what Cygni says or does. She's her own person."

"Let us endeavor to keep the number of double entendres in the single digits." I was practically pleading at this point. "That is all I'm asking."

He burst out laughing in my face. "I'll do what I can, but you know how much Cyg likes her wordplay."

My eyes narrowed involuntarily. "I'm familiar. Yes."

It was my turn to look out over the pond in contemplation. Ildrit's problem still persisted, but I hoped that our conversation had at least rid him of some degree of the angst involved. He hadn't quite made a place for himself in the city the way that his girlfriend had, but at least now he might take some steps towards such a thing. Cygni was settled and happy now that she had a project to turn her hand to, Ig's degeneration had been cured with the power of self-belief, and I . . . was content. Perhaps for the first time in my life, I was content. Not striving for more power that I didn't really need, or delving for some discovery that nobody had ever made so I could lord it over everyone just how much smarter I was than them. Through my little misadventure, I had opened up a whole new world of magic for my studious compatriots, and while I had no doubt that in my remaining years I would turn my mind to some of the new problems that we would invent alongside our new systems of casting, it would be out of a desire to leave the world in a better place than I had found it. Not for the ego boost of self-aggrandizement.

This was my happy ever after. The end of my tale. I could drift along for the rest of my life making no greater contribution to the study of magic than serving tea at the meetings of the Council of the Wise and I could call it a life well spent. For the first time ever, I felt complete.

Which was of course the moment that the sun blinked out in the sky.

CHAPTER 10

THE DOOM THAT CAME TO ARPANPHOLIGON

Typically when the sun goes out and the world is plunged into perpetual darkness, people turn to religion. Not so in Arpanpholigon. Here there is a far more accessible option than some all-powerful bearded figure in the sky. Well, no, actually, there is exactly that. Unfortunately that all-powerful bearded figure in the sky was currently in the park watching ducks and hadn't the faintest idea of what was going on. So as I was approached by swathes of people who rushed to my pointed hat like it was a beacon, I had no answers to give them.

"Yes, I realize it is very frightening. No, I do not know what impact this will have on your begonias. Yes, I'm aware that people in other places don't have to deal with cosmic objects vanishing without warning. No, I do not know why the sun has gone out, but if all of you lovely people will get out of my bloody way, I can get back to the college and look into it. Yes, I am aware that the sun has gone out, thank you for informing me all the same. Yes, I am the head wizard and should really know why the sun has gone out. No, I do not have all the answers for you right now because you are all currently crowding in around me and preventing me from going and finding those answers. Yes, I will let you all know exactly what is going on just as soon as I have learned what is going on, if you could just give me . . . if you could just give me a little bit of room, please?" The press of bodies around me was crushing, and since I wasn't willing to accidentally dematerialize any of these random bystanders just so I could teleport away, I had no immediate means of dealing with the situation. What luck that Ildrit was more accustomed to dealing with trouble on this more personal and physical level.

"Back off if you want to keep your face attached!" he roared.

I must admit it was rather effective. He placed himself between me and the gathered crowd and shouted over the more aggressive questioners who were still trying to get an answer out of me that I didn't have. "The wizard is going up to the college to find out what has happened, and if any of you take one more step forward, you're going to feel the flat of my blade, do you hear me?!"

The vast majority of the crowd reflexively took a step back, leaving one rather perplexed-looking old woman who was a little hard of hearing, who was still standing there holding the plant pot containing her prized begonias. Cradling it in her arms like a baby, really. Thankfully Ildrit did not introduce her to the flat side of Widowtaker, and instead waited while some brave soul stepped up to guide her out of the blast radius. From the corner of his mouth, he hissed to me, "Go. I'll hold them off."

It was my sincerest hope that his holding them off wouldn't involve him brutalizing anyone, but I needed to put my money where my mouth was in terms of trusting him to make the right decisions. Besides, the sun going out was pretty concerning, and I really needed to get on that. I nodded Ildrit my thanks, invoked a variety of gases, and vanished up to my office with all haste.

It would not occur to me until afterwards that he was in the radius in which he might very well have been dragged along in the spell, and I had cast it simply assuming that it wouldn't take a hold of him. Interesting little bit of subconscious action that I'd have to examine later when I wasn't dealing with the fact that the sun had just gone out like someone snuffing a candle.

Cygni, Ig, Sabrinia, and old Balthazagar all came bursting through the door of my somewhat disheveled-looking study at about the same moment that I materialized there, presumably on their way to ask me where in the nine hecks the sun had gone to. I was already in mid-shrug before the questions could begin.

There was a yammering of questions from all quarters that I couldn't really make out due to the sheer volume of noise. Not to mention the slow but steady arrival of every other member of the Council of the Wise, and a particularly bedraggled-looking knight herald demanding my presence at the palace to explain the absence of the sun, presumably, though heavens forbid that the king could actually say what he wanted rather than demanding I toddle over there to find out.

I closed my eyes.

After spending a decent amount of time in Ig's head, I had become accustomed to constant shouting and screaming going on in the background as I thought about more serious and important things, so I was quite comfortable ignoring them all as I closed my eyes and reached out with my arcane senses to the heavens. It was quite a distance between here and the sun, probably a greater distance than anyone else in the world knew about, but I was the greatest living wizard for a reason, and I could extend my touch beyond the Quintessence I extended from within myself and feel the vibrations of the Quintessence that occupied all space. The real trouble was not perceiving what had been done, but in avoiding perceiving everything else that was happening in the cosmos at the same time.

There was magic being worked to blot out the sun's light, but the heat of it still washed down on us. If I had not been so diligent in working on the curse that was wrapped around Ildrit, then I likely wouldn't have sensed it or understood it, because of the vastness of the spell, and the way that it was woven into the fundamental building blocks of the universe. But I had been diligent, I was familiar, and I recognized traces of my own magic within it. Not the Quintessence that I had personally wielded, but the shape of it. The little quirks of the spell's construction. It had been done in a mockery of my own magic, wrought by some arcane power so far beyond mortal ken that any lesser wizard probably would have looked upon it and thought it an act of nature, or an act of a god.

I opened my eyes, and Cygni met my gaze with a kind of stoic dread in her expression that mirrored my own. She asked what I was dreading she would ask now that everyone else had fallen silent after feeling me pulling at the vast tides of Quintessence all around us in some vast invisible working. "Is it him?"

"It was him." I shuddered at the memory of his touch. The dark one.

Nun-Mhorgoth.

Finally Knight Herald Uhp shouldered his way through the gathered elderly academics and called out through the hubbub. "There is an army of monsters at the walls."

More good news.

"Please inform His Majesty that I will be heading to the wall shortly to investigate and disperse it. Also inform him that the sun is not gone, it is still there, just obscured by a shroud placed by a hostile power that I shall be removing promptly. Once this monster army matter has been dealt with in the Badlands."

The gathered wizards were barged out of the way once more and they all looked askance to me. All the old and wise, powerful and confused, all looking to me for leadership as they always had. "I suppose that you had all best accompany us. Cygni can fill you in while I deal with the diplomacy."

I took somewhat more care to teleport the whole room full of people across the country to the Great Wall. Not a lot more, but a little bit. My own cells were feeling a little bit too loose after the second journey as gas in as many minutes, so I took a moment to pull myself together, figuratively, before heading across to the wall to see how many ogres the lawyer one had managed to pull together to file their second complaint about us not handing over Ig. The rest of the company should have been deep in conversation with Cygni about Nun-Mhorgoth and the ancient dwarves who had bound him, but they were all inexplicably silent, staring out over the wall. Perhaps they were as taken with the scenery as I had been on my last visit.

Looking out, I could not see the scenery. To see the scenery, there would have had to be considerably fewer monsters on top of it. As far as the eye could see, there were monsters. It was hard to make out exactly which monsters they were by the dim starlight, but by heck, there were a lot of them. Every inch of the Badlands seemed to be covered in them.

All the forests that we had passed through beyond the river had been downed to construct the rather gigantic ladders that were currently being passed forward towards our walls. Crowd-surfing atop the ladders were a few creatures I could firmly identify as ogres, but there were so many more monsters of varying sizes and varieties that my attempts at identification more or less ended there and then.

The ogres that we had encountered before had been attempting to be civilized, but now they seemed to have let go of that idea, at least for so long as it would take them to invade and slaughter us all. It is possible that I may have underestimated the force that they'd be able to pull together at short notice.

Balthazagar cracked his neck from side to side, then stretched out his arms to crack his knuckles too. "Rain of fire, anyone? Rain of fire?"

"Um, actually, ogre hide is resistant to flame damage," Copernicrust piped up.

To his left, Iomedania already had golden lightning crackling between her fingers, but that was markedly less concerning than what was happening towards the rear of the group where Arturo had conjured up a chalkboard and was doing some intense calculations. Whatever he planned to cast looked like it would involve unleashing the hecks themselves directly amidst the monstrous horde. Or possibly one of the other more obscure dimensions full of things that didn't quite line up with the regular geometry of the world. The sort that gave you a headache to look at, and let you see the three-dimensional picture behind blocks of pattern.

I stepped between the monstrous horde and the wizards and held up my hands for silence and calm. "Ladies, gentlemen, and miscellanea, please refrain from any catastrophic violence for a moment." I sighed. "I shall go down and parley with them."

Ig squeaked up, "No go well last time."

"Well, last time we weren't on the verge of committing annihilation upon them," I snapped back, feeling a tinge stressed by the vanishing sun. "I feel it provides a degree of leverage."

"Don't think they'll think they've got the leverage, with the whole army?" Cygni asked grimly.

"Ogres aren't entirely unintelligent, and it appears they've allied with other folk who are liable to be smarter still. I'm sure whoever their leader might be will have the sense not to charge directly into the gates of heck. You'd have to be some kind of egotistical megalomaniac to send your minions to die without any hope of victory."

With a little conjured cloud to cushion my fall, I drifted down to the battlefield on our doorstep, with all the gathered beasts of war drawing back at my approach. "Parley!" I called out. "I call for a parley. Who is your leader?"

Up close it was easier to make out the Badlands conglomerate's component parts. Orcs were here, presumably all the ones that had been driven from their city when the ogres moved in. Some werewolves, dire wolves, regular wolves with a bad attitude, and goblins riding on top. Vampires, sapient plant creatures, vampiric sapient plant creatures. Rock trolls, river trolls, cave trolls, taiga trolls who were clearly lost. Goblins aplenty. A mothman, wyverns and wampus cats. Three cockatrices a-laying. A pair of hippogryphs with the front of a bird and the rear of a horse, a gryphohip, with the front of a horse and the rear of a bird. Two questing beasts with diverging goals. An ouroboros being worn as a necklace by a very angry-looking dryad. A variety of dinosaurs and dire animals of varying stripes. A pig-dragon. Some mummies who I suspect were lost. Redcaps, catoblepas and a gargoyle being hauled around in a wagon. Four cyclopses moving in a square formation so nothing could sneak up on them. A yeti with a hangover. Some miscellaneous elementals, zombies, skeletons, presumably a necromancer or two somewhere to explain those. And a partridge in a man-eating tree.

All that was just what was up here in the front ranks. There were some distinctly dragon-looking things farther back as well as giants, titans, and other creatures that are distinct from humanity only by virtue of being exceptionally tall. Also a dire gnome, which was basically human sized, but with a very large and pointed hat that made even mine look paltry by comparison. She was riding a dire hamster.

They all stood around awkwardly as the message got passed back along the ranks that somebody wanted to talk to the boss. I caught myself tapping my toe and stopped it. None of the assembled creatures would meet my gaze, perhaps fearing that I'd put the evil eye upon them, perhaps feeling the awkwardness of hanging around with the enemy and not being allowed to murder them currently.

It came at first like the thunder of drums. A percussive beat, made not of skin being struck, but of breath being unleashed. A rhythmic huffing, that soon began to grow in volume until all the monsters that had lungs were grunting in time. Then from the rear ranks, there came the distant echo of words. "One. Two. Three. One. Two. Three. One. Two. Three. Nun. Mhor. Goth. Nun. Mhor.

Goth." Getting louder and louder as it swept through the ranks, creeping closer and closer until I was surrounded by the deafening cacophony and finally the bodies of the enemy parted to reveal it.

It was much improved since last I laid eyes upon it. Soot-stained armor was layered over its amorphous form to give it more of a fixed shape. Still wearing black from head to toe, but in a more martial manner now.

"Nun Mhor Goth! Nun Mhor Goth!" the minions chanted. "Nun Mhor Goth!" And then silence fell.

For a moment it was as though we were the only people in the universe, me and this creature that claimed to be a good. It had no eyes, only a dark void beneath the holes of its helmet where eyes should have lain, but nonetheless I could feel the crushing weight of its gaze, its will. "Absalom, baby. How you doing, kid?"

It took all of my composure not to flinch as its awful voice flooded into my mind. Via my ears. "I have been well since we parted, Nun-Mhorgoth."

"Ooh-hoo-hoo you know it gives me shivers when you say my name like that." It chortled with delight. "Go on, say it again. Say it like you mean it."

My skin felt as though it were attempting to crawl off my body. Specifically the skin on the side facing the creature in armor felt as though it were attempting to migrate to the back of my body so as to get away from it. It was entirely possible that I was now devoid of wrinkles. Still, I was not going to show weakness to this puffed-up shadow. "May I enquire as to the purpose of this visit?"

It flung its arms out to the sides as though about to lunge in for a hug, and once more I had to restrain myself from fleeing. "You know me, baby, I was always going to take this show on the road. I need the limelight of the big city. I need an audience. I need to conquer the world and bring it to heel. Starting with the home of the only man who's ever crossed me and lived."

"And these gathered . . . people." I glanced around the surrounding army as the various monsters leered at me. "Might I enquire why they are accompanying you?"

Nun-Mhorgoth raised its voice to be heard by all the gathered creatures. It echoed out across the plains before the Great Wall and then bounced back. "Seems like I'm not the only beefcake that's got beef with you highfalutin civilized folk. Everybody out in the Badlands has had it with your crap. You've got the best land, the best of everything, and what have they got? Dirt. Not even good dirt. Lowdown, no-good dirty dirt. You need to learn how to share your toys."

However it may have irked me, I did not meet the alleged god's bellowing with a raised voice of my own. I did not need to bandy my words about to rile anyone up. My actions would speak for me. "People's lives aren't toys. Nun-Mhorgoth."

"Not with that attitude they ain't." It threw back its helmeted head and laughed uproariously. Then paused and looked around at all the monsters who had until now just been watching placidly. They all started laughing on cue, only for him to cut them off again after a moment. "When you're all grown up and get a little perspective, then you'll see. This is a game, they're pieces, I'm the only player, and the way I win . . . Well, I win if I'm having fun. Ripping down your wall, slaughtering your people, destroying everything you've spent a lifetime trying to preserve. Oh baby, that sounds like a real good time."

This was, of course, an attempt at intimidation, and when you have legions of monsters at your back and enough raw arcane power to remake the universe as you see fit, it is quite easy to appear intimidating. I suppose that if it had been attempting to be meek and friendly in such company, being convincing would have been a much more impressive feat. It was this that I kept in my mind as I answered Nun-Mhorgoth loud enough that its little minions could overhear this time. How very unimpressive I found all of this. "You seem rather confident that we shall simply allow you to do as you wish."

"Scryne, baby, you're a doll." It threw back his head and laughed some more. I wondered briefly if it was ever actually amused, or if this strange performance actually had any meaning, but then abruptly it was there, nose to nose with me, figuratively. It stood a head taller in his new outfit, and I wasn't entirely sure that it had any olfactory organs to speak of behind the metal plate. "I mean it. You are a doll. All of you are toys. Ain't nothing you can do if the big hand comes down to pick you up. Ain't nothing you can do if that big hand twists off your arms and your legs. Didn't you ever play as a kid?"

For a moment I felt it scratching at the surface of my mind, trying to get in and pillage my thoughts the way that it had done when I was a defenseless hat. No longer would I succumb to such ill-conceived assaults. The wards placed around my mind were unassailable, bound to my own certainty in my power and reinforced through a lifetime of repetition. But it didn't need to dig in my head for my memories. It already had most of them, having gobbled them up like Ig at a buffet when it last had the opportunity. "Stupid question. Of course you didn't. You sad sack."

Once more it sought to get what the youths refer to as "a rise" out of me, and it was to no avail: I had been bullied by the best of the best through the years, and every one of those bullies had ended up beneath me in the end. "I had more pressing concerns on my mind."

"Of course you did! You had to get powerful, right?" It treated me to a waggle of hands. Mockery of the sort commonly seen among preteens. Such showmanship as the world had never before seen. Truly remarkable, to mock someone while surrounded by your own legions. Everything radiating off Nun-Mhorgoth spoke of power and superiority, and by disbelieving it, I could not help but feel that I was robbing the creature of its power. Even if it was only its power to intimidate me. "Well, let me tell you a little something about being powerful. Either you are, or you ain't. All the books in the world won't change that you were born a worm in the garden of gods."

It was becoming increasingly apparent that there was not going to be an equitable agreement at the end of this conversation. Whether the millennia bound in stone had driven the creature to madness, or if madness had led to it being bound in stone for millennia, the net result was entirely the same. I was confronted with a creature that was deranged and heck-bent on rampaging across the world. Lashing out endlessly against some perceived slight.

Still, I would not allow such a thing to occur if it could be avoided, and ultimately, though they followed Nun-Mhorgoth, I had no wish to see all of these monsters murdered any more than I would the people of Arpanpholigon. That was the unfortunate side effect of spending time in their company and finding a portion of them likeable—it left me vulnerable to believing that they were people and not the mindless ravening beasts of evil I had been taught they were. They were people, just as capable of right and wrong as any one of us born human.

For the most part at least. I was pretty sure that the dire gnome was bad to the bone.

I made my offer. "If you have issues with me, then might I suggest that we settle them between the two of us rather than involving the entire nation-state of Arpanpholigon in what is essentially a private matter?"

"You got me all wrong, baby," Nun-Mhorgoth cooed. "Conquering the world? I'm doing that anyway. Hurting you so bad you regret ever being born, that's just gravy."

I drew myself up to my full height, unimpressive as that may have been surrounded by all of these giants and monsters. "Gravy?"

"It tastes nice, but it ain't the meat of the thing, you know?"

"I cannot claim that I do know," I replied drily. "No."

My feigned ignorance seemed to have put a crimp in the creature's good mood. "Ain't you meant to be a smart cookie? Well, I guess we're just going to have to see how the cookie crumbles."

It was in motion so swiftly that I scant could have believed it had I not already seen it moving at such speeds down in the deep dark. Lashing out the wickedly clawed gauntlet on the appendage it had decided was its arm with the intent to tear my throat out.

"Fugio!" I snapped, evaporating into a puff of air and reforming but a moment later, back atop the Great Wall.

Tremors ran through me, not just the vibration of my atoms still getting accustomed to being bound together into solid form once more, but nervous energy too. Perhaps Ig had rubbed off on me more than I would have liked to admit. Infecting me with that same adrenaline-fueled twitchiness.

"Negotiations went well then?" Cygni asked from by my hip.

I jumped.

After a steadying breath, I informed her, "As well as could be expected."

"That bad?" She chuckled. It was nice that someone could see the funny side of all this.

And then the gathered crowd of wizards and guards descended on me.

"What is happening?!" Iomedania seized me by the front of my robe before remembering herself and quickly letting go.

Arturo had abandoned his calculations and had apparently been watching through a spyglass. "Who was that?"

"Weh?" Ig weighed in with his usual insightful contribution, afraid of being excluded.

One of the despairing guards shoved his way to the fore. "Why are they here?"

"Wuh-what do they want?!" Poindextrous asked. I really should have left him at the college; fieldwork like this brought him out in hives.

The only one asking actually important questions was, of course, Cygni. "How long before they attack?"

I counted off my answers on my fingers as I jogged across the breadth of the wall. "We are under attack by an alliance of all the monsters in the world. Their leader is Nun-Mhorgoth, who claims to be the dark god of evil and darkness. He has rallied them all to claim the altogether nicer patch of land that we live on. As to what they want, they want to despoil and slaughter until all the world is in ruins under the guise of seeking to right the injustice they believe we have perpetrated against them by hoarding all the benefits of civilization while they festered in obscurity."

I paused as I reached the edge of the wall and looked down over the ramparts at the incoming tide. "And by my estimate, they're attacking now."

CHAPTER 11

WALL, DWARF, SALAD

The Great Wall of Arpanpholigon is one of the wonders of the world. Those few wizards who had made the trip into space claimed that it was the only man-made structure visible from that distance, but since the majority of wizards who willingly launched themselves up into the cosmos were thoroughly deranged, this was taken with a grain of salt. Even if it were not for the architectural prowess involved in producing a single continuous wall that stretched the full length of civilization's borders with the Badlands, even a single square foot of it was an impressive work of magic. For you see, long ago, when the world was divided between those who wished to live comfortably with some constraints and those who wished to live free and occasionally resort to cannibalism, one of my predecessors had involved herself in the plans. I believe that it was Archmage Gennifer Gwendolyn Eggleton herself who cast the first of the many layers of protection upon the wall, tapping into ancient magics almost as potent as those currently blocking the sun and cursing Ildrit. The ancient magics now superseded by superstition about the need to invite a stranger in, the laws of hospitality and the invisible barrier of the threshold. This wall marked the threshold of civilization, and to cross it one had to be invited in or enter with no ill intentions. That was the primal principle on which the magic and wall had first been built, and every generation that followed in her footsteps, developing new spells and protections, had layered them atop it, using it as the foundation and root. All other magic of protection in the Great Wall sprang forth from that same wellspring, and all that it really took was for a wizard of sufficient power, with sufficient loyalty to civilization, to activate it.

Confronted with these overwhelming hordes of monsters fully intent on charging in and despoiling all that dwelled beyond, it was almost easier to activate that magic than to not. The ancient wards buried deep in the foundations of the wall burned to life. A barrier of magic far stronger than any stone could ever be pulsed into place before the first rank of goblins, gremlins, or whatever else the monsters had to throw at us reached that threshold. They rebounded off that invisible barrier before they came close to scratching the stone, knocked away by the sheer power of how unwelcome they were.

Of course, goblins, orcs, ogres, and their like were not inclined to careful pondering of the situation that they were in. As soon as they had regained their feet, they charged again, and again, and again, each time being rebuffed with the same satisfying "ping" sound.

"That should buy us a little time to think." I clapped my hands together.

The wall beneath our feet made a very distressing whine. It was not meant to do that. I reached out with my arcane senses and caught, for the very briefest moment, a glimpse of what it would have been like to be born a beetle-grub, spending months, if not years, gestating down in the comforting darkness of the soil, only to find myself slowly but inexorably changing within a shell of my own flesh and dirt into a creature of armor and deliberate movement, feeling safe and powerful within the construct of myself, only to scurry at last towards the place beyond, the place above and be blinded by the sun. Seen for the very first time.

All the floes of Quintessence were visible to me, but what was pressed up against the other side of the barrier so haphazardly assembled over the centuries by my predecessors was not a stream or a river, it was an ocean. The power at Nun-Mhorgoth's disposal was so great as to be beyond comprehension. Once more I had the sense of the vastness of it all, as though I were capturing a glimpse of something so impossibly large that I could not take it all in.

All of that nigh-infinite gathered power touched against the barrier conjured from the wall, and it pushed.

Cracks began to form in the stone where the spells were rooted. In the very concept of protection itself. You cannot protect against the inevitable, Nun-Mhorgoth's magic whispered insidiously into the soul of the stone. You cannot ward against hostility when all of creation is your enemy. When all the universe wishes you were dead and cold.

Dust began to drift up in the air around us as the ancient spells of my forebearers began to unravel.

"That not good," Ig informed me, helpfully.

"Yes, thank you so much for the update." I did my best not to snarl as all the wizards spun to look at me as if I had all the answers.

Well, I am the greatest living wizard, it is only natural. "Philodephina, I need as heavy a Quintessence flow as you can bring down to this point. Arturo, scrap your calculations and start over; you're creating a dimensional fold that will create infinite distance the further you proceed into it, layered along the front of the wall. Behind that, we'll have Sabrinia's time-slowing spell. Even if they make it across infinite distance, I want them traveling at an absolute crawl. Copernicrust, I need Philodephina's supply divided up amongst the different protections we're assembling. Archimendo, tap the old magic, the unwritten stuff; this is the threshold to our home, and while Nun-Mhorgoth might be trying to siphon the importance from that, I believe you can reinforce it. You know tradition like nobody else, it is time to put it to work. Repetition and reinforcement. Danyeel, come here, you nervous wreck, I need the most elaborate illusion you have ever constructed, running the length of the wall, convincing anyone that walks into Sabrinia and Arturo's infinite distance of infinite slowness that they are in fact walking in the wrong direction. Send them sideways, curve the light, whatever needs to be done. Balthazagar, I need you working with Iomedania—she is about to invent the most ingenious protection spell ever concocted and she'll need an extra set of hands casting it. Poindextrous, I need you working with Cygni; she knows stone like nobody else, and you know the mathematics of the forces involved. I need this wall impenetrable."

Cygni was the first to react, catching Poindextrous by the belt before he could run for his life as he'd clearly intended to. "Come on, longshanks, you and me are going to make stone harder than stone."

The others, to their credit, took only a moment before jumping to their assigned tasks, with the exception of Iomedania, who stared at me blankly. "I'm about to invent the most ingenious protection spell ever concocted?"

"Yes, yes you are." I managed a smile.

I had not expected that I'd need to hold her hand, of all people. She was typically the most bullish of the whole Council of the Wise, though she had the sense to hide it, as a rule. "How . . . how do you know that I am?"

"Two reasons." I leaned in close to take her into my confidence. "The first is that you are one of the most brilliant and inventive wizards I have ever had the pleasure of working with, and the one I would have chosen as my successor until only recently given your incredible drive and your capacity to make the necessary logical leaps to truly advance the art of magic into its next phase. And the second, is that if you don't then you are going to die a horrible and gruesome death, and I feel that is typically one of the better motivators. Wouldn't you say?"

By the end of that little speech, I will admit that my voice had gone from the soothing cadence I had sought to a sort of manic pitch, but the pep talk seemed to do its job. She conjured a slate board from out of somewhere and started frantically scribbling.

Excellent. Their combined efforts would have bought us infinite time against an average foe, and probably a few hours against Nun-Mhorgoth. Assuming that the wall stood long enough for them to get everything working.

"What me do?" Ig asked from where he'd somehow slunk up to my side.

"You, my friend, are going to have the most onerous task of all the gathered wizards. You will be helping me."

"Me like help you," Ig said.

"Well." I patted him on the head. "You don't know what we're doing yet."

Even with all of the considerable power at its disposal, what Nun-Mhorgoth lacked was finesse. It attempted to completely overwhelm the spells already in effect with raw force of will, when magic is, after all, a subtle art.

With no small amount of trepidation, I opened up my senses once more to the tidal wave of power pressing against us. I saw the shape of it now that the shock had passed. Saw the way that he worked to unweave the vast magic's arrayed against him. It was vast and powerful, but also insidious, just like the water I had described it as in metaphor, it pressed and it pressed, with any tiny crack in the wall allowing a trickle more of it to push inside and erode what was already there. I would not be able to stop it. There was simply too much of it, pissing in through too many different gaps in our defenses.

Laying a hand on Ig's head, feeling the Crown of Cognition brush against my fingertips, I let him see what I saw. To which, in his wisdom, he responded, "Weh?"

"That is Nun-Mhorgoth's magic." I bit my lip as I considered my next words carefully, then I said what needed to be said. "I need you to push it back."

"Weh?!" Ig exclaimed once more. "How I push that?!"

"In the same way you stopped a flight of arrows. In the same way that you perform all your wonders. If his magic gets through, it is going to kill you. So everywhere that you see it coming through, I need you to push it back. Can you do that for me?"

He looked up at me, wide-eyed at the awful burden I was putting on him, the terror that I had just placed in his heart so that he could do what needed to be done, and bless his little kobold heart, he nodded. Raising his paws, he reached out with the paltry Quintessence within him, and he pushed.

It should have been impossible to turn back the tide. It should have been impossible to use what little magic he had to grab hold of a vast arcane working of such magnitude. It should have been impossible to stop Nun-Mhorgoth's advance. But Ig didn't know that, so it worked. All along the watchtowers atop the Great Wall, in every place that Nun-Mhorgoth's influence was starting to filter through, it was halted, and inch by painful inch, Ig drove it back. Sweat slicked him already, and the fight had scarcely even begun. Through where my hand rested upon his head, I let my confidence in his abilities flow along with the comparatively vast supplies of Quintessence that I had on hand. Running down into his head, along his arms, and out to push the dark lord's power back with force of will and blind terror alone.

All of my attention should have had to remain upon Ig, to keep the flow of magic steady, to drag in more and cycle it through to him, but luckily for us both, I had two minds. One contained within my skull and the other perched atop it. I let the mind of the hat take over the operation of my body and the flows of Quintessence, and I turned my attentions to the puzzle that I had been presented with before.

Nun-Mhorgoth would win through intimidation if he could. If he broke the faith of the defenders, of my wizards, then their spells had no hope of standing up against him. What they needed right now was hope. Hope to spur them on, to get them thinking and casting instead of being consumed by the blind terror that seemed to wash against our defenses as surely as the dark one's will. They needed a sign that this fight was not over before it began, and what luck, our enemy had hand-delivered me not only such a sign, but the means to uncover it.

Nun-Mhorgoth may have learned my magic when it ripped the memories from my hat, but I was not like it. I was not some stagnant ancient creature that could no longer grow and change—regardless of what my students through the years might have said otherwise—so I was not reliant upon stealing the work of others. Instead I did what all geniuses do. I borrowed heavily from the work of others without outright plagiarism by putting my own slant on things.

The working of unweaving that Nun-Mhorgoth had cast upon the spells of the Great Wall had a distinctive shape and flavor to it. A pattern that I could discern now that I'd been given long enough to study it. A working that I could replicate.

I began to cast, murmuring words of Archaic to myself as I readied the spell for its long journey. Flickering from one element to the next, constructing counterbalances, and using Ig's incredible method of allowing the subconscious mind to keep track of one spell while my conscious mind worked on the other. My brain stem began to ache with the effort of all the different fragments of spells I had it maintaining, but it kept the figurative plates spinning until I was ready to do what I should have done from the start.

With a heave and one final snappish word of the Archaic tongue of the Arcane Archons, I launched my spell up into the sky.

It traveled across the cosmos, not at the speed of light, which was altogether slower than I should have liked, but at the speed of thought. Traversing the vast distance between our world and our sun in moments, striking on the vast shadow that had been cast betwixt us and light, and undoing it.

I staggered with the effort of such a potent and complex spell, performed simultaneously with my Quintessence reserves being drained by Ig, but I did not fall. He stood stalwart as a walking stick, keeping me upright.

The whoops and cheers of the guards and the less focused of the Council of the Wise took a few seconds to begin, but once they had, I opened up my eyes and saw the battlefield once more. Bathed in sunlight.

"How do you like that gravy?" I hissed at the distant figure of the dark lord, still bathed in a pool of shadows despite the abrupt end to its little eclipse. A comment that earned me a confused look from Ig, and that I was frankly quite ashamed of. I was a wizard. We aren't meant to attempt pithy one-liners. For obvious reasons.

In an instant, every troll on the battlefield was afflicted with their native curse, turning to stone and creating huge blockades in the path of the charge. The vampire contingent of the dark one's armies immediately burst into flames and evaporated away, as though in counterpoint to the trolls' persistent presence.

All around me I could feel the magic of my people swirling through the air, contorting into new shapes as it was pulled this way and that by all the different spells at work. Then, abruptly, Philodephina's work was complete and we were all flooded with more Quintessence than even the most spendthrift of us could not hope to use. I replenished my reserves, and poured yet more power down into Ig, who was now so slick with sweat that I began to suspect that I'd been accompanied all of this time by some sort of gelatinous creature in the shape of a kobold.

"Me doing it!" he squeaked out, before he had to turn his full attention back to Nun-Mhorgoth's persistent pressure.

With the first of the Council's spells active, it would only be a matter of moments before the others were done with casting theirs. The lack of Quintessence would have stymied progress until now, but with the arrival of all that raw magic, they began to reach completion. Danyeel's came first, and I got to see with my own eyes as dozens of charging orcs suddenly swiveled to go running along the length of the wall instead. Nun-Mhorgoth would soon have that illusion dispelled if he had half a moment, so we ensured that he did not get that half a moment. I threw a borrowed version of his spell of unraveling directly into his original spell of unraveling, setting it to unravel even as it tried to unravel our spells. He tried to patch it and get back to destroying all we knew and loved, but my borrowed version of his spell proved entirely too effective at disrupting his own spell for a quick fix. In fact, the two workings soon began working to consume one another.

Ig slumped, and my hand upon his head had to grip lest he fall to the ground entirely. He let out an undignified squeak, but it didn't have much energy behind it. It was more of an acknowledgement than anything else. All at once the other spells began to fire off, and Copernicrust's filtration system got to work divvying up the available Quintessence to each of them so that no one could starve any of the others by drinking up too much of the available resources.

Iomedania's spell, completely unknown to magic before today, came into effect first. A solid but invisible barrier stretching up into the sky just in time to catch those clever wyverns who had attempted to circumvent the whole wall problem by flying up and over. It was joined a moment later by Arturo's spatial fold, Sabrinia's time warp and Archimendo followed up the rear, reaffirming the connection with the ancient magics already rooted in the wall and bringing the original wards back to full effectiveness despite the best efforts of the dark maybe-god to unmake them.

Cygni shouldered up beside me on the opposite side to Ig, and she grinned. "Watch this."

Poindextrous looked entirely out of his element, standing there and actually casting magic instead of making spreadsheets. His glasses sat askew, his hair, as much of it was left, was disheveled by the whipping wind, and his face was contorted into an expression of what I could only describe as delight as he rattled through the entire litany of Archaic that he needed to say to cast the spell with nary a stutter in sight.

The stone beneath our feet hardened. The cracks that had appeared in it healed. More than that, though, in addition to becoming more and more dense, to the point that I could swear that gravity began to increase where we were standing, the wall began to become more and more real. It had been real before, of course. But with magic involved, a certain amount of unreality would begin to bleed through. These were the metaphysical cracks in which Nun-Mhorgoth had been able to insert its will. Working magic on something that was 99 percent real was considerably more difficult than something that hovered around the usual 75 percent mark of most solid objects. And what Cygni and Poindextrous had achieved went even beyond that. They had cranked up the solidity and the reality of the wall beyond the point of all other matter. This wall was now at least 10 percent more real than everyone standing on top of it. It was the most wall to have ever walled.

It made one a little queasy to experience being less real than one's surroundings, but needs must.

"Excellent work, everyone." I graced them with a smile, even as my mind rushed ahead to the next steps that we needed to take. "Poindextrous, while I am sure that you are feeling quite exhausted after all of that . . ."

"I feel great!" he yelled. "Let's do some more magic!"

I couldn't help but notice that both his slouch and stutter had entirely vanished now that he'd tasted power, making me wonder how much both of them were an affectation. Regardless, it seemed that fieldwork did agree with him, if it came with a handy rush of adrenaline.

"Unfortunately, more magic is not actually our current requirement. Rather, I need your amazing powers of calculation."

"Oh." He deflated a little. "I guh-guess that's fine too."

Pinching the bridge of my nose to hold back the impending headache, I assured him, "I promise there will be more magic later. Now can you please chart out how long it is going to take for our defensive spells to fail."

"Fuh-fail? They'll never fail! We're the best wizards in the world, using the most up-to-date techniques; those protections will stand until . . ."

With a shudder felt along the length of the wall, Danyeel's illusion shattered. It was hardly a surprise that it had been the easiest to pick apart. Not because he was in any way less competent than my other casters, but because illusion is fundamentally rooted in misdirection, and Nun-Mhorgoth had a pretty clear view of the spell as it had activated, since it popped up ahead of all the rest.

"Damn it," he grumbled, mostly to himself. He rolled up his sleeves, getting ready to cast it again.

I laid a hand on his shoulder, and he froze as though mine were the grip of death itself. "Save your strength, Danyeel. I've no doubt we shall have need of it soon enough."

"Yes, Archmage." He looked down at his boots.

"They will all fall to Nun-Mhorgoth's power." I sighed. "Yours just happened to be first."

The gathered wizards went from looking victorious to desolate in a matter of moments. "Um, actually, what was the point, if it's all going to come tumbling down anyway?" Copernicrust complained.

"Time, my dear man." I pushed off my exhaustion like I was shrugging off a mantle and rose to my full height once more. "We have bought ourselves time to think, to plan, to prepare."

They all still looked miserable, so with no small amount of trepidation, I launched into a pep talk. "And what more has a wizard ever needed to defeat any foe than a little time to prepare the right spell?"

Cygni piped up. "A bloody army."

"I beg pardon?" I blinked down at her in surprise.

She jerked her head to the wyverns splattering off the side of the protective field between us and the Badlands. "Goth's got an army, we need one too."

Archimendo scoffed, "Girl, we are wizards. More puissant than any army. We could wipe all of our foes from the battlefield in a single . . ."

"Except you can't. Or you would have already. Goth can block your magic. And even if it couldn't, there's stuff out there magic won't scratch." She glanced to Ig for support, which was a bold move if ever there was one. "Remember the werewolves?"

"Magic no workie," he confirmed.

"Had I were-creatures at my disposal, I would most likely set them to biting everyone in my army with all haste . . ." Iomedania trailed off at the betrayed expression on old Archimendo's wrinkled leathery face.

"So, who's got an army?" Cygni clapped her hands together. Bringing us back to the question nobody really wanted to answer.

Sabrinia replied just to break up the deathly silence, punctuated by wyvern splats. "I suppose the king has some knights?"

"Need more than some," Cygni grumbled.

"We could send messages to the other city states, requesting aid." Balthazagar snapped his fingers arthritically. "They probably have something like an army?"

Copernicrust added, "Um, actually, we could ask the Elves of Verdance Wood."

"Good luck getting an answer this century." Iomedania rolled her eyes at that.

"What about summoning help?" Sabrinia suggested. "Mister Arturo, you could pull an army through from somewhere or other, right?"

The voluminous gentleman in question flapped his mouth open and shut a few times, surprised to be put on the spot, before finally sighing, "Ah . . . No."

Surprise held everyone's tongues for a moment, then Philodephina pushed him. "All those different dimensions and you can't get help from any of them?"

He had already been sweating from all the exertions involved in casting his dimensional fold spell, but now he reached for a handkerchief and wiped at his face as a fresh flood came forth. "Ah . . . you see . . . we're not very popular in those other dimensions. We've used a lot of them for waste disposal over the years and . . ."

My palm met my face as Danyeel groaned. "Oh come on, really?"

"How were we meant to know that we would someday be reliant upon them for aid?" Arturo shouted at him, clearly feeling picked on at this point.

"I think it may have just been common decency not to dump toxic arcane waste in other dimensions," Philodephina replied coldly. "I assume it was toxic arcane waste?"

"Perhaps." He confirmed her suspicions entirely with that one word.

With another catastrophic explosion, the dimensional fold collapsed in on itself. That kind of magic was already inherently unstable, otherwise we'd use it all the time for everything. Still, I had hoped that it would have been unfamiliar enough to Nun-Mhorgoth that that it could have bought us a little longer.

"Seventeen hours and twenty-four minutes." Poindextrous finally joined back into the conversation. "Give or take."

"Not long enough," Cygni noted.

To gather armies and march them here could take weeks. Even if I borrowed Arturo's expertise and students to set up portals, we'd be looking at a day or more. We needed more time. "Calculate for the addition of illusory defenses by Danyeel."

Maximus Arturo had finally dabbed himself mostly dry and tucked the soggy kerchief up his sleeve. "I can bring back the fold, just give me . . ."

I stopped him with an upheld palm. "We'll need you elsewhere if we're moving troops, Max."

"I've got to go," Cygni said, out of nowhere.

Ig startled out of whatever daydream he'd drifted off into. "Weh?"

Incredulity straining at every inch of me, I strived to maintain my composure. "I beg your pardon?"

I must have sounded sufficiently deranged at that moment that Philodephina actually stepped between us. As though I were going to lunge at the dwarf.

She stared me down. "It isn't her fight, let her go."

That was patently not the case. I'd argue that it was more Cygni's fight than anyone else's, given that she was the fool that had released the dark maybe-god from his imprisonment underground. But I digress.

"Not staying gone," she grumbled. "I'll get King Khnute. Raise the dwarves. That's an army for you."

There wasn't really a polite way to ask if she was going to be executed for stealing my hat self and escaping the dwarven kingdom, so I tried for a gentler approach. "Do you think that your mother is going to be . . . receptive to such an invitation?"

"Got to. Her responsibility."

I could see the dwarf logic of that: if the dwarves could be reminded that they were the ones to bind Nun-Mhorgoth in stone originally, then I suppose their internal logic would dictate that maintaining said imprisonment was their duty. And dwarves would jump on anything even vaguely resembling a duty.

With that stated, Cygni strode clear of everyone and readied herself to cast one of the myriad spells of transportation that would carry her home. Though the barrier along the wall would prevent anyone attempting to come from the outside in, the reverse was not so. Iomedania had been very clever in that regard. Not that she wasn't very clever in every regard.

I strode right after her, and after an awkward moment where we both looked like we were going for a hug, but the height differential made it too awkward, she extended a hand for me to shake. I was surprised to realize just how upset her departure was making me. As if I'd thought she'd stay by my side forever like a good little apprentice despite her having already learned more in a week than most wizards accomplish in a lifetime. "Good luck to you, my friend."

She cleared her throat and looked away, clearly uncomfortable. "Project I was working on for you is done. Just needs some polish."

Hope may have taken root in the heart of the others when I'd lit up the sun again, but in my heart there had remained the burden of reality. The reality of our situation was that however powerful or clever I might be, Nun-Mhorgoth was more powerful. Not more clever, obviously, because I'm the cleverest, but in terms of raw power, it had me beat. This disparity was unusual for me. I was accustomed to being able to bull through any trouble with raw arcane might. And as such, I was feeling a little unmanned by the whole experience. Cygni's project being complete changed that. I allowed myself to hope genuinely, once again. "That is exceptionally good news."

"Try not to break it before I get back." She tried her best to grumble.

I waited and watched as she evaporated off into the wind with a heavy heart. To my immense surprise, I felt a leathery little paw slip into my hand, and I almost jumped away before realizing that it was Ig trying to give me comfort.

I'd have to remember to wash that hand later, thoroughly. It was the same one I'd used to touch his greasy, loose-skinned scalp.

With a heavy sigh, I turned back to the wizards. "Let us purchase some more time for the dwarves to arrive, shall we?"

"Nineteen hours and eleven minutes." Poindextrous supplied the number at last.

"Nowhere near enough." I groaned. "If I stay here, directly countering his magic, as I did before. How long will we get?"

Poindextrous had the good grace to look surprised. "You cuh-can't? You'd need to be fighting him every minute. Yuh-you'd exhaust yourself in . . ."

"Assume for a moment that I can." I showed my teeth in what I had hoped was a smile but which Ig's startled expression suggested was something somewhat more sinister. "Assume for a moment that you are addressing the greatest living wizard in this world and that he has been spurred to action for the first time in his life."

Balthazagar was the one to answer, having taken the measure of me and my intentions. "You would hold him off until you collapse of exhaustion, then the ticking timer of the static defenses would run down."

"Giving me nineteen hours to recover my strength before he broke through."

"Unless it kills you," Iomedania was quick to point out.

"Dying is the last thing I mean to do." I forced a smile to hide the quaver of fear I could feel deep in my stomach. She was right, of course, exhaustion could very well end my tenure in this ancient and increasingly decrepit body, which was why I would need to reinforce it before I began.

I clapped my hands for their attention once more. "Right. Danyeel, get those illusions up, whatever you think will work best. Everyone else, go to see the king, explain the situation as best you can, and get him to work gathering allies for the battle to come. Leave Arturo with him to start shipping in troops from anywhere that will loan them, then head back out to the wall and start clearing the countryside. I want everyone between here and Arpanpholigon inside the city before the wall falls."

"Surely our time would be better spent . . ." Philodelphina objected. Inevitably. But I spoke over her.

"The preservation of innocent life is our highest goal. There shall be plenty of time for great feats of magical destruction later." It was hard to argue with someone talking about defending innocent lives. As far as moral high ground goes, it is pretty unassailable. As such, she shut up. "Ig and I shall accompany you back to the city, albeit briefly, in case there is any issue with the king."

Sabrinia cocked her head to one side, silky hair falling about her face. "How's the kobold going to help with that?"

"Given his track record with authority figures, I'd imagine he'll either end up wearing the crown by the end of the conversation or choking the man on a piece of fruit." Ig had the good grace to look away, ashamed. "Either way, we will get what needs done, done."

"Um, actually . . . what are you going to do in the city?" Archimendo asked me slyly as the others began getting organized for their departure. Clearly expecting me to have some magical artifact of supreme power squirreled away somewhere to trivialize the battles to come.

"I am going to get some dinner and a nap," I announced firmly. Best to prepare as best I could for the arduous work ahead.

"Me help," Ig volunteered immediately.

"I thought that you might."

I should have gone with Ig directly to the keep and dealt with the politics and organized everyone and everything, but there was a clock ticking away now. The longer that I spent getting myself ready, the less time I would have to recover on the other side, and given that I was already wobbling a little after the singular attempt to drive back Nun-Mhorgoth's magic, I could not imagine that my recovery time after spending hours doing so was going to be brief.

Thus, as the others departed to go about their terribly important business, I located the familiar signature of Widowtaker, and allowed the winds to carry me and Ig there instead of following after the rest of the Council of the Wise.

We materialized in a rather shabby-looking tavern with a low ceiling to find Ildrit already there, with four places set at his table and a heap of greenery and mushrooms in a wooden bowl between them. The famed dwarven cuisine that I'd heard so much about. Of course they had gone wild on greens—such a thing was poverty food on the surface but the rarest of luxuries to the underworld-dwelling dwarves.

After my departure, I'd hoped that there wouldn't be any sort of trouble, but it was quite impossible to tell from looking at him if there had been or not. I'd seen him emerge from bloody battles looking completely unmarred before. The man knew his way around a fight, if nothing else.

He rose when he noticed our arrival with a cheerful smile, greeted Ig with a wave, and then looked moderately confused that his girlfriend hadn't arrived yet.

His girlfriend, who had just gone off on what very well might have been a suicide mission behind enemy lines, without mentioning it to him. Oops.

"Got the sun back on, then?" he asked me jovially.

This was going to be a very awkward conversation.

CHAPTER 12

A GREAT GAME OF THRONES AND CROWNS

Dealing with diplomacy with the monsters had been infinitely easier than dealing with diplomacy between the various human nations. The monsters were united in their goals, straightforward in their speech and relatively sensible about such things as whether or not their massive army of monsters actually existed or not. The same could not be said for the leadership of the human race, which was responding to threats of its impending annihilation with outright denial for the most part.

What I'd assumed would have been the briefest part of our job, mobilizing all the forces of civilization to defend itself, had turned into something arduous. Something that made me long to return to the Great Wall and slam my face into it repeatedly rather than listening to any more blithering.

Ildrit had been the smart one. After dinner he had made himself scarce. He announced that he was going to go and round up his old friends to help us out, by which I assumed he meant all of the monsters, murderers, and madmen that he'd hung around with prior to becoming an adventurer, though I imagine that there was a lot of crossover between adventurers and monsters, murderers, and madmen anyway, so we'd probably be seeing a mix.

Ig had offered to go off into the Badlands by himself and gather up all of kobold-kind to join us in our battle, but . . . well, there really wasn't any polite way to say that having a load of kobolds milling around pooping themselves every time there was a loud noise probably wasn't going to be conducive to mounting a successful defense against the encroaching foes of civilization. He was going to stay with me while the others went off on their little side quests, so as to avoid him accidentally making a misstep and causing some other vast cataclysm while I wasn't there to keep him right.

Currently he was lying on the floor by my feet, snoring just loudly enough that it was making the world leaders that we were chatting with through a variety of head-height portals flinch with each droning warble.

I wished that I could join him in the realms of the unconscious.

"I can assure you that there is in fact a massive army of various monsters outside of the Great Wall, I have literally just come here from there. If you wish, I can have one of my staff come and collect you from where you are, and show you the army in question," I informed the sultan of Frogaria.

"Ah-hah!" he declared to his tired-looking vizier on the left periphery of the frame. "They seek to kidnap me!"

"Well, no, if we sought to kidnap you, we probably wouldn't be extending you an invitation that you can refuse at any time, we'd probably just teleport you away from where you are to wherever we wanted to. We are wizards, you see."

I could see the vizier nodding along to this statement of fact and trying not to roll his eyes when the sultan looked askance to him.

"What does it matter to us if you have some monsters?" the grand duke of Ellington asked with a sneer from his little porthole portal. "They are not Ellington's concern. Nor is it our concern if they should do away with Arpanpholigon, the most arrogant of all nations."

"Well"—I tried to maintain my composure—"I am not sure if you grasp the concept of linear time, but there is this thing called 'after' which occurs when the current moment in time has passed. And after Arpanpholigon falls to this overwhelming horde, it will march on your kingdoms and lay them to waste."

He roared, startling Ig awake, albeit briefly. "The brave Knights of Ellington can repulse any foe!"

"Then might I suggest that you prove that by sending them here? Now?"

It was worth a try.

He crossed his arms. "We have nothing to prove to you!"

"Spoken like someone who is quite certain that they'll be found wanting," sniped the queen of Regaldria.

Oh, they were all going to start bickering again and we were going to lose another half an hour. I held up my hands for silence as though they were a class full of bickering undergrads, and to my immense surprise, they actually shut up.

I guess the fact that there were portals aimed at their faces and I was capable of conjuring fireballs had not entirely escaped their notice.

"I do not speak now as the Archmage of Arpanpholigon, but as a fellow human being. We face an existential threat. If we do not come together now and face it, then all will be lost."

The viscount of Ravensby-By-Sea fiddled with his mustache. "Yes, but you'll all lose your stuff first. And by the time the monsters get to us, after fighting through all of you, there won't be many left."

Idiots. Every single one of them. I did not know if it was a result of the endless interbreeding betwixt the royal houses, or if they were simply morons as a result of having spent every waking moment coddled with no need to engage with reality, but either way the result was the same. We were all doomed.

Uproar had kicked off again. The kingdoms that lay closer to Arpanpholigon and the Great Wall abruptly realized they would be the first on the chopping block, leading to fierce screaming arguments with those situated a little further from the front lines. The viscount of Ravensby-By-Sea was looking incredibly pleased with himself where he sat on the other end of the continent.

The king of Arpanpholigon was seated upon his throne by my side, and I looked to him now for some sort of assistance in this sphere that was supposed to be his area of expertise, and he gave me absolutely nothing. Not even a shrug. He just stared off into space. Presumably lost in contemplation of potential escape routes from the country.

Ig was more helpful. At least his snoring sometimes interrupted a filibuster.

I raised my voice to be heard over the hubbub, and since our keep was the nexus point for all the various portals, I was relatively successful in drowning out all the yammering.

It was time for one of my patented inspirational speeches. "Ladies, gentlemen, and miscellaneous, we are at a crisis point in the lifespan of civilization, where we stand on the precipice of losing everything. If troops do not arrive today, then the Great Wall will fall. Whether you care for Arpanpholigon or not, the fact remains that we have served diligently as a buffer between you and the Badlands throughout history. A buffer that I sincerely doubt any of you shall survive without. Do not think of this matter in terms of kingdoms in contest or personal gain, but all the more simply as this: Ever have we been a shield, protecting the realms of humanity from its enemies. You do not allow a shield to drop just because you cannot be bothered to raise it in your own defense."

Were I a religious man, I would have silently prayed that my words would get through to them, but I was not a religious man. I was a wizard.

"Let me explain even more simply than your clumsy metaphor," the king of Crudmudgeon sneered. "You expect us to abandon our own defenses to come to yours."

That earned a significant amount of babbling approval from the other bobbing heads of state. It reaffirmed their view of the world, so of course they approved.

I took a deep breath and tried not to scream.

"There is only one place where the spreading tide of darkness might be stemmed. Only one place, and one time. The place is here, the time is now. I am not some peasant, come begging for help. I come before you with my hand outstretched, offering you the only opportunity that you will ever have to escape from inevitable ruin." I actually extended my hand out towards the assorted portals and resisted the urge to invoke sulfur. "Will you take my hand, or will you let all of mankind die?"

They all shuffled on their various thrones, looking uncomfortable at the prospect of having to do something decent for once in their life. The moment stretched on, longer and longer as the rubber band musculature of my old arm began to ache with the effort of keeping it up.

Finally the queen of Regaldria piped up. "I'm not sending anyone unless everyone else is."

I could work with this.

"And nobody would ask you to, Your Grace. Arpanpholigon is committing the full breadth of its army to fending off this invasion. We are committing every soldier and knight at our disposal, a full four thousand men in all. Who will match us?"

What followed was an hour of painstaking negotiation over who was willing to commit what. With everyone insisting on sending slightly less than their nearest neighbor until at one point we were bickering over Ravensby-By-Sea only offering up three elderly guardsmen from one of its lighthouses. Gradually, painstakingly, we brought the numbers up and up, until every kingdom had agreed to match the soldiers that Arpanpholigon was fielding. It would be the largest army ever assembled, assuming all the various warring factions didn't immediately turn on each other instead of fighting the enemy.

I turned over the remaining negotiations to the king with a hearty handshake that was mostly hearty because I was trying to shake him awake, and departed with all haste as soon as that commitment was made. Let him worry about housing and feeding all of them, and the refugees already streaming into the city from the farmland outside. I had more pressing concerns.

Time was my trouble, and time had caught up to me, it seemed. There would be no time for rest before I went back to the wall, and already I could feel myself wrought by tremors. It was the exhaustion, you see, definitely not any sort of mortal dread of going out there and pitting my will and wits against the most terrifyingly powerful creature I had ever encountered in my entire life. I'm an old man, after all. It was probably past my bedtime.

Ig was there by my side all the same, looking up at me with those beady yet doleful eyes. He believed in me to a degree that was almost comical. He believed in me to the point that when I was not around, he stopped believing in himself. It was . . . probably not healthy, but we could pick that apart later when we didn't have legions of monsters to fight. Then when all was said and done, perhaps I could settle comfortably back into my worn and overstuffed chair and write up a treatise on kobold codependence.

There was probably a good laugh to be had, about drawing courage from a kobold, but at this point in my life, I was willing to take courage wherever I could find it.

Our journey back to the wall was blessedly swift and painless. Far easier to move just the two of us, and easier still when the two of us were, despite our differences, so markedly similar.

Knights had found their way to the Great Wall in my absence and were now barking orders at the rather beleaguered guards who until now had only had to deal with the authority of a sporadic letter from the city informing them that they were doing a great job standing around and staring into space for months at a time. I'd wager that their nap time for the day had been canceled too.

Danyeel was already there ahead of me, casting his illusions to turn the tide of monsters around, to trick them into thinking that their best friends in the world had suddenly become their most bitter enemies, whispering false orders into ears, where he could find them. Conjuring up oversized ogres of various genders to flirt with their counterparts and lead them away for discreet rendezvous far away from the battle soon to rage. For all that he was young in comparison to the others on the council, and for all that his particular specialty in the realms of the arcane was considered by most to be purely for entertainment purposes, there could be no denying that he was doing a good job, layering illusion upon illusion until the monsters out there probably didn't know left from right, up from down, or friend from foe.

I gave him an encouraging pat on the shoulder as I passed, and he almost jumped off the wall in fright. "Good grief, man, pull yourself together. I'm on your side."

It felt like a microcosm of the endless arguments between kings then and there, all of them jumping and shadows and running away from one another as I desperately tried to convince them that we were all in this together.

It takes a great deal to surprise me, given my long tenure in this mortal coil and the varied experiences held within that tenure, but Sabrinia certainly succeeded in startling me a little when she appeared out of nowhere. Literally nowhere; she had been a puff of gases but a moment before.

"Wait," she said, panting for breath with lungs that had until a moment before been composed of mostly breath. "Wait a moment, before you begin."

I did as requested, waiting a moment. It only seemed fair, given that I'd just wasted infinitely more time on far less helpful people.

"Balthazagar said . . ." She panted. "That you didn't get to rest."

"Well, no. Sadly the affairs of state kept me occupied through such time as I would have devoted to . . ."

"Then you . . . should take a nap." She finally managed to get her lungs convinced that they were solid again.

"Thank you for your consideration, but I don't really have time to spare." I turned to face out towards Nun-Mhorgoth and its armies.

She caught me by the sleeve. "I do."

I raised a querulous eyebrow. She certainly couldn't have been proposing to take my place in countering the alleged dark god's magic. Talented as she may have been, she wasn't my match, or its.

"I can give you eight hours, in a minute." Now that she had her breath, she managed something vaguely resembling a smile. As if she'd only read about them. "Just like my time fold on the wall, but backwards."

"Then let us find a bed with all haste!" I declared a little too loudly, drawing snickering from the nearby guards, along with some mutters regarding predatory age gaps, workplace sexual harassment, and questions about the potency of the elderly.

"So that I can sleep!" I added, awkwardly.

True to her word, I got my eight hours, though in truth I probably only slept half of them. It was a disconcerting thing, to see Sabrinia staring down at me and Ig in my borrowed guardsman's bed, moving in slow motion so extreme that even a blink took minutes. Not to mention the overwhelming stress of knowing that as soon as I rose, I would be facing off with a creature that described itself as a god with some pretty substantial evidence in its favor. I tossed and turned, not helped by Sabrinia staring at me or Ig's little feet kicking as he dreamed of being chased by things considerably larger than him, which is to say, most things. Yet despite these indignities and discomforts, I woke an hour or a minute later—depending on your perspective—with a spring in my step and the aches of the day before abated.

"My thanks to you. You have done more for me, and humanity, than you can ever know." I said as I passed her by, carefully not patting her on the back as I would have done Danyeel. I didn't need the hassle from HR after my bumbling up on the wall.

And so at last I came once more to look out on the armies of the dark one, my mind still filled with thoughts of the ticking clock, counting down until all of our wards and magics came apart. Ig gave me a nod, and I began.

The overwhelming power. The overwhelming vastness of the strokes with which Nun-Mhorgoth painted magic. It seemed insurmountable when first I laid my eyes, and other more arcane senses, upon it. Yet I knew that this tide of power could be stemmed, disrupted, and turned aside, for I had already done it once.

I raised my hands and I cast.

What followed, I shall not recount here, for just grasping the complexities of the spells being cast, countered, and unraveled would render the sanest quite the opposite. We struggled and strained against one another. His techniques becoming more refined as he learned from his mistakes, my counters becoming more precise and effective as I learned from mine. He mimicked my magic at every turn, using the knowledge that he plucked from me as a hat like a scalpel to slice at the delicate threads of my art, but seeing things through his eyes, observing how he used his magic taught me new ways of thinking. He had been thinking in the same way for millennia, and once I learned how he did it, I thought better. Thinking was my area of expertise, after all.

From the outside it would have appeared nothing was happening at all. Just an old man in a pointy hat waving his hands around and staring off into the falling night. Even those blessed with a sight for the arcane could have taken a lifetime to decipher the complex game we played.

Our battle for the destruction or preservation of the Great Wall raged like a storm so vast it could encompass the world.

The sun went down.

The sun rose.

Ig was there by my side through it all. Clambering onto a wooden crate to press a waterskin to my parched lips in between incantations. Carefully positioning a seat behind me so that when my legs gave out, I did not fall to the ground. Time lost all meaning to me. All that I knew was the gentle ebb and flow of the magic around me. The press of the tide coming in, the release as I drove it back. I was lost in it. My mind, my wonderful mind, entirely turned over from rational thought to action, reaction, contraction, revulsion. I would have gone on forever, if I had the strength in my body that I had in my will, but slowly, steadily the darkness all around me crept in closer and closer. I ignored it when I could, shoved it back when I couldn't.

I would not be defeated. I would not be afraid. I would not show weakness to this pitiless thing.

When I finally passed out, I had no recollection afterwards of the precise moment. It was the same as any of the others of our endless stalemate. Our endless game with no winner.

It would not be until much later, when I was stirred from my slumber in that same guard's bed where I had taken my last nap, that I would be shaken back to life with the realization that I had been fighting on only in my dreams.

It would not be until later still when I emerged blinking and bleary into the dim sunlight and learn that I had fought on for more than twenty hours before my body gave out.

Not too shabby for an old man, eh?

I will admit that Ig had to help me a little with the stairs. Apparently, I had only been entirely insensible for a matter of some four or five hours, leaving us with the vast majority of Poindextrous's prediction, some fourteen hours, for us still to go before the wall fell, and with it all hope of survival.

"You do good," Ig informed me, as I looked out at the enemy stretched as far as the horizon. They were legion, but we had something that they did not.

We had a kobold with an upbeat attitude. Surely that would be enough to carry the day in defiance of all odds.

I spat over the edge of the wall in defiance of the inevitable doom lurking beyond, and then we headed back to the beautiful Arpanpholigon, while it still stood.

CHAPTER 13

CRY HAVOC

The tenuous alliance of humanity was gathered in the city, presided over by the hovering porthole portals through which their rulers viewed their comings and goings in comfort. The dicks.

The closest that we came to aristocracy among those who had been dispatched to our aid were those knights and cataphracts who were entirely delusional about their importance in the grand scheme of things. At least a solid half of those were not yet old enough to grow whiskers, yet they talked of the great feats of prowess they would soon display on the battlefield with the vigor of battle-hardened veterans. Mostly those battle-hardened veterans who had suffered heavy blows to the head.

The subtle hint that none of the gathered knights and miscellanea were actually important members of their respective courts was the fact that they were here. Fodder for the meat grinder.

The king of Arpanpholigon sat amidst them all upon his throne, surrounded by knight protectors that were positively bristling with armaments in case any of these pompous oafs happened to be assassins putting on a very well-executed performance. Not that it would matter much, as any assassination attempt would likely dissolve the tenuous alliance we'd cobbled together rather rapidly, whether it succeeded or failed, and then we would all be corpses anyway. He gestured at me imperiously on my arrival.

Proving once again just how much I had grown as a person in the past few months, I elected not to gesture back. Instead I waded my way through the sycophants and fools, most of whom politely parted before my approach quite sensibly, though a few treated me instead to some bullying leers. If you are a man with a long beard and what is essentially a dress on, you come to expect some degree of this from people who don't quite grasp exactly how many pieces you could turn them into with a single word.

Amidst the leerers was one gentleman—and I use the term loosely—who I suspect was a bastard child of the sultan of Frogaria. He looked me up and down slowly. "This is the wizard who snaps his fingers and expects us all to come running?"

I had a fair few short words that I would have liked to say to him then. Few of them in Archaic. I resisted, and I graced him with a bow. "It is a pleasure to make your acquaintance, oh Prince of the Blood."

It was exquisitely polite if he were in fact a legitimate son of the sultan and a crushing ego blow if he was not. Either way, he was flabbergasted into silence, and I sidled on by to deal with the member of royalty that I was in fact obliged to speak to.

"Your Grace, thank you for all that you have accomplished here in so short a time." Flattery was always a good plan with these people.

From at my heels, Ig peeked out from behind my skirts and said, "Hi."

"It was for the most part the work of your servants, old friend," the king said from behind a hedgehog of polearms. Spoken loudly enough that everyone could hear that he was friends with the archmage, who despite matters of blood and lineage was still somehow in command.

"Then I am most pleased that my associates could be of help to you," I said, carefully sidestepping the word *servants*. If I started calling the faculty my servants, that would be another uncomfortable conversation with HR.

"From those same servants, I have come to understand that the Great Wall has been reinforced with powerful magics and you have ordered a full clearance of all the lands between here and there." There was a little bit of an edge when he said the word "ordered," as if I had somehow overstepped my bounds by moving the average working man out of a field where he was liable to die messily and into a city where he was at least moderately less likely to die messily. "We have of course offered all due comfort to those poor refugees."

They were all over the place, clogging up the roads, shoved up against the walls so that the various armies that were also squeezed into the city could fit. There was perhaps one blanket to share between a dozen or so of them for when night fell and they discovered that as welcoming as the people of Arpanpholigon could be, that welcome ended at their own front doors. Such rooming houses as the city possessed were packed beyond bursting, and I'd heard through the grapevine that Maximus Arturo had received requests from several of the more well-informed doss-houses to perform some dimensional manipulation so that they could cram some more bodies in, sardine-style.

It was still better than the requests that one of my myriad secretaries had passed along to me from the royal family requesting that we opened up the Invisible College itself as a hall of rest for these charming country bumpkins. A request that I had politely lost amidst the piles of paperwork that had accrued on my desk in my absence.

By now I am sure you know all too well what a soft heart I have developed, but there were limits to my kindness, and one of those limits was sanity. It would be all very well letting these farmers and their children into the college, but there would be no stopping them from roaming and touching things, the way that the uneducated and the young do. Something which would invariably result in some experiment or another being disrupted at a crucial point and the whole place exploding.

Better that they slept on the streets below the shelter of the hovering college than were splattered across them in a maelstrom of rubble.

The king pressed on when I gave no immediate answer to his blatant lie. "So now we must turn to the rather more troubling news that your servants conveyed. That the Great Wall, raised so many generations ago by our respective forebears, is on the verge of destruction."

While it was clear that my "servants" had conveyed some of the situation to the king, it was also apparent that they hadn't mentioned the alleged god of darkness in our enemy's midst. Presumably as a means of avoiding the harm to morale that would result from hearing that we were matching our mortal strength against divinity. I too would have to tread carefully, to make him understand some portion of the danger that Nun-Mhorgoth represented without entirely cutting out his heart and hope.

"There is a leader among the assembly of monsters, Your Grace. One who is extremely powerful in the ways of the arcane. As we speak, it works to disassemble all of the spells that we have laid to block the path of the invasion."

"It big bad," Ig affirmed.

I couldn't see the king, but I had a suspicion that he had just raised an eyebrow. "And you mean to allow this?"

"With respect, Your Grace, once it has unbound our wards once, it will be far less difficult for it to do so again. Repeating the process of layering on protections is liable to buy us only moments instead of hours." It was a gross simplification of the situation, of course. Once Nun-Mhorgoth had dissembled all of our magics and unwritten the fundamental laws that they stood upon, there would have been no more point in defending the wall. It would no longer function as a wall. No longer be a barrier. Simply a lump of rock that he could cast aside as easily as sweeping a table clean.

The king scoffed in disdain. This conversation was not going well. "So you will let the Great Wall fall instead of defending it?"

"It has served its purpose well, both through the centuries and on this day. It has held back the enemy for long enough for us to assemble a grand alliance of all the free people to fight back against the invaders." There, that should have satisfied him. The wall did its job, we were ready to fight back. He should have taken some comfort in that.

"But surely the best defensive position to engage our foe would be . . ."

I cut him off more or less accidentally, entirely too accustomed to talking to people who didn't think they were my better. "In terms of the craft of war, I have no doubt. But it is not a clash of warriors alone that will settle this matter. To linger on the wall when its more arcane protections have been stripped away would be folly. Why, there is not a student in the college above that could not level that wall given a little time to plan."

Cutting him off mid-sentence was a mistake. I realized that as soon as I'd done it. He was already spoiling for a fight with all these foreign dignitaries prodding at him, and I'd just painted a target on myself.

There was a low heat in his voice as he gave me my orders. "Then perhaps it is time to turn your students loose. For you and your servants to sally forth and demonstrate these incredible destructive powers that you speak of so casually."

"Your Grace . . ." This was the trouble with talking to people who thought that they were clever. They hear about magic and think that it can solve any problem, then they present their problem and an assumed solution to you. "It would result in much the same outcome as if we simply gave ground to the enemy. The utter annihilation of all the lands betwixt here and the wall. Our powers of destruction are truly as great as you have doubtless heard us brag, and were it not for our adversary's ability to unravel our spells, then I have no doubt we could wipe all of the gathered enemies away in one fell swoop. But there would be little left of the land you know and love when we were done. It would be naught but desolation so far as the eye could see. No more farms, no more food. No more Arpanpholigon."

"Surely your students could simply conjure us food." Once more, the problem of magic in the hands of the uneducated arose. Of course we could feed everyone forever, that was what magic did, right? It solved problems without any cost.

"In the short term, they most assuredly could. But it would be a stop-gap measure at best. Humanity cannot live on magic alone. With time, the quality of our conjurings would degrade as a result of endless repetition of the same magics in the same space. It would slow the city's decline, but it would not stop it." I tried to give him some more assurance that we were on the same side. "I do not mean to win the fight today if it costs us all our future."

"So you wouldn't help us?" There was some subtle venom to that, presenting the second half of the problem of magic in the hands of the uneducated. Once you believe that someone has the solution to all of your problems, you come to also believe that every time your whims are not fulfilled to the letter, you believe that your prize is being withheld out of malice.

"I am helping you now, Your Grace." I spoke softly now, hoping against hope that we could move past this poisonous line of thinking. "I am helping you to avoid a terrible mistake."

"Would you rather see Arpanpholigon fall than risk some dirt-farmer's mud patch?" He was shouting now. Trying to stand up, but still invisible behind the huddle of bodyguards. Including the happily married Lhoin and Racha, I noticed.

That had put me on the spot a little. This sort of thing was why I tried to avoid politics. When wizards come down from our castles in the sky and interfere with matters on the ground, it always ends in recriminations. If I had not spoken up against the wild use of magic of mass destruction, then it would have come later, when the king realized all that he had sacrificed for his victory. Instead it was now.

"Did you know that everything you know about how magic works could be inscribed on the head of a pin? That your knowledge across the full breadth of human experience is as narrow as the width of that same pin? A pin that is nonetheless markedly larger than your withered genitalia. Did you know that my contempt for you is so complete that I didn't even learn your name until a few days ago despite allegedly living under your rule? Have you considered that you are a complete cretin who only sits on that fancy chair because somewhere down in the roots of your family tree there was some deranged half-starved barbarian who slaughtered friends, family, and everyone else that they met with such vigor that the only way to get them to stop was for the entire human race to collectively say uncle and give them a shiny hat? Are you aware that inbreeding throughout countless generations has rendered said family tree into more of a wreath? Did you know that with a fraction of the power at my disposal, I could reach out and pluck your whole nervous system from your body, then submerge it in electrified vinegar until I've wrung the very last spark of agony from you? Were you aware of that? Of course you were not aware of any of that, because to be aware one must be sapient, and all that you are is an animate mass of meat that someone mistook for a person. Afterbirth crowned." Is what I would have said, if I wasn't so polite and good at politics.

"In this, as in all things, I am yours to command, Your Grace." Is what I said instead.

This personal growth thing is absolutely terrible, I cannot recommend it, I would have had infinitely more fun tearing this moron a new one, but here I was kowtowing to him as if convincing a bunch of other idiots that you are in charge was real power.

"Then listen to my command and obey. I want you to go out there and drive the enemies off!" He was shouting once more, despite me rolling over like a good little lapdog. It was quite frustrating how emotionally incontinent this raving man-child actually was, given that we were meant to trust him to govern a nation.

I didn't even struggle to unclench my jaw to say, "As you wish, Your Grace."

Turning on my heel, I departed from the Grand Hall with all haste, and this time the staring and snickering of the dignitaries felt more deserved. Here was some fool so bad at making nice with his own king that he had been condemned to face a whole army alone. Quite deserving of mockery, I suppose.

We broke out into the night air, still moving apace, and Ig caught me by the sleeve. "What we do? We no can magic all monsters! If take all wizards then land go boog!"

"Boog?" I halted my stride for just a moment.

"Boom argh," he elaborated, and I gave a nod of concession. Boog indeed.

"You're quite correct, of course. But you will note that our last command from the sovereign was not to marshal our forces and cause an arcane cataclysm, but to go out and fight ourselves." I laid a hand upon Ig's shoulder. "Or rather, myself. I shall not take you into danger, my friend. You have suffered enough for one lifetime."

Without a moment's hesitation, Ig replied, "Me come with."

I brought myself down into a crouch so that we were eye to eye, even though my knees truly did not appreciate it. "Ig, it is going to be very frightening."

He stared right back at me. "Me is fright everywhere. Me rather be fright with you."

Distressingly, that was the nicest thing that anyone had ever said to me. I drew the little fellow into a brief hug, then used him to drag myself back up to my feet. "Then let us show the world what we are truly capable of."

There were some matters that I needed to attend to first so we made a jaunt up to my office in the college. It was in a state of disarray not dissimilar to when we had an all-out magical brawl in the place, though not, this time, as a result of conflict, but rather as a result of my having settled in to come up with ideas to save us all from certain death for an hour or so earlier in the day before being summoned to attend the king yet again. A brainstorm had swept through.

I settled at my desk for a moment and looked down at all the myriad plans I had outlined in the frenzy of activity. There were twenty-five of them in all, once they had been collated, and after arranging them in order of desperation, I labeled them with the letters A through Y.

Should I fall in battle, then at least some portion of them could be enacted by my faculty and friends with a possibility of increasing their survival, and should I manage to not die in the coming hours, then they could be enacted in my absence at various stages to better increase our chances of success in this whole endeavor. I affixed a note atop the pile to that effect, and then went to one of the various hidden chambers adjoining this one to gather up all the magical artifacts that I had available to me.

Some of them would serve no real purpose in combat, and these I loaded onto my loyal pack-kobold, just in case. I also equipped him with as many pieces of jewelry with protective enchantments and wards as I could, until he jangled with every step. I briefly contemplated whether we had time to get him some body piercings so that we could fit more magic rings on him, then decided that I would rather not experience the noises that he made during that process. For myself, I slipped on twenty separate magic rings of varying potency, even though the ones on my toes were causing me a great deal of discomfort. For the briefest of moments I examined those that remained in storage and contemplated my nipples.

Better not.

Enchanted rings tended to activate only when worn, and I couldn't say with certainty if I would have been wearing them or them me if I went through with some reckless body modification. I could, of course, grow more fingers onto each of my hands, but I worried it would interfere with my concentration. Better to just go with what I had.

When it came to magical belts, however, I went whole hog. Some cinched in my robes at the waist, some became bandoliers that I would use to hold my various wands and staves. A few, clearly designed for gnomes and their kin, became garters under my robes. Finally, looking like some hideous hybrid cross between a fetish model, elderly librarian, and action hero, I tramped back through my office and out into the hall.

Where I was confronted by an assembly composing the entire Council of the Wise, standing with their arms crossed, blocking my path.

"Ah."

"You cannot go," Iomedania announced. "It is reckless."

"Is reckless," Ig agreed, nodding. Treacherous little toad.

"Reckless or not, it is as I have been commanded to go forth by our king."

Ig now turned to Iomedania, nodding. "Is true. Commandered."

"Oh bugger the king and all his horses too." Balthazagar appeared surprisingly incensed. "You're too important to squander like this."

Ig looked back to me. "Big impotent."

I ignored all of them and pushed on. "I have prepared instructions for all of you, labeled in order. Some, you may have to discard as matters progress, others will become viable only if things go according to my predictions. Please enact them to the best of your ability."

Copernicrust spoke up next. "Um, actually, you don't get to throw your life away and leave us to deal with this mess."

Ig pointed at the old man as though he were making a particularly salient point. "Is messy mess."

"My friends . . ." That was a stretch too far. "Well . . . coworkers . . . you do not need to fear. I have faith in the abilities of each and every one of you in the face of this adversity. What have we studied all our lives and trained for if not a situation just so dire as this one?"

"Why do study?" Ig asked them all, presumably attempting to back me up but seeming more like a gibbering buffoon with each passing second.

"I mostly studied because if I didn't, I thought you'd yell at me," Danyeel replied, entirely too honestly.

"Do be shouty looking," Ig pointed out.

Once again, I ignored them all to push on. "You are the most powerful and learned wizards in the world, perhaps in all of history. This army that we face is nothing to the likes of you."

"It isn't the army we're wuh-worried about," Poindextrous replied. "It's Nuh-Nun-Muh-Mhorgoth."

I think that I liked him better when he was drunk on power and on the verge of deranged.

Philodephina was the next to speak, with considerably more eloquence than those that came before her. "The fact of the matter is that none of us can match the . . . creature. None of us but you. If you throw your life away, then you leave us all at its mercy. As the greatest living wizard, you are a bulwark against such nightmares. As the greatest dead wizard, you will be naught but a memory, forgotten all too soon."

She was doing her damnedest to convince me not to go, which truly came as a surprise. I would have thought she'd be happy to be rid of me, given our history. Perhaps that was why she'd been elected by the group to say that particular piece. To add more weight to it.

To give her yet more credibility, Ig added, "Dead be bad."

It wasn't entirely clear why he had become so needlessly vocal, but I had to hope it was something that one of the myriad enchanted pieces of equipment strapped to him was doing, otherwise it would continue after he had shucked it all off.

I forced what I hoped was a smile rather than a grimace onto my face. "Would it please you to know that I have no intentions of dying?"

A sea of angry frowns met my timid smile. Archimendo grumbled, "Nobody intends on dying."

"Um, actually . . ." Copernicrust began before all of the angry frowns turned on him and he shut the heck up.

Balthazagar took another swing at things. "What the king has to say does not matter. We are the ones who hold true power over Arpanpholigon; we could depose him in an instant. You do not need to do this."

"Not need," Ig concurred, switching sides for what felt like the hundredth time in this one conversation.

"Nonetheless." I took a deep breath and squared my shoulders. "I mean to."

"But why?!" Sabrinia shocked us all with her sudden outburst. Usually so stoic, it seemed that her icy demeanor was finally melting.

"If I can put an end to this without anyone else being hurt, or put at risk, then that is what I mean to do." I met her gaze and was mystified to see that there were tears in her eyes. "I could not live with myself if I didn't try."

"Got try," Ig agreed, patting me on the back. Though I could scarcely feel the impact through all the belts.

"Then wuh-we all go with you," Poindextrous announced, surprising everyone at his sudden bravery after a lifetime of being a wilting flower.

The rest of them may not have wanted me to go, but they certainly hadn't been volunteering to come along. Poindextrous was receiving some very serious glares, and the others had all found extremely interesting bits of carpet to look at.

"Um, actually . . ." Copernicrust began.

"You all have far greater roles to play in all of this. I beg of you, please proceed to my office, examine the plans that I have outlined, and begin to enact them. If I fail to stop Nun-Mhorgoth alone, then we shall be reliant upon them to succeed." I only realized afterwards what a supreme act of ego it was, assuming that none of them had any plans of their own. That I was the only one capable of rational thought. Of course, all of my plans did happen to be better than anything they could have come up with, but that was neither here nor there.

I stepped out of the doorway of my office and ushered them in. Clearly thinking that our conversation was going to continue inside, they all proceeded in, and didn't even notice my absence until I carefully closed the doors behind them.

"Ready, Ig?"

Once more, the kobold nodded. "Me ready."

I prepared myself to cast, and then paused. "And you definitely don't need the bathroom before we go?"

His eyes briefly crossed as he concentrated. When they uncrossed again, I had my answer. "No need go."

Smiling, I began to ready my spell, then paused once more. "You're sure?"

"Me sure." Ig nodded.

I leaned in a little closer to ask again, so as not to embarrass him. "Because last time, you said you were sure and then . . ."

The wizards in my office had discovered my deception and started banging on the door trying to get out.

"Ah . . . never mind."

With a word of Archaic, we exploded apart into nitrogen and the wind carried us off.

CHAPTER 14

AND LET SLIP THE KOBOLD OF WAR

On arrival at the Great Wall, we found it to be quite different from the last time that we had attended. Now aware of the inevitability of its fall, all of the brave knights who had shown up to defend it had buggered off back home, leaving the poor guards in attendance to try and tidy up all the mess they'd left behind. Each guardsman was strolling along the ramparts with a burlap sack, gathering up discarded oddments and trash.

The magic maintaining the barrier was on the verge of collapse, evaporating around us into its component elements and drifting off in vast colored clouds that spontaneously imploded every so often. The reality of the wall was the only thing that had remained relatively untouched. Cygni and Poindextrous had done such good work on it that even Nun-Mhorgoth had not been able to scratch it yet. It hovered somewhere about 90 percent real, which was still a good deal realer than everything around it, and this was despite everything that had happened in the past couple of days. On spotting me, the guardsmen all came running, abandoning their sacks where they stood.

"Is it true the wall's coming down?" one had the courage to ask.

I couldn't keep the exasperation out of my voice. "Why haven't you all been evacuated back to the city yet?"

"Nobody told us to!" He replied with surprising courage for a man who could so easily become a newt.

"Nobody tell," Ig repeated in case I'd missed it.

I rolled my eyes at this latest idiocy. "If nobody had told you not to jump off the top of the wall, would you have thrown yourself off, bodily, at the first opportunity? When you saw everyone else in the whole country fleeing for safety, did it at no point occur to you that perhaps you ought to be heading in the same direction?"

"No jumpy," Ig noted.

"Yes, thank you," I said to him with barely restrained irritation.

"You welcome." The little turd bobbed up and down happily at my side.

Turning back to the rather disgruntled-looking guards, I realized that they were still waiting to be told they could leave. "Oh for the love of . . ." I raised my arms in the air like I was trying to startle a bear and yelled, "Fly, you fools!"

They did depart then, but not at the sort of pace that they really should have. They had to take their time getting their belongings and grumbling about how rude I was.

"Oh, do forgive me for saving all your lives," I yelled after them. "It won't happen again!"

With a sigh, I turned back to Ig. Finally, we were ready to begin.

I took my time ascending the stairs to the ramparts, letting my senses snake out and sample everything that was happening around me. The barriers were thinning now, paper thin, really. A concerted enough attack right then and there would break through despite all that we'd done to prevent it.

At the top of the wall, I looked out and immediately regretted it. The numbers of the monstrous army hadn't grown since I last looked, but that was probably because I couldn't actually see its back ranks because of how far it stretched off. The segments that had been filled with vampires had now definitely been refilled with other creatures, and while the petrified trolls were still scattered around the field, some enterprising orcs and goblins seemed to be using them as watchtowers now.

Wherever Nun-Mhorgoth was in all of those heaving masses of bodies, I could not say, but his presence could be felt everywhere. The insidious press of his will and his power. It didn't matter. He couldn't stop what I was about to do any more than I could stop him unraveling the wards on the wall.

With great care, I channeled oxygen, nitrogen, argon, and traces of dozens of other elements to weave together a great construct of air, which I carefully fitted to my mouth.

"Hello!"

The sound of my voice was sufficiently loud to knock Ig off his feet, even though he had been forewarned. His hands remained flat over the sides of his head where any decent species would put their ears.

Alright, the voice amplification spell worked. It was time to begin.

PLAN A: Make Peace

"Greetings to you, assembled peoples of the Badlands. My name is Absalom Scryne, and I am the Archmage of Arpanpholigon, Master of All Magics, and representative of all the folk of the civilized lands."

There were some sparse boos from the crowd, but for the most part they seemed to be listening. It was quite surprising really that they hadn't been conditioned to ignore my words; I'd have thought that Nun-Mhorgoth would have realized I was going to try this. He had, after all, read through a copy of my brain. Though perhaps the me that he had read was not so bold as the me of now.

"It is my understanding that you have some grievances with the civilized lands. You feel that we have created a monopoly on ease of living and magic. That you have been excluded and left to fend for yourselves." I paused for dramatic effect. "I am here to tell you that those grievances are entirely justified."

All of the booing had now ceased abruptly. Apparently, I had just got their attention.

"The people of civilization did not trust you. They called you monsters. Assumed the worst about you at every turn. With the raising of this Great Wall, they segregated you from us. And for that I am truly sorry. Because I know now that there are good people among you, just as there are bad people among the allegedly civilized. Beside me stands a creature that most would call a monster, and he is . . . he is the dearest friend I have ever known.

"So I extend this offer to you now. An offer of amnesty. If there are any among you who want all the benefits of being a part of civilization and do not wish to despoil and slaughter innocent people to get those benefits, I will now grant you entry into these lands. I will guarantee you safe passage, and assistance in building lives for yourselves on this side of the wall. I will personally see to it that each of you is comfortably integrated into the kind of life that I know you want. All that I ask in return is peace. No fighting with the other civilized peoples. No stealing, or wanton slaughter. You can live the rest of your lives without fear of violence, you can become whoever and whatever you want to become, and I will do everything in my power to help you. Everyone will."

Alright, that last part about everyone else in civilization being onboard with this plan may have been a slight exaggeration. In fact, I was fairly certain that back in my office, the faculty were currently reading the memo with Plan A on it and screaming that I was insane, but so long as I survived this day, I would always have the power to enforce my will on others, because that was, unfortunately, the nature of power. And this time, I would force them to see that they can live in peace and harmony with their neighbors. Even if said neighbors happen to be ogres.

"I know that you might fear being seen as a traitor if you step forward now. I know that you might fear reprisal from your kinfolk. So I offer you this. Simply stand where you are and think of peace. Dream of the life that you will have. This Great Wall which once divided us will now bring us together. It is the threshold to my home, and if you mean no harm, I welcome you in. The magic of the threshold will do the rest. Think now of peace, and you will come to be on my side of the wall!"

And now came the tricky bit. I dispelled the construct of air by cutting off its supply of Quintessence and turned to Ig. "Are you ready for this, my friend?"

Ig cracked his little neck from side to side, straightened out his crown and gave a curt nod. "Me is."

The wall had lost all of its protections by now and it was beginning to crumble as the integrity of even the stone was being eaten away, but that invisible sense of inside and outside still remained, reinforced by both Cygni and Archimendo's workings. The wall was about to cease being a solid object, but the fundamental nature of it was still a wall, a barrier, a threshold.

Lifting us off the wall on a platform of that crumbling stone to hover above it was a relatively simple bit of enchanting. Channeling Quintessence into Ig so that he could do what he needed to was going to be the hard bit.

Just as Ig had learned to do, I drew in more Quintessence, even as my reserves filled to bursting, letting the raw stuff of magic pour through me, down through my palm, and into him. The faster it flowed out of me, the faster I could draw it in, until there was a veritable vacuum in the spiritual core of me that started dragging the Quintessence from all around us in without me even consciously trying. All of the magic that had been dispelled, all the powdered remnants of the ancient spells that had held up for centuries, none of it had vanished. It was all still here, lingering in the charged air around us. I dragged it all in, and poured it into Ig, and with so much power overflowing from him that bunnies started spontaneously hopping into existence all around him, he held it for as long as he could.

Then, at last, in one great push, he let it out.

For a moment at least, the wall held. Then, all at once, it didn't. He pushed the whole wall as if it was a single object. Throwing raw Quintessence out into low magic. Something that everyone would have said was impossible before today.

The wall lurched forward, like a cart that had just lost its brake blocks, and as it moved out towards the legions of monsters, it began to pick up speed. The reality of it had already started fading away, and true to form, as Nun-Mhorgoth saw it speeding towards him and his minions, he pushed in harder with his magic to dissolve it into nothing all the quicker, but that only served our purposes all the better. Even as the rock faded into nothingness, that invisible barrier of the threshold went on.

Every monster that it hit was pushed back, knocked over, and sent tumbling away. The whole front rank of Nun-Mhorgoth's army was flung back. A great gouge was left all along the border of Arpanpholigon as the wall surged across it, slowly fading to only flattened grass as it lost its structural integrity.

With the last of our combined strength, and that ancient strength left behind by the wards of my ancestors, he shoved that wall until it swept off over the horizon and vanished. Taking with it all the enemies of Arpanpholigon and civilization before at last, somewhere far from sight, it finally came apart.

Ig flopped to the ground on our little hovering rock, and I was frankly amazed that he'd managed to push the wall as far as he had before running out of steam. Momentum may have carried it a fair distance, but he was the engine that had gotten the whole thing moving. I brought us slowly down towards the ground, gently as I could, then let the last remaining piece of the Great Wall crumble away to dust.

Looking out across the barren field we had made, it did not take long before I started to make out figures plodding towards us. Those monsters who had decided that they'd rather be friends than enemies. There were less of them than I had hoped, but more than I had expected. Ogres made up the greater part of their numbers—there were enough ogres to populate several small villages, in fact. The ones who'd had a taste of civilization in New Orc and decided that they needed more. Next came an absolute plethora of goblins. That I had expected. After seeing how badly they were picked upon by the other monstrous races, it was no surprise that a life of peace was appealing to them. If there had been kobolds among the armies of Nun-Mhorgoth I would have expected to see them in equal numbers, but of course, no dark lord worth their salt would have gone around recruiting kobolds. Some orcs came lumbering along too, a lot of them actually. No trolls, probably because we had inadvertently turned them all to rubble. Whoops.

Various were-beasts of different descriptions made their presence known, with most of them shapeshifting back into human forms that made their decision to live among humans considerably more understandable. Beyond that, when we were getting into the more extravagantly monstrous kinds of monsters, I could count only a handful of each kind. Wyverns, the gryphohip, a few great shaggy beasts that I suspect were lamassu. One dragon, who was probably in his late second century, which is to say the dragon equivalent of a teen. He had painted his claws black and had some smaller creatures inscribe a skull tattoo on his wing. He would probably regret that in a millennium or two.

"Greetings to you, my new friends and neighbors," I announced to the gathered crowd after a half hour or so. "To my immediate left you will see a very tired little kobold. He is going to guide you back to the city of Arpanpholigon, where you will be greeted by my coworkers from the Invisible College. They will see to it that you are sequestered away somewhere safe until the current crisis is over, and then we can get to work on building your exciting new lives."

The dragon raised a claw. "Excuse me."

"Yes?"

"Will there be gold in the city?"

This did not seem like a safe line of questioning. "I believe that there is some gold within the city, yes."

The dragon nodded. "And will you be offering economics lessons?"

I wet my lips, still completely flatfooted. "Uh, I believe that we can probably arrange for you to take some classes if you desire . . ."

The dragon nodded again, more firmly this time. "And will I be able to become a stockbroker and make gold appear out of nothing?"

My mouth flapped open and shut a few times before my brain caught up. "I believe that you will fit in very well within the banking sector."

One final firm nod and the dragon spread its wings, readying itself for takeoff.

"Just a moment!" I called to it, before it could launch.

The dragon cocked its head to one side. "Hmm?"

"I wonder if you might do me a little favor. In a short while, Nun-Mhorgoth and his invaders will be arriving here, and I would prefer to know that everyone present is safe and accounted for behind the safety of Arpanpholigon's walls. Do you suppose that you and the wyverns might be able to give them a lift?"

A brief period of haggling ensued and after what felt like entirely too long, we settled on a fixed fare to be paid from my own bank account for each monster transported in such a manner, with the dragon then proceeding to hash out the details of how little he was going to be paying each of the wyvern that were now going to be in his employ in Draconic. I take back all that I said about it being a teenager. This was a go-getter if ever I saw one. No more than half an hour in the country and he had already founded our first flying taxi service and employed a handful of other immigrants to do all his dirty work. Truly living the Arpanpholigon Dream.

With a well-placed slap or two, Ig was roused from his stupor and loaded onto the back of the dragon alongside the orcs, who helpfully held on to him when he realized what was going on and tried to escape back to my side. "I shall be seeing you soon, my dear friend."

"Me no need go!" Ig cried out. "Me no need go!"

"Well that's good," I reassured him. "It is a short flight, but it doesn't look like there are any bathrooms on board."

With that, the new taxis took off and I was left truly alone for the first time.

I turned to look at the distant horizon and the dark mass that was already on its way across it. All of the monsters that had survived being slapped in the face with a giant wall. All of the monsters, minus the ones that didn't actually want to be slaughtering innocent people. All of the monsters of the Badlands, considered by some to be the homeland of all monsters. All charging at me.

Marvelous. Just how I wanted my day to go.

There was something that I had not admitted when justifying myself to the faculty of the college. Something that I had barely admitted to myself. I felt guilty. Cygni may have been the one to physically unleash the dark probably-not-a-god from its stasis beneath the earth, but if I'd thought just a little faster I could have prevented it. All of this fighting, all of the misery it was sure to bring, it was because of me. I'd failed, and now all of civilization was going to pay the price for it.

This was an opportunity to fix that mistake. I didn't much care if it killed me, so long as Nun-Mhorgoth died first. I wouldn't care so long as I knew that Ig and Cygni and Ildrit were all safe, not to mention all the people in Arpanpholigon and the lands beyond, and now these monsters who had shucked off such a title and stepped forward with good faith to start over as people. Gosh, there were a lot of people relying on me.

No pressure, old man. No pressure.

It was my own voice but speaking into my head. My offboard brain that I'd more or less entirely forgotten about.

"I work best under pressure," I declared to the empty field of battle.

Actually, you work best under absolutely no pressure other than your own drive to succeed, which is already crushing.

I corrected him. "That's still pressure."

Pressure that you generate for yourself isn't pressure, it is just . . . are you really arguing with yourself right now?

Backing down from an argument just proved that he wasn't the real Absalom Scryne, and I was. "It does seem that way."

So you will do literally anything other than engage with your feelings about having inadvertently unleashed a minor apocalypse on the world.

"Minor nothing." I bickered with the voice in my head, even knowing that it was me. "That . . . creature is going to wipe out everyone and everything we hold dear."

I am aware of that, I was there. I just meant that the actual world itself isn't going to be cracked open like an egg, now is it?

"Hmmph," was my terribly witty response.

Would you like to talk about your feelings?

"I would rather die, as you well know," I grumped.

Then would you like to engage in some entirely cathartic violence?

"You know what, me? I really would."

I drew all of the wands, staves, staffs, and the like from off my back where they had been making me sound like an off-kilter xylophone, and I stuck them into the fresh-turned earth all around me so that they would be easy to draw swiftly. How I would remember which was which in the middle of fighting was going to be the only trouble.

I can keep track for you, if you'd like?

"That would actually be incredibly helpful, thank you, me."

Quite alright, me.

With that done and my Quintessence reserves fully restored after the half hour since my last big exertion, I began casting my spells. Not one, or two, or even a dozen, but every spell of death and destruction that I could think of. Suspending each and every one of them in the air at the last moment, strolling along in a line and lining up my artillery to either side of my central position, where it bristled with sticks. Those spells that couldn't be trapped in the tiny time-folds I was making to be activated later because of their inherent instability, I kept going using my subconscious. Just as Ig did. I could recall every single one of them, and what elements need to be invoked when to activate them despite their being dozens upon dozens hanging around. Just as Cygni did. I could have been casting them one by one as I prepared them, but instead I meant to hold them back until my foes had closed the distance somewhat, so that they knew it was me doing it to them, and the very sight of me began to fill them with dread. Just as Ildrit would have done to wage psychological warfare on the enemy as well as the literal kind.

Everyone that I had been as a hat was a part of me now. All of the things that made them unique, made me even more unique. I was truly the most special little wizard in all the world. The greatest living wizard, in fact. Finally given the opportunity to prove it.

The were and dire animals, along with the larger quadruped monsters, loped ahead of the main force, using their four legs to great effect to outpace their dawdling upright-walking allies. This unfortunately meant that I was about to murder a significant number of creatures that Ig would have called "puppies." It was lucky that he wasn't here to see it.

Once they were close enough to see me, to know me, even by the dim light of the moon and stars, I lit the fuses on my spells and drew the first pair of wands from the dirt.

It was party time.

PLAN B: Make War

The charging mass of monsters in the lead fell. Some to lightning, some to acid, some to rays of rainbow light. Others burst apart on contact with the spell that had touched them, unwillingly transformed into some noxious chemical that would eat away at them and at the feet of anyone unfortunate enough to charge through them. Next came sweeping waves of invisible energies, a shimmer in the night that came upon them and simply robbed them of life. The front-runners took the worst of the punishment, wiped out of existence as though they had never been, but the were-beasts with their resistance to magic fared better. Admittedly, all of them would later develop cancer after being doused in so much radiation, but as devastating as that would be to them and their families, it didn't actually help me all that much in the short term.

One particularly fast were-badger closed on my position ahead of all the rest, triangulating in on the source of the barrage of spells that I was raining down on them all. It slipped and skidded over patches of ice, slime, and other fluids that I dared not attempt to name, slowing its wild sprint to more of a confused jog, but in spite of that it was still coming on. Coming for me.

I raised a pale white wooden wand—*Valantrine's Rod of Silent Thunder,* my other self helpfully informed me—and I cast the spell bound within.

The badger had been mid-leap when the magic struck him and launched him away. Not a short distance away either. It was as though some great boot had descended from the heavens and kicked him back over the curvature of the earth. It didn't matter if the magic itself didn't do the badger any harm; the landing most assuredly would.

If it had been Ig, he would have said something mind-numbingly stupid, like "this is my boom stick," but I had learned to keep the pithy one-liners to myself at this point.

A were-pangolin burst up from amidst the storm of magic. Its heavy hide had protected it from the worst of the ongoing artillery fire, barring a few acid streaks along its back. The tip of the staff in my off hand followed its motion. *Laon Cherie's Puckering Lancet,* I informed myself. The bright yellow beam shot clean through whatever protection the were-beast had against magic and through its soft pink underbelly too, leaving behind a fresh lemon scent and a gaping hole two feet across.

There was nothing then, but motion and light and magic. My hands, I gave over to the hat to control as more and more of the magic-resistant monsters broke through and required more direct attention. My mouth, my mind, I turned them instead to conjuring a small army of Phosgene Elementals that charged headlong at the enemy lines beneath the blinding streaks of my ongoing bombardment. They clubbed down the front-runners before dispersing into poisonous gas that choked out the next rank, leaving them gasping and frothing on the floor.

With the wands in my hands spent, the hat reached for the next pair. *Cochrane's Velocity Rapture,* and *Pukka's Profane Propagator,* he informed me as he brought them about.

My initial volley of spells was now all but spent with only a few still sputtering out fireballs along the line, here and there. I needed to cast something considerably more impressive to deal with the oncoming horde. By now the were-beasts were a dim memory. I was now faced with ogres for the most part, which made sense, what with them making up the vast majority of Nun-Mhorgoth's army.

This actually made things a lot easier. That magic immunity some of the were-creatures had was no longer in the equation. Now I could really cut loose.

My hat kept at work, blasting away with both wands in harmony, Velocity Rapture creating areas of super-accelerated air that shot out towards the enemy and Pukka's wand duplicating each of these effects dozens upon dozens of times. The second wand would invariably run out of Quintessence before the first, as it was soon duplicating its own duplicates, but by then who knew if there would even be any ogres left.

This once more left me to focus on more important matters, like a modified version of the Golden Flames of Galgalagrin, which would launch not a single bolt of unquenchable potassium flame at my foes, but instead a great band of it that should have eaten through the whole front rank of them. It cast far quicker than I could have anticipated, mere moments after I'd come up with the idea at all, and then it was made all the better by my two wands carrying segments of it off to strike at enemies farther back into the push of bodies and then multiplying the Golden Flames over and over and over again until the power within Pukka's wand was entirely spent and it crumbled to ashes in my palm.

One rank of ogres fell, then the next, and the next. Over and over the spell washed out towards them, and it was only on the ninth or so iteration that I realized I was no longer hearing the horrific screams as it consumed the ogres. By then the wand was gone, and I'd been casting my own versions on repeat.

With that odd quieting, I stilled my motions and silenced my own voice, listening so that I might understand what was happening beyond the veritable wall of fire that I'd created.

It was only then that I could see that the long line of fire had stopped dead, with the later castings only piling up against that first one. It was launched up into the air with a jerk on Nun-Mhorgoth's armored gauntlet. It had learned Ig's trick of grasping spells and moving them around.

This was less than ideal.

I fired off a few rounds of Velocity Rapture towards the towering black-clad alleged god, now lit from above by the golden halo of my spells. It did not even bother to counter them, letting each spike of accelerated air simply plink off its armor. Armor that I now realized was most likely enchanted, given how easily it could shrug off such attacks.

The mass charge towards me had stopped now. Nun-Mhorgoth strode forwards in its stead. Never hurried, never rushing. Calm as only the coolest water in the deepest of wells could be. Well, I was going to drop a rock down that well.

With a tug of low magic, I yanked a chunk of the broken Great Wall from out the dirt and fired Velocity Rapture at it. Instead of super-accelerating the air, this time the wand launched that rock at Nun-Mhorgoth.

It didn't even use magic. Simply reached up and caught the boulder twice its size in a single hand like it was a ball and we were playing catch, then casually tossed it away. "I got to tell you, kid, you put on one heck of a show, but its curtains for you now."

With a shaky breath, I calmed myself. "We do not need to fight, Nun-Mhorgoth. I have no quarrel with you. Nor need you press on for domination; a full half of the world lies empty by my wager. All of the Badlands is already yours. If you would settle for ruling just half the world instead of it all, we need not come into conflict."

"Scryne, baby, I don't know what to tell you. I ain't a glass-half-full kind of god. I'm more of the all or nothing kind. The total war, total domination, sum total. I want it all, and I want it now." It flexed the clawed gauntlet that it had used to catch the boulder. "And you made one other mistake too, kid. This ain't a fight. It was never going to be a fight. I'm a god, you're a teeny tiny little wrinkled bit of jerky. But cheer up. You can't spell slaughter, without a laugh!"

It didn't lunge at me this time with those pointy claws, instead casually casting a bolt of black flame with a flick of the wrist that sizzled and crackled its way across towards my chest, heading straight for my heart.

It could cast without speaking Archaic. That would make things somewhat more difficult.

Leaping aside clearly wasn't going to work, since the spell was targeting my heart. If it had been coming from a great distance away, I probably could have stilled my heartbeat and shaken it off my trail using a few different poisonous elements cycled briefly through my body. Without any sense of what elements were involved in the creation of the black flame dart, I could hardly counter it with a neutralizing counter-element, and without the Archaic component to identify what type of spell it was . . .

The hat was still in control of my hands, and while I was trying to come up with clever solutions, it simply acted, leveling Velocity Rapture with both my chest and the spell, and firing it off.

It caught the black bolt, launched it back along its own trajectory and smacked Nun-Mhorgoth directly in the face. I felt, very briefly, like Ig with a banana.

The force of the impact was enough to jerk the jerk's head back, and when it returned its level night-black stare to me, I could see that the whole side of the helm where its own spell had struck was sheared away. That would have made a real mess of me if it had struck home.

Incensed, the dark alleged god launched another bolt of blackfire at me, then another, a veritable barrage of spells, firing from both of its palms at a speed that I could not have even hoped to match with my own casting. Yet time after time, the hat guided my wand to blast them off course.

The first shot back along its own route towards Nun-Mhorgoth, who casually sidestepped it now that it knew what to expect. The bolt that had missed the dark one did not miss the unfortunate ogre standing behind it. Within an instant it was entirely consumed and sizzled abruptly out of existence.

My other return shots were not so lucky. Some did get struck, of course, and intercept with another monster that promptly died. Including a wyvern up in the sky above us at one point. But none came close to hitting Nun-Mhorgoth, and as his torrent of wicked little spells ran dry, so too did the wand's charge. It crumbled away to nothing in my grasp and I sighed.

It had taken both of my minds working in harmony to deflect all of those nasty little blasts, but now that the hat was no longer preoccupied with preventing my inevitable death, it reached out my hands and low magic to pluck a fresh pair of wands from the ground.

Things were about to get tricky.

Although Nun-Mhorgoth may have been somewhat lacking in the looks department, and moderately unimaginative in the way in which it applied its incredible power, after however many millennia it had been kicking around, it had definitely mastered consistency. Seeing no reason to stop doing exactly the same thing, just because it hadn't worked before, it raised both hands towards me and unleashed another stuttering rapid-fire torrent of blackfire bolts.

One of the many bracelets that I had jangling on my wrist contained a prepared spell for just such an occasion, so I willed a little Quintessence that way to activate it, while trying to come up with some better solution for the long term. A bubble rippled out from my wrist to encompass me, and where the blackfire struck it, instead of colliding, the curvature of reality was shifted just enough for the spells to slither around the side of me before blasting off into the dirt behind.

So it went with each consecutive bolt, though by the end, each was leaving a dark oily streak across my bubble that I began to worry indicated that it was decaying. Regardless, Nun-Mhorgoth's patience ran out long before my amulet did. The barrage came to a halt.

"Come on, kid, just let me hit you. It'll only hurt for a second," the still-in-sisted-that-it-was-a-god said with irritation in its voice. "It'll feel like an eternity of agony for you, but really, just a second, honest."

Whatever element it was invoking to create those bolts was not yet known to magical study, but that did not mean there was no counter to it. In fact, I had learned the perfect counter just the other day. As Nun-Mhorgoth had been unleashing torrents of lightless-fire and talking to itself, I'd been casting the same unraveling spell that I'd used to counter its presence at the wall over and over again.

My shield-bubble popped audibly, and the dark one launched two last great big blackfire balls at me, flung underhand with both hands like it was bowling down two lanes at once.

Time slowed to a crawl as the solid dark spheres of inevitable death flew towards me above the churned mud of the battlefield, but time need not have bothered, I was ready before Nun-Mhorgoth had even launched his big black balls at me.

My counterspell didn't try to touch the elements being invoked, it attacked the magic binding the whole thing together, the structure of woven Quintessence that made up the spell itself instead of the effect. With that done, the blackfire simply dissipated into puffs of smoke.

Time continued to move at a crawl. I could see the nearby ogres' expressions changing from the jeers of the victorious to the dismay of those who just saw their leader's balls disappear before their very eyes.

"Are you doing this?" I asked the hat version of myself.

I had assumed that it was your doing. You did have a very good look at Sabrinia's spellwork when she was putting us down for a nap.

"Hmm." Oh well, I wasn't one to look a gift horse in the mouth. As all my foes continued to move in slow motion, I turned on them with my wands and let loose.

Wands are, as a general rule, useless. They only work if you're already capable of performing magic, which somewhat defies the point of putting all the time and effort into acquiring a device that can do so for you. They are expensive and time-consuming to construct. Not to mention the inherent limitations of any enchanted object being that eventually whatever Quintessence you have stored in them runs out. Not to mention the negative effect that they have on your growth as a wizard. If you use a wand to cast, then you never learn the ins and outs of the spell being used itself, and as such you can never improve upon it. All in all, I could not recommend them for any situation.

Except for possibly if you are in an unfortunate situation with no time to cast spells.

I can't say exactly why so many wizards, when afforded the opportunity to craft a wand decide to imbue it with their most potent destructive magics rather than, say, a handy stain remover, but in this particular moment I was glad of it.

The spells from my wands rebounded hopelessly off Nun-Mhorgoth and, more specifically, its armor, but all of the creatures around it were unprotected. At least until the supposed dark god recognized what was happening and started countering me the same way that I'd just countered it.

As soon as it recognized that every spell I cast could be undone in the same manner as the clash over the Great Wall, I was entirely beyond saving. I would end up locked in a battle with Nun-Mhorgoth, pushing backwards and forwards, outwitting it, but never by enough to make progress, and all the while the various minions at his disposal could stroll over and hack me to bits.

The hat and the wands, working in harmony, were intended to prevent this sort of deadlock from immediately rendering me dead but I had a more than sneaking suspicion that they would be insufficient, as each wand would only get a single cast in Nun-Mhorgoth's direction before it learned how to counter that one's effect, and as vast a hoard of wands as I had bristling around me in the mud, they were not infinite. Not to mention the rather more pressing concern that nothing short of lobbing the whole Great Wall at Nun-Mhorgoth had done so much as scratch it thus far. And even the wall had been a temporary inconvenience.

The time dilation effect gave me a chance at least. A chance to unload everything that I had at Nun-Mhorgoth to see what stuck and to clear away enough of its allies that when the inevitable deadlock came, their morale might have been broken enough to preserve me from their tender ministrations.

My hopes were not high, but there was a reason that this had not been Plan A.

To be entirely clear, I was not sitting idle while my hat and hands did all of the work for me. I was in the midst of casting two very important spells simultaneously, using that kobold-style magic that everyone was so envious of.

The effects of the various wands that I worked through prior to the time dilation effect collapsing were as wide ranging as they were destructive. Some froze my foes in place and then shattered them with sonic booms. Others launched streams of acids and alkalis to eat through their flesh. All the various traditional elements were there too, tidal waves washing out, icicles shooting through, fireballs, so many fireballs, in all the colors of the rainbow. Lightning lanced out through them, illuminating nervous systems and skeletons in the brief moments it passed through. Ogre skulls are extremely thick, as it turns out, and they have more ribs than one might expect. It was a slaughter. The kind of thing that one might have nightmares about, if one were so inclined. I suspect that if I could have looked away, or closed my eyes against what I was doing, then I would have, but to aim, the hat needed to see. So I just did my best to focus on my spells instead.

Time snapped back into its normal alignment as the last of my wands dissolved in my hands. I had spent the entire lot of them in what must have amounted to no more than a few seconds of real time. A dilation as sharp as the eight hours in a minute that dear Sabrinia had granted me before.

"That was certainly efficient" was her only compliment to the abject annihilation before her, from somewhere behind my left ear. It had been obvious that she'd arrived on the wind, to me at least, ever since the hat had failed to take credit for that handy little spell that had saved our lives.

"I assume that you are invisible?" I asked as softly as I dared.

"Of course. Danyeel has us both covered."

"Just the two of you came?"

"Three of us," Danyeel amended, in my right ear. It was wise of them to stay close, to shelter behind the protections I would be casting for myself as much as possible.

"Who . . ." I began before being rudely interrupted.

"Absalom, baby, that was a neat trick. It won't help, I'm still going to gut you, and all that other fish stuff, but I might have to steal that one for later."

"You and what army?" I snipped back.

It did still have an army, of course. Even unloading the entire destructive arsenal of every wand that every previous archmage had gathered throughout the illustrious history of the college had not been quite sufficient to completely eliminate all of them. But, for now at least, that army was at a distance, driven back or simply wiped away by the awful violence, and to all appearances, I stood alone against Nun-Mhorgoth.

When its arms jerked forward this time, it was not a dart or a ball but a relentless stream of blackfire that was unleashed. An unstoppable blast of boiling death that I had no chance to stop.

CHAPTER 15

LONG DIVISION

But it did stop. It stopped dead, six feet away from me, not as though it had struck some obstruction, but as though it were some solid object that had simply become fixed in place.

Ig was here.

I had hoped that he would have stayed away, given the pretty clear send-off that I'd given him. But perhaps to a kobold it hadn't been clear enough, perhaps I should have outright told him, *I do not wish to see you harmed and I need for you to stay as far from the fighting as you can be.*

At least he was invisible for now, and whatever cleverness Danyeel had used to ensure that they were hidden from the eye had also extended to all other senses too. I could hear them when they spoke, because it was being deliberately projected beyond the illusion, but the natural sounds of their movement, their breathing, all obscured. Likewise, to my arcane senses, I was alone here, with the exception of the towering inferno of power that was Nun-Mhorgoth.

"Now how about that." Speak of the dark one . . . "That's a real neat trick too. You're just full of them. I might have to suck them all out of you before I'm done."

"At least buy him dinner first," Danyeel quipped in my ear, resulting in a snort in the other from Sabrinia. It seemed that she did have some sense of humor after all.

I maintained a straight face, of course. If whispered jibes had been sufficient to ruffle my feathers, I would never have made it to the celebrated title of Archmage. "Given the great many 'tricks' at my disposal, might you at least briefly acknowledge that there may be some value in communication rather than conflict?"

"Just when you were starting to get interesting, you go and spoil it." Nun-Mhorgoth's shoulders slumped, bringing down its spiky pauldrons for just a moment before it flung its arms up and unleashed another furious outburst of blackfire. To his credit, Ig caught every ball, blast dart, and sickle without hesitation, and with surprising aggression from a creature usually known to cower at the sound of a raised voice, he flung it all back at the dark alleged god in an equally impressive torrent.

Nun-Mhorgoth had fashioned this magic and knew the way that it had been woven far too well to be caught off guard again. Each spark of it sputtered and died long before it reached him. Still, it had been an impressive show of force that would have made any sane opponent rethink their strategy.

"Pretty neat, kid, pretty neat. But let's see how you handle this!"

It thrust out its gauntlet at me again, and I was ready for more of the same black fire. Ig was probably all set to catch it too. Though I hadn't yet heard a peep from him. But what came at me wasn't fire or death-rays or any other conjuration. What came at me was the gauntlet. It shot forward so fast that if you blinked, you'd miss it, and slapped me squarely across the face. All my trinkets and knickknacks had been designed to stop magic, not slapping. And while a regular slap would likely have hurt my ego more than my face, this was a solid metal gauntlet moving a little over the speed of sound.

Crack. I heard the impact long before I felt anything. I toppled over backwards, only failing to fall entirely thanks to the two wizards at my back catching me. It fouled Danyeel's spell and the pair came into view with a rippling of light. Even if the spell hadn't failed, they probably would have been visible to Nun-Mhorgoth now though, what with all my blood all over them. The pain showed up at about the same time that I reached up to touch my face where I'd been struck and realized that my whole lower jaw was dangling off to one side.

Oh, that isn't good.

I tried to say as much, and it came out as, "Oooo aaaa iiinn gooo."

With a single strike, Nun-Mhorgoth had robbed me of my ability to cast.

Its gauntlet had fallen after it struck me, but now it weaved its way back to its owner, still attached by the sinuous oily tentacle that was the dark god's true body-shape. It had been playing so well at being humanoid that I'd completely forgotten its true nature. Stupid.

And now I was entirely disarmed, the spells that I had been preparing still hung in helpless stasis, impossible to complete without the final words of Archaic and I could not speak at all.

Breathing hurt. Moving hurt. Near enough everything hurt. I may have experienced death in other bodies, but there was a unique unpleasantness to experiencing a maiming in my own. It was harder to shrug off and forget about.

"Iiiii," I tried to call out to my apprentice. "I eee iiii."

The two new Council of the Wise members looked at me, looked at one another, and then panicked. Starting to run, and dragging me along bodily behind them.

The jostling made my dislodged jaw waggle from side to side, and if I were not so incredibly disciplined and wise, I imagine that I would have been screaming all the way. As it was, my back arched and my toes curled as I tried to constrain the anguish gathered in my throat.

The helm-clad darkness that I'd been tricked into thinking was Nun-Mhorgoth's head tilted back and its laughter rolled out in peals. "Don't want to talk no more? What's the matter, baby? Cat got your tongue?"

In desperation, I pulled the hat from my head and tossed it awkwardly up at Sabrinia. She caught it, even though it meant dropping me, and looked back and forth between it and me in confusion. "Uuu iii ooon," I urged her.

She seemed to parse that just well enough to do as I asked, and then my hat-self immediately explained to her what I had been trying to communicate all along. She turned her head, now topped by the most fashionable item in her whole wardrobe. "Ig?"

"Bring him back over here, I ain't done with him yet," Nun-Mhorgoth called after us. "There's so many joints in a human body, I want to pop them all. Don't you want to see your old boss turned into spaghetti?"

Unlike these buffoons, Ig had maintained the good sense to remain hidden until now, or the cowardice, I suppose. So when he did cast aside the illusory shroud rendering him invisible, I was quite shocked to realize that he had been creeping across towards Nun-Mhorgoth the whole time, trying to get around behind him. What magic he meant to use on the dark one, I could not have guessed, though striking the creature with a banana was a novel approach, if not one that I'd have hoped would be successful. Regardless he'd covered most of the distance back to us with a capering scamper before the shroud broke.

"Oh gross, that's what an Ig looks like?"

I did not feel that a creature composed primarily of darkness and tentacles really had a leg to stand on when judging the physical appearance of others, but kobolds did seem to provoke that response in other species regardless of their own makeup.

"Kid, that thing looks like a wart that grew another wart. That thing looks like it fell out the ugly tree, missed every branch, and slammed face first into the ugly ground and all the ugly roots. If I was that thing, I'd kill myself just in case I ever met a mirror. If I was that ugly . . . well, I'm just glad I ain't that ugly is all I'm saying."

By now, I suspect Ig had heard enough commentary on his appearance to last a lifetime of therapy, and the new verbal assaults ran off him like water off a duck's back. He looked down at my broken face in unabashed horror once the distance had been closed. It must not have been a pretty sight. My chin and beard all askew.

With grasping hands I reached for the hat still atop Sabrinia, and with a heaving sigh of relief she parted from it. A moment later it was atop Ig, and

I could see the moment that my own intellect slipped into place behind his otherwise vacant eyes.

We did not waste time bandying words about. Ig's lipless muzzle was already in motion, whispering Archaic as I seized full control over his flesh. That was the one thing that Ig had going for him that none of the others I'd been worn by had: he was quite willing to completely absent himself and let me take over. With time the two of us had grown more and more alike, our minds working in similar ways, if not similar speeds. So as he rattled through oxygen, carbon, hydrogen, nitrogen, calcium, phosphorus, potassium, sulfur, sodium, chlorine, magnesium, fluorine, bromine, boron, silicon, vanadium, and nickel faster than any wizard in the world barring me could channel, I was unsurprised. He had become a smaller and less handsome me, at least for a moment. Giving himself over entirely to the hat, the way that I had surrendered control of my hands.

Reattaching my jaw would have taken time. It would have been a perilous exercise crossing the borders of medicine, surgery, and magic. Growing me a whole new one was much easier. It was the choice I would have made, given the rush that we were in.

Of course, that was a choice that was probably easier to make when one didn't have to experience what it felt like to have a jaw spontaneously grow out of your face, dislodging the old one and ripping it free. Which is to say, no matter how stalwart and strong willed one might be, there is always going to come a point when the pain is simply too much, and one must scream a little.

In my case, I screamed rather like a bleating lamb that had just had its whole jaw forcibly removed and regrown. But I retained control of my bowels, so I was counting it as a win. At my age, that's a win any day.

"That was incredibly unpleasant," I announced, rubbing at my shiny new chin, now devoid of the beard I'd spent decades growing.

"Terribly sorry," I replied from Ig's mouth. "But we are in something of a crunch for time."

I hauled myself free of the wizards, staggering to my feet to face Nun-Mhorgoth once more. With conscious effort, I raised my hand, and while the alleged god braced itself for an outburst of magic, I instead made a gesture towards it that was not in any way arcane but was good for starting a brawl. Then I finally hissed out the final words needed to complete one of the spells that my brainstem had been so kindly holding in stasis. "*Calcitrare asinum suum!*"

One of the most complex workings of magic ever committed burst into life, draining me to almost the last drop of Quintessence. It went beyond the mere elements that I had used to compose it, beyond even the more refined magic that my compatriots at the college had managed to manipulate time and space, this was purely conceptual magic, purely theoretical before I cast it that day. What I unleashed upon him tapped into those same ancient forces that had empowered the Great Wall's invisible threshold, that ensured the rising of the sun, that caused gravity to hold us down and the world to keep spinning. I cast a beam of highly refined and infinitely dense destruction at Nun-Mhorgoth and it shone as a solid beam of blinding light projecting from the none-too-arcane gesture I was making towards the supposed god.

The dark armored form was consumed in light. Behind him, still a half mile off by my wager, the armies of darkness that had been charging towards us now found a whole column of their troops absent. Everything that beam touched was not burned or electrified or frozen or washed away, it was quite simply made to no longer exist.

That spell was the culmination of all my life's work, everything that the college had been researching for lifetimes, a spell of such perfect purity of purpose that nothing could have stood against it.

When the light died and I was left standing there on legs like jelly, so too stood Nun-Mhorgoth.

It was not unharmed. Far from it. All of the layers of clever protection that it had surrounded itself with in terms of armor and magic and magical armor had been sheared away. The protruding tendrils of darkness that had expanded out in every direction from its central core the first time that I'd encountered it were all pruned back, until only the central, vaguely humanoid, mass remained. It swayed from the force of the impact, having to stick out the thicker trunk like tentacle that was its leg to stop itself from falling. But it was still alive.

Even after everything I'd done. It was still alive.

"Oh no." My words came as a breathless whisper, tickling my stalwartly remaining mustache.

PLAN C: Tactical Retreat

For a moment Nun-Mhorgoth simply stood there, then with an awful shrieking roar it exploded outwards. Tendrils of darkness lashing out and waving in every direction. "You little bitch!"

"I think it is time for us to regroup," I informed my compatriots, but on turning it appeared that both wizards had already taken off at a full sprint, and the only reason Ig wasn't halfway back to Arpanpholigon already was because he was too busy pissing himself in terror.

I snatched Ig up by the scruff and ran as fast as my geriatric hips would allow, which, when under threat from an eldritch beast that had now degenerated into cussing at me because it was so angry, turned out to be surprisingly quickly. We were not going to make it on foot of course. Even without a backwards glance

I could hear the wet slaps of tentacles rapidly approaching us from the rear. We were merely running until I'd had time to cultivate enough Quintessence within me to teleport us away. Something I was distressed to find was taking much longer than usual, given how badly I'd just overextended myself with what I'd hoped would be a killing blow.

The version of me on Ig's head forced out words. "*Ig's reserves are full, let him do it!*"

"And end up scattered across the four winds?" I croaked back, still getting used to my newly regrown teeth. "I think not."

"*Oh for . . .*"

Ig and I were both lifted from our feet by the kobold's low magic, flung into the air just as one of the vast black tentacles of Nun-Mhorgoth whipped through the space we had but a moment ago occupied. It was a tricky thing to fling a person with low magic, their own internal Quintessence usually resisted. Easier by far to latch onto some inanimate object, like their shoes, as Ig had done to me just now.

Another tentacle came for us while I was still surprised, and it was only a swift blast of heckfire from Ig, accompanied by a squeak of, "*Fragor!*" that stopped it snatching us from the sky.

"You know you really shouldn't channel sulfur so freely, you're going to . . ."

Ig had been slowly rotating in my grasp as he dangled from the bunched up loose skin on the back of his neck, but by now he was facing me, able to see what was happening behind us. His eyes went wide in terror and then my presence washed down into him once more, shouting out through his mouth, "*Nos auferet!*"

It was at that exact moment that every molecule in my body decided all at once that rather than being a wizard, it would like to be a puff of nitrogen instead. The same with Ig's from the look of it.

With a lightening of spirits as well as atoms, we both exploded apart and started flying off towards distant Arpanpholigon. To home and safety, however brief that respite might have been. And we would have gotten away with it too if it weren't for that meddling eldritch monster behind us reaching out with its magic and fouling up the spell.

We were ripped from the air and back into our physical forms by Nun-Mhorgoth's arcane unraveling, dashed against the earth by our sudden fall from grace and sky. It hurt, but not nearly so badly as having my jaw slapped off, so I recovered much quicker than I would have anticipated, hauling Ig up too. I probably should have counted myself lucky that the undoing of the spell hadn't simply scattered us to the winds as I'd feared before, or worse yet, coagulated us into a single unfortunate creature.

We'd already done that when I was a hat, I had no intention of doing it again so soon.

The dark god—alright, I was willing to concede at this point that there may have been some divinity to the creature, however twisted it might have been—towered over us on the open plain, a darkness so deep that it blotted out the stars behind it, surrounded in all directions by the gentle undulations of its tentacles. "I gotta tell you, kid, that hurt! Do you know how long it has been since anything was able to hurt me? Me?!" It lowered itself slowly towards us. "I've always said you've got cajónes, standing up to a god, but now . . . now I'm going to tear them off and wear them as earrings."

"Well, that doesn't sound like it is going to be very pleasant for either one of us." I stalled for time, still backpedaling away with the catatonic kobold gripped firmly in my arms. "Wouldn't it make much more sense to leave them where they are and talk this through like two sensible, sapient . . ."

A tentacle as thick as a sapling lashed out at my legs, knocking me rather heavily onto my rump.

"There ain't no talking your way out of this one, buddy, no running from it neither. No matter where you go, I'm going to find you. No matter how far you run, I'm going to hunt you down. You get me?"

Quintessence flowed into me again, my contracted and collapsed core shocked back into operation by the jolt of landing. It flowed not just from all the world around me, but from Ig too. He was pushing power into me with such force that it was making me lightheaded. Not the version of me that was riding around on Ig's head, but Ig himself. "Me no like him."

I patted him gently on the head. "Me neither, Ig."

"Don't you talk to that thing like I ain't even here," Nun-Mhorgoth roared, expanding out, larger and larger. Like some great sea-star composed of oil. Slicking out across the landscape and sky. "And don't look away when I'm talking to you. Do you even know how bad you've messed up here? Do you even know WHO I AM?!"

My reserves brimmed with power once more, all that Ig had and all that I'd been able to haul in. Nowhere near as much as I could carry, but more than enough to finish up the spell that I'd still been holding onto through all of this, just a word away from completion. I set the kobold down, then used his shoulder as a pushing-off point to get myself back onto my feet.

"LOOK AT ME, SCRYNE. LOOK AT THE BIGGEST MISTAKE YOU EVER MADE."

I did look up at it then, meeting what I suppose you could have called its gaze, even though I'm sure its senses were so thoroughly alien to humanity that it wasn't even in the vicinity of the right word.

"I offered you half the world if you'd leave in peace." I heard my voice cracking with exhaustion and pushed on all the same. "I offered you half the world . . . Now I'm giving it to you whether you want it or not."

Slamming my hands down into the dirt, I called out the final word of my spell.

"Confractus!"

PLAN D: Break the World in Half

The Quintessence drained from me once more. All the power I'd begged, borrowed, and stolen from the universe, rushing out of me into this titanic spell. It cut far too close to the edge of my limitations. My vision darkened around the periphery as I had to drag tiny sparks of Quintessence back into me or risk unconsciousness.

By the time that my sight had cleared, the awful force that I had unleashed had already taken hold. It was not a clean cut, you see—to do that would have required a degree of precision that was simply beyond me at present. I hadn't the time or the calculations required, so instead I had simply shattered what I could and sliced through what I couldn't, relying heavily on entirely abstract knowledge of the stratum of the world to guess whether or not we would see success. A crack stretched out betwixt the dark god and I, already stretching out to each horizon, and, in truth, far beyond.

The spell was not yet finished its work. To my arcane senses, it still shone bright from deep down in the earth as it went down and down, drawn by that weak force gravity towards the center of our planet.

Heat rushed up through the ever-widening crack as lava and still deeper layers of the world were exposed to the open air for the first time. If heck was really down there rather than being on an alternate plane—as had often been suggested in children's literature—then all the demons and devils were about to get the shock of their lives.

Nun-Mhorgoth still hung on the opposite side of the ever-widening ravine, its tentacles waving around, its expression unreadable by virtue of it having no actual face. "What did you just do?"

It was probably a grave injustice to describe what we were feeling now, as the spell tore down through the planet's core and neatly severed It Into two parts as being an earthquake. For one thing, an earthquake isn't typically the death knell of an entire world, and more pressingly it didn't contain all of the fascinating gravitational fluctuations that splitting the celestial object's center had caused. Ig floated beside me.

"Did you . . . How did you just do what you did?" Nun-Mhorgoth was becoming increasingly distressed. The usual spasmodic twitching of its tentacles now upgraded to a writhing. It seemed that for all of its talk about destroying the world, it did still need an actual planet to stand on. This was a creature that craved an audience, and global extinction would leave it deprived of one, even if it did somehow manage to survive the cataclysm I'd put into play.

Strictly speaking, most people probably would have put the destruction of the planet that they lived on further down the pile. Maybe somewhere around Plan X, but I, as you may have noticed by this point in our tale, am not most people, I am in fact as unlike most people as dear Ig, or Nun-Mhorgoth or any of the other unique little freaks that make existence ever so interesting.

Regardless of what Nun-Mhorgoth might have been, regarding deity, it was nonetheless defined by how extremely powerful it was. I, for my part was defined by my intellect. It was not my ability to collect vast amounts of Quintessence that made me the greatest living wizard, after all, but my ability to process vast amounts of information. To take all that others had learned before me and use it as a stepping stone.

This did not merely encompass the study of the arcane, of course. I had been studying Nun-Mhorgoth since the first moment I laid eyes upon it. I had been parsing through everything that it said and did, composing a profile that I could refer to so that I might predict what it would do next. That profile was of course still incomplete, but at this stage I felt that I could place solid bets on what it would do given the correct stimulus.

It said it wanted to destroy everything, but what it meant was that it wanted to destroy some things and impress everyone with how much it could destroy. So when confronted with the destruction of the whole planet and everyone on it, it did the only rational thing that it could. It saved the world.

The tentacles that had until now been flailing around so wildly now lashed out, reaching for the opposite side of the ever-widening trench that stretched down all the way through the planet and out the other side. The two hemispheres were drifting apart. The explosive force of my spell had seen to that. Gravity and centripetal force were simultaneously trying to pull the halves back together as momentum carried them apart, slowing the whole process to a crawl. Slowing the process to such a speed that if you were say, a giant tentacle monster with immense power, you might look at the drifting apart of the two parts and convince yourself that you could grab on and pull them back together with your incredible power and strength.

My only hope was that Nun-Mhorgoth's arrogance in this matter wasn't wrong. If it didn't save the world, I didn't have the strength left to do it myself.

Regardless, the important thing was that while Nun-Mhorgoth was grappling with the two broken halves of this big sphere we call home, it was not able to pursue Ig and I. Assuming that it took even half as long as it should have to pull the two bits back together and meld them, then we had a couple of hours to put Plan E through Y into effect.

While I began gathering Quintessence for the journey home, I caught Ig by the ankle and dragged him back down to earth. He asked, "Do good?"

"You were perfect in every way, as always, my dear friend." I gave him a tentative pat on the head. "Thank you."

It seemed Nun-Mhorgoth was so preoccupied with its task that it didn't even have time to shout obscenities after us as we strolled off across the barren plain towards home, and finally vanished into a puff of smoke.

CHAPTER 16

THE BEST LAID PLANS OF KOBOLDS AND MEN

We arrived not in the college or even the city itself, but out in the farmland beyond. Iomedania had set up the same sort of snare as had been used to direct me to her laboratories earlier so as to prevent any magically talented enemy of Arpanpholigon from just popping inside. On the one hand it was very sensible, on the other, I really could have done with a nice comfortable chair about now. We came through, staggering, both Ig and I. The gravity here was so much more solid than where we had just departed.

All around us knights bristled with weaponry. All of it pointed in our direction. This was the other advantage of wearing the pointy hat and robes, I suppose. Nobody was going to mistake you for anyone else and accidentally stab you. "We return victorious!" I announced to the gathered crowd.

That brought a cheer from all around.

One young knight pushed up his faceplate, relief painted across his sweaty features. "So the monsters are defeated?"

"Well, no, there are still quite a lot of them headed this way." There was a certain wilting among the cheerful. "But I have definitely thinned their numbers a good bit."

A different knight asked with a little more cynicism, "And the magical monster that tore down the Great Wall is dead?"

"Well, no, it is currently distracted for an hour or two, after which it will probably be marching on us with all its forces."

A third, and the most cynical of all of the knights, then asked, "How's this returning victorious then?"

"Well I'm bloody alive!" I snapped, then stormed off with all haste to where I could see Plan E being enacted.

The college remained invisible, despite how it had been repositioned, but you could tell from the heavy outline of shadow where it lay against the outside of the city walls. It took me a moment or two to orient myself correctly to it, as there had been some degree of rotation as it had drifted down to ensure it lined up correctly with this section of city wall. All around it, wizards scurried and cast with the kind of frantic energy you usually only saw from them around exam time. Amidst them all, Balthazagar was barking orders. He gave us a hearty wave on our approach. "How did B through D go?"

"As well as is to be expected." I brushed over the details, not wanting to see any more disappointment. "How is Plan E proceeding?"

"We're just about to try her out and see if we tear the whole city in half. All the soldiers are out and all the normal people in. That much we have managed."

"Do you need our assistance?" I asked, swaying with exhaustion.

He looked us up and down. "Philodephina has us covered, but thanks all the same."

What sounded like an earthquake rattled through the ground beneath us, possibly as a result of the planet cracking in two, but more likely as a result of . . . Before our eyes, the city began to rise. The spell which ensured the levitation of the college had been expanded out to encompass the whole of Arpanpholigon. Every innocent that might have been injured was being carried up and away from the hordes of the dark one.

PLAN E: Get Everyone Out of the Way

It had been a stroke of genius on my part, even amidst all the usual strokes of genius. A way to keep the city as a tasty prize for the monsters and ensure that they didn't split their forces to spread out across all the civilized lands, while also ensuring that none of them might actually be able to get into town.

As the city continued to rise, all of the plumbing and sewers dangling beneath it were hauled out in a rain of dirt. Like the roots of some vast shrub.

"Oh wait." I jumped into motion with the realization that the college was rising too, and I needed to be in it. I seized Ig by the wrist and took off running. Not something that my arthritic knees cared for, but a necessity all the same. Where the entryway to the college happened to be situated was a little difficult to ascertain, given that the whole place was invisible and swiveled around. But I did manage to leap and catch on the edge of a doorway. Hopefully. If it was a window ledge, I was in for a rather unpleasant surprise. Swinging Ig up and using him as a doorknocker, it took only a half dozen knocks before we gained entry.

From there we proceeded to that secret room in which Cygni had been conducting her secret project for me. Ig had been entirely unaware of what we were doing, and remained unaware until I plucked my hat off his head and put it elsewhere.

"This work?" he asked me, surprisingly shrewdly.

"I believe so. We must simply give it a little time to activate."

With that done, I proceeded to my office, where I was immediately beset by all of the other members of staff who were exceedingly unhappy about the vast majority of the plans that I had left behind for them to work with, particularly the now operative Plan F, given that it was a blank page titled—

PLAN F: Activate the Secret Project.

"You cannot seriously think that this is going to work?" Philodephina demanded, waving a handful of my carefully constructed plans as though they were scrap paper for her calculations.

"Um, actually, he probably thinks everything is going to work, because he is insane." Copernicrust sighed.

Arturo's head popped around the side of the doorframe. "Would anyone care to elucidate me on why my scrying devices are informing me that the planet is breaking in half?"

I held up my hand. "Oh, that was me. I broke it."

"You what?!" Danyeel bellowed, before slapping a hand over his own mouth.

"It is like you people didn't even read my memos in my absence. Check Plan D."

Danyeel dove for the desk and started digging through the papers.

"The king is not very pleased that there is a dragon in his treasury explaining compound interest to the chancellor of the exchequer," Sabrinia mentioned, quite casually.

"One would have hoped that the chancellor already knew about compound interest . . ." I chuckled. "How are things proceeding for Plan G, Danyeel?"

He had managed to pull himself together by now. "The illusory copies of the city are already in place in the sky, all that remains is to move on to Plan H: The Old Cup and Ball Trick."

"Excellent." I turned to the other most furious wizard in the room. "Philodephina, would you be kind enough to assist our young master of illusions in the physical shuffling of the city amidst the various others in the sky?"

"Are you . . . You have got to . . . I am . . . . . ." She schooled her enraged expression, bit her lip to bring about her own silence, and seized Danyeel by the sleeve, storming towards the door.

I laid a hand on her shoulder to stop her advance. "Before you depart, I feel it would be appropriate to give you the opportunity to slap me. I know you have been wanting to do so for a great many years, and now it seems that you might never have another chance if things go awry. In fact . . ."

Her open palm caught me right on my freshly regrown face with enough ringing force to send me flying across the room. The shock of the impact, like the shock of my earlier fall, was sufficient to get my Quintessence channels unseized and my reserves refilling.

She let out a sigh, calm returning to her at last. "Thank you, Archmage."

"Any time," I mumbled back from halfway under my desk.

Ig did his best to pick me up again, but the best he could manage with his weedy arms was getting me into a seated position. That was fine, I'd stay down here a little longer until the room stopped its slow spin around me.

PLAN I: Trapping

My fellow wizards had, despite my complaints to the contrary, been quite assiduous in reading through my various memos, and had made such contributions to said memos as I had demanded. There were laid before me such an assortment of ingenious spells that could be laid upon the battlefield as traps that I could scant believe the bounty of them. Things that I will readily admit that I had never even contemplated doing. Some so vicious as to be depraved, some so simple as to be entirely overlooked. Over a hundred suggestions in all.

When it was finished putting the world back together, Nun-Mhorgoth would be more than capable of dissolving any one of these spells. But the question was, would it bother? All those monsters that had been slaughtered up until now, and it hadn't shown the faintest sign of giving even a fraction of a damn. Would it waste time disarming the traps that we laid to thin out the herd? I thought not. So with as many wizards as I could have gathered up, we marched to the expansive balconies arranged around the outside of our floating hub of education and we began to cast. It probably took a solid hour in all, the completion of Plan I, but I believed that it would be time fruitfully spent. Particularly the rather vicious explosives set to detonate with proximity that had been hidden the various illusory copies of the city dotted around the sky behind us.

I felt, rather than saw any sign, of Nun-Mhorgoth successfully slapping the fractured halves of the world back together just as I felt rather than saw the approach of its armies before they crossed the horizon.

PLAN J: Trusting in Our Allies

Of all the plans that I had come up with, this had seemed, from the very beginning to be the one most liable to fall apart on contact with the enemy. Both Nun-Mhorgoth and I knew that if we went head-to-head, we could achieve a stalemate. It might not have been willing to admit it, but I was. Clever and quick and strong as the dark god was, I couldn't overpower it any more that it could overpower me. Which meant that despite our respective egos, this fight would actually be settled not by either one of us, but by those that fought alongside us. Nun-Mhorgoth had assembled the most powerful monsters that it could find, I had gathered whatever useless little idiots in armor the various armies of civilization deigned fit to share. It hardly felt like a fair match up, but then I had wiped out a solid half of its army on my own before Nun-Mhorgoth intervened, so perhaps it would be fairer than any of us could have hoped.

It wasn't, as it turned out. The monsters still outnumbered our troops three-to-one, not even mentioning that most of them would quite literally be able to eat our soldiers for breakfast. Certainly the magical snares we'd laid would be effective in thinning their numbers a little more, but even so, we were likely looking defeat in its face.

Alongside me, the various members of faculty and the student body who had the stomach for it lined the balconies once more, raining arcane destruction down on the enemy army to surprisingly little effect. We were trying not to destroy everything, you see. Silly of us, really, given that our enemy intended to destroy everything, thinking it was our duty to preserve it. But we are, despite our incredible gifts and education, only human, and susceptible to silly notions like sentimentality.

Wyverns and dragons and other miscellaneous flying monsters swooped about in the air, level with us, and for the most part they were brought low by the various invisible traps and barriers that we had cast up there. Of the few that got through, only some swept over towards the real Arpanpholigon, with the majority mistakenly pursuing one of the illusory copies, from which it appeared that magical barrage that was slaughtering their troops was also being unleashed.

The monsters came pouring across the battlefield towards the knights in shining armor that we'd left down below. The knights went bravely charging out to meet them, though not at such a speed that the clash was likely to happen anywhere near the myriad curses and enchantments that we'd buried about the place to ensure the liquification of as many monsters as was physically possible in the time frame. The two battle lines clashed and held for only a moment, before sheer weight of numbers and bulk began driving civilization's soldiers back inch by agonizing inch.

Step by step, our armies were pushed back, but the wholesale rout that one might have expected in the face of such impossible odds did not arrive. They held true. Which was, all in all, a rather pleasant surprise.

One that was immediately supplanted by the altogether unpleasant surprise of Nun-Mhorgoth's bombardment.

Those big black balls he'd been throwing at me earlier had swollen to hitherto unseen proportions and came soaring through the air towards our unfortunate forces. Titanic spheres of destruction that would leave naught behind but a gruesome splatter of carnage.

Ig caught them with low magic and surprisingly little effort, juggled them about clumsily when it seemed they'd slip from his grasp, and then lobbed them back in the direction from which they'd came. Most of them went nowhere near to his intended target, but given the breadth of the opposing force, he still managed to slaughter more orcs, goblins, ogres and miscellanea than any other wizard in that one little parry.

Then, abruptly all of the magic being cast against our enemy came to an abrupt halt, just as Nun-Mhorgoth's bombardment of us had. Not by any choice of ours, but because the dark one willed it. The same working of unraveling that he had used to disassemble the wards of the Great Wall came into play, blocking any spell that we might cast, sweeping through those hidden spells that were already out there, lying in wait for the right time to trigger.

It had come to this far sooner than I had anticipated, but I was prepared for it. All the details of my other plans were in the hands of those who needed them, all the plans within plans explained to those who needed to know. All that was left was to trust, to trust in my friends, coworkers, and allies to do precisely what they had promised to do.

Trust did not come easily to me, but here at the end of all things, it was all that I had left.

PLAN K: Neutralize Nun-Mhorgoth

Ultimately, the clash between the dark god and I was always going to be self-contained with neither one of us capable of performing any magic or entirely undoing the other's spells. We were evenly matched and becoming ever more so as we both learned more about the intricacies of how the other cast.

All of the monsters were occupied fighting against our army, and if nothing else were to happen, that clash would be the deciding factor in who won the day. Nun-Mhorgoth and I would be at a stalemate until everything on its side or mine died, and then the winner of that secondary conflict could interfere in ours, leading to ultimate success for one or the other of us.

I could make the dark form of the dark god out now, an ink splotch down on the field of battle, and while I'm sure Danyeel's illusions held, I couldn't entirely shake the sense that it was staring right up at me despite the absence of eyes.

Then there was no more time for such petty things as seeing and understanding what was going on. I was locked in against Nun-Mhorgoth's immense power once more with only my wits and power to keep it at bay. To pretend that there wasn't some small part of me that was thrilled at this challenge would be deceitful, but it was a far smaller part than it might have been but a few months ago. Before I had anything that I cared about. Before I had a thing to lose.

We clashed and we fought and we wrestled and ducked and dodged and countered and time lost all meaning as it dragged on and on. Moment by moment, I was holding him at bay, but moment by moment, I was losing. Not because the conflict between us was going against me, no, never that. Because the trust that I had placed in my allies had been misplaced. I may not have been able to see anything that was going on, with all of my senses attuned to the occult world for now, but Ig was providing a running commentary for my benefit all the same.

"Ogres be fighting horse shiny-mens. Horse picked up. Horse club now. Man go splat. Other mans no happy. Wizards be zapping lots. Lots monsters. Too many lots monsters. Horse broke. Shiny mans run away. Shiny mans stop. Shiny mans run back."

It was not the most enlightening overview of the tactical reality of the battle, but I could at least extrapolate some portion of what was happening from it all the same, when I could spare the tiniest sliver of cognition.

"Shiny mans is walking backwards real silly and ogreses and lizardses is big happy. All monsters be shouty happy."

That continued to be bad news, and with the inevitable faltering of my morale also came more mistakes in my defense than I would like to admit. As my people faltered, so too did I. The full weight of Nun-Mhorgoth's will fell upon me, driving me to my knees. I could distantly feel Ig trying to haul me back up, but that moment of weakness had cost me dearly. A wave of unmaking passed over us all, and the illusory cities in the sky vanished. We now hung alone, the proverbial sitting duck.

The sight of our magic failing filled the enemy with renewed vigor, if all the excitable roaring was anything to go by.

What luck then, that Plan F was finally in position.

There were tunnels beneath the world, complex subsystems of them stretching out in every direction, an entire underworld of them, in truth. And before her departure, Cygni had conveyed to me as decent a map of those beneath the battlefield where we now fought as she possibly could.

It was along those tunnels that my hat had journeyed, carrying its perfect copy of my mind within it. Traversing the distance behind enemy lines until it arrived directly underneath the position where Nun-Mhorgoth now stood.

With a cataclysmic explosion worthy of the finest fireworks display, Plan F emerged now. A perfectly carved, identical replica of me, made about two times my size, and composed entirely from the material that I was reluctant to call Cygnite, but I now had no choice but to describe in that manner. Pure condensed magic, made solid, made into a golem, which my mind now piloted.

In short, as my doppelganger rose from beneath the earth, still riding atop the vast explosion it had just used to destroy Nun-Mhorgoth's commanders with a fist pointed directly up. It was shot, like a bullet, directly into the underside of the dark mass of Nun-Mhorgoth.

He got Plan F'd right in the ass.

The impact cost Nun-Mhorgoth its grip upon the earth, flinging it up into the air to such a great height as to bring it level with my gaze. Which was when I, no longer encumbered with having to deal with the weight of its arcane attention, unleashed the same spell of catastrophic destruction that had failed earlier to end its life. I knew that beam of blinding white wouldn't be sufficient, it had already proven itself insufficient after all, but this time I had every single wizard in the city standing alongside me, unleashing all of their most deadly spells at the same time. All of us at once, focusing fire exclusively on the one dark shape flung up into the sky.

For several moments afterwards we would be blinking the shadowy aftereffects of that torrent of magic away. Moments in which the ravaged body of Nun-Mhorgoth tumbled, stunned, back towards the ground.

Then the version of me standing underneath it unleashed the very same spell again. Firing straight up into Nun-Mhorgoth's underbelly.

Falling less like a comet this time, and more like a burnt-out meteor, Nun-Mhorgoth returned to the ravaged land below with a thump that could be heard even up here.

For a moment I allowed myself to hope. I allowed myself to dream that we had succeeded. But scant moments after the dark god's landing it was rising to its feet, or rather, tentacles, once more.

It turned on the towering crystalline perfection that Cygni had spent the majority of her time at the college constructing and doubtless made some very threatening comments. The other me didn't seem to acknowledge it, instead being rather more focused upon spellcraft. Spells that the dark god would have of course been able to directly counter were it not for the fact that I had now returned to my task of unraveling every spell of unraveling that he could conjure up, faster than he could bring them to bear. Another blast of that blinding light from my spell of utter destruction struck him, then another. The way that lesser mages cast around fireballs, my doppelganger golem was able to wield the cosmic power of pure annihilation.

Over and over again he struck out, wiping out veritable legions of enemy monsters entirely by happenstance. Breaking the enemy army's focus on charging forward into our stalwart defenders by destroying their lines of communication and sowing confusion, dissent and corpses. So many charred and jellified corpses.

Nun-Mhorgoth, once so colossal and unstoppable in everyone's eyes, was now diminished. Extremities seared away. Mass reduced, until the dark form of it had shrunk to half the size of my crystalline copy. It leapt forward, trying to tackle my golem to the ground and caught another blast directly to what on any other creature I would have called a face. It could not muster any magic, each time that it tried, I tore its spells apart. All that it had left was its pseudopods and brute force to face off with an idealized copy of the world's greatest living mage, and it was clearly being found wanting.

Needless to say, it was at this moment that the tide began to turn. The monsters that had been so certain of their victory with Nun-Mhorgoth leading them suddenly began to develop doubts, something that it was extremely untimely to do when one was in the midst of mortal combat.

Something that was exacerbated even further by the abrupt arrival of our reinforcements.

PLAN L: Trust in My Friends

Cygni had returned home to the dwarvish kingdoms beneath the world I knew, and she had gathered all of the support that she could, which in this case appeared to have been every single dwarf in the world, or at least every single dwarf that could be brought here within the allotted time. There were as many dwarves pouring out of myriad holes onto the battlefield as we had soldiers at the start of the battle, and while our knights had been full of pomposity and grandeur, the dwarves brought a dreadful practicality to the battlefield. They had no care for a glorious victory, they only sought to kill the enemy faster than they could be killed in turn. In addition, they also had the great advantage of having spent their entire history in direct conflict with all of these various monstrous people while elves hid in their forests, and we cowered behind our walls. They knew what they were doing, and they did it ever so well.

The dwarves swept in from one side, and on the opposite end of the battlefield, Ildrit returned.

My assumption had been that he had gone off to find all the lowlifes and ruffians that he had encountered throughout his life, rallying them with an iron fist and bringing them back to do some good instead of evil. What I had not assumed was that he would go directly to the people who loathed him the most in all of creation. The Elves of Verdance Woods had, quite rightly, put a fairly substantial bounty on the head of Ildrit Elfbane, so it must have come as quite a surprise to them when he showed up at their doorstep with his figurative hat in his hands, a sad story about an elf named Wyn, who had marked the man before them as an elf friend instead of elf bane, and a short political and philosophical treatise on the subject of redemption.

Whatever he'd said to them, it worked. They had turned out in force. Far fewer in number than the dwarves, primarily because there were so many less elves in the world, but none the less effective for it.

It also helped that while the monstrous peoples of the world had spent centuries in bloody conflict with the dwarves, they had built the elves who had once been their primary antagonists up into legendary figures. Tales to tell a baby orc if it wouldn't go to sleep. Close your eyes or the elves will come get you.

The side of the battlefield faced with dwarves fell back under the ferocity of their assault. The side faced with elves fell back out of blind terror under volley after volley of arrows. Dropping away before the very intense looking elves with glaives got into range.

In short, a pincer movement had been effected upon the flanks of the enemy and they were suffering tremendous casualties as a result, with their only route to rout being positioned directly away from the human troops who had until now been rather hard pressed. With a renewed energy born of hope, they surged back into the havoc.

Nun-Mhorgoth had an array of sensory apparatus that was entirely beyond what we mere mortals could lay claim, it was aware of everything going on around it, and most likely aware that the tides of battle had quite firmly turned against it. Moreover, it appeared to have recognized that it was going to have no luck going head-to-head with my golem.

The sensible thing in this moment would of course have been to beat a hasty retreat and live to fight another day, but for a creature entirely unfamiliar with the prospect of mortality, I suppose such a thing simply did not occur to it. Instead it took off, in an unexpected direction, bolting betwixt its own soldiers and the greater monsters scattered amongst them in an attempt to use said monsters as a living shield against my golem's ongoing arcane bombardment.

It might have worked too, if the other me had been lobbing fireballs or lightning around, but it was firing beams of pure disintegrating light and power that didn't really need to account for anything getting between them and their target by virtue of destroying anything between them and their target. Again and again strobe lightning played out across the gathered armies as Nun-Mhorgoth was struck and lessened. More and more of the darkness that composed it sloughing off. More and more of its power diminished.

Then, all of a sudden the bombardment, which had looked liable to put an end to Nun-Mhorgoth once and for all, came to a halt.

It had shot off into the mass of monsters that were being hemmed in betwixt the two opposing armies of our newfound allies, into the wedge that was being formed as the monsters failed to beat a sensible retreat, and instead drew towards their center of mass where they felt that weight of numbers might better protect them. In the sky, there were scant few monsters left, with so many of them having attempted their own assaults on Arpanpholigon on high and encountering my faculty's most vicious rebuttals. But those that had still flown now met their end at the tip of carefully placed dwarven arrows. It cleared my vision, and let me see precisely why my counterpart had ceased his attacks.

In its strangling tendrils, Nun-Mhorgoth held Cygni.

With her to hand, it had finally found something that I could not, or would not, blast through to get to my target. Its tentacles looked noodle thin from this distance, but were nonetheless encircling her throat and choking her off from using any magic of her own. For one long awful moment I thought that the dark one meant to kill her and abandon its only defense against my golem, but it seemed that despite its loudly professed desire for destruction, it was quite capable of staying its hand when it became necessary.

We all stood frozen for a moment. Ig staring down through oversized binoculars to take in what my arcane sense were telling me. Only one thing still moved. One piece of magic as vast and potent as anything that either god or I had been able to muster. Ildrit burst out through the flank of an unfortunate hippogryph with Widowtaker in hand, clearing the distance between them in a single leap and bringing its black blade down upon the tentacles that held Cygni.

It seemed that much as he sought to deny it, he had to be a hero after all.

There was a moment, one glorious moment, when Cygni and Ildrit were both loose of the dark god's grasp, and then just as swiftly, that moment passed. From its central mass a new mycelium expansion of tentacles burst forth, like an anemone reaching out for fodder, and the two of them were caught, and then drawn in close.

I could stand it no longer, with a single barked word of Archaic, both Ig and I were carried down through the winds to stand before Nun-Mhorgoth and its hostages. My counterpart golem met my gaze for the briefest moment, before we both moved to place ourselves on opposing sides. It was I that Nun-Mhorgoth chose to watch, to twist around and follow.

"Absalom, baby, that was another real good one. A real bring-the-house-down kind of number." It paused for a moment, twisting out what might have been a head to peer up at Arpanpholigon. "Bringing the house down, yeah, that sounds like a good idea."

Its magic lashed out towards the college, and in my distraction over the lives of my friends I was too slow to counter the unmaking it struck the hovering building with. The invisibility spell that had lasted generations faded away to naught, revealing that almost every inch of the college, inside and out, was entirely coated in naughty limericks in the form of graffiti. Bloody students.

But it was not the visibility of the place that gave me concern so much as the way that it began to lilt to one side. The enchantment that had been holding it, and the city, aloft, had been broken.

"That ought to be all she wrote for that old town." The dark god cackled.

Ig was already moving, reaching out, the distance was too great, the strain too much, the raw Quintessence that he needed far beyond what he could replenish in time stop such a thing draining him dry. But as been said all too often, kobolds are stupid. With low magic, he caught hold of the distant city and held it aloft. Sweat beaded all over the poor little creature, and already I could see the tell-tale paleness as he drained his body's reserves. We had mere seconds before he fell, and Arpanpholigon with him.

I dragged my eyes away from that and back to the dark one's gloating. "This is your last chance, Nun-Mhorgoth."

"Again with the threats? You think you can threaten me?" The dark god swung them forward, Ildrit and Cygni, both ensnared in a dense web of oily slick tendrils. "I've got your kids right here, both of them. One little squeeze and they go pop."

Time was ticking out for Ig, for all three of them.

"Down in that cave when I first shucked you like an oyster from a shell, you touched my mind, Nun-Mhorgoth. You ripped all of my history from me when I was but a hat. Think back through it now. Find any single moment where I gave a damn about another living being." I grinned at him. "Find a single memory that suggests for a moment that I won't burn through everyone else to get to you."

Cygni and Ildrit both started squirming all the more frantically as if they truly believed it. Perhaps they did. Perhaps I had not made so kindly an impression on anyone as I might have hoped.

It seemed it was enough to sell the deception though, Nun-Mhorgoth flung them at me instead of trying to crush them. Hoping to buy itself more time to escape. It turned tentacle and fled directly away from me, and directly into my other self. More specifically into the rising uppercut of my other self.

Nun-Mhorgoth soared through the air, cussing and cursing all the way. And it was up there, in the air, that one final incinerating blast of blinding white magic struck him. From me instead of my duplicate. It mattered nothing to me now if I spent every last speck of Quintessence within me, so long as the dark one perished too. So long as it kept the others safe.

He vanished in that pillar of light and when it faded, no trace of him remained to be seen. I blinked hard, trying to rid myself of the black bar across my vision. The darkness encroaching from all around.

I staggered to Ig, forcing the last tremulous sparkles of Quintessence that I had into him as I had before. I reached out a flailing hand for help from somebody, anybody, and my golem caught it. My golem, built from solid Quintessence. I drew from it like I would not have dared from anyone else lest I killed them, and I poured every drop into Ig. I hung there on the precipice of death until my other self reached past me and laid his own oversized hand on Ig's back, flooding him with raw power. Enough to go on holding the city up forever if need be.

Finally. Finally it was over.

From amidst the routing ogres, Nun-Mhorgoth surged like a tide. A tide that had admittedly been reduced to a large bath's worth of water, but a tide all the same. It sloshed out from between them, launched itself into the air and coiled into a single angular spike that it buried not in me, as I would have expected, but in the broad Cygnite back of my golem.

For a moment both golem and god swayed together in their stillness, then with an awful crackling sound, the crystalline structure of the Cygnite began to shatter. Fault lines spread from where the blow had been struck. "Oh, bugger," I said.

Then my double-sized visage exploded into chunks and rained down around us.

It got some good distance too, I'd imagine a few of the smaller bits of shrapnel went miles. And when all was said and done, all that remained was my hat, drifting down to land beside the black puddle on the ground.

Ig had been knocked to his knees by the explosion, but one tremulous paw was still held high, and though Arpanpholigon lilted once more, drifting over towards us, it remained at a steady height all the same. He would need my strength to keep on holding it aloft, but between me and Ig, the slick form of Nun-Mhorgoth rose once more.

"You just don't get it, Absalom, baby. You're never going to get it. You can't beat me. Not because you're getting it wrong." He said it almost like it was a kindness. "I just can't be beat. You'd be better getting mad at the sun for rising than me for winning."

"Bollocks."

All heads turned to Cygni, where she stood still held in Ildrit's overprotective embrace.

"Did that lawn ornament just speak?" Nun-Mhorgoth hissed.

"If you couldn't be beat, how come we beat you?" Cygni pulled away from her lover and stalked towards the dark god. "Stuck you in a rock for so long nobody could even remember your name."

"I was biding my time, I was waiting for . . ."

"Bollocks," Cygni repeated, and it was all that I could do to resist the urge to guffaw.

A tentacle lashed out, spiked like the one that had killed my golem. Ildrit was already in motion, blade already swinging, deflecting the blow, turning it aside.

Enraged, the dark god exploded out into a seething leech swarm of tendrils, reaching out for every one of us, raking across the hasty shields that Ig and my enchanted equipment had raised. Cygni had no such protection, but Ildrit, to my continued amazement, fended off every blow as it was struck with a spin and flourish of Widowtaker. With a fierce grin fixed on his face. Ildrit fought the dark god's outburst to a standstill.

"Nun-Mhorgoth." I spoke the name softly, soft enough that by all rights nobody should have heard it on the battlefield, yet the creature contorted to look at me all the same. "We have unfinished business."

"You're right, kid." It lashed out all of its tentacles once more, not at me, but up into the air, latching onto the low hanging plumbing of Arpanpholigon with three elongated noodles of itself and beginning to pull. "Let's wrap this up."

The city fell from the sky. Not as fast as it would have without magic holding it up and Ig straining against every inch of the fall, but not slow enough that the landing wasn't going to cause some real problems for everybody inside. I threw up my own hands and reached out with my own magic, lending my strength to Ig.

The maniac god pulled all the harder, trying to bring the whole city down on top of us. It probably assumed that it would survive the impact, while the rest of us were ground to pulp, and it was entirely correct in that assumption.

We pushed back, it pulled down, and weak as gravity may have been on the grand scale of things, it didn't help that it was working against us too. All the weight of the whole city and college, all bearing down on us. All about us the monsters, men, elves, and dwarves fled. Running for their lives as a city was dropped out of the sky upon them.

I wish that I had a fraction of their good sense, as I went on fighting. For my life, for my friends' lives, for the lives of everyone in the city above. All the innocent unfortunates who had gotten into Nun-Mhorgoth's way.

Ig surged to his feet, giving the falling city one last hearty shove with the last of his strength before passing out. Abandoning Arpanpholigon to the terrible fate of falling about six feet, I lunged for Ig, scooped up my hat, and met Cygni's eyes just as she completed her teleportation spell.

Caught in Iomedania's snare, we were returned to our point of origin. Now a good mile off from where Arpanpholigon had fallen to earth. I had Ig dangling from one arm like a rag doll, and my hat danglin from the other hand. I was, to put it mildly, a bit done. I was exhausted. My bones were aching, my teeth felt like they might fall out at any moment, and more importantly, I felt that I had upheld my moral obligation to save everyone to the best of my ability. This was the end of that definition. That had been the best I had, and it hadn't worked.

Cygni was already moving off, Ildrit falling into step beside her. She cast a glance back. "Come on, got to get the city back in the air before monsters get in."

She was so sure of herself. So sure of what we were meant to do. So sure of it in fact that she had convinced every dwarf in her sphere of influence to follow her into battle against an unbeatable foe. So sure that even my useless old body had taken a step after her without a second thought.

I put my hat on, took a deep breath, and then began to cast.

CHAPTER 17

THE GREATEST LIVING WIZARD

Traveling by the elements was blocked by the same snare that had pulled us here to safety, so I folded space to transport us back to the city. One of Arturo's tricks that he hadn't known that I knew. The way that he was always at the front of the line in the cafeteria, even though his offices were the farthest from it.

We arrived outside the keep of Arpanpholigon, which was inevitably swarming with all sorts of very important people who had to look like they were busy doing something when not a one of them could have done anything at all. Some courtier or other called my name, but I didn't bother to turn. All of my attention was for the kobold in my arms that I was coaxing back to awareness with a slow and steady flow of Quintessence.

His eyes bugged out as they opened, and he gasped. "Me no need go."

"Well that is certainly a relief." I smiled down at him, before dropping him back to the ground and giving him a pat on the head. "I doubt we'll have much time for bathroom breaks now."

Cygni fell into step with me as I hurried off towards the college. "What's the plan?"

"You are going to the university to get the levitation spell back into operation." I pushed her in that direction. "I am going to find Nun-Mhorgoth before it can run riot throughout my city."

"You think it's here?" Ildrit caught me by the sleeve, eyes wide with fear.

"Inevitably." I groaned, trying to work a kink out of my shoulder that turned out to be a hunk of embedded Cygnite shrapnel. Well, that was probably going to be a problem, but a problem for later.

I had expected Ildrit to go with Cygni, to shepherd her through the packed streets, but she was very proficient with her elbows, and already well on her way before I realized that she'd departed. "How are you going to find it?"

Pausing for a moment I cocked my head to the side, listening, then the screaming began. "Follow me."

Ig stumbled after us in his usual clumsy gait, only going untrampled by the stampeding crowds because he was in the lee of Ildrit, who despite how much of a rush they were in, nobody seemed to want to bump into. For my part, I suspect that the hat and robe would have been more than enough to shift crowds like parting seas, but with Ildrit's company I would never know for certain. There was a certain wolfishness to his snarl that had everyone scampering aside. Very helpful.

The screaming came from one of the market squares of the city, where the dark god had just emerged through one of the sewer grates and risen to its full height. It was wiggling its tentacles and looming over everyone and doing its best to make a spectacle of itself, but it had entirely failed to account for exactly which town it was messing with. This was not some village of country bumpkins, these were the people of Arpanpholigon, city of magic, this was not their first eldritch abomination. It wasn't even their first eldritch abomination this week. Mere moments after the initial fright had passed, a child threw the first tomato.

It splatted against one of the low hanging tentacles and then slithered along the curve of it. Soon to be joined by a half dozen more from some of the town's more ambitious young rapscallions. One particularly vicious little street tough picked up a potato and threw that. If it had been anyone else, that most certainly would have been a concussion when it bopped off their noggin. And then, with that initial embarrassment out of the way, the grown-ups stepped in. Levelling crossbows, bows, wands, staves, and a half brick on a rope at the dark one and advancing menacingly.

"Whoa, tough crowd," it managed to say before the bombardment began driving it back towards the sewer it crawled out of.

I could not allow Nun-Mhorgoth to retreat back into the underworld of the city. Not when it could emerge once more from anywhere with plumbing. As it tried to slither in, Ig caught onto it with low magic and hauled it back out. Only then did Nun-Mhorgoth lay eyes on me. "Absalom, baby, can you tell these people to chill out or I'm going to have to turn them all into mincemeat?"

"As you have said so vigorously and continuously, Nun-Mhorgoth, I am not a god. Just a man. I cannot hand out commandments."

It lashed out with a tentacle at the next tomato thrower, only to have the blow intercepted by Ildrit's blade. When it tried it again in the other direction, it caught a fireball to the face from someone's "in-case-of-shoplifters" wand.

"I COULD ANNIHILATE ALL OF YOU!" the dark god bellowed, reaching for its magic and finding me already there, locking it out.

With a strop, it flung itself up onto the rooftops and cartwheeled away, with Ig, Ildrit, and I in swift pursuit on the ground.

The city lurched suddenly, almost knocking us from our feet as we rounded a familiar corner and I caught sight of Nun-Mhorgoth held up at one of the canals by a traffic sign. The canal itself had emptied sometime during the departure from the ground and return, but still presented a gap, and the enchanted sign was currently giving right of way to a small troop of ducks and ducklings waddling their way towards the park. Nun-Mhorgoth lifted a brutal tentacle, thickening it and hardening into the same lethal spike it had used to slay my golem.

"Oh no you don't," I declared, as Ig and I raised our hands in sync while belting out, "*Fragor!*"

The two bolts could not have been more different. Mine was a blast of pure concussive force. Ig's was a curved yellow fruit. Yet both flew true and struck the dark one solidly. Ig's proceeded to fall with a splat, delighting the ducks that now had a nutritious snack. Mine launched Nun-Mhorgoth tumbling through the air to land in the vacant lot at the end of the road. The lot that had once contained a burgeoning coffee shop, and now contained the world-famous . . .

"The acid pit!" Ildrit yelped in delight.

The noises that the dark god made down in the acid pit were not delighted. Quite the opposite in fact. Its initial form that it had presented itself to us in had been all but impervious to the elements, but that had been before the top few layers had been nuked off a few dozen times. What was left apparently could be affected by acid. I hoped it could also be affected by soap, as it needed its mouth washed out. The ducklings would have had a lot of questions for their parents tonight about what some of those words meant. I glanced down at Ig. He'd probably have a lot of questions too.

With another clunk, the city began to rise into the sky once more.

The battle down on the ground was all but won, but this would not be over until Nun-Mhorgoth was dealt with and judging by the sloshing and swearing from up ahead, it was not anywhere close to being dealt with yet. It slithered out onto the cobblestones, which began to sizzle and it let out an awful guttural sound that had to be its version of a groan. "Is there a doctor in the house?"

Ig was by my side, staring up at me with the faith that he always had in my incredible intellect, and I was drawing a blank. All of the plans from M through Y had been entirely buggered up by contact with the enemy. With the majority having been terribly clever ways to defeat the army of Nun-Mhorgoth rather than the critter itself. Part of that was because I'd assumed that my incredibly lethal white beam of death would have been entirely sufficient for that task, and part of that had been because I didn't have even the slightest inkling of what I could actually do to kill a god. If that was what it was.

I looked down at Ig, and I felt like crying. I dropped to my knee by his side, just as Nun-Mhorgoth surged back to a halfway upright position at the end of the road. "I don't know what to do."

Ig took this very seriously. Reaching up to remove my hat and carefully set it on the ground, before reaching up and plucking the entirely useless Crown of Cognition from off his own head and place it on mine. It didn't fit me, what with my brain being that much bigger. It pinched, and it didn't do anything at all. It was just a stupid trick I'd used to solve a problem, not an actual solution to the problem at hand. I . . .

The idea came to me fully formed.

"Thank you, Ig." I removed the crown and gave it back. Carefully returning my hat to my own head for just a moment to take a fresh copy of my own cognition, before slapping it down on top of Ig's crown. "The hat knows what to do."

"Oh!" Ig exclaimed. "Me know now."

It took him a long moment to parse all of the information being downloaded into his little brain, but once it had, he frowned. "Me no like plan."

"Yet you cannot deny that it will work." I smiled down at him. "Ildrit, you are with me." I moved off towards Nun-Mhorgoth with no greater farewell to my young apprentice than that. There was no need; I would always be with him. Literally. I was in the hat on his head.

The burly warrior fell into lockstep with me. "We've got a plan?"

"Ig is enacting the first part now. I need you to stay close to me, no matter what occurs. Will you do that for me?" I cast him a glance and saw his terse nod.

Nun-Mhorgoth surged forward, only to be caught in mid leap by an invisible barrier. He splatted against it. I glanced around and spotted Balthazagar, entirely coated in dust from head to toe, staggering forwards with his pipe still inexplicably lit. He made a rude gesture at the dark god, and then staggered on. I suspected a head injury, but I'd been suspecting something similar about Balthazagar since more or less the day I'd met him.

The dark god rallied fast, took stock of our new position and lanced forward again, only to hit another wall, this one having been rendered invisible by a quick spell by Danyeel.

It seemed like it took it forever to turn around and find us again, courtesy of the slowing spell from Sabrinia. And then it only saw us for a moment before two dimensional portals popped open to either side of it, one connected to the elemental plane of fire, blasting Nun-Mhorgoth like it was inside a furnace, and the other connected to the elemental plane of ice, freezing Nun-Mhorgoth so badly that its liquid like tentacles became jagged icicles down that one side.

It lashed out with its magic and disrupted the portals after only a moment, but by then it was already caught in Copernicrust's curse, a rather wicked and long reaching one that would ensure that Nun-Mhorgoth could never successfully have children or even keep a pet for any length of time. Probably not terribly useful in the current situation, but we liked to let the old man feel like he was still involved. Iomedania and Philodephina worked together for their spell, ripping all of the Quintessence out of the unsuspecting god, funneling it all into a recursive pocket dimension, and then dumping it out again into a ray of destruction that I have to say looked remarkably like the big white one that I'd come up with. Albeit considerably more focused thanks to originating on a convex curve.

Nun-Mhorgoth sizzled like an ant under a magnifying glass, rupturing down its middle. Then it was my turn again and I hit it with a spell that crossed the borders between illusion and psychology. Plunging my will past the dark one's defenses and into the center of its mind. Flaring light out there in the dark place and stoking the fires of fear that were now burning bright.

Throughout this protracted beatdown, we had been leading Nun-Mhorgoth through the city, avoiding those places where refugees were gathered, where important structures stood, and generally having a merry time of it, combining all our collective centuries of experience and talent into a single long tableau of violence.

By the time Nun-Mhorgoth emerged from all of that with enough awareness to strike back, I was already in place, locking its magic back down. We were in the now empty field where the circus had been staked out but a few days before. A completely empty place, perfect for my purposes. Cygni was flung bodily over the wall from wherever she had been when Ig found her, and she was wearing my hat, intended to be returned to me. It would have been informing her of the details of the plan as she crossed the distance and threw the hat right at me.

"This ain't right," she growled.

I shrugged my shoulders. "We cannot kill a god, so we must do what can be done instead."

Drifting up all around the city, rose the fragments of Cygnite that had been my golem. The most precious mineral in all of creation, left scattered on a battlefield, only to be retrieved by a kobold. There was probably some irony in there, but I'd been too inured to absurdity at this point to be able to decipher it.

It was from those beacons of raw power that Cygni drew when she began casting. A spell that had been included in Plan Y, for the other members of the faculty to peruse at their leisure. They joined in, one by one, young, and old. Every one of them serving as a conduit for the power of the stone, every one of them channeling that power into Nun-Mhorgoth.

"What do you apes think you're doing?" It knew precisely what we were doing, because it had borne witness to precisely the same spell the last time that it was imprisoned.

"We are binding you, Nun-Mhorgoth. You have made it clear to us that you cannot be destroyed, so we are returning you to imprisonment."

"You ain't got the stones, kid," the dark one rumbled. "Those dwarves, they knew what they were doing, they had some conviction. You're just playing at it."

"Because we choose to bind you using the power accumulated in the Cygnite rather than sacrificing our lives, you feel it will be less effective? Don't be so sentimental, Nun-Mhorgoth. Magic is magic." I treated him to my own most fearsome grin. Rendered all the more fearsome by the mustache that was now flying solo after the loss of my beard. "Power is power."

"They put their souls in it; you're only putting up some shiny rocks." It snarled, still pinned in place by the flows of Quintessence pouring into it. Held still by Ig's low magic, even as he brought all of the Cygnite and himself up and over the city walls to look over proceedings.

"Power is power, Nun-Mhorgoth. And power is what I know best. I am the world's greatest living wizard." I took a step closer. "Even if they are not enough, I will be."

There is some turn of phrase about rats and how you should never corner them because they will lash out, but I had not thought it applicable to cephalopods or deities. As such, when Nun-Mhorgoth suddenly lunged forward against its restraints and launched a desperate, pinched-off dart of blackfire at me, it caught me unawares.

Ildrit stepped sharply into its path.

The fire that had consumed ogres and left nothing behind washed over him. His eyes went wide, then closed as he whispered. "Guess this is what I deserve."

Blackness swallowed him up. Blazing so dark it seemed to sap all light from the city around us. The curse set on him didn't know what to do with that. He had just done one of those incredibly big good deeds that people write legends about. He'd sacrificed himself to save my life, not out of any real love for me, though we got on fine, but because he knew that taking the hit meant that I'd be able to go on and do the magic that I do so well, preventing the end of the world as we know it and defeating Nun-Mhorgoth. That was the sort of thing that karma really needed to pay back in kind, otherwise everything was going to be seriously unbalanced.

Do you remember when I told you it was important to remember that Ildrit had been a werewolf? This is why. Because being cursed with lycanthropy renders you immune to just about every kind of magical attack that you can think of, and direct magical damage like the blackfire was the sort of thing a lot of were-beasts could shrug right off. And while, technically, Ildrit was no longer a werewolf, he had been proving oddly resistant to magic all the same. As if the curse hadn't worked itself fully out of his system. Maybe getting tangled up in the curse that he already had, or maybe lingering because fate understood that at some point in the near future it was going to have to balance the books rapidly.

The fire washed over Ildrit, and then it washed away, and he was none the worse for wear.

I slammed my will into Nun-Mhorgoth anew. Stopping any attempt to cast, and slowly, oh so slowly, stone began to grow across the dark one's oily skin. I stepped in closer then, clapping Ildrit on the shoulder as I went.

"Nobody is going to forget you this time, Nun-Mhorgoth. You aren't going to be abandoned in some long-forgotten dungeon until nobody even knows your name. Everyone is going to know what you are, who you are, and because of that, nobody will ever set you free."

"I'll be back, kid. Sooner than you could have guessed." The dark one scoffed. "You people forget your history from one generation to the next. How are you planning on keeping my name on everybody's lips?"

"Why, isn't it obvious?" I chuckled. "I'm going to make everyone love you."

"What?" Cygni interrupted her casting for a brief moment.

"What?!" Nun-Mhorgoth said in harmony with her.

"You are going to be the mechanism by which we manufacture Cygnite. A mineral so valuable to magic that it will be used the world over." I couldn't keep a grin from splitting my face now. "You are going to help so many people, Nun-Mhorgoth. More than you ever could have hurt. And you are going to be alive and aware and helpless the whole time that you're doing it."

The dark god bucked and struggled now, straining against the magic pouring in, wrestling with it and pushing it back and unmaking it as fast as I could move to block him. It was frantic, like an animal in a trap lashing about, willing to tear its own leg from its body.

I stepped in closer, until I was nose to endless black void with Nun-Mhorgoth. "Of course, there is an alternative."

"I ain't going back in the slammer." The dark one shuddered. "Name your price, and it's yours, kid."

"First, you will acknowledge me as your equal." I counted off my demands on my fingers.

"No!" Ig cried out. "No let go!"

"You want me to lie to you, I'll lie to you," it sneered. How I could tell it was sneering when it was a throbbing mass of tentacles, I could not tell you, but it was sneering.

I counted the next finger. "Then you will agree to my terms from before, but with further caveats. Half of the world will be mine, half yours. Anything either one of us happens to conquer becomes equal share of the other. A partnership."

That seemed to throw Nun-Mhorgoth, but only for a moment. It was so certain of its own importance, that it didn't even think to consider any problems that might arise from such an arrangement. "Okay, kid, you want to hitch your wagon to this black star, I ain't going to stop you. You did some good work today, running rings around me. Imagine what we could do if we were on the same side."

I let some of my wicked desire for power and domination bleed through into my smile. "Precisely my thoughts."

"You cannot do this, Archmage!" Philodephina cried out in dismay. The spell was already beginning to falter, either through the failing concentration of the casters, or because Nun-Mhorgoth had been right from the start and my people simply didn't have the conviction to pour their all into this working.

I spun on my heel to face her and was almost startled to find that Ildrit was still staying right there beside me, like I'd told him to. "I think, my dear coworker, that you will find that I am well within my rights. It is the duty and privilege of being the captain of a ship, or the leader of an institute of learning that one can conduct ceremonies of marriage. I am merely exercising that right."

"Weh?" Ig inquired.

"What?" Ildrit gawked.

"Huh?" said Nun-Mhorgoth for only the briefest moment before I lunged in and pressed my lips against the slick surface of what surely would have been the face of a humanoid.

"By this kiss, we are wed," I announced to the gathered crowd. It hadn't quite been the traditional ceremony, but a glance to Copernicrust confirmed my suspicion that it had been close enough. The ancient magic that had underlined the construction of the Great Wall and Ildrit's curse had been invoked. In the eyes of the universe, we were married. "I now pronounce us husband and abomination."

I turned to Ildrit at last and tilted up my chin. "Strike true, my friend."

He took a moment to process precisely what I was saying to him. Still somewhat stunned with his own brush with death. He looked down at the enchanted blade Widowtaker in his hand, and the pieces clicked into place. "No."

Behind me, my gender-neutral life partner had begun tearing its way loose of the spell that had been binding it. The spell that I had known we didn't have enough of the original construction to recreate completely. Just enough to make Nun-Mhorgoth think we had it all.

The dark creature that I was married to hadn't worked out how to use the connection that I'd just forged between us against me, but it would, given sufficient time. It was clever like that, in the cruelest sort of way. However it could contort to do harm and cause misery, it would. It was in its nature.

Ildrit looked from me to the sword. "I don't want to . . ."

"I know." I gave him a soft smile. "But this is how we win."

The enchantment on the sword, much like the curse on Ildrit, tapped into those same primal forces again. It traced the connection from one partner in a marriage to the other, and inflicted death on both if one should fall to its edge. It too had a nature of cruelty.

But for its faults, there was one thing I could not complain about with the Widowtaker. Its edge was still sharp. Even after all the years.

PLAN Z: Die

It sliced cleanly through my neck, my spine, everything, and I was treated to a wonderful tumbling view of events unfolding as my head fell to earth.

The magic in the sword may have been primal, but I had not been certain that it would be enough. That was why it had to be Ildrit using the sword. It needed to be empowered, not by the balancing of karma that his curse created, but by the cataclysmic energy of that curse coming undone.

He was committing a truly evil act; he was killing the only man powerful enough to stop Nun-Mhorgoth from having its wicked way with the world.

He was committing a truly good act, sacrificing one of his only friends in the world so that a great evil could be defeated, even though it was going to cause him immense grief.

The contradiction of the two broke his curse, and with nowhere else to go, all of that conflicting energy tried to escape, following along the lines of fate that it had always followed, snared in the line that Widowtaker had made between me and Nun-Mhorgoth.

The dark god Nun-Mhorgoth died with me. The core where all of its tentacles were rooted made a wet farting sound, and all of those tentacles fell off, writhing about in the mud for a moment before finally going still, then turning to ashes. It was an ignoble death for an ignoble creature. And on the subject of ignoble creatures, here came Ig now, crashing down into the mud beside my severed head, snot already bubbling out his nose as he sobbed.

Ildrit tried to give him comfort, but the kobold was having none of it. He shoved wildly with his low magic, and sent everyone staggering back. He cradled my head in his hands and sobbed. "How you be so stupid?"

For obvious reasons my severed head could not reply. Though actually, why couldn't it? It still had vocal chords and all the rest, I'd worked with less.

"I'm not dead, you whittering buffoon. I'm just no longer in that particular corporeal body." If I had thought that the gathered wizards and friends had looked shocked before during the impromptu wedding ceremony and execution, then it was nothing compared to how they all looked now that my severed head had begun telling them off.

"You is in hat!?" Ig cried.

"Of course I'm in the bloody hat, where else would I be? Heaven?"

That drew some chuckles from the faculty.

"Put me on, would you? There is something profoundly obscene about puppeteering one's own severed head." Ig reached for the hat carefully, snot still bubbling about his nose-holes. "Actually could you blow your nose first. Use my robe if you like, I'm not going to be wearing it anymore."

Ig did, in fact, wipe his nose on my dead body before plucking me from my own severed head. There was a brief moment of blissful nothingness, then I was back on Ig's head. To my immediate distress, it felt like home.

And we're back to this again.

Ig shrugged. "Me no mind sharing."

Well I do mind sharing your mind. It is in desperate need of a cleanup around here. Do you have any idea how messy your filing system is . . . I'll be spending the rest of my life trying to get your thoughts in order.

"Thank all," Ig announced to the gathered wizards and Ildrit, who was looking more than a little shell-shocked after his curse broke. "We wins."

This is what you think a victory speech is meant to sound like? Stand aside and let me take over the mouth . . .

THE ARCHMAGE OF ARPANPHOLIGON

There came to the Invisible College of Arpanpholigon a young girl of no more than fifteen years. It was her intention to become a wizard, and though she was not human, she had been informed in no uncertain terms that this would provide absolutely no impediment to her entry, if she proved herself sharp of wit and capable of learning.

She traversed the city like a native, standing aside as an illusory fox darted through, pursued by far younger children, who were nonetheless almost her height, and seeming to intuit which backstreets led to where she desired to be and which took a left turn into some pocket dimension that was populated by sapient roaches descended from the first pair that had gotten lost in there.

At the base of the vast flight of stairs leading up into the college proper, she had remembered an old family story and pressed her hand to the crystal on the wall, allowing magic to carry her up to the top instead of sweaty effort, and with further foreknowledge, she traversed the various halls and corridors that composed the outer areas of the college with a practiced ease. Her memory, like her mother's, was eidetic. And when her mother had recounted tales of this place, every detail had been ingrained in the impressionable young lady's mind.

She had been told that the archmage was an old man now, far older than he really should have gotten to be. Some whispered that he enhanced his lifespan with magic, as if it were scandalous and not exactly what every single wizard since the beginning of history had been doing. Regardless, other whispers said that he no longer held court in an office, but out on the Quint instead. A little patch of grass in the sunshine, where he claimed his old bones were soothed by the warmth.

It was to the Quint that the girl traversed with all haste, carefully dipping back into the shadows when she feared that she might be spotted.

Finally she came out into sunlight and grass soft underfoot. For a moment she had to blink against the light, pupils contracting to wolflike slits before she could see what lay before her.

On the ground on some grass, there sat a kobold. This was not a grubby dirty kobold of the sort that you might have expected to find in some hole in the ground out in the Badlands, but a very refined and polished sort of kobold. It wore clothes, for starters. Not particularly fancy clothes, of course, as no tailor worth their salt would cater to a kobold, but clothes nonetheless.

The girl crept closer, and one of the kobold's eyes languidly opened. "Weh?"

"Excuse me . . . sir?" She tried for the right honorific, but it was diffi-cult to say any without sounding like she was being insincere. "I'm looking for Archmage Scryne. Would you be able to tell me where he is?"

"Scryne?" the kobold asked, scratching the side of its neck with its rear foot. "Me not know no Scryne. Who you?"

The girl drew herself up to her full height, little taller than the kobold would have been if it weren't sitting on the ground. "I am Rhinolyta Cygnisdottir, and I'm here to learn how to be a wizard."

The name seemed to catch the kobold's attention, as it should have. She was the daughter of the dwarven king after all. Queen. Pronouns were a complex subject for dwarves, and more so for dwarves talking with outsiders, and more so still for half-dwarf, half-human hybrids who had no real place in either world.

"Weh? Why want be wizard?" the kobold asked, looking genuinely confused.

"Because my mother's the greatest living wizard of all dwarf-kind, and I want to be better."

The kobold chortled at that. "No likey Cygni?"

"I love my mother," the girl said severely. "But I can still be better."

"*Perhaps it is time for me to speak to the girl, Ig?*" Another voice, a strange voice, came from the kobold's mouth.

"Who's that?" she asked, glancing around as though somebody might have been performing some trick of ventriloquism.

"*The one that you seek, dear girl. The friend of your mother and father, the savior of the world, and currently, a hat. I am Absalom Scryne, this is Ig, and it is he who will take you on as an apprentice if I judge you to be worthy of his teachings.*" The kobold leaned in closer, and there was an uncanny focus to his gaze now that the wizard inside was peering out. "*So tell me, Rhine, beyond burning ambition to be the greatest living wizard, why would you seek to master the High Art of magic? And, perhaps more importantly even than that, I must ask you, do you like bananas? Because everyone is so very tired of eating them, but Ig just won't stop making more.*"

ABOUT THE AUTHORS

Luke Chmilenko is the author of the Ascend Online series, among others. He grew up in Mississauga, Ontario, and now lives in Burlington, Ontario, with his wife, daughter, and two cats. Visit his website at lukechmilenko.com.

G. D. Penman is the author of more books than you can shake a reasonable-size stick at. Before finally realizing that his guidance counselor had lied about one's not being able to make a living as an author, Penman worked as an editor, tabletop game designer, and literally every awful demeaning job that you can think of in between. Nowadays, he can mostly be found smoking a pipe in the sunshine and pretending that deadlines aren't lurking behind him with a club. He lives in Dundee, Scotland, with his menagerie.

Podium